ALBERT E. IDELL

❧ ❧ ❧

Centennial Summer

❧ ❧ ❧

NEW YORK

HENRY HOLT AND COMPANY

Contents

Characters

JESSE ROGERS—Philadelphia Quaker who married "out of Meeting."

AUGUSTINA ROGERS—Called "Gussie" by her husband and "Tina" by her sister. Daughter of an impecunious Italian nobleman, Count Borelli, who was a member of the entourage of Joseph Napoleon as "Mr. Repetto."

TERESINA (ZENIE)
JULIA
GEORGINA (Gene)
HENRY
} their children

TERESINA LASCALLES—Sister of Augustina, called "Aunt Zena" by everyone. The widow of a rich French merchant.

PHILIPPE LASCALLES—Her nephew, a son of her husband's brother.

AUGUSTUS PALMER (GUS)—A medical student and suitor of Zenie Rogers.

HENRY LONGFELLOW NAYLOR (HARRY)—A young politician and suitor of Zenie Rogers.

AL, LIZZIE, AND CARRIE NAYLOR—His brother and sisters.

MR. AND MRS. SOLOMON PEALE AND ADA—Next-door neighbors of the Rogerses.

FATHER DUFFY—Priest of the parish.

MARY GALLAGHER—The Rogers' maid of all work.

MARTHA LEARY—The Rogers' cook.

LUCIUS—The Rogers' "boy."

DENISE AND CÉLESTE—Aunt Zena's maids.

MR. QUINBY—The finest horse in Kensington.

TOTAL ECLIPSE—Mr. Rogers' horse.

NELLIE—The Dalmatian.

MOODY AND SANKEY—Not the revivalists.

❦ ❦ ❦

November and December

❦ ❦ ❦

1875

"While the people retain their virtue and vigilance, no administration, by any extreme of wickedness or folly, can very seriously injure the government in the short space of four years."

—ABRAHAM LINCOLN.

Chapter 1

THE FRENCH clock struck the hour. It was a bronze figure of Venus on a pedestal of crystal and marble, with the clock face let into the lovely lady's middle. Mary counted the five tinkled notes. She shook her head and hurried to complete the setting of the table. From the buffet she took plates and cups and saucers. It was the French service decorated with roses, pink sprays alternating with pearly white ones; it was always used with the rose linen tablecloth. She put the heavy, cut-glass tumblers in place and set the matching water pitcher on a corner of the sideboard. Piece by piece she took the silver from a folded roll of cotton flannel and wiped each spoon and fork on her apron before placing it on the table. Cocking her head, she inspected the heavy steel knives, putting away one or two that showed marks of tarnish, blew on the others, and repolished them. From time to time she darted anxious eyes at the clock which seemed to move toward five-thirty with an inexorable speed.

A problem presented itself. She stopped in her hurried limping movements, thought a moment, then moved to the kitchen door. She listened for untoward sounds, but everything seemed quiet. Pushing the door slightly, she called through the crack:

"Clean napkins? D'ye want clean napkins, ma'am, or shall I use them that's in the rings, from yesterday?"

Mrs. Rogers kicked against the door from the other side

3

so violently that Mary was pushed backward. She would have fallen if she had not been able to clutch one of the high-backed dining-room chairs. Completely oblivious of the near-catastrophe, Mrs. Rogers glared at the old woman.

"Of course there will be clean napkins! With Henry home for the first time in months, would you ask us to welcome him with soiled napkins? My best linen table-cloth, the rose service, the solid silver Aunt Zena brought me from Paris, and soiled napkins! I never heard of such a thing! Mary, I'm surprised I keep you in the house with your sloppy Irish ways. Every time I open the front door I expect to see a pig in the parlor, and that's the truth." Mrs. Rogers drew herself up to a regal five feet two. "Of course there will be clean napkins!"

Mary answered sullenly, "I was just askin'. A body has got to ask, ain't they?"

She glanced with little gray eyes at the door closing on Mrs. Rogers' back, then turned to the buffet. Pulling open the linen drawer, she picked out a stack of clean napkins and dealt them on the upturned dinner plates as if they were huge cards, giving each square of folded linen a little spin that sent it fluttering to its place. She practically threw the last one at Mrs. Rogers' plate just as the master of the house came into the dining room.

"Hooray, Mary, a perfect shot!" Mr. Rogers applauded vigorously and threw up his hands in pretended amazement.

With his entrance the room became alive. The large, ornamented fleurs-de-lis which formed a funereal design on the wallpaper lost their drabness and became grotesque, grinning faces that welcomed him. From an oil portrait hanging over the mantelpiece, Grandfather Rogers smiled down on his son. On the sideboard, the circlet of little

4

goblets pendant from metal hooks on the large cut-glass punch bowl chimed and rattled as he shouted.

Mary peered up at him through puckered eyes, after making a gesture of trying to recapture the angrily thrown napkin, and he shook his head, judiciously.

"You will never do it better, Mary, though you can try it if you want to. I didn't know there was so much life in the old girl."

"Stop it, Mr. Rogers, quit blarneying me, now." Mary's eyes almost closed in a smile of pleasure.

Mr. Rogers felt her right arm carefully.

"Tremendous power, there," he judged, in mock seriousness.

"Be gone with you. You're worse than a flannel-mouthed Irishman, so you are." Mary hobbled from his reach and laughed.

Mr. Rogers also laughed, but suddenly he was serious. He looked at the fragile numerals on the French clock, with its hands pointing the half-hour, and his frown deepened. He seized the massive gold chain that spanned his vest. Taking the great links between thumb and all four fingers, he pulled the watch from its vest pocket like a seaman hauling on an anchor. He compared the time of the clock and that of his watch, and his voice boomed in protesting thunder.

"It's slow. That gilt gewgaw, that marble mausoleum of dead hours, that useless, dusty dirt-catcher is slow!" Walking over to the clock, he peered at it from different angles, to establish the greatest possible degree of inexactitude. "Mother!" he shouted. His voice boomed *"Mother!"* until the punch-bowl glasses rattled again, and the French clock all but stopped running entirely.

Mrs. Rogers came in from the kitchen, her black eyes sparkling with a deceptive look of surprise.

5

"Why, Father! You startled me!" She spoke gently to Mary. "Run and tell the children dinner is served. Hurry now, Mary, I know Father is hungry."

Mr. Rogers' face showed apoplectic above the line of his beard. He pointed accusingly at the offending clock. "That poor excuse for a timepiece is a fair symbol of the way this household is managed. No thought or regard for time. It's all of two minutes slow, and you look at me complacently. If our railroad . . ."

"Tell the children to hurry, Mary," Mrs. Rogers interrupted, "Father has been working hard all day, out in the air, and he's hungry."

The brass chains that supported the chandelier shook with his rejoinder. "I am not *hungry*. I *am not hungry*." He changed to a comparatively calm tone, as if anger was being controlled by a terrific display of will power. "I merely offer my feeble protest because that miserable clock is slow. A timepiece that has its center in a woman's navel is an abomination to art and science both. It has disrupted the calm of this household. It has allowed you to slip behind schedule. I demand promptness—I am a railroad man, and I must work on schedule."

His wife looked up at him pertly, like a sparrow unmindful of the lion's roar. "I know how hungry you must be, working in the air all day. Things will be ready in just a moment."

Mr. Rogers clenched his fists and beat them in the air in fury. His voice echoed and re-echoed in the narrow confines of the dining room.

"Mother, I am not hungry. I am never hungry. Understand that I do not allow the desires of the body to affect me." His voice lowered almost to a whisper, and he began to speak slowly, as if reasoning with a very small child. "I merely plead for a small measure of the exactitude to

6

which I have been trained. This family must be taught the value of time. If the trains of the Philadelphia & Reading Railroad pulled out two minutes late on every trip, how long . . ."

Mrs. Rogers picked an imaginary thread from her husband's black coat. "Jesse, Jesse, how you do run on—and a thread on your coat. You men never will look out for your appearance." She caught his arm with her fingers and skipped as she led him to the head of the table. In spite of her graying hair, as she pulled at his giant, broadshouldered figure, she was like a plump, schoolgirlish hoyden. His great bulk, and the froth of brown beard that covered most of his face with luxuriant growth, made him appear to be much the older, but he joined in her play, skipping like a huge trained bear and roaring with laughter. In a moment he had forgotten completely the whole matter of the clock. Without waiting for the others, he seated himself ponderously in the armchair; Mrs. Rogers returned to the kitchen.

Julia was the first of the children to appear. She took her place unobtrusively at her father's left, and said, "Good evening, Papa." Although she was too slender, her features were beautiful. She took after the Borellis, her mother's family, with perfect oval face, straight nose, and heavily shadowed dark-brown eyes. She had a clear, high forehead, thick brows like tiny bird wings, and glorious black hair that made one forget the meager curves of her figure. In her father's presence she lowered her eyes and turned over a plate, reading the pottery mark she had deciphered a hundred times before.

The twins raced in, Georgina flushed and happy. She ran and placed a little kiss on her father's cheek, above the edge of his whiskers. "You surprised us, Father dear —you must have sneaked in, we never heard you."

7

Henry said, "Hello, Dad!" He swaggered down the length of the table and seated himself at the corner farthest from his father.

Mr. Rogers squeezed his napkin into a tight ball and threw the crumpled linen against his plate in anger.

"In this household I will be called 'Father.'" He leveled a forbidding glance at Julia, trembling at his side. "I want no daughter of mine mincing 'Good evening, Papa.'" In his deep, lusty voice he attempted an imitation of her reedy tones, "Good evening, Pa-pa," he mimicked.

Georgina laughed and clapped her hands. "That was wonderful, Father. Mother . . . Mother . . . you should hear Father! Do it again, do!"

Mr. Rogers beamed. "By Jove, it was a good imitation." He tried it again several times. "Good *evening*, Pa-pa." No, more like this, "G'd ev'ning, Pa-pa." It did sound like Julia, he thought. He glanced around at his family. Julia was hurt, her eyebrows drawn together in dismay. Georgina, his favorite daughter, and Henry were grinning at him. Then his voice almost blasted his son from his chair, and startled the others afresh. "And you, sir, shall also address me properly. That syllable you directed to me a moment or so ago, I hesitate to pronounce it, Dad. *Dad!* It is no term of respect for an indulgent father, but a flippant word. Not a word, a hideous noise, completely without meaning. Here in my house I demand a modicum of respect, at least a shred of dignity to cover such human weaknesses as we may have. By God, sir . . ."

Julia laid a slender, admonishing hand on her father's sleeve. "You mustn't. It's sacrilegious."

Mary came in, bearing soup in shallow wide-brimmed plates, but Mr. Rogers was not to be distracted by the

8

appearance of food. His voice drove the soup in waves against the plate rims.

"By the Lord Harry, I'll not be corrected by my own children! Leave your puerile cant behind when you sit at this table."

Julia shrank in her chair. Her smooth olive skin lost some of its color and the oval of her face seemed to lengthen, but she bent her head dutifully. She said a silent prayer for strength, as she had been taught at the convent.

Teresina peeped in at the door and speculated whether she could reach her seat while her father was distracted by Julia. She took a chance and won her goal, aided by a new diversion. Mary, who had been in the kitchen when Henry entered, noticed his presence as she served him. She placed her tray on the table and threw her arms around his neck. "Me darlin' boy. Me darlin' boy." The soup for Teresina and Mr. Rogers had not yet been served, but they waited the end of the exuberant greeting, Mr. Rogers impatiently, and Teresina with tolerant acceptance, because she was not yet sure her own lateness had passed unnoticed.

When Father's soup at last reached him, it was almost cold, but he seized his soupspoon. Holding his napkin over his beard with his left hand, he conveyed soup to his mouth as expeditiously as possible with the right hand.

Mrs. Rogers stood in the doorway between the dining room and kitchen until the room was quiet again. Well, he was eating at last. Things were safe for a while. She followed Mary into the kitchen, and as the door closed behind them, scolded Martha, the cook. "If you'd had dinner ready on time, he wouldn't have started on poor Julia."

The cook was enormously stout, one of those heavy

9

people who arrange their work to save every possible step, but once in the position they have selected, can move hands and arms with quick precision. Her station was directly in front of the large built-in range. Years of standing in the direct radiation of heat had given her face a permanent flush. Her fat acted as a cushion against Mrs. Rogers' frequent criticisms; the only sign that she had heard, and resented, the accusation was an increase in the tempo with which she moved utensils and handled condiments.

Mrs. Rogers turned toward Mary, busily filling the water pitcher from the pot of boiled water. "And you, lazy good-for-nothing!"

Mary escaped, pushing open the door in the middle of the tirade, which immediately ceased. She hurried into the turmoil of the dining room and Mrs. Rogers followed, smiling pleasantly and graciously, to take her seat by her husband. She picked up her soupspoon delicately, and held it to show her small jeweled hand to advantage. Mr. Rogers was on his third helping of soup. Henry was excitedly whispering to Georgina about school adventures. Teresina was eating slowly, with an air of abstraction. Mary hobbled about.

Dinner had begun quite auspiciously for the Rogers family.

2

The roast was a huge rib, lugged in triumphantly by Mary, whose nose was quivering at the smell. The meat was surrounded with a double bank of roasted potatoes, the whole done in Italian style, drenched in claret, which gave both roast and vegetables a purplish hue. Mr. Rogers stood up to carve. He examined the long blade of the knife and gave it several dexterous passes with the steel.

There was a regular order in the serving, according to the tastes of the family. Mrs. Rogers liked the brown crust, and received the first slab, all of a half-inch thick. Next came Julia, and then Teresina. That disposed of the well-done members of the family. Now the twins, who shared his own taste, received generous pink slices. Then a tremendous slice, fully an inch through, and practically raw in the center, for himself. Potatoes were served as lavishly, two or three to every plate. Mary brought in a large bowl filled with chicory salad, but this Mr. Rogers pushed aside contemptuously. "Who wants rabbit food? Meat and potatoes are good enough for me—for any human being—but if there are rabbits in our company, let them speak up!"

Everyone ignored the challenge, but in due course the two older girls and Mrs. Rogers helped themselves to the greens. Mrs. Rogers ate slowly, picking delicately at her beef and nibbling at minute pieces of potato. She acted the part of a great lady who never forgot her noble blood.

Mr. Rogers carved the rest of the roast into slices quite as large as those of the first serving, and all but Julia took the second helping. As Mary moved about with the refilled plates, Mrs. Rogers' eyes roamed quickly over the faces of her family. It seemed incredible, she told herself, that these children could be hers: Teresina twenty-one, though not yet married, Julia two years younger, and the twins fifteen; that she was married to this great bulk of a man who ate noisily from a fork piled high with food. Her husband disturbed her reverie. In the voice that carried across freight yards, he spoke to Henry:

"If you can spare a few of the confidences you are whispering to Gene, an interested father would like to share them. Of course, if they are secrets to which I have no right, forgive the interruption."

11

Abashed at the sudden interest of the table, Henry sat with his head bent over his plate. Georgina nudged him with her elbow. She was so glad to have her twin brother with her again that she radiated her pleasure, and was anxious to share it with her father. "Tell him," she whispered, excitedly. Henry began in the middle of a story of an escapade at school.

"We had two cats with their tails tied together and let 'em loose under the Master's window. It was a joke on the Master, supposed to be, but they jumped on me and my neck's not healed up yet where they scratched." Henry felt ruefully at the sore place, and Georgina whispered:

"That's not how you told it to me. It was funny the way you were saying it."

His father laughed. "There's nothing like two cats tied by their tails for fun. Except a good terrier with a lot of rats. When we were children there was nothing like rat-baiting—one terrier to a hundred rats, and the dog didn't always get the best of it, I tell you!"

Mrs. Rogers made a little grimace of disgust. "I suppose you learned that at the same place Henry invented his unpleasant cruelty. What can you expect of a boy, sending him to a heathen institution?"

Julia awaited her father's explosive rejoinder, but he changed his mood to one of quiet forcefulness.

"Mother, I take this moment to reiterate. The souls of my daughters have been delivered into the arms of Holy Church, but my son at least shall see the pleasant vistas of a healthy, unregenerate life before entering that embrace. When the time comes, the decision shall be his own. His school is the one that gave his father and grandfather a sound practical education, and I will not hear it unjustly criticized."

As he talked, he impressed his points with a light tapping of his knife handle on the tablecloth, until his wife objected plaintively:

"Father, I wish you wouldn't tap that way. It's a sign that you are nervous, and it gives me a headache." Before he could frame an answer, she cut off the necessity for one by an order: "Mary, I believe you can remove the plates."

Teresina pushed back her chair. Her mother watched her with open admiration. What a perfect, patrician face! And a lovely figure! A true Borelli, beautiful, and religious enough to ensure a not too grim hereafter. There was no need for those extremes of piety indulged in by Julia. Religion could, and should, be sensible. The mother's thoughts continued as her oldest daughter rose from the table. "I don't want dessert," she announced, "I think I'll read." She closed the door into the hall-way carefully behind her, and Mr. Rogers gave a whistle.

"We are having, I know, a delicious roly-poly, prepared as only Martha can, and our beauty, who would sell her soul to add another ounce of charming curve to an already luscious frame, eschews it! Mother, what is the meaning of this?"

"It's young Gus Palmer. She expects to meet him, I think. You know he is very much interested in Zenie."

"I don't know why he should be. She is beautiful, I admit, but I never saw a girl with less spirit, unless it's our Julia here."

"It is a good match for Zenie—a good family—not much money, but they are comfortable. And he's studying to be a doctor. With Zenie for a wife he could go far. Who knows, they might become really wealthy. My heart goes out to the poor child. There's so little we can give her, and she is so dissatisfied with our reduced circumstances."

Mr. Rogers looked about the room as if searching for something he could not see.

13

"Reduced circumstances? Reduced circumstances? I see a table groaning with food. I notice voluptuous hangings, and rich plate. Haviland china graces the sideboard, and we have just dined from the finest of French porcelains. There are family retainers, and my wife's fingers sparkle with jewels. In fact, we are so fat with good living we have become the prey of a constant and ever increasing army of priests, who live from the bounty of this house." His voice ended in a suddenly arrested crescendo of sound, as if he could no longer go on reciting the glories of the family and the hazards to which it was exposed.

"What I give is my own," Mrs. Rogers answered sharply, "out of the little that remains from what my father left." She lifted her hands above her head in a dramatic gesture. "Poor Father! Your heritage of wealth is spent, but I prize still more another heritage you left me—my faith and the traditions of an old and noble family." When she spoke in this manner, she adopted an affected accent she fondly believed to be Italian. It put her out a good deal when Georgina clapped her hands.

"That was wonderful, Mother. It was better than Fanny Davenport." She called down the table to her father. "You didn't miss a thing when you wouldn't go to see her. Mother is much more grand."

Julia spoke in a mild, quiet voice: "I forgot to say that Father Duffy is coming in the morning. They are having a collection for the new church."

Mrs. Rogers thought, "Julie can be just too stupid." She saw her husband framing a new outburst in his mind and jumped to her feet in a well-simulated appearance of distress.

"I do believe Martha left the pudding in the oven. I smell it burning." She pushed open the kitchen door. "Martha, the roly-poly! Please remove it from the oven."

14

"It's out, mum," Martha answered.

Mrs. Rogers stamped her foot impatiently. "Don't answer back that way. I distinctly smell something burning."

Martha's voice was firm. "It's out, mum," she repeated.

Mrs. Rogers resumed her seat by her husband. "How I ever get along with that cook!" She sighed. She gave a quick, curious glance sideways. Julia had provoked a trying moment, mentioning Father Duffy when Jesse was in a bad mood, but evidently her trumped-up crisis had succeeded in diverting him.

He smiled in a patronizing manner.

"You have exercised a remarkable degree of restraint the nineteen years you have put up with her. Besides, she cooks atrociously, as we all can testify. In a moment, when the roly-poly makes its appearance, not one of the family will touch it."

No one attempted a rejoinder; in this mood Mr. Rogers was to be handled only by diversion.

"Mr. Quinby has been restless, Father," Georgina spoke up. "Maybe you had better look in at the stable after dinner."

"I always look in at the stable after dinner. Mr. Quinby would only be nervous if you children have been pestering him."

Julia said: "It's the puppies. Nellie's puppies are so tiny, and I think Mr. Quinby is afraid of treading on them. You know how much he loves Nellie. Whenever she has a litter he's that way. His heart would be broken if he hurt one of the dear little things." When Julia talked about animals, her expression became warm and tender. "They are so little and soft, Papa."

She stopped aghast. The word was out, and it could not be recalled. Her father, all ready to be moved to a comfortable, sentimental feeling by a recital of the puppies' doings, bristled anew. He turned to his wife and delivered himself.

"Mother, I know this child has had opportunities denied to us. Through the munificence of your sister she has been given the advantages of an education within the saintly spheres of a French convent. I implore you, however, to intercede with her so that a commonplace, ordinarily educated American father and a less fortunate brother and sister may be spared the visible and outward signs of her superior training."

As Mr. Rogers talked, his voice sank lower and lower, until the last words were like the distant rumbles of thunder preceding a summer storm. The originally furious convolutions of his beard slowed to a gentle waving. As he finished, the family sank into complete silence, which Mr. Rogers broke with a shout that brought Mary on the hop from the kitchen, and seemed about to shatter the cut-glass magnificence of the punch bowl. "By God, I will not be called *Papa*," he roared.

The pronouncement made, Mary served the dessert. After each crisis passed the family went on as if its life ran an even, placid course. There was no sound but the scrapings of spoon against dish as its members devoted themselves to the roly-poly.

Henry was the first to be finished. "I'm going over to the Naylors'," he announced. "I want to see Al. Do you want to come, Gene?"

She nodded, with a mouth still full of the pudding. They hurried around the high-backed chairs to their father's place. Henry put his arm around his father's shoulder while his sister jumped into his lap. The three pairs of gray-blue eyes were astonishingly alike. It was as if Mr. Rogers looked into twin replicas of his own. Georgina

16

slipped her arms around him, hugging furiously, while his lips, framed by the tawny hair of his whiskers, opened in a grin.

Julia watched her sister's display of affection, and thought: "If only I could sit on his lap like that, but he wouldn't have me. It's only Gene he cares about. He'd say I was just bones, or something." Her eyes began to fill with tears as she felt the injustice of her father's attitude. "If he knew how much I love him! Gene can't possibly love him more than I do." She rose and walked through the doorway; the twins romped by her, dashing down the narrow hall. Slowly she climbed the stairs toward the quiet of her fourth-floor room. It was pleasant to look forward to this refuge.

Chapter 2 Georgina followed Henry from the house. The wooden frame that covered the marble steps for the winter rattled and banged with their passing.

"Gee, I like to be home!" Henry said. He ran down the uneven brick pavement. A gas street light, lit too soon, burned vainly in the autumnal afternoon. He got to the post, climbed up until he caught the crossbars at the base of the lamp, and chinned himself. "Look, Gene, I bet you can't do this!"

Georgina repressed a desire to join him. Of course she could shinny up the lamppost, but she was growing up, and shouldn't.

Henry shouted: "Watch, Gene! Watch me do this one!" He drew his feet up under him and pushed against the post. When his body stuck out almost at a right angle,

17

he let go and swung violently, the crossbars wearing against his palms.

Forgetting the restraint she had imposed upon herself, Georgina climbed up and caught the bracket opposite her brother's. Laughing and screaming, they clung there until the mood passed.

"Listen, Gene," Henry suggested, "let's go down to Paddy's. We'll have fun with old Paddy." They dropped from the lamppost and ran. Turning the corner, they pounded down Richmond Street to the saloon that sat back in heavy respectability behind twin frosted-glass windows. Closed heavy doors had replaced the short swinging summer ones.

The twins began an old game. Georgina tiptoed up to the saloon door and pushed it open, and Henry stuck in his head. His eyes rested for a moment on the secrets of the interior, and then he shouted: "Paddy, Paddy, want a pig? Keep it in your parlor."

They slammed the door and ran to a safe distance, to wait for Paddy's irate appearance. The saloonkeeper was evidently in no mood for the game. They waited a reasonable interval, and then tiptoed back to push open the door again and peer inside. The saloon was incandescent with gaslight. The fan-shaped flames made a glare that was dazzling, and behind the bar a long mirror reflected the light and doubled a display of bottles. This was an array which included every conceivable brand and kind of liquor, and Georgina, who had seen it before, admired anew its richness and variety.

Evidently old Paddy had decided to ignore the doings of the Rogers twins. He didn't even chase them from the doorway. They could see him plainly, a striking figure with snow-white hair but intensely black mustache and sideburns. Georgina whispered: "Henry, do you really

18

think he keeps them black with stove polish, as people say?"

Henry shook his head, and pressed his finger to his lips as a sign for quiet. "They say he dips them in ink every day," he whispered back.

Three or four men stood at the bar. They were all neighbors, and Georgina appraised each one of them curiously, with wide-open eyes. She nudged her brother as he bent over to peek through the same crack. "Look, Mr. Peale has almost got a load." They watched the parent of one of their playmates as he argued violently at the bar. Ordinarily one of the quietest and most unobtrusive of men, Mr. Peale was undoubtedly feeling his liquor now.

The pleasant tinkle of a piano came from the back room of the saloon, and a musical tenor voice burst into song. This was more entertaining than to wait for Old Man Peale to stagger home. The children tiptoed up the alley to the side door, where the sign LADIES' ENTRANCE was illumined by a single gas jet.

"It's Gus Palmer," Georgina whispered. "Don't you remember, he was singing that song last Sunday, down at the Bauerles'. He sings it wonderful."

They listened enraptured to the words:

> I've just been learning the lesson of life,
> The sad, sad lesson of loving,
> And all of its powers for pleasure or pain
> Been slowly and sadly proving;
> And all that's left of the bright, bright dream,
> With its thousand brilliant phases,
> Is a handful of dust in a coffin hid,
> A coffin under the daisies.

"That's it, the same song. It's 'Under the Daisies.' Doesn't he sing it beautifully? It's so sad." Georgina

19

kept time with her foot and hummed the tune. The last
lines she remembered, and sang them softly to Henry.

> And far better than life with two hearts estranged,
> Is a low grave starred with daisies,
> The beautiful, beautiful daisies—
> The snowy, snowy daisies.

Henry thought "Gosh, Gene is beautiful when she's
sad." She interrupted her singing to ask: "What do you
suppose Gus is doing in there? I bet he and Zenie had
a fight."

"Maybe poor Gus is drowning his sorrows. They're
always scrapping about something or other."

"I'm glad they are. I like Gus Palmer, and I'd hate to
see him stuck with Zenie. I hope they had a fight." She
repeated more loudly, "I hope they had a fight."

Henry said: "Shut up, Gene. He'll hear you right
through the window."

"I don't care. I hope they had a fight. . . . I hope they
had a fight. . . . I hope they . . ."

"Gene, shut up, or I'll crack you!"

Georgina backed down the street, away from Paddy's
saloon, singing "I hope they had a fight" in an approxi-
mation of the tune of "Under the Daisies."

Henry shouted, "If you don't shut up, I'll shut you up!"

Georgina stuck her tongue out at him. "You would
if you could catch me." She started to run before Henry
lunged forward, and she maintained a fair lead as they
raced, now in the cobbled street and again on the uneven
brick pavement.

They stopped by mutual understanding before the Naylor house. In spite of the lateness of the year, the evening
was warm, and Georgina fanned herself with her handkerchief as she recovered her breath. Her face glowed with

color, and her hair, damp from the exertion, lay in wet ringlets on her forehead. It was now quite dark, and there were no lights in the Naylor windows, but they pulled at the doorbell and banged on the door. When there was no answer, Henry yoohooed. It was of no use —evidently Al and Carrie were out with their parents.

Georgina was still warm. "Let's sit down on the steps and cool off," she proposed. "Say, Henry, have you told Father why you're home?"

"Uh, uh. I guess he thinks maybe it's just the vacation. When he finds out I'll get skinned alive."

Georgina shook her head. "Not if you handle it right, you won't. I'll tell you why. He insisted on your going to a Quaker school, and if he makes a fuss now, Mother will say 'I told you so,' so he can't. And besides, he's already laughed at what caused the trouble. He took tying the cats together as a big joke. You won't get a licking for that." She paused a moment, in deep thought, honestly evaluating her brother's chances. "Of course, he might give you a hiding for that and blame it on something else not so important. He does that sometimes. It might not be altogether fair—I don't know—but he does do it."

"I don't see why Dad has to whip us like he does. He whips harder than anybody's father in the neighborhood. Seems to me he just gives us beatings for the fun of it. . . . Besides, we're too grown up to get licked like little kids."

Georgina's eyes flashed. "Henry Rogers, how can you sit there on that step and say that about your own father, the kindest, best, and jolliest father ever lived? You know every whack he gives with that old cat-o'-nine-tails hurts him more than it does us."

"Shoot, I don't believe that, or he wouldn't do it so much." Henry examined the scuffed toes of his shoes for

21

a long time. "Gene, I can hardly look kids in the face after I've had a walloping. The way he hits, everyone in the neighborhood can hear."

"I don't see how you can say such things. He hits harder just because he's a real man. I bet there's nobody else in Kensington as big and strong as he is. . . . It's natural he hits harder. And it's all for your own good. . . . Spare the rod . . ."

"Oh, I know, and spoil the child," Henry interrupted. "But shoot, there isn't any danger of our getting spoiled, if that meant anything, and yet I feel cusseder after I get whaled than I did before."

Georgina's voice hissed in excitement. "Look, here comes Zenie down the street. She *did* have a fight with Gus. Look how she's walking!"

"She's not walking any different than usual."

"She is too. She'd never walk with her head like that, looking straight ahead, if she wasn't mad. And look at her skirt!"

Teresina's blue serge suit was unruffled above, but the skirt churned, frothed, and swirled along the pavement, sweeping before it all the dust, paper, and trash of the sidewalk. This was a strange thing about Zenie, Georgina thought. When she was angry, she looked placid and quiet, as if nothing was wrong, but things around her went slam-bang, the way her skirt was doing.

As she drew opposite the twins, Henry assumed a knowing air that Teresina pretended not to notice as she prepared to run the gantlet of their eyes.

Georgina spoke first. "Hello, Zenie. Where's Gus?"

Teresina made the mistake of answering. She raised her head higher, so that the line of her chin made a square angle above her whaleboned crocheted collar. "I'm sure

22

I don't know. I haven't seen him all evening, and I don't care if I never do."

"We just saw him a little bit ago." Georgina waited to be asked further particulars, and Henry nodded. "We wondered where you were."

In spite of herself, Teresina asked: "You did? Where was he? Tell me, what was he doing when you saw him?"

Her sister turned malicious without any seeming change in her expression. "He seemed to be having a good time, too."

"I don't believe you saw him at all."

"He was down in Paddy's." Georgina embroidered on the truth. "A lot of them were in the back room, singing and cutting up. We saw them right through the door. Gus was singing that daisy song. He sings it beautiful— you could just cry when you hear him."

Teresina shook with indignation. "I don't believe it. I don't believe you saw him at all, with anybody. Why, it's not more than an hour since I left him . . ." She stopped, conscious of her mistake, and hurried on, supported by the tide of serge that beat along the pavement with her.

Georgina's eyes hardened, and her lips made a thin line, as she ran along by her sister, now frankly taunting her. "You were lying, that's what—lying. I know you had a scrap with Gus. Let me tell you, Zenie Rogers, Gus Palmer is too good for you. You can be a queen lording it over Mother and Julia, but you can't with anybody like Gus. There's lots about you I'd like to tell him—and some day I will, too."

Henry began a jeering chant. "Zenie had a fight with Gus. Zenie had a fight with Gus." Suddenly Teresina's calm was gone. Her eyes blazed and she revealed twin rows of even teeth biting tensely together. She made a

23

dash for Henry while Georgina stood by, enjoying the futile effort to catch their agile brother. Before Georgina knew what was happening, Teresina, failing to reach the flying Henry, swung quickly upon her other tormentor. She caught her sister's blond hair and pulled until Georgina cried in anguish. "You dirty little heathen, you little vixen, you mean, contemptible, lying . . ." Teresina yanked and Georgina howled until neighbors on both sides of the street peered out with wondering faces and then turned away, bored when they saw it was only the Rogers children, fighting again.

Henry came to the rescue of his twin. He made a flying leap, like a Comanche mounting a horse, and landed astride the curve of Teresina's corset. His legs wound about the narrowest section of an already painfully constricted waist and he found two curls on which to pull, like imaginary reins.

Teresina's screams far outdid her sister's of a few moments before. She forgot her other tormentor and ran up the street, with Henry astride. He was enjoying the experience tremendously, adding war whoops of his own to the already deafening sound. He swung around on the saddle of Teresina's artificially spreading hips long enough to shout to his twin: "Look, Gene, look! I'm Father, riding Total Eclipse." He let loose a terrific slap that stung his sister right through her heavily corseted thigh. Then he gave another jerk on the curls, as if to rein in.

There was a last agonizing shriek, and then silence, complete and awful. Mr. Rogers had appeared! A moment ago the street had been empty but for themselves, and now here he was, gazing with concentrated frown upon the three of them.

No one had seen him come, but there he was. Georgina

24

thought: "Father is like God. He knows when you do something, and he's there watching when you realize, all of a sudden, it was something wrong."

Mr. Rogers, while preserving a Jovian exterior, actually enjoyed the scene and his part in it, although his eyes seemed dark with wrath. "Those little devils have certainly got Zenie going," he thought. "I haven't seen her so mad since the last time I beat her, and that must be five, no, six years ago."

Here, he mustn't be getting soft, he had a duty to perform. "What kind of hoodlums do we have here?" His beard waved like a flag, and the sound seemed not to come from his mouth but from some mammoth cavern hidden behind that curtain of hair. "I see I have been a too indulgent parent. First of all, I have just learned that my son has been expelled from school. I excuse the childish play that was the cause of this incident, and ascribe it to healthy animal spirits. Now what do I find?" He swung around as if addressing a nonexistent audience. "I find him and his sister engaged in unseemly horseplay, sundering the quiet night with wild, abandoned shrieks, disturbing the peace of a community at repose." He turned toward Teresina, and his voice took on a throbbing note of pain. "Need I say how hurt, how shocked, surprised, overcome, I am to see you behaving like this—like a hoyden, a . . ."

Teresina looked up, amazed. "Father, you don't for a moment think this was play. Those little fiends attacked . . ."

"I have the evidence of my own eyes. I saw you myself, racing your brother pickaback. What is the meaning of a young lady of your years prancing down the street like a tomboy? Is this the ladylike carriage your mother taught you?" He did not wait for an answer, although he savored Teresina's helpless anger. He turned again to Henry.

25

"Young man, we have an engagement in the shed in fifteen minutes. I shall expect you there."

His gaze seemed to enlarge its field until it included Georgina, who stood meekly by. Her face had taken on a look of almost angelic sweetness, and she glanced up through a veil of long blond lashes. "Georgina, my dear, need I tell you how glad I am that you were not taking part in this outrageous performance? By your ladylike behavior you furnish an example your older sister would do well to follow."

2

The shed formed a frame extension to the brick house. Twice a week Louisa, the wife of Lucius, the colored stable boy, washed and ironed there. Large washtubs exuded an odor of cedarwood and soap that Henry never forgot. It was this smell he always associated with those terrifying moments before his father's punishments. In addition to the tubs, there was a squat laundry stove, cold and rusty-looking except on washdays. His father's gloves lay on a windowsill, the ones he used for odd jobs and fire-tending. During the winter, a snow shovel stood in a corner, and various emergency wraps were kept handy for Mrs. Rogers and the children to use when they ran to the stable on errands.

Henry paid no attention to any of these things. As he waited for his father, his gaze rested upon the whip that hung by a loop upon a nail in back of the shed door. He was like a bird fascinated by the serpent waiting to devour it. He feared and hated the whip, although he seemed entirely composed as he endured this extra torture of suspense which his father always imposed.

The doorknob turned, and he lifted his chin a little higher. He did not intend, when his father came in, to reveal for an instant how frightened he really was. But it was Georgina's flushed, excited face that appeared in the doorway. She whispered loudly:

"He won't be in for a few minutes. He's talking to Gus Palmer out on the pavement. Gus wants to come in and talk with Zenie, but he's been drinking, and Father won't let him." Henry nodded and relaxed; Georgina glanced back over her shoulder. "Look, I brought this down. It's part of Zenie's stays. You could stuff it under your shirt and pants and it wouldn't hurt so much." She drew from behind her the long boned stays, with side laces straggling. "She's upstairs gloating, waiting to hear you catch it, so I grabbed them." She held out the garment for him to take, but he shook his head.

"It wouldn't do any good. Besides, he would find it. When he hit, the noise would be different."

"I know what I'll do. I'll steal the old whip and cut it up in pieces." She grasped the knotted leather thongs, but Henry dissuaded her.

"It's no use. We'd just get it worse later, when he got another one."

"Anyhow, I'll go down to the stable and pray hard for you. I'll pray to St. Stephen the Martyr. I'll pray . . ."

Henry interrupted, scornfully. "Shoot, prayin' won't do any good. You needn't bother. I'll take it and get it over with."

Georgina peered back toward the house. "I better run. I'll be in the stable waiting. Come down when it's over with. Say, Henry, I'll never forget, long as I live, how Zenie looked with you riding her."

Henry laughed, a small edition of his father's roar. "And me shouting 'Giddap, Total Eclipse,' remember?"

There was a noise and Georgina hissed a final injunction,

27

"Come down—I'll be waiting." She was off, and in a moment Henry heard her run down the path outside.

The knob turned again, and this time it was Mr. Rogers. He stood for a moment, measuring his son. He hadn't realized how tall Henry was. "Must be all of five foot eight," he thought. "He'll be me all over again, a real chip off the old block." His beard and his impassive features hid his thoughts as he removed coat and waistcoat and laid them on the washtubs. He undid the steel cuff-holders that clamped cuff and sleeve together, and untied his black cravat. He placed these articles on top of his coat carefully, moving slowly and methodically, to prove to himself that what he was about to do was not from anger but purely for the future well-being of his son. A warm and agreeable sense of power emanated from a conviction of his absolute rightness; a knowledge that *he* had made of his son this erect and fearless youth. "Nothing sniveling about my Henry," he said to himself. He watched to detect a quiver, a sign of weakness, in his attitude and went on with his thoughts. "A fine boy, hard as they come. That's what a good licking now and then does for a youngster—gives him character. Look at him standing up to me now. Ready to take his punishment like a man. He'll always be that way, too, if I know anything."

He walked over to the door, took down the whip, and counted the separate knotted thongs. For a time, he didn't know how long, he had been whipping with only five of the thongs, instead of nine. One of the children had cut out some of them! The remembrance made him grin now, and he said to himself: "They put one over on me then, and I bet it was either Henry or Georgina. They're the only ones with spirit enough."

Henry noticed the smile, and thought bitterly, "Father

28

likes whipping us, in spite of all he says." His parent's voice seemed far away and unimportant as he said, "You know, son, this hurts me more than it does you."

Chapter 3

THE ROGERS house stood like a huge book end that held erect a long row of uniformly bound volumes of narrow-fronted homes. It was wider, and a full story higher, than others in the row. A brownstone trim ornamented a first floor which in the others was of plain red brick. Even its white marble steps were higher, wider, and more ostentatious. As Mrs. Rogers returned from marketing, she began her regular morning inspection of the place. Her chip basket was heaped high with food for the Christmas dinner, and she was glad to rest it on the wooden step cover which hid the shining white marble underneath. There were few Kensingtonian habits of which she approved, but going to market in person was an exception. Imagine letting Mary or Martha spend a cent of the household funds, or select a family roast! It was ridiculous even to think about.

She jerked the handle of the brass bell pull. Martha answered, and picked up the basket with more effort than Mrs. Rogers had used to carry it. "How you manage to lug that, I don't see, mum—all the way from the market."

"It's not heavy—I didn't find it so, at any rate. Of course, if you're too tired, or lazy . . ."

Martha was not one to bandy words. She fairly yanked the basket through the door and banged the door shut afterward.

Mrs. Rogers gave a little inward smile of contentment. Inspection of the house began in earnest.

The brass bell pull, the lock escutcheon, and the door-knobs were all polished. The double front doors were varnished, with an artificial graining on the wood that made an attractive display. They were heavy doors, richly ornamented with heavy molding, and were washed down twice a week by Mary. There was a smudge on the plate glass! Mrs. Rogers noted it mentally. She was conscious at this moment of a gap in her routine. Of course, the steps! Now that they were covered there was no need to see if they had been properly scoured, right into the corners. This brought another thought. What did Mary do with the time saved from scouring? She was vexed that it had not occurred to her before. In all the twenty-six years Mary had been with them, during the winter months she had been wasting daily an hour or more that in summer was used for scouring the steps. "That awful woman. No honor, no principle . . . she's been shirking that time, you see," she told herself.

She looked up at the front of the house. The bricks had been painted over a bright red, with the lines of mortar simulated in white paint. The job had been completed in October, but she still found a satisfaction in it. It was so much more distinguished than the bare natural-brick color of the other houses. The deeper, garnet shade of the paint and the brilliant white of the striping gave a richer tone.

There was a side garden that ran clear to the stable on the back street, and a cast-iron fence enclosed it. It was a handsome fence, Mrs. Rogers always thought. The design gave an effect of crisscrossed wickerwork, with open diamond-shaped spaces between. What gave it character, however, was the ornamentation in the center of each panel. The little iron baskets, filled with iron roses and tied with long streamers of metal ribbon, had delighted her ever

30

since the day she had picked the design at the ironmonger's.

Although she worked so hard to keep it up, there was little one could do with an old row house. "All that keeps this place distinctive is my taste, my flair for the unusual," she thought. She had not always felt this way about it. When she had gone there as a bride it had seemed a very grand and imposing home, but with the passage of years, and more frequent imaginings of ancestral castles in Italy, she had come to question its magnificence.

From where she stood, by the gate to the garden, she could see to the river, and the tall spars reminded her of an old regret. If Grandfather Rogers had not lost all his money in his ridiculous ventures, those spars would belong to them. The wide sails that filled on the river would be spreading to get riches for her spending. She thought back with anguish to the time, marriage vows barely made but already irrevocable, when she had learned that the wealth she had thought attained and ready for spending had fled her fingers like quicksilver. She remembered the anger of her father, who had been duped with her. Poor Papa! Count Borelli had lacked business acumen to sense the approaching disaster. He had been no match for the shrewd American merchant. He had looked forward so much to her union with traditionally substantial Quaker wealth as a solution of his own embarrassing problems. Even today, at this moment, it seemed impossible to her that wealth so real, so tangible, did not exist, and had not existed for more than twenty years.

She remembered how her husband's father had stood on the hard, solid deck of the *Sally Rogers* as he had expounded the seaworthiness of the beautiful craft. "What a deceitful old man!" she thought, as she had done many times before. Even at that moment, the bottom of the *Sally Rogers* had been honeycombed with the hidden

31

worms of debt, and its cargo, those solid casks she had seen slung ashore, mortgaged and distrained upon! She and her father had both met their disappointment with true Christian fortitude, she thought. For him, the dear, sweet man, it had not been for long. He had died, she was convinced, of a broken heart. It was she who had paid for that one mistake, for that fatal confidence in the integrity of the Rogers fortune. Her thought ran on. "No one will ever know what I suffered."

She caught herself from her daydreaming. Looking away from the points of spars stabbing the sky above the line of rooftops, she again scanned the front of the house. The busybody at the second floor window was dirty. "That lazy, impossible Mary," she thought. "I'll give her a talking-to. If I have told her once about that busybody . . ."

But this morning the past held claim on her. Her mind went back to her early married life. She stood with one hand grasping the spike in the center of the garden gate. Those early days! The years when Grandfather Rogers had lived with them, a broken old man; his last bedridden months, when he had been completely under her care. She fumbled for the gate latch, pressed it, and walked into the garden, to be reminded of another, a greater sorrow. There was the maple tree from which Raphael had fallen. Dark, slender Raphael, who had looked like her father for whom he was named, and whom she had loved more than any of her other children. Her first son had been a true born Borelli, not a Rogers, like Henry.

There was the limb, the treacherous limb from which he had slipped. The anguish of that hour! Her husband's refusal, his stubborn refusal, to procure a priest! What if that had been their bargain, anyone could see Raphael was no Quaker. Even now, twelve years later, she clenched her fists in anger.

Poor Raphael! Noble Raphael. Her beautiful, adorable man-child who had been injured in that fall, and died in three days, despite her constant attendance. Neither Julia, the pious and dutiful, nor Teresina, the tall and beautiful, had compensated for that loss, while the twins, with their obvious Rogers traits, had been sent to mock her.

That evil tree—every time she saw it she felt this way, but her husband would not allow it to be cut down. Now, with the leaves almost gone, its bare branches writhing in the fall breeze, the tree was to her more than ever a symbol of death.

And there was the hateful little pond Henry had dug two years before. She knew it bred mosquitoes, but Jesse insisted that it stay. It annoyed her anew to pass it now, and she hurried down through the garden to the stables.

Lucius had been careless in preparing the garden for winter. A heap of dry weeds lay against the stable wall, and dead stems of phlox and hollyhock plants needed cutting. She made another note in her mind. "I'll tell a few things to that lazy black scoundrel," she said to herself. She bit her lip and shook her head till her curls danced, thinking of Lucius' delinquency.

In the stable, she forgot unpleasant memories and household cares. She looked at the smooth, rounded rump of Mr. Quinby, nickering from his stall. Mr. Quinby loved her, she knew, and the affection was returned. "The finest horse in Kensington," she told herself. She rubbed her hand over the trotter's chestnut coat, and stepped close to stroke the soft, grain-sweet velvet of his muzzle. Mr. Quinby danced delightedly with little mincing steps. He accepted delicately a tribute of a few wisps of hay caught up from the side of his manger. In the far stall, Total

33

Eclipse whinnied for attention. The big old black horse was Mr. Rogers' favorite, although in the stable this made little difference to his wife. She stroked the black before giving her attention to the puppies. Nellie, the coach dog, always had her litter in the straw in the far corner of Mr. Quinby's stall. It had been so ever since her very first puppies. Time after time that first litter had been removed from the stall, and the danger of Mr. Quinby's hoofs, and on each occasion she had immediately picked up her brood, one by one, and returned them to the place she had selected. Her judgment had been good. There had never been an accident; Mr. Quinby seemed to realize his responsibility; he took the greatest care with each hoof as he lowered it, and gradually Nellie's choice was accepted.

Nellie looked up with soft brown eyes, following her mistress's movements until she turned toward her place in the straw. She pushed away the puppies and stood with both paws scratching against Mrs. Rogers' dress until her head was scratched, her long ears smoothed and rubbed. Mrs. Rogers knelt in the straw to play with the puppies. She gathered them in her lap and stroked their fat pink stomachs. It was too soon yet to be sure, but the little Dalmatians gave promise of being as beautifully spotted as the mother. Nellie licked her face with soft, warm tongue—wide licks of tongue that brushed wetly over nose and cheek and ear.

There was something soothing about the dog's lickings, about the animal warmth of the stable, about the smell of straw, hay, and grain, of the horses, of oil and soap from the carriage room. She picked out the two male puppies and held them up under her chin. Their noses ran in thin, cold, blindly questing circles until Mrs. Rogers laughed delightedly and placed them back by the satisfied mother.

34

She jumped from the straw and shook clinging bits of it from her dress. She felt a sudden happiness and began to sing in a clear, bell-like soprano that sustained a note until it became a transparent fragility in the air. "Funiculi, funiculá!" she sang. There was work to do in the house. Tomorrow was Christmas, and there would be company in for Christmas Eve: the Naylor children, probably, and Gus Palmer, and the Peales from next door. And Father would begin one of his political arguments with Harry Naylor. . . . She stopped singing and sighed. Then, determinedly, she began again, though not so freely as before. She walked back toward the house, by the vegetable garden with its last hilled-up row of celery, through the grape arbor and up the wooden steps into the shed, and all the way she sang "Some think the world is made for fun and frolic, and so do I! And so do I!"

2

The three women spent most of the day in the kitchen, completing preparations for the morrow. They cleaned and dressed the goose, which had been hanging in the shed for a week, ever since it had been brought from a farm near Fox Chase. Apples were pared and made into sauce. Oysters, brought up from the lower Jersey coves, were dumped in the sink, and Mary shucked them with all the skill of an old oysterman. She drew a tubful of water, added cornmeal, and placed the shelled oysters in it to "fatten" overnight. Three plum puddings, in flour sacks, were hung to drain on a hook by the goose.

Mrs. Rogers added more brandy to the crocks of mincemeat maturing in the cellar. Lucius was sent out to dig up some of the celery that was blanching in a row down one side of the garden, and this was cleaned and trimmed.

35

He next brought in a pumpkin from the pile covered with earth to keep off the frost.

The kitchen was redolent with odors heightened by the intense heat of the coal range. There was the sharp fragrance of spices and cooking sherry, the subtlety of onion, and the fruitiness of apples stewing. Mary's nose kept sniffing appreciatively in anticipation of the coming feast, and even Martha forgot her usual silence long enough to observe, "Smells good, don't it?"

Mrs. Rogers' curls shook and bobbed with each toss of her head. She executed a few steps of a polka while carrying the pumpkin, holding it high so that it appeared to be the head of a dancing partner with whom she was engaging in animated conversation. She waltzed the goose twice around the table before rehanging it. She sang a funny song she had heard years ago:

> Will you go with me, my Phyllis dear,
> To yon blue mountain free?
> Where the blossoms smell the sweetest,
> Come ride along with me.
> This very Sunday morning,
> When I am by your side,
> We'll jump into the wagon
> And all take a ride.

When she reached the chorus, she insisted that Mary and Martha join in. Mary surpassed herself, topping the others in a trembling falsetto while she thought: "There's no one like her. On the go every minute—a body can't tell what's coming next." She remembered all the good times there had been in the house since the mistress had come to it, a sweet little lady of a bride. "Brimming over with song and fun, like the suds on a bucket of beer," Mary phrased it in her mind. At moments like these she

36

would have hotly resented any allusion to her mistress's less amiable characteristics.

"Mary, that was good—the alto was fine," Mrs. Rogers pronounced. "But, Martha, you flatted on the last note. It goes this way." She la-la-ed the line. "We'll try it again, and louder this time."

The three women put their heads together, with the mistress in the center. Her short left arm barely encircled the cook's ample waist, while her right hand beat the time with a large nickeled spoon.

> Wait for the wagon,
> Wait for the wagon,
> Wait for the wagon,
> And we'll all take a ride.

This time it was perfect, as they all took the ride together in perfect harmony.

"My, I'll never forget the first time I heard that. It was in Boston—dear Father took me there on a visit, before Zena married. We went to the minstrels—Buckley's Minstrels, it was—and Mr. Buckley himself sang it, and the minstrels, all in blackface, sang the chorus." She stood for a moment, pensively, while Martha and Mary watched her, love in their hearts. Simultaneously, they became conscious of tasks undone and began to work again. But Mrs. Rogers' spirits were too ebullient to allow her to remain quiet long. She sang again as she mixed butter and sugar together for the hard sauce on the pudding. "Shoo, fly, don't bother me," she sang. Each time she reached "Shoo, fly," she made a motion with her hand as if to brush away the annoying insect. "What dear Father used to say was that sauce made with song never lasted long. You see what he meant, Mary? It tasted better, and got eaten up quicker. . . . Oh, my dear father—a

37

nobleman he was, in every sense of the word. The times we had when he was alive!"

Suddenly she wondered where Julia was and what she was doing. She stopped in the middle of adding the rum to the hard sauce, and handed the wooden bowl containing the buttery mixture to the cook.

"Here, Martha, finish this. I have to look up Julia. She's probably moping by herself, up in her room." As she went through the door, she turned around, put her head on one side, cut a little caper, brushed away a whole swarm of flies, and sang the last lines again: "Shoo, fly, don't bother me, for I belong to Company G."

Mary took the bowl from the cook. "Let me finish up the sauce for you. It's time you got started on dinner. If it's not ready on time there'll be the very devil to pay."

Martha began to throw pots and pans about the range, and Mary talked on. "Ain't she the case though? There's somethin' doin' every minute with her around."

The cook nodded her head sententiously. "The madam is like a cow that gives good milk 'n' then kicks the bucket over."

"You took the very words out of my mouth," Mary agreed, nodding her head furiously, "but there ain't anyone better when she wants to be—with fun in her heart, and she'd give up the shirt from her back."

"Gives good milk, and then when you ain't thinkin', or just lookin' that way, kicks over the bucket," Martha elaborated.

3

Mrs. Rogers sang "Shoo, fly," all the way to the second floor, but by the time she reached the third all her energy was required for breathing. "Why Julia wants to live in the garret I can't understand," she said to herself. She slowly mounted the narrow stairway that led from the third floor to the low-ceilinged room under the roof, and her good-natured mood evaporated completely. Her thought ran on. "I declare there's no sense to it. Wanting to be away where it's quiet!"

Julia heard her mother's sharp, hasty steps on the bare floor of the hall, and straightened up in her chair by the frame holding her lacework.

"You shouldn't work so steadily, Julia, it's so hard on your eyes. It will ruin them, doing anything so fine."

Julia gave a shrug of resignation. "The nuns at the school . . ."

"Nonsense, it's all right for the nuns. It doesn't matter whether they wear glasses or not, but I'll have no daughter of mine disfiguring herself with them. How would you ever catch a man with those things on?" She gazed out the narrow window that gave upon the areaway separating that part of the house from the Peales'. "No view, and no air. All you can see is the stable, and rooftops. Nothing but rooftops, clear to the river. Why you stay in this room when you could have the one next to Gene's, I can't see."

"It reminds me so of Paris." Julia bent over the lace frame and began to stitch painstakingly.

"You might still be there if you had played your cards right. Your aunt would have kept you on, but she wanted someone young and gay, and you turned saint on her." Mrs. Rogers scolded her daughter with mounting anger. "You knew your aunt was disappointed when you came. You could have played up to her just a little. Who knows, with all her money, she might have left you her entire fortune, then you would never have to worry."

Julia shrugged her shoulders. "Other things mean more to me."

"Don't try pretty speeches on me, young lady. You were in Paris, with everything a girl could want, an aunt who wanted someone to dote over, and you made a fool of yourself. She wanted me to send Zenie because she's named after her, but I thought she could get along anywhere, and sent you."

Julia bent her head closer to her work and made a series of minute stitches while her mother talked on. "She wrote me a hot letter, I can tell you." She plumped herself down in the straight-backed wooden chair that stood by the bed, and talked in a series of angry outbursts. "But she put you in school, gave you everything. Zena couldn't have done more for you if you had been her own, I must say."

Julia remained silent. She tried by her dutiful expression to make her mother stop, but Mrs. Rogers was rehearsing a favorite plaint.

"In another year or so you could have met the most charming men in Paris. If instead of starving yourself you'd stuffed a bit and put some meat on your bones, you could have been attractive. There is nothing Frenchmen like more than a well-rounded figure. You have a pretty face, and you might have caught someone really wealthy."

"I'm afraid I wasn't interested. You forget I was going to school. In the convent . . ."

"Stop this holy business with me. My faith is just as strong as yours, but it doesn't prevent me from knowing a good thing when I see it." She turned her eyes upward. "When poor Father died, his faith was the greatest heritage he could leave me. If you have any religion at all, it's certainly because of me. If your father had his way, you'd all be heathens." She gave a snort of anger. "I can see you all, wearing gray bonnets and those outlandish Quaker rigs. Mark my words, you have me to thank."

"I've often prayed Papa might become a Catholic, or

just a good Quaker. He never even goes to their Meeting."
Julia shook her head.

"We'll leave your father out of this. He is my problem
and you are my problem, and just when I thought you
were settled, with a future ensured, you had to spoil everything."

Mrs. Rogers stopped only for want of breath to go on.
She jumped from the chair and walked to the window with
quick steps. Down near the stable she saw Lucius spreading manure on the garden with an aimless, languid fork.
"That boy!" She threw open the window, and the cold
December air made Julia shiver. "You there, Lucius!"
Her voice was a thin, piercing scream that cut the colored
man like a whip. He sprang into quick activity, throwing
about him with great abandon. "Get on with that manur-
ing. It'll snow, and then where will you be?"

The question remained unanswered, and Mrs. Rogers
banged the window in closing it so that the glass shivered.
"I always have to be after that boy." She returned to the
chair and sat wearily in it as if the responsibilities of housekeeping had completely overcome her.

Julia looked out. Lucius had returned to his original
indolent pace, idly casting the brown clots of manure. She
smiled as she turned and prepared herself for the continu-
ation of her mother's lecture.

"What to do with that boy—lazy and good-for-nothing
. . . Why I put up with him I don't know. I tell you,
I'd send him packing if we didn't need a boy for the horse,
and Mr. Quinby does love him. He'd be disconsolate without Lucius. . . . Why, I don't know. Of all the shiftless,
irresponsible boys in Kensington!"

"Why, Mother, you couldn't get rid of Lucius. He
came when you married—it always seems funny when you
call him a boy—and what would all his children do if you

41

turned him off?" Julia smiled in remembrance. "His babies always remind me of Nellie's puppies. There are always more coming and they all have the same soft, pleading brown eyes."

Mrs. Rogers jumped up. "I'm sitting here when there's still work to do, but before I go, let me tell you, young lady, there are some things you ought to think about, and one of them is putting more meat on your bones. I haven't seen what you weigh lately, but I'd lay a wager it's less than a hundred and thirty, and that's not enough. You need to fatten yourself up. If you had stayed in Paris, and really made an effort, who knows, perhaps . . ."

Julia tried to stem the tirade, but it was not until her mother tired that she could break in, with a protesting, injured air. "Really, need we start this again?" She rose from her lace frame. "I've made some things for Lucius' new baby. He's named it Jupiter. I know the poor little thing will get called 'Jupe,' and won't that sound just awful? I have some little gifts for the others, too, so I think I'll walk down while Louisa is there." She kissed her mother on the forehead with an air of patience and forbearance. Her calmness of manner infuriated the older woman; she shrugged her shoulders despairingly.

"You walk in front, Julia. I'll follow you down. The stairs are so steep I'm afraid of giddiness. . . . Why you have to stay up here, away from everyone, I don't see."

Chapter 4

Mrs. Rogers stood patiently while her husband buttoned her up the back. She pretended to be unaware of the storm brewing behind her, of the constant low rumble of protest, the sibilant noises of vexation when an unwilling button shied from its too-small hole. One popped loose, and there was a sharp lightning of expletive, but before the storm could break she said:

"Really, Jesse, you make so much fuss about those buttons, I'd rather let Mary do them for me."

"Mary! Mary with her poor, rheumatic fingers manage these devilish little spheres that elude the touch like mercury? Pah! If you depended on Mary to button you into this strait jacket, this eelskin, this . . ." Mr. Rogers stopped for a moment to invent further comparisons, lost the train of his sentence, and continued: "Besides, so long as I am part of it, this family shall dress itself. Your sister can have her French maid, but there will be none in my house."

Mrs. Rogers gave an affected, girlish giggle. "Father, your sense of extremes is amusing. Zena's maid and our Mary! You know what Zena would do with Mary? She'd send her to the old folks' home, where she belongs—that's what she'd do."

At that moment, Mr. Rogers' fingers were desperately engaged with a recalcitrant button in the small of her back, and she moved instinctively.

"Whoa, there! By the Lord Harry, woman, if I must button you up the back, hold still. *Hold still.*"

"Not so loud, Jesse. It's hardly modest in you to announce to the whole of Kensington that you are helping with my dress." She had the uncomfortable feeling that a game of tittattoe was in progress down the length of her spine. ". . . Forty-three, forty-four . . ." Mr. Rogers' voice boomed triumphantly as he counted the buttons, "forty-five, forty-six." Then the storm broke, that she had tried so hard to evade. "*Forty-six*—six more than the last dress. Woman, you have tried my patience too far.

43

This is no longer fashion, but pure folly. It is grounds for divorce—far past the end of human endurance. When this home is broken up, our poor children entered in eleemosynary institutions, our faithful servitors dispersed, the cause of it will be buttons, buttons, *buttons.*"

Mrs. Rogers arched her head coquettishly, and ran a hand down the ample folds of stiff silk. "Why, Jesse, you should like your wife to be fashionable. This is the most beautiful dress I have ever had, and you know it. You'll be proud of your Augustina tonight. Now admit it is really beautiful." She walked a step or two, to display the full drapery of the material, its rich rustle along the carpet; she forgot entirely that her husband was still struggling with the final button. It pulled out of his fingers and evaded the buttonhole just when it had seemed ready to submit. Instinctively she winced, a reaction of her nervous system to another roar of protest, but this time there was none. With sudden determination and a facility he ordinarily refused to display, Mr. Rogers recaptured the button and popped it easily into place. When she turned around he was standing with an almost fatuous expression of admiration on his face. The claret-colored stiff watered silk was richly trimmed with heavy braid, and it did enhance her dark coquettish beauty, while her face could recapture, at moments like this, a girlish expression that created an illusion of youth.

"It's lovely silk, Father, real Lyons silk—look at the weight of it. Zena sent it on to me a year or so ago, and I just had it made up." She arched her body, confined in a tight vise of corset, so that the deep curving line of her back was emphasized. "How do you like the cut of it in back? It's the very latest mode—the Grecian bend, they call it."

Mr. Rogers roared with laughter until the photographs

that adorned the wall shook in their varnished walnut frames. His mouth opened like a cave of the winds, from which a hurricane of sound emanated. "The Grecian bend! Ha, ha . . . ho, ho!" He drew a handkerchief from the pocket in the tail of his coat and dabbed it to his eyes as if reduced to tears from laughter unrestrained. "My darling Gussie, you are possessed of endless combinations of curves and bends, all of which I recollect with sensations of extreme pleasure, but I say to you, if Phidias had beheld that ridiculous, artificially contrived posture you call the Grecian bend, he would have cried out in horrified protest at such distortion of the female form. Later, if you wish, I'll recall to you your Grecian bends—Grecian bends, indeed!" He walked over and sat down on the side of the huge walnut bed that filled the end of the room. His weight rattled the slats under the box spring.

"Land sakes, Jesse, you'll push the bottom right out of that bed."

In his really jovial moments, Mr. Rogers was louder, if anything, than when angry. "Push the bottom through this bed? You should know better than that, Mother. . . . This is none of your light modern stuff, made for namby-pambys, but a tried—and well tried—article of furniture."

Mrs. Rogers colored prettily. "Jesse, there is no need to be downright vulgar."

"Nonsense. There's nothing like a little good wholesome vulgarity, but let who will stand up and say that the testing of our bed was vulgar and I shall rise to refute him.

"And what is vulgarity? I shall tell you. It is lack of restraint. Anything can be carried too far, and it is the extreme to which I offer protest. This costume of yours is extreme, and therefore vulgar. It is the product of a decadent civilization. It accents the lush, matronly

45

charms of your lovely bosom until one would think a cow represented the ideal of fashion, and the natural amplitude of the feminine posterior is increased . . . magnified . . . distorted, to proportions such as voluptuaries conjure in their most obscene imaginings. There, madam, is vulgarity."

Mrs. Rogers put her hands before her face so that mischievous black eyes peered out between plump jeweled fingers. "Mr. Rogers, indeed you shock me." She turned with a sharp rustle of her gown and began to adjust a curl before the bureau mirror. Her husband's long arm reached out and encircled her waist. She tried to pry loose the great hand that pressed against her. "Jesse, behave yourself. My best French silk—you'll ruin it." There was no evading him. As the easiest way to prevent damage to her costume, Mrs. Rogers seated herself upon his knee; his beard tickled her neck and ear.

"Fashions or no, Gussie, you're as sweet and girlish as the day I married you, and that's more than can be said for most women over twenty years married. Is it the love of an adoring husband keeps you young, or is there some mystical fountain of youth in that handsome zinc bathtub you pestered me into buying for you? Perhaps I should use it, instead of the wooden tub in the shed."

At the first opportunity, Mrs. Rogers jumped up quickly, eluded her husband's restraining hand, and moved over to the bureau. If it is possible to scamper in a French silk dress, well lined and made of ample material, she scampered over to the marble-topped bureau, and began a frantic search among cut-glass cologne and bay-rum bottles and silver-backed brush and comb. She pushed aside the green vial of smelling salts and the jar of pomade Mr. Rogers used for dressing his beard. She moved each

46

article so that it clattered against the bureau top until her husband said:

"Good heavens, Gussie, what have you lost? You'll break one of those bottles, if you don't crack that handsome marble top."

"It's a letter from Zena. I intended to show it to you, but it slipped my mind until this moment." As she continued her pretense of rummaging in the bureau, her eyes kept keen watch in the mirror, to read in its reflection any change from her husband's benign mood. She debated whether this was really a good time to bring forth Zena's letter from its hiding place in her jewel case.

For all their married life, Mrs. Rogers' sister had been the subject of much contention in the family. Thoughts of Zena's good fortune always made her dissatisfied with her own life, and she could never resist reminding her husband of the difference in their stations. Zena had enjoyed just the career Augustina wanted, or thought she wanted. She had married a man with a large fortune who died shortly after, leaving to her the spending of it. Her youth and middle age had been given over to flirtations and love affairs, and scandal borne clear across the Atlantic still rumored her exploits.

It was not her sister's love affairs, or her own carping at her wealth, that furnished the chief irritant in the Rogers household. It was Zena's generosities. She had sent as a present the French clock in the dining room, the spindly-legged chairs in the parlor, and half the gimcracks that filled every shelf, mantelpiece, table top, or other flat surface that could be utilized for their display—useless things that got in Mr. Rogers' way, or were knocked over inadvertently and broken. Zena had given Julia convent schooling, she had . . . Almost every month brought some token of her affection. It was only unfortunate that so many of her gifts were of an impractical nature.

Mrs. Rogers decided to take the risk. Nothing chanced, nothing gained, she thought, and aloud, her mind groping frantically for some divertissement, in case of ill reception:

"Well, wherever I've put it I don't know, but Zena writes she's coming over for the Centennial. She'll arrive in March, to be here for the opening."

Her unpredictable husband beamed his pleasure. "Hooray! Both of the Borelli beauties at one time. Of course she'll stay with us"—and then the first hint of displeasure —"or perhaps our humble little quarters, with only two servants in the house, won't be sufficiently grand?"

"Oh, la, Father, of course she'll stay with us. She asked particularly for a room on the second floor, as she's gout-ish." Mrs. Rogers lied magnificently and with adequate imagination, for the whole last page of Zena's letter had been given over to the matter of hotel reservations.

"Evidently she can't trip as lightly as you, Mother. You can see, my dear, there is nothing like the bearing of children to keep one youthful."

"Go on with you, Jesse Rogers. A little while ago it was my bathtub, which you refuse to use, and now it's childbearing. You might as well admit we are just an unpleasant old couple, and stop your flattery."

She picked up her chatelaine, which accompanied her always, and Mr. Rogers offered his arm in heavy, playful gallantry. As they walked downstairs she used his good humor to press home a last request.

"Now, Pet, this is Christmas Eve, and it's for the young people. Don't start on politics with Harry Naylor. He's becoming quite interested in Teresina, and the way her affair with Gus Palmer is going, I'm not at all sure it wouldn't be a better match." When Mrs. Rogers said

"Pet" she was being as persuasive as she could, for it was a term dating from their honeymoon days and carried special significance.

While Mr. Rogers nodded in seeming consent, he was already marshaling in his mind the arguments with which to overwhelm the young politician. As they entered the long narrow front parlor, everyone stood up to welcome them and began a murmur of Merry Christmases. They were lost like the chirp of sparrows in a storm when Mr. Rogers thundered, "Merry Christmas . . . and a Happy New Year!" The parlor was quite filled, which meant a good audience for his monologue on the evils of the Republican party. He always looked forward to Harry Naylor's infrequent visits from Harrisburg, to engage in one of their "little chats on the state of the nation" or to obtain the "inside story of affairs at the Capitol," as he variously termed their one-sided conversations.

He assisted his wife into the large, comfortable chair close to the parlor stove, the one he ordinarily occupied, and took for himself the seat closest to the young state senator. The chair was one of the slender French ones sent over by Aunt Zena, and at any other time nothing could have forced him to sit in it. Tonight was different. The country would soon have a new national election, which to his mind would reform the United States or damn the country utterly, and it was a burning necessity to attempt the conversion of young Naylor to his views.

It was rumored in the neighborhood that the Naylors were half Indian, and Harry looked the part. He was tall and broad-shouldered, with very dark skin. His eyes were an opaque black that allowed no passage outward of the thoughts behind them, and seemed to absorb none of the outside light. He had a large strong nose that stood out like a cliff over a heavy, drooping black mustache, and

49

square white teeth that startled one when he laughed. He was the complete opposite in appearance of Augustus Palmer, and in Mr. Rogers' opinion, except for his political beliefs a much more suitable husband for his eldest daughter. "Teresina needs someone to hold the whip hand over her," he phrased the thought to himself, "and Gus just ain't man enough."

Gus was at the piano now, playing a soft prelude to one of his favorite ballads. He was not as tall as Harry, and of a more slender build. He had fair curly hair, a lock of which constantly fell over his eyes, and a luxuriant though pale mustache. His expression was usually serious, and his chin could be hard and strong, but when he played or sang, he became another person. If he sang a sea chantey, he seemed instantly to become a rollicking sailor just come into port. When he sang a comic song, his eyes lighted and his smile became infectious. A moment later, he would be the romantic lover, sighing a lovesick strain to the moon. The whole family was fond of Gus. Georgina actually adored him, and Julia might have fallen in love with him had not the standard of her father blinded her to lesser men.

Mr. Rogers, like Julia, measured other men by himself, and was not always too perceptive. In judging Gus, he mistook a slighter build for a weaker one. He missed the strength of purpose that had carried the comparatively poor boy through college and medical school, and saw only an adoring suitor whom Teresina ordered around at will. Teresina was the chink in Gus's armor. Against her he had no real defense. He argued with her, they had serious quarrels, but in the end he always capitulated. This Mr. Rogers saw, and it contributed to his belief that Augustus Palmer was too spineless ever to achieve success, with Teresina or in his profession. That was another thing—

he had nothing but respect for the general practice of medicine, but he objected to Gus's avowed intention of specializing in obstetrical practice. It seemed indelicate to Mr. Rogers that males should preside at time of birth, and he suspected that no real man would deliberately choose such a career.

Teresina sat between the two suitors—if Harry could be called a suitor, for until recently he had shown nothing but a most polite interest. She wore a dress of striped silk, with wide bands of rose against a cream-colored background. It was a tasteful combination, and she looked very beautiful in it, Mr. Rogers thought, although he always resented the cool poise that seemed to remove her from whatever company she found herself in.

Lizzie and Carrie Naylor sat in the love seat. They wore unbecoming black, and their short, fat bodies so filled the little chair, with their dresses run together in an indistinguishable whole, that they seemed to comprise a single double-headed monster. While both sisters had bodies of the same proportions, Lizzie had a thin, hawklike face, not unlike Harry's, and Carrie had fat, pudgy features, more in keeping with her form. The gaze of both centered on their eldest brother, whom they adored, and avoided Al, the family black sheep, who was talking animatedly with the twins. This trio occupied an ornate backless chair, or cricket, that stood at the end of the room, wedged in between piano and wall. It was an uncomfortable seat for three, since it was highest in the middle, where Georgina sat, and the two boys kept sliding off to the sides; but she solved the problem. She had each boy put an arm about her waist, and then shouted to the company:

"Look, we're the Three Musketeers—'All for one, one for all, that is our device.' "

As usual, Julia sat quietly in a corner, the one farthest

51

from the piano, and hidden partly by the whatnot and its collection of mementos and souvenirs. She was shocked by Georgina's action. It was bad enough for her to allow Henry to put his arm around her waist, and absolutely shameless for Al's to be there also, but no one reproved her. Julia tried to think of an excuse to retire to her room, but Gus began to sing again. Along with the others, she forgot everything but the charm of his tenor voice. "The spell is past, the dream is o'er, and though we meet, we love no more." Julia could imagine the poignancy of a situation such as the ballad described, and her eyes filled with tears that gave them unusual brilliance.

Mrs. Rogers' glance, darting restlessly from one to another of the company, lighted on Julia at this moment, and she thought: "The girl is positively ravishing—Zenie isn't one, two, three with her for looks! If she would only eat more, and put on twenty or thirty pounds, she might still be the first of my girls married, and to real money, too." Her attention was distracted from such a prospect by ominous mutterings, puffs, blows, and ejaculations emanating from her husband's beard, which she recognized as vocal exercises preparatory to a discussion of the sins of General Grant and his Cabinet. For just an ordinary political argument concerning Pennsylvania politics and Messrs. Cameron and Quay, no such warming-up noises were required. Only the national scene demanded such preparations.

"No politics—at all costs, no politics," Mrs. Rogers determined mentally. She jumped from her chair as Gus finished his lover's lament. "Gus, won't you play for Father while he sings 'The Beggar Girl'? You remember how beautifully he sang it at Ada Peale's birthday party?" She ran over to Mr. Rogers' chair and began to coax him with a pretty show of affected gestures, wheedlings, and poutings.

Ordinarily he would have been delighted to sing—once at the piano it was difficult to get him away—but tonight he was distinctly annoyed, as she knew he would be, and it required all her charm to cajole him. "Come, Father, everybody is waiting!" She caught one of his large hands in both of hers, and pouted when he resisted.

"Now, Mother. They've all heard me sing that song— they don't want to hear it again. Besides, I want to chat with Harry a little, about affairs at Washington."

"Come, Jesse, you can't get off. You must oblige the company."

Harry said: "Yes, by all means, sir. I haven't heard that song, although I have reports from others of the robust and musical qualities of your voice."

Mrs. Rogers sent Harry a grateful look as she led her husband to the piano. Everyone applauded loudly, the twins with more noise than the rest, while Mrs. Rogers thought: "I know what makes Harry such a good politician. He knows how to butter people up. Thank heaven, he put Jesse in a good mood again."

Once in the public eye, Mr. Rogers forgot his chagrin and reacted to his love of dominating the scene. He stroked his beard with both hands, and then coughed politely, as Gus played through the introduction. With studied grace, he placed a hand on the tasseled scarf that ornamented the piano top, and sang in a strong baritone better suited to sea chanteys:

> Pity, kind gentlemen, friends of humanity.
> Cold blows the wind, and the night's coming on.

He paid a great deal of attention to appropriate gesture and intonation. When he sang "pity," the foundations of

53

the house shook with the persuasive tones, while his right hand stretched forth, palm upward. Georgina giggled, and met a hard look of stern reproval. Singing was a serious business to her parent. "I can almost see Father, beard and all, begging in a tattered skirt and the wind whipping it about his ankles," she whispered to Henry, which caused him to titter as well. As Mr. Rogers sang on, he made a resolve to reprove his favorite children later.

> Give me some food for my mother for charity,
> Give me some food, and then I'll be gone.

But he wasn't gone, for there were verses and verses still to be sung. In the next, about a poor dead father who perished of hunger while he wandered the night, bare-footed, Mr. Rogers really spread himself, with sentimental tremolos and explanatory waves of his hand that were marvels of interpretive gesture.

Julia was enraptured, the twins amused, Teresina aloof, Mrs. Rogers relieved, Lizzie and Carrie Naylor unaware of anyone but their brother, while no one could tell at all what Harry thought.

Teresina was aloof. Her mind was engaged in a problem only remotely connected with anyone present. She had decided to give up Gus as a marital prospect. A doctor without money required so many years to become a success, and Teresina did not intend to wait until Gus had proved himself. Nor did she wish to chance a marriage that might mean a future of comparative poverty. As for Harry Naylor, although he was already a top-ranking office-holder in the Cameron-Quay political machine, she did not really like him, and felt uncomfortable in his presence. "You can't tell what he's thinking," was her mental criticism. "He might be getting ready to kiss or to scalp you, and from his expression you couldn't tell which."

During her father's performance, Teresina was speculating upon the problem of meeting eligible men. "I'd be throwing myself away on anyone here in Kensington," she thought. "If I could stay at Long Branch for the summer, now that the President has the summer capital there, perhaps I could make a real conquest—but Father would put his foot down, and Mother—well, Mother thinks anyone with a few thousands is a catch." Her mind reverted to the great disappointment in her life, so far. "If Mother had only let me go to Paris, instead of Julia, I would have made something of it. The men I could meet in Paris!" She applauded dutifully when "The Beggar Girl" came to an end. Joined to the hearty handclapping of the others, it made a gratifying reception which demanded an encore, and Mr. Rogers was delighted to give one.

The time seemed opportune to Mrs. Rogers to leave the scene and supervise Mary in the preparation of a collation. "So long as Father is singing he won't get started on politics, and it will be safe for me to get things ready," she thought. She gave the dining-room table a last quick inspection. It was gay with a centerpiece of holly; she rearranged it and then stood back to view the effect. Her thoughts ran on. "There, that's better." She nodded, then pursed up her lips. "Mary has no sense of decoration, and heaven knows what she is up to right this minute."

In the kitchen, Mary was turning the ice-cream freezer. Her feeble strength barely moved the crank impeded by the almost frozen mixture, and she was perspiring freely from her efforts.

"Good heavens! After nine o'clock, and the ice cream not ready yet! Mary, what are you thinking of?"

"It's almost set, ma'am. I've just been givin' it a last lick before icing it up." Her old eyes peered slyly, to see how Mrs. Rogers was taking her explanation. Her mistress nodded her head slowly, and then suspicion sharpened her features. "I'm in for it," Mary thought. "The woman has eyes can look right through a body's mind."

"A last lick—a good many licks, is my guess. I know what you've been up to, you wretch. You've been eating it. I should know by this time I can't leave you alone with ice cream in the house. It's a passion—a curse—a greedy, selfish habit. The idea of eating the top off that whole freezer of cream, and then churning it up again so I can't tell the difference!"

Mary regretted her unfortunate choice of words, but denied the charge strenuously, the more so because it was true. The love of ice cream was her greatest weakness. It was the only delicacy she could eat without pain to her bare gums. It was so cold, so rich and satisfying, that what had begun as a taste on a spoon tip had ended as an orgy. She said to herself: "If she had only stayed out a minute longer, no one would have ever knowed the difference." She was more hurt that Mrs. Rogers had not trusted her than that she had been found out. "Imagine her sneaking out before time; while they're still singing— suspicious, she is—trying to catch me taking something. Well, she didn't, but I'm telling you, life in this house is hard."

"Here, give me that freezer," Mrs. Rogers commanded. She took the handle that Mary had been barely able to turn, and spun it around. "It's a pretty pass when I have to make my own ice cream with two servants in the house."

Mary hustled around the kitchen as if to give the lie to all her mistress said about her, grumbling to herself, "There ain't no use in denying anything to her, she knows it all, right or wrong."

Mrs. Rogers cocked an ear toward the parlor. Everyone

was singing, now, and the song was "Kitty Clyde," another of her husband's favorites. She could hear his voice above the others: "In a sweet little nook, by the babbling brook, there lies my sweet Kitty Clyde."

As yet, no politics. She began to hope she had staved off that disaster.

2

The late arrival of the Peale family cut short the singing. When the doorbell rang, Kitty Clyde had been buried for the third or fourth time in "the sweet little nook" of the chorus. The company accepted the uselessness of further interment, and the single volume of the singing shattered into a number of conversational fragments. Al Naylor began a spirited argument with Georgina about the relative merits of neighborhood horses. His sisters discussed together the clothing to be packed for Harry's return trip to Harrisburg; that gentleman began some heavy pleasantries with Teresina, who answered them too automatically, so their conversational ball dribbled loggily instead of bouncing resiliently in approved fashion.

A draft of cold air entered with the Peales, and it was not alone from the terrific Merry Christmases that Mr. Rogers typhooned after them from down the hall. It had definitely turned colder. "Winter at last! It's cold enough out to crack a fifty-pound rail!" Mr. Rogers shouted above the din of welcome. The Peales had only crossed over their joint front steps, but each of them described the reaction to that moment in the cold, and followed with explanations and apologies for their lateness. They had been visiting in Northern Liberties. For some reason there had been no horsecars running, and they had walked the several miles back to Kensington.

Ada Peale joined Georgina and the boys. When Henry

was away, she and Georgina were inseparable, but since his expulsion from school after the cat episode they had seen comparatively little of each other, and now had endless confidences to exchange. Ada was a short, stocky girl, a year younger than Georgina, with a tolerant, cheerful personality. She had curly brown hair and laughing, light-brown eyes with none of the malice in them Georgina so often displayed.

Mrs. Peale was a tall woman of ample girth, whose corsets succeeded in giving her body a forward thrust which conveyed a feeling of movement even when she stood still. Her husband was a quiet man not nearly so tall as herself. He suffered from a feeling of inferiority excepting at those times when he forgot himself in discussing the movement nearest his heart, the Knights of Labor, a secret society for workingmen in which he was an officer.

Mrs. Rogers came in from the kitchen. She always took a high tone with the Peales, whom she considered far beneath her in the social scale, and her attitude now was that of a duchess graciously welcoming the tenantry to an annual Christmas celebration. She held forth her hand at almost shoulder height, making her wrist affectedly limp. "Why, dear Mrs. Peale! It's so good you could come." She spoke in tones quite different from those she regularly used in chatting with her next-door neighbor, but if Mrs. Peale noticed, she paid no attention. She had a real liking for her neighbor and ascribed all her peculiarities to her foreign birth.

The state of the weather was gone over again in great detail. Mrs. Rogers tried desperately to keep her husband engaged in polite conversation. It had been an open winter, so far. Who remembered when there had been skating on the Delaware at Christmas time? The snows had been light, and of short duration. The cold snaps were

58

less cold than in former years. When each point was established by the group as a whole, Mrs. Rogers interceded with "Don't you think so, Jesse?" or a pert "I'm sure I don't remember that far back, but Father would know"—which allowed him to describe in detail every winter (as he remembered it) from childhood days to the present. Curiously enough, no one was ever bored by Mr. Rogers' accounts. They were so larded with boisterous laughs, humorous stories, and strange expletives having a railroad flavor that people forgot entirely their pointlessness.

In her anxiety to keep her husband away from dangerous topics, Mrs. Rogers neglected her other guests, and was chagrined to discover that during her preoccupation with the weather, a full-bodied argument concerning the scandals of the Grant Administration was in progress. It was Mr. Peale who had begun it. Who would have thought it of him? He was usually so gentle, so mild, so unassertive, and here he was describing the villainies that caused the panic quite as if Harry Naylor himself had been responsible for it. In Mrs. Rogers' code, polite parlor talk consisted of inanities gracefully delivered, obvious little double-entendres not too indelicate, and similar amiable chatter. Her husband's refusal to conform to this standard was always a source of great unhappiness to her, especially during the war years, when his forthright denunciation of the Union cause had embarrassed her and subjected him to discomfort and actual danger. Now, when things had been going so well, it was unfair of her neighbor to undo all her efforts to spend Christmas Eve without bringing up that man Grant again—and the panic.

So far, the Rogerses had been fortunate. Although the panic had started two years ago, and business depression was extreme, the remnants of the Rogers fortune were conservatively invested, with no dimunition of income, and

Mr. Rogers' salary and position with the railroad had not changed. Mrs. Rogers measured any question by its effect upon herself, and after the restrictions of the war years, General Grant seemed to have done quite a good job. Supposing he had been dishonest, and his Cabinet members were rascals? It was just like Jesse to fuss and fume over such things, but she couldn't see where he had been hurt. In fact, she wished *he* were smart enough to pick up a fortune out of a whisky ring, or railroads—in an honest way, of course.

Mr. Rogers, realizing suddenly that another conversation was going on under cover of his reminiscences about the weather, waited to discern the depth, strength, and direction of its current before plunging in. It took only a second to get his bearings. Evidently Sol Peale had been reproaching Harry with the evils of the Cameron-Quay machine, dominant in Pennsylvania politics and Republican, and as defense, Harry countered with a description of the equal corruptions of the Democratic Tweed Ring until recently in control of New York. Mr. Rogers huffed and puffed in his whiskers, then rose and stood as if on a rostrum. His cough blew Mr. Peale's arguments clean from his mind. Hitching a thumb through his watch chain, he rumbled:

"Gentlemen, in one short week we shall enter upon the hundredth year of our life as a nation. In our own fair city a celebration is planned in honor of that event—an Exposition, in which nothing of our internal condition will be exposed. I say to you, democracy has failed in these states if the only excuse for its knaveries the Republican party can make is that there was also a rascal on the other side."

Mr. Rogers paused, not for want of words, but for rhetorical effect, which was largely spoiled by his wife, still determined upon a genteel, unpolitical evening. She used the pause to inject "Jesse, was it in seventy-one or seventy-two we had the blizzard?"

He was certain there hadn't been a blizzard since sixty-nine, and at any other time would have braved hell and high water to prove it, but now he pretended not to have heard, and continued, in a less rounded flow of words:

"The hotheads in the North, Republicans all, who brought on the war and almost caused our destruction, were at least actuated by some humanitarian impulse, however misguided, but war, as it must always do, wrecks the moral sense, and you have the spectacle of martial heroes raping the very country they pretended to defend. For my part, I despise every man who waves a bloody shirt, and says, 'Look at my wounds, I deserve election to office and all the graft I can get.'"

Harry attempted to interpose a word, but Mr. Rogers drowned him out.

"As for Butcher Grant and his ilk of thieves and scoundrels . . ."

Now Harry interrupted more loudly. "Oh, come, Mr. Rogers, you can't mean that. . . . While I admit the Crédit Mobilier went a little far, not a breath of scandal has ever touched the President himself."

"Sir, when a man's closest friends, his immediate underlings in office, engage in thievery of the most open and notorious sort, one must imagine he is either a fool if he does not know it, or a rascal if, knowing, he does not expose them. Do I understand you to intimate that the President of the United States is a fool?"

Harry shrugged his shoulders. "No, of course not, but don't you see, he's really a military man, and not just up on business."

"That's my point exactly." Mr. Rogers held out his fist

61

and beat the air with it, emphasizing his words. "It is because General Grant is a military man that he has no moral sense. I also am not a businessman, but I can tell right from wrong. He doesn't know the difference. All he knows is expediency. When his very Cabinet members were found guilty of plain theft, he attempted to shield them from prosecution, and that was lapse of duty. When a President of the United States fails in his trust, what is the reason we are willing to blind our eyes to his misdeeds, and invent all kinds of apologies to excuse him?"

Mr. Peale spoke up, hesitatingly, as if afraid of being outshouted by his vehement neighbor.

"I sort of think that is going too far myself, Mr. Rogers. The country looks up to General Grant; it would be too bad if there wasn't anyone in office they could trust. Besides, he was a great soldier, and he has to be given the benefit of the doubt."

"I am not able to measure military greatness. I know his men called him 'Butcher Grant.' If a great soldier is one who spends human lives like pennies to overwhelm, eventually, a force half his size, Lee in defeat was a greater. I do know that as man and as President Grant has accomplished the wrecking of this country."

"What the Republican party needs is some new leadership," Mr. Peale suggested.

"What the country needs is a new party. If the Democratic party doesn't get in office next year, the country's ruined, take my word for it."

"La, Jesse, you said that four years ago, and nothing happened." Mrs. Rogers threw up her hands in a gesture intended to express the futility of her husband's pronouncement. "The country is still going on just the same."

"My dear Gussie, my dear Gussie. Your interests and talents lie within the precincts of this home of ours. Out-

62

side its door you venture only under the most sheltered circumstances. You can't see the faces of the men laid off by the railroad. I hate to hand them their notices, Saturdays. You don't know the hopelessness of the employees of the banks and business houses that have closed, the hungry stomachs and weary hearts. We have had a panic, madam. We are in the midst of a depression that gripes the guts of America like a colic, and yearly we grow thinner with it."

"Jesse, you shame me—such an expression!"

"Like it or no, wife and friends, this country has guts, and at this moment they are empty. Worms feed in its intestines—fat slugs named Gould and Fisk and Vanderbilt, lesser parasites like Tweed and Cameron and Quay. Our banks fail, business languishes, the rails rust on our railroads. I hate to think of the losses of the road in which I am a minor cog. The country is ruined, I maintain, but there is still hope of rehabilitating it. A change in parties . . ."

A fresh, eager voice broke into the peroration, and Mr. Rogers looked in the direction of Al Naylor with some annoyance. Couldn't he ever get his say said without these interruptions? The younger Naylor boy had been listening with intent, flushed face.

"Don't you think, sir, what you say about the Republican party, the same thing is true of the Democrats as well? They are both managed by people such as you mention, and they are both used to rob the worker and the farmer. Here in Pennsylvania it's Quay and Cameron, and in New York it's Tweed. What we need, I think, is a new party to represent ordinary folks, like us, and the farmers and the workers."

Mr. Rogers gave a snort that threatened disaster to his most prominent feature. "That's the idea some of the railroad men are talking, and I don't hold with it. There's enough parties. I'm a Democrat, and I intend to stay a Democrat."

"I'm no Democrat—I can't hold with states' rights and free trade and that business," Mr. Peale interrupted. "The Republican party will do me when the Knights of Labor and the Grange control it and clean house of the rascals. All it needs is reforming."

Al had difficulty in restraining himself, but he waited politely until Mr. Peale had finished. "But don't you see, when the controlling machinery of the party is in the hands of capitalists and grafters, what chance is there for honest men to get them out? Labor and the farmers need a party they can run themselves."

The older men all looked pityingly at the youth, as if he were a child they allowed to speak out of politeness, and his face flushed with realization as he paused abruptly.

Mrs. Rogers used the silence to announce brightly: "My sister Zena, Teresina's namesake, is coming over for the Exposition. I received a letter from her today." This time she succeeded in breaking up the talk of panics and politics.

Harry Naylor, uncomfortable under the criticisms directed at his chiefs, and anxious for a diversion of subject, asked: "Is that your only sister? I have never met her, I believe?"

Simultaneously, Teresina and Georgina both questioned: "Aunt Zena? Coming to Philadelphia? When does she get here, Mother?"

Instead of answering their questions directly, Mrs. Rogers turned to Mrs. Peale and explained: "My older sister, you know. She is extremely wealthy—married into the Lascalles family—extremely prominent in France. We have many French connections. Dear Papa was in the

64

entourage of Joseph Bonaparte, the Count de Survilliers, you know, at Bordentown. He was extremely . . ."

Mr. Rogers shouted: "Ha, the third time, Gussie. Are there no other adjectives you can use to describe your family? 'Extremely' has worn pretty thin!"

"She hasn't been in this country since she was a mere girl, Mr. Naylor," Mrs. Rogers went on, ignoring the interruption. "She has never met Father, imagine! She has talked about coming on many occasions, but she is so afraid of the crossing. Now she is determined, she writes me . . ."

"Oh, Mother, when? When?" Teresina showed vast impatience with her mother's slowness at arriving at the point.

"She's planning on March, Zenie. . . . My goodness, don't rush me so. Philippe Lascalles, her nephew—her husband's brother's child—has to come on official business. He has some post with the French exhibit at the Centennial—that determined her."

Teresina seemed to have no further interest in the conversation, but her mind raced on with plans of turning her aunt's visit to her own account. "After all, I'm named after her, she ought to do something for me," she thought, "and she will, too, if I handle her just right."

Georgina effervesced with excitement. "Just think, Henry, all the way from Paris! Won't it be fun seeing Aunt Zena? We've heard so much about her she always seemed like someone out of a fairy book. The good fairy of the family! I hope she buys me just one new dress that isn't a made-over of one of Zenie's."

"Oh, shoot, what I want is a gold-mounted toothpick, like she sent Dad for Christmas last year—and nice shirt studs, gold ones."

"Why, Henry Rogers! Anyone would think you were

65

a fop. You'll get Father's studs someday, and that's time enough."

Julia alone heard the news without pleasurable anticipations, but then she was the only one of the children who had ever met their aunt. The memory still made her quiver. "Mother can be indelicate at times, but Aunt Zenie is just a coarse woman," she thought.

Mrs. Rogers hadn't planned on serving her collation for another half-hour, but she feared a resumption of the political discussion, so she announced:

"Mary has made some ice cream. I know it is cold for ice cream, but it was warm enough this afternoon, when . . ."

"No excuses, Mother!" Mr. Rogers shouted. The thought of eating always put him in a boisterous mood. "Mary's ice cream is acceptable at any time, hot or cold. Come, Gus—strike up the Grand March, we're off to the dining room." Then, in his best freight-yard manner, so that his voice made Total Eclipse whinny all the way out in his stall, he shouted: "Mary, we're coming!"

Chapter 5   On Sunday morning, the last before the New Year, Mr. Rogers took the twins with him, and they drove out the Frankford road behind Total Eclipse. It had continued to grow colder after Christmas, and then it snowed, crisp, fine flakes that made ideal sleighing. It was fun to crouch down in the sleigh, well tucked in with buffalo robes. The hair of the robes had matted, and moths had played havoc with the linings, but nothing affected their warmth. Georgina sat close to her father, enjoying his nearness,

66

his shouts of exuberant vitality, the rime-coated beard that occasionally tickled her cheek. She found a comfort in his strong hands, gloved now but no less masterful as one held the reins and the other used, occasionally, the light carriage whip. As they drove along she was almost hypnotized by the sway of the horse's rump, the steady swish of tail, and the slow seesaw of the breeching as the sleigh sped along on noiseless runners. Her silence was shared by the others, and they passed through Frankford before anyone spoke. Then Georgina thought of Nellie, and her love for the sleigh. "It's too bad Nellie couldn't come along—she would have enjoyed the run!" she shouted in her father's ear.

He shook his head and called back, the blast of his master's voice causing Total Eclipse to break into a gallop that was quickly checked. "Your mother said Nellie shouldn't go for a few weeks yet, on account of her pups, but I think it would have done her good."

They were gone three or four hours, and when they got back to Richmond Street, all three Rogers faces had been so worked on by wind and temperature that they were more alike than ever, with cheeks redly painted by the wind and eyes weeping.

With bells jingling in a last-minute burst of speed, they pulled up before the stable. Nellie greeted them with excited barks. Mr. Rogers shouted to arouse Lucius, who was probably asleep in the hayloft. He succeeded also in waking anyone else who might be sleeping within the distance of a square. Lucius ran out, grinning, hastily rubbed off Total Eclipse's steaming flanks, and threw an old blanket over his damp shoulders. Mr. Rogers and the children went into the stable.

Although Mr. Rogers would have denied the charge, he had no real love for animals. He merely went through

67

the motions of liking them. They were possessions to be cared for and they repaid the trouble by providing transportation and pleasure, or in the case of Nellie, affection and decoration. He stooped to pat the dog and stuck a thick finger into the midst of her polka-dotted puppies. He petted Mr. Quinby's soft muzzle, and gave the rump of Total Eclipse a hearty slap, before turning houseward. However, if either horse developed a spavin, or other injury, he would have wanted it traded immediately, and when the Dalmatians grew too old to follow the carriage, it required all of Mrs. Rogers' persuasion to keep them alive. Or if Nellie were to run around the stable twice and produce a mongrel litter, he would have had it drowned forthwith. As a result, he got from the horses and the dog none of the affection they gave Mrs. Rogers, although the deep bond between his wife and their animals—which he recognized but did not comprehend—seemed to him to exist because of some weakness in her attitude, some feminine foible.

In the shed, father and children divested themselves of huge quantities of clothing and stamped hungrily into the kitchen, where Mary, glad to cater to her favorites, soon prepared snacks for each of them; a whole turkey leg and a segment of apple pie for Mr. Rogers, part of the Christmas goose and slabs of cold plum pudding for the children.

Mrs. Rogers heard the excited voices, and called down from upstairs: "Father, is Gene there? Send her in to the piano. She hasn't done her practicing yet."

The times that her mother remembered her practice hours were rare, and Georgina had learned the uselessness of protest. She ran into the parlor and clumped over to the piano with as much noise as possible. It was not until then that she noticed Teresina was in the room, receiving Gus, and she grinned joyfully. Gus was going through

68

the torture of a Sunday-afternoon call, and she planned to end it for him.

Teresina was being ungracious. She sat in one of the straight-backed chairs gazing sullenly at the stern, aristocratic features of Grandfather Borelli. Not only did the old man have a very ornate gold frame to enhance his portrait, but it was also draped with a chenille-fringed valance giving the impression that he sat in state in the center of the household. He seemed to be encouraging his granddaughter in her attitude of hauteur, and enjoying the discomfiture of her suitor.

As was often the case, Gus was extremely unhappy in Teresina's company. His sensitive face showed his hurt at the impression she conveyed that while listening to him her thoughts were elsewhere, and more pleasantly engaged. She derived a perverse satisfaction from watching his dejection, but fed him sufficient slight encouragement to keep him dancing attention. When she did consider his importunate offers of marriage, which was seldom, it was because she was sure that she could dominate him as a husband as she had always done.

Georgina ignored her sister entirely, but shouted, "Hello, Gus!" to her swain. Teresina held her irritation in slight check. "Really, Gene, I don't see why you have to come running in here when you can see Gus and I are talking."

It wasn't often that Georgina had so valid a defense for hanging around in Gus's presence. "Mother sent me in to practice," she replied, happily. She laid back the piano scarf carefully, removed the bric-a-brac, and opened the case of the square rosewood piano. "What will make Teresina the maddest?" she asked herself. Of course, scales. . . . She began to bang them out rapidly, and apparently with the utmost seriousness.

Teresina concealed her irritation beneath her usual mask

of indifference. She swept into the hallway and called upstairs in a modulated voice:

"Really, Mother, can't Gene practice at some other time? This terrible banging of hers will give me migraine, I fear, and you know she hasn't the least talent."

Before her mother could answer, Mr. Rogers made his entrance from the kitchen, still carrying in one hand the turkey leg on which he had been munching. He wiped his mouth and beard with the back of the other hand, and objected:

"Nonsense, Zenie! How do you expect our young virtuoso to execute her arpeggios and other musical do-funnies if she doesn't practice them? And when could she ever practice if she waits for the parlor to be unoccupied? Why doesn't Gus have Lucius hitch up Mr. Quinby, and the two of you go for a sleigh ride? The horse needs a workout, and the air will do you both good. I don't see how you can be in the house on a day like this."

"You forget Mother made us go to mass this morning. If you think it was any fun getting up at six o'clock in this frigid weather . . . I was stiff when we got there!"

"One blessing the Church has given a decadent civilization—early rising on Sunday mornings! Perhaps, my dear daughter, you realize it was your father who stoked the early morning fires against your arising. I am glad you were appreciative of the comfort they provided."

Gus spoke up, eagerly. "Let's go, Zenie, Mr. Quinby is like a flash in the sleigh. I'll drive you over to the park, and we'll stop somewhere and eat."

Georgina, playing softly the better to hear the conversation, decided this was the critical moment. She banged away, slowly, upon an unrhythmic do-re-me-fa-fa-fa-fa until the tones vibrated in Teresina's ears.

70

"Anything is better than listening to that din," she assented ungraciously. "I'll go upstairs and change into warmer clothes."

Gus hastened out to the stable to give orders to Lucius, and Georgina, triumphantly and careless of tempo or expression, hammered out an unoperatic rendition of the "Soldiers' Chorus" from *Faust* which continued until Teresina was out of the house.

2

That Mr. Quinby was the fastest horse in Kensington was the favorite boast of the family, and he was proving himself now. The snow was packed and polished by the steel runners of hundreds of sleighs and sleds. It provided a noise-deadening cushion between iron-shod hoofs and cobbled streets, so that the horse seemed to be trotting along on air and the sleigh moved with the noiseless, buoyant flight of an arrow.

The front seat was low, and well within the body of the sleigh. The footboard curved up in a graceful sweep, and then turned over, to offer still further protection from the cold. Gus could feel the warmth of Teresina's body next to his, and this intimacy added so much to his transport of pleasure that he felt more than ever that they were flying through space, completely unsupported by any terrestrial foundations. As usual, a ballad occurred to him that seemed to express the sensation he enjoyed, and he began to sing it in a soft but sprightly manner as he turned the speeding Mr. Quinby into Girard Avenue.

> . . . and we talked by the light of the moon;
> There was squeezing of hands, followed up by a kiss,
> And so far's I remember, I felt just like this:

Up in a balloon, boys, up in a balloon,
All among the little stars,
Sailing round the moon.

Teresina laughed, a chill musical note that hung bell-like in the air. "Gus, you're a case. I do believe nothing could keep you from singing."

"By Judas, Zenie, isn't this wonderful—the sky is that blue canopy of heaven poets talk about—and the crystal whiteness of the snow . . ."

Teresina was completely unaffected by the exhilaration of the speed, the rhythm of Mr. Quinby's muted pace, the intoxicating wine of the air, or the beauty of white snow and blue sky. She was heavily veiled to protect her complexion from the wind. She would die of mortification if she were to get a flushed or wind-roughened face. Moreover, she was in no mood for Gus's poetics, although as she watched him from behind the protection of her veil she admitted he was handsome. His blue eyes laughed at her, pale curls showed beneath his cap, and his eager face searched continually for a smile, a hint of approbation.

In record time they passed the Girard College building. It looked more beautiful than ever as the snow accented the massive simplicity of its Grecian lines. Thin featherings of snow lay in the flutings of the columns and increased the height of their capitals.

"The glory that was Greece, Zenie! Isn't it wonderful to have just a little of it here in America—instead of some of those overdecorated monstrosities they are building nowadays?"

"I don't know. I like things a little richer, myself. If you ask me, I think the new French styles are much handsomer. If it had a mansard roof, now, and fewer of those columns, it would be nicer, I think."

72

Gus maintained a discreet silence for a little while, but his exuberance had to find expression.

"You know, Zenie, we should make these excursions more often. It's too bad Sundays are the only days I'm free. It gives us so little time together, but as soon as I graduate—just think, less than six months from now—I'll be seeing more of you. Perhaps then you will learn to like me better."

"What do you mean, see more of me? You practically live at our house now when you're not studying, or at the university."

"Zenie, tell me, don't you like me a little?"

"Of course I do. I'm very fond of you, Gus, but I'm just not ready to think of anything more." Her languid voice gave the lie to any hopes Gus might have tried to build from her words.

"There must be someone else." He gave voice to one of the thoughts that constantly tortured him. "It's Harry Naylor, that's who it is. He kept looking at you the other night just as if he owned you."

Teresina did not trouble to deny the charge with any vehemence. "Harry just comes in to talk to Father—besides, he is so much older than I am. I'd never think of marrying an older man, unless he had a great deal . . ." Teresina caught herself before she gave too frank expression to her thoughts. ". . . a great deal of personality. And Harry is just like an Indian, whether he really is, like they say, or not."

"If it isn't him, it must be somebody. . . . Oh, Zenie, if you would just wait a little while! I'll soon have a practice, and I'm specializing in a new field. I just can't help being a success."

Teresina shook her head. "No—I can't make any promises, Gus. I want to be very sure myself of what I

73

do. I don't want to make any mistakes, that's all. Mother made a mistake. She has had a very unhappy life, and I don't want the same thing to happen to me."

Gus was shocked. "Why, Zenie, how can you say that? Your father dotes on your mother. I think they are the happiest pair in Kensington."

"She made a mistake, all the same." Teresina shook her head. "She's confided in me when she just had to tell someone, I guess. Of course she makes the best of it, and puts up with things. I'm not going to have to make the best of my marriage. I'm going to be right. . . . I'm going to be sure, first."

Mr. Quinby sped over the bridge crossing the Schuylkill, and below, the frozen river was alive with skaters in vari-colored costumes. "It would be fun skating. Shall we hire skates, and try it awhile?"

"Don't be tiresome. Besides, I'm not dressed for it, and think what it would do to my complexion."

"And it would be bad for Mr. Quinby to stand after he's been heated," Gus agreed. "I'll drive through the Centennial grounds and see how the buildings are coming along. It doesn't seem possible 1876 is just a couple of days away, does it, Zenie?" Mr. Quinby's flying hoofs turned down Elm Avenue, along the boundary of the Exposition grounds. Gus was amazed at the progress made in the buildings since the preceding summer. The great Transcontinental Hotel, which took up a huge triangle opposite the entrance building, at Belmont Avenue, was almost completed, as was the Globe Hotel around the corner from it.

"There must be hundreds of rooms in each of those buildings. I don't see where all the people will come from to fill them," Teresina said.

"Why, all the world is coming to Philadelphia next

74

summer. It will be the largest fair ever held in the history of the world. They plan to spend five times as much on it as was spent for the great London exhibition, before the war." Gus reined in on Mr. Quinby while he pointed out some of the buildings. "Along here is the Main Building —and over on that side is the Machinery Building. The largest engine ever built is being erected there.

"You know, Zenie, I was thinking the other night, when your father and the rest of them were talking, everything they say about America may be true. I guess it is rotten politically, when even President Grant doesn't seem to be really upright, and they buy Senators and Congressmen with bribes—but there is still something grand about a country that can go ahead with a project like this, right when it would seem from outside it was on its last legs."

Teresina nodded, with no particular interest. She gave more attention to some of the other turnouts. All the Philadelphians who possessed horses and sleighs seemed to be there inspecting the progress of the work. There were beautifully matched pairs of spirited horses, richly harnessed and driven by coachmen with a flair for whip-cracking and smart maneuvers, and farmers' sledges pulled with plow horses, and over everything, the tremendous noise of jingling bells—musical, matched-toned silver bells on the most expensive outfits, the merry notes of ordinary brass sleigh bells, and an occasional husky, tin-can bang of an old cowbell. Together they formed a carillon of winter, and even Teresina found pleasure in the impromptu glockenspiel.

Gus continued to point out the buildings, many of them still scaffold-covered, others practically completed. "Beyond the lake—way over there on that high ground—that's Horticultural Hall. It will be all glass-covered when it's finished, and I hear there will be a whole tropical jungle inside: banana trees, and huge palms, with bright-colored birds flying through them.

"And up there somewhere is the French Building. I guess that is where your cousin—or whatever kind of relative he is—that's where he'll be."

For the first time since she had heard of Aunt Zena's coming, the mention of her nephew had some significance. Why, he must be wealthy, too! And handsome, if he was French. And surely he couldn't be already married, or Aunt Zena would have mentioned it. Teresina paid no further attention to the Exposition, only nodding automatically as Gus named each site. Her mind was busy again with the question that preoccupied her to the exclusion of almost everything else: the choice of a husband. "Gus is handsome, really," she thought, "and he can be amusing company, too. Everyone would think he'd make a good catch, but he's too much of a gamble. Supposing he doesn't make good with his idea of being a female specialist—supposing women wouldn't go to him? Personally, I'd die of mortification if I let any man, doctor or no, examine me—yet there are women, shameless ones . . . But Philippe Lascalles, now, Aunt Zena's nephew . . ."

She didn't hear Gus at all as he said: "This will be the parade ground. Isn't it a noble avenue? It's wide enough and long enough for whole regiments to pass in review. And over there . . ."

3

Julia watched from her fourth-floor window as the sleigh returned. She saw Gus solicitously help Teresina to alight. It was quite a task for her sister to gather her full skirts about her, to avoid snagging them on some part of the sleigh and still allow decent covering for her ankles. For

Gus it was equally difficult to furnish adequate support for Teresina's descent while preserving the distance modesty required. Julia sighed. He was such a fine young man. He was not only good-looking, he had such an air of refinement. He was forbearing, and clever, where Teresina was not concerned. It was too bad she did not treat him more kindly.

"It is so unfortunate Gus can't see through Teresina, how hard and cold and selfish she is," she thought. "Here she lives with us, her family, and none of us has ever felt her love. She just ignores or tolerates us, and just because she is the most beautiful, she thinks that is all that matters. I would rather be like Georgina than like Teresina. At least Gene isn't thinking of herself all the time. . . . She may be full of mischief, and is a little troublemaker, but she really loves Henry, even if she doesn't like me. And of course, she loves Papa." . . .

By this tortuous route Julia came around in her thoughts to her own unhappiness. Her father, whom she loved so devotedly, preferred the other children to herself! It had always been that way, even before she had been sent to the convent. She had been a sensitive child, easily hurt by jibes or criticism, and he had continually made fun of her. While the other children were often naughty and disobedient, and were punished for it, she was ridiculed for always being good. It was so unfair of her father, especially when she tried so hard to please him. She thought: "If he would be really nice to me only once, so I knew the other times were only a kind of joke, I would be the happiest girl."

His thoughtless attitude robbed her of self-confidence. If even her father couldn't like her, how could strangers? It made her shy and unsure of herself. The interest a marriageable girl of nineteen should have felt in the oppo-

77

site sex was not entirely lacking, although to her parents she seemed completely unaware of the young men about her, and she insisted herself that she had no wish to marry. The fact was that her father had become the standard by which she measured the opposite sex, and the youths who came her way were all from a smaller mold. Julia was in love with the very male qualities which disturbed and distressed her the most.

"Julia! Don't stay up there in your room, moping. Come downstairs!" Mrs. Rogers' voice carried up the stair well from below.

"I wish Mother wouldn't shriek so when she calls, it's not refined," Julia thought. "But I suppose that's Italian." She went to the stairs and called down, "I'll be down presently, Mama." She gave a last glance out the window, at the pattern of snow-covered ground and houses that stretched clear over to the river, where green water still showed in midstream. It was beautiful, the outlook from her room, especially at that moment, with the early winter night already graying the sky and reflections from the setting sun gilding the snow on the rooftops. Then she turned toward the stairway, and the family, and her father.

PART - - - TWO

❧ ❧ ❧

January through March

❧ ❧ ❧

1876

"Society waits unformed and is for a while between things ended and things begun."

—WALT WHITMAN.

Chapter 1

$\mathcal{E}$xCEPT for the right of way of the horsecar line, the street and pavements were piled high with snow. Drifts buried the steps and rose like a tide against the doors of buildings. The proportions of the red-brick houses were so changed by this blotting out of parts of their first stories that they seemed more like tight little Old World homes than the high three- and four-storied modern residences they actually were.

The shovelers had cleared the tracks, and the cars raced through a deep trench of snow above which only their roofs could be seen. The pedestrians who were abroad walked along this miniature snow canyon, protected from the wind, rather than brave the drifts on either side. When a car passed, they climbed the side walls of snow to avoid being run down, breaching the trench in many places and causing small snow slides that here and there covered the track.

Ordinarily, Mr. Rogers would have enjoyed this bout with the elements. He would have made of the car trench a strategic route of advance. He would have climbed the packed snow when the cars passed, with zest, and bellowed at the freezing passengers, huddled miserably inside the windows, their feet vainly seeking warmth in the straw that filled the car floor. The snow would have been a personal enemy, to be fought and vanquished, and he would have arrived home with the glint of a victor in his eye.

Tonight he merely plodded along, his heavy boots crunching in the packed snow, kicking aside the horse droppings frozen hard as stones. When the cries of a car-driver were heard, he phlegmatically pushed his bulk into the snow to the side just enough to avoid being hit. At Richmond Street a narrow path turned off, trod down by those who had passed earlier. It seemed to offer escape from the streetcar right of way, and he followed its tortuous windings between drifts until it ended where its maker had reached home. He had still almost a square to go, and no one had yet attempted clearing the pavements.

One of two other men who also were returning early from their work stopped behind Mr. Rogers. Sol Peale, enveloped in greatcoat and fur cap, spoke: "Well, Neighbor Rogers, we're waiting for you to lead the way. There's no use standing here, and you're the biggest of the lot of us." If he expected a characteristically boisterous and boastful answer, he didn't receive it. Mr. Rogers merely nodded. He put his head down to the wind so that his beard protected his whole face. Hunching his shoulders, he breasted the drift a foot at a time; the others followed shouting encouragement. Gradually, the fight against the drifting snow aroused his combative instinct, and he overcame his feeling of depression with a renewed and personalized battle with the weather.

When he and Mr. Peale parted on their common doorstep, he seemed almost his usual self, and paused a moment to shout encouragement to several of the men following him, who had now to break the path into the next square. "Go to it, boys!" he cried. "I'm sorry, but this old snowplow is due in the roundhouse for refueling and water."

Once within the house, his spirits drooped again. For the first time since their marriage, Mrs. Rogers was unaware of her husband's entrance until she heard his heavy steps on the stairs. The slow, deliberate footfalls carried a premonition of disaster, and she dropped her sewing, a dress of Teresina's she was making over for Georgina, and rushed to the stair. "Why, Pet! What in heaven's name! What's wrong? And you're early." Before that moment, she would have insisted that nothing in the world disturbed her so much as her husband's loud and boisterous manner. Now she found his new quiet much less to her taste. He climbed the last stair and placed a heavy hand on her shoulder before answering, and then he said, quietly:

"It's nothing, Gussie—I'm a little winded. The drifts are heavy and I had to break a path."

"Jesse Rogers, you tell me what's the matter, and tell me right away. If you think you can pull the wool over my eyes you're very much mistaken. A few snowdrifts, indeed! Anybody who loves snow the way you do!"

Mr. Rogers plumped down on the bed and the massive walnut bedstead creaked and groaned in protest. He took his wife's constricted waist in both hands and sat her on his knees as easily as though she were a child. His mouth found her ear, hidden beneath a row of tight cylindrical curls, and he kissed her there.

"Jesse, behave yourself. I declare! And your beard tickles. Besides, all your mush won't make me forget there's something wrong." Her voice was quite sharp as she waited for the ill news she knew was in store.

" 'How fair and how pleasant art thou, O love,' as the Bible has it."

"You are the most aggravating man! If the Bible says any such thing, which I don't for a moment believe, it still has nothing to do with this. I want to know what's happened that makes you like this. Tell me the worst, and tell me right away."

"My dear, I'm trying to tell you, but it's hard to begin. I hardly know how."

"Don't begin. Just come out with it. It's something to do with the railroad?"

"Gussie, you've heard me speak of the iniquities of the Republican Administration. You know of the suffering and hardship that is going on around us, but until now, we ourselves have been unaffected."

"The worst, Jesse! The worst, and quickly, and spare me this. You know I care nothing for politics, and know less. Have you lost your position with the railroad? Is that it?" Her voice, which had sharpened with exasperation, became calm as she began to plan what must be done. At last, as she had always suspected would happen, they were to be practically penniless! Until this moment, her husband's position had seemed a very poor one. She felt sure he was underpaid, and the work was beneath his dignity. On the other hand, it had always seemed secure, as solid as the very roadbed on which the trains ran. The shock of contemplating the fact that it might be gone was eased by a slow shake of Mr. Rogers' head.

"No, Gussie, I'm not turned out of the railroad entirely, thank heaven, but the company is hard hit, and has had to take drastic measures. Economies have been carried right down the line, beginning with the very highest officials. The state of the country is such that we've been losing constantly . . ."

"Bother the state of the country. It's the state of us I care about. Now what is it?"

"I've been demoted, Gussie. Demoted—back where I was years ago."

Mrs. Rogers thought, "Well, there will still be money coming in." Her face brightened, and she assumed a carefree attitude she did not altogether feel. "La, Father, you gave me a turn for a minute, and now I find you come home grumpy as an old bear over nothing at all. What if we do have to economize a little? I'm surprised at you!"

"It's not only the severe loss in salary, Gussie. I'll be back on night work again. You remember how you used to hate it when I worked nights, when Teresina was little? It will be the same job I had then—Yard Superintendent."

"Well, we got along then, and we'll get along now. Leave it to me. And, Jesse Rogers, if you give me a fright like that again, I'll be angry with you. Now come on, and cheer up." She slyly ran her hands under his coat, and then, without warning, pushed him over onto the bed, and began to tickle him in the ribs. He let out a scream of hysterical laughter, and lay back with feet kicking high in the air. Mrs. Rogers remorselessly followed up her advantage; her hands moved quickly from armpits to thighs and back again, while her husband gave way to continued paroxysms of laughter, his arms flailing about in vain attempts to catch her.

Finally, as they both tired, he caught her in a crushing embrace and the laughter ceased.

Much later, Mr. Rogers spoke. "Gussie, my dear, you know the solace a man needs after he is defeated and disappointed. . . . I can again face the world with confidence. With your love, nothing can overwhelm me."

"How you go on . . . and we've been behaving atrociously—not even waiting for bedtime. I'm ashamed of myself. And we're going to be late for dinner. What will the children think? They must know you've been home for an hour."

"Dinner? By Harry, yes. It's past time now, and I'm starved. What's for dinner, Mother?"

"Smoked herring. Your favorite dish, Pet. Mary got

85

them at the smokehouse yesterday, before the storm broke."

"And potatoes, I hope—none of those Italian rabbit foods you do up for the girls."

"And potatoes. Come, Jesse, hurry and get tidied up." Mrs. Rogers' face took on a calculating look. With her husband in a complaisant mood, it was a moment not to be wasted. "While you're dressing, do you mind if we discuss a little what's to be done? We will have to economize somewhere, and I want your approval."

He grunted as he struggled with a fresh collar, and she went on: "There's the servants. Of course we have to keep Mary, the poor soul. No one else would put up with her, crippled the way she is—but Martha. To most people she would be a good cook. It ought to be possible for her to get another place, and I could take over the cooking. I have to supervise it anyhow."

"Now, Mother, our servants are part of our family. We have a duty toward them, for their years of patient service, and so long as we have anything coming in we must share it with them. . . . I suppose I could sell the horses."

"Not Mr. Quinby, Father! Why, he's as much one of the family as any of us. He'd be desolate with anyone else. I'd work my fingers to the bone, go in rags . . ."

"I know, my dear, and take in washing—that's always the third of your threats, and I don't intend you to fulfill any of them. We are not destitute yet."

"Besides, there's that good-for-nothing Lucius. We'd have to keep him on anyway, because of that parcel of young ones, so there would be little economy there."

"I'm afraid, Gussie, it's going to be hard to cut down." Mr. Rogers threw up his hands in a gesture of futility. "I leave it all to your instinct for management. Now let's go and eat dinner. I crave the fragrance of herring broiled as only a Philadelphia housewife can do them."

86

"There's one thing I shall have to do." Mrs. Rogers now broached the subject for which all that preceded it had been only an elaborate build-up. "I'll have to write Zena and tell her we won't have room to put her up."

"Nonsense, we can't put up your own sister?" Mr. Rogers was hurt. "We must. We must, I say. I'd rather starve myself. We'll go without herring tonight. We'll cook soupbones twice. From now on I eschew roast beef. . . . Nonsense again! I tell you we'll manage somehow. Besides, I'm hungry. Let's eat, and consider these things afterward."

Relentlessly, Mrs. Rogers went on to gain her point. "Now listen, Pet. Zena will understand. She would want to be with me, naturally, but in her letter she expressed doubts that we would have room for her. You know she is so helpless; she must have her maids constantly. There will be at least four extra mouths to feed, and we couldn't set a mean table. It will be expensive, I assure you. . . .

"No, I insist, Jesse, that I have my way in this. There will be other sacrifices you can make later. This is one upon which I am determined."

Still troubled in appearance, Mr. Rogers gave grudging assent, and his wife put on her most sprightly manner to say: "Now that's that. Forget about it, Father, and leave it to me." As she spoke, she thought: "There, that's settled, thank goodness. It does keep a body at wit's end, smoothing things out in this family. . . . And that reminds me, I must burn Zena's letter. If he should ever come across it he'd be furious. Imagine anyone thinking for a moment that Zena would put up with a household like this!"

The family were all seated at the table, uncertain of what to do in so unprecedented a circumstance, when their parents entered, with faces still somewhat flushed. It was the first time in anyone's memory that Mr. Rogers had been in the house without being first at table, and Mary hobbled around excitedly, sure that some crisis impended, while in the kitchen Martha complained that the herring would soon be as dry as chips and the potatoes were already ruined.

Ignoring his own lateness, Mr. Rogers rushed to his chair, unrolled his napkin, tucked his beard in carefully, and shouted: "Come, come, Mary! In spite of all I say, we've gotten behind schedule. The victuals, Mary, the victuals, and hurry!"

2

After dinner Teresina waited impatiently for the arrival of Harry Naylor. It would be the third time within the month he had called, a sure sign of his growing interest, although up to now he had made no declaration. Not that she was more inclined to him than heretofore. He was too self-centered, she told herself. The evenings with him had been given over to nothing but discussions of his opportunities for making money, of his past political coups and those he meditated.

Gus Palmer was much better company, for he usually spent the time in telling stories, of which he had a store, or in singing. Between whiles, he talked about Teresina herself, most interesting subject of all. It was indeed difficult to make a decision. The successful man was boring, and the amusing one not yet assured of success.

Of course, she could send the politician packing and be done with his orations, but he was important, and he was becoming famous. Who knew, perhaps some day he would be Governor, or even President. She couldn't afford to make a decision too soon. And then too, the more prospects she had, the greater her value in the eyes of future suitors. Teresina intended to keep a string of males to dangle before each new one.

And there was one thing she would have to do—she would have to cure Harry of lateness. It was almost seven-thirty now, a preposterous hour to make a call. While she waited, she idly thumbed through her autograph album. It was a handsome volume, bound in green moiré silk that had yellowed slightly, but was still beautiful. A bouquet of forget-me-nots was stamped on the center of the cover in gold, and the title page had the name FORGET-ME-NOT exquisitely fashioned in type that simulated many sprays of the little flower. As Teresina turned the pages, delicately tinted in pastel shades of blue and pink and orchid, almost every one of them was a record of earlier conquests. There was Bob Pitcairn—her first real beau. . . . She had not seen him for years and years, all of three, certainly. She read the verse he had written in a large but unformed hand.

> When some forgotten air you hear
> Brings past scenes back to thee
> And gently claims your listening ear,
> Think one kind thought of me.

It was too bad later suitors had not read through the book before making their contributions. Variations of this same stanza were repeated a number of times, as were several other verses and mottoes.

Ed McClain she had never liked—even now she could see his round, freckled face grinning at her. Of course his effort was a humorous one.

> On a log sat a frog, sneezing at his daughter,
> Tears he shed, till his eyes were red,
> And then jumped into the water.

89

Teresina wrinkled her nose in distaste. At least he might have written something nice about her. But then, he was a silly thing.

And young Darby, and Tommy Evers, and Alonzo Peace. . . . Going over the list in this manner, she was surprised when she added up how many of her young men had failed to remain on her string. It was as irritating as the lateness of Harry Naylor. He had told her he might be delayed, but she was angry nevertheless, and said to herself: "I shall have to take him down a peg or two. He should feel lucky I allow him to call at all—and then to keep me waiting in this fashion."

Alone in the parlor, there was no need to pretend the aloofness that usually protected her from the world. She stamped her foot angrily, and in her pettish temper was more beautiful than ever. The doorbell in the kitchen began clanging; her anger forgotten, she lifted her skirts high to run upstairs more easily, showing lovely ankles in tightly laced high-topped shoes. Even a few inches of stockings, dyed in horizontal stripes of red and white in the newest style, were revealed in a manner that would have entranced an observer.

Mary answered the door, using the formula Teresina had taught her after many exasperating failures. "Indeed, I don't know whether Miss Zenie is in or not, Mr. Naylor. Won't you be having a seat in the parlor, and I'll find out." As this did not seem to her hospitable soul an adequate greeting, she winked, and whispered reassuringly: "She's waitin' for you. I'll tell her you're here."

It was a good fifteen minutes later when Teresina floated down the stairway on a cloud of crackling skirt, the heavy material supporting a figure that seemed to begin with the narrow waist and above it, the swelling bosom and serene lovely features of the belle of the Rogers household. "Why, Harry, I had given up expecting you, and had just retired," she announced, sweetly.

Harry stood fingering his mustache with his left hand, holding his right arm forward. It was a pose of easy nonchalance that he used when called upon at political meetings, but now, instead of saying "Friends and citizens," he began sonorously, "My dear Teresina," and went on: "It grieves me to have been late, but I was detained at a most important meeting that may have a vital effect on national affairs. Matt and I—perhaps I should say, Mr. Quay and myself . . ."

Teresina sat down with a look of resignation that Harry failed to notice. She observed something about the arrangement of his hair that almost made her giggle, although she was not easily amused. The black locks that were carefully drawn across his forehead from a part to the left dipped low over the bridge of his nose, climbed in a high sweep, and fell abruptly at the right. His black mustache made a similar pattern, and glistened with pomade. The hawk nose, opaque eyes, and leather-colored cheeks seemed to be a mask decorated at top and bottom with black silk frills, behind which the real Harry Naylor lived.

It was hard to restrain this thought, which amused Teresina during an evening that ran the usual course, beginning with a talk on the advantages of being a Republican.

"There's no chance for a Democrat to make real money in Pennsylvania. For the life of me, I can't see why anyone belongs to them." He extolled the beneficent despotism of the Quay-Cameron machine. "Still people kick," he complained. "You can't expect anybody to go into politics just for their health. It isn't human nature."

Teresina brought out the autograph album to change the subject. Harry thought a while before making his contribution. He ran his hand over his hair to make sure it was not misplaced. He twisted anew the ends of his mustache and toyed with a handsome goose-quill tooth-pick. It had an ornate gold holder, with an inscription on it which he carefully pointed out. "The boys at the Union League presented it to me when I became the youngest senator in the history of Pennsylvania," he boasted, and explained the ingenious way in which old quills could be removed when they wore out, and new ones inserted.

By this time he had made the momentous selection among the several quotations he was considering. Seizing the pen Teresina held out to him, and turning over the leaf to a fresh page, he made two or three preparatory flourishes, and then commenced writing. He used a hand laboriously modeled after John Hancock's Declaration sig-nature, with a few added curlicues of his own, and the effort filled the whole page:

Courage, brother! do not stumble,
Though the path be dark as night;
There's a star to guide the humble,
Trust in God and do the Right.

HENRY LONGFELLOW NAYLOR,
State Senator (Pa.)
January 14th, 1876

Chapter 2

ONE EFFECT of the change in Mr. Rogers' hours was an alteration in mealtimes. After working outside all night—checking freight manifests, tracing the numbers of cars, adjusting disputes between conductors and brakemen, and attending to all the other duties connected with the handling of freight—he came home ravenously hungry. After an early breakfast, he retired to sleep before the rest of the family made its appearance. Early in the afternoon he awakened hungry again, so dinner, hitherto set inflexibly for five-thirty, was moved forward to one-thirty.

It broke up the day for everyone, but worse than the change of mealtimes to Mrs. Rogers was the presence of her husband in the house all afternoon. After an exasperating week, she expressed herself to Mary:

"I declare, the man will drive me raving crazy. All he does is snoop, snoop, snoop. Of all the calamities visited upon womankind, the presence of a man around the house during working hours is the worst. I tell you, Mary, what I have put up with from that man this week would try the patience of a saint." Mrs. Rogers pointed dramatically toward the stable. "One moment he's snooping in the stable—the oats are musty, or the hay has thistles in it." She pointed heavenward. "The next, he's going through the Lord knows what up in the attic."

Mary tsk-tsked commiseratingly, and Mrs. Rogers, thoroughly warmed up to her subject, went on. "What I've put up with during the years no one will ever know, but this is the worst. Mary, I tell you, never marry a Quaker. They'll get the best of you every time. My sister warned me when I married. Not even a Protestant, which would be bad enough, she said, but a Quaker—and she was right. Of all the snoopy, hardheaded, deceiving, impossible people, they are the worst. The very worst!"

A bellow from the cellar seemed timed to confirm her. "There, what did I tell you?" she grumbled.

"Gussie, Gussie—oh, Gussie." Mr. Rogers' voice filled the house.

His wife made a series of expressive gestures to convey soundlessly the extent of her exasperation. She threw a dishcloth into the sink with considerable force, and opened the cellar door in time to be blown back by another blast: "Gussie! Come here a moment, can't you?"

"Oh, Father, for heaven's sake, what is it now?"

"The wine I made from those Concord grapes, from the arbor . . . It's not here, and I remember distinctly where I put it. It was along these shelves, I'm positive."

"Jesse Rogers, did you bring me down this cellar to ask about wine you drank up yourself long ago? It's four years since you made that wine—you never made it before or since—and you drank it all up the very next Christmas. A spectacle you were, too. Drunk as a lord, and contentious the whole evening. The Peales were over, and I was so ashamed. Before Mrs. Peale, of all people. She's an ordinary sort of woman, and there you went on, arguing and arguing. You fought the Civil War all over again. I remember you knew more than the generals on either side. And all the time you were arguing about the wrong battle. . . . It was mortifying."

When his wife mentioned the one and only binge of his married life, Mr. Rogers recalled it with a smirk of complacent remembrance. As the tirade continued, he turned sheepish. Finally, with the insinuation that he had been wrong in his argument, he became angry.

"Stop! Cease this harangue. I won't be browbeaten in my own home, and it was the siege of Vicksburg!" he shouted. "And there was some of that wine left, I'd swear it. It's a providence, I believe, that I'm here for a while in the daytime, to observe the waste; the appalling lack of efficiency in this household. If the railroad . . ."

Mrs. Rogers let loose the full force of her Latin temper. Her head went forward between her hunched-up shoulders, and her eyes narrowed to thin slits. Her voice rose to a shriek. "You despicable worm—get out of this cellar and

94

stay out. *Stay out,* do you hear? You've been home all week, and you've done nothing but snoop, snoop, snoop until I'm sick and tired of it. The way I scrimp and slave and wear my fingers to the bone for you, ungrateful wretch that you are . . . Get out of here. Get out! I have work to do, and I have no time to be at your beck and call."

Up in the kitchen, Mary listened to the controversy with unconcealed relish, but Martha shook her head, sadly. "When this is over, she'll be takin' it out on us," she predicted.

In a moment, a chastened and crestfallen man, no longer, as he was himself thinking, master in his own house, beat a retreat through the kitchen to escape his wife's furious onslaught. Even his beard seemed lifeless, instead of frothing up in its usual unrestraint. Both the servants turned their heads away as their mistress followed and, with a final gesture of anger and supreme contempt, removed a slipper and threw it full force against the door closing behind her husband.

2

The arrival of Father Duffy put an end to the scene. The prolonged clanging of the bell in the kitchen began as Mrs. Rogers pushed open the kitchen door to hurl shrewish accusations after her discomfited spouse. The bell had not stopped vibrating on its coiled spring before she completed one of her amazing transformations of mood. Her scream ended in the middle of a choice insult. She reached down and retrieved the slipper she had thrown. Without pausing to put it on, she began a dash for the stairway, to observe who the visitor might be from the second-story busybody. Her uneven, one-slippered gait did not prevent her reaching her room in almost record time. She peered through the front window into the arrangement of mirrors that

cunningly reflected the entire front doorstep without showing oneself. "Of all people to arrive at such a moment,"
she thought in exasperation as she saw the clerical black
of her visitor. "Father Duffy, imagine!"

The new priest in the parish had become very popular
during his six months' incumbency, and Mrs. Rogers had
been trying very hard to impress him. Frantically patting
her curls in shape, she wondered if he could have heard her
imprecations through the front door. This unpleasant concern was succeeded by another: How would Father behave?
Although it was years since he had met any of the clergy
that stopped frequently at the house, he was always fulmi-
nating against them, and magnifying the amounts of her
contributions.

And why wasn't Mary answering the bell? She was just
impossibly slow. She ran to the head of the stairs and
called down in her sweetest, most refined accents, "Mary,
Father Duffy is at the door," and then she saw the broad
back of her husband already in the vestibule. She stamped
her foot impatiently. Ordinarily the bell could be pulled
from its spring before he would answer it, but this time he
would go, of course—she might have known.

It was too late now to do anything. Events would have
to take their course, but she thought: "If he dares to insult
Father Duffy it's the finish. I've put up with all I intend
to."

There was a mumble of voices from the open door,
suave, quiet, but indistinguishable sounds easily identifiable
as the priest's voice, and Father's heavy, rumbling undercurrent. It was impossible from that distance to know the
mood of the rumble, and Mrs. Rogers strained for a first
indication of it. "It's just like a man to come when I'm
completely unpresentable," she thought. She was too curious to return to the front room and put on her slipper, so

96

she stood with her stockinged foot resting on the shod one while the conversation outside continued. "In heaven's name, why doesn't he bring him in?" she asked herself in exasperation. She called downstairs in tones that were a triumph of the art of inflection. "Jesse, dear, why don't you ask Father Duffy into the parlor? And tell him I'll be right down." Her voice combined an indication of connubial felicity, respect for the cloth, pleasure at the appearance of a guest, concern for his comfort, and underneath all, a veiled threat, to be heard and understood only by her husband, that he'd better behave himself or there would be trouble afterward.

A good five minutes must have passed before the two men finally left the front step to find their way into the parlor. Mrs. Rogers was relieved to see that her husband was seemingly in fine spirits, and already on good terms with the priest.

"Right in there, sir," he boomed, and then he surpassed himself in the volume of sound with which he called up the stairs, "Gussie! *Gussie*—there's a visitor down here for you."

Her answer was drowned by his cry, and he shouted again before she could make herself heard. She hastened back to her room and began frantic repairs to her toilet. "I must get down there before Jesse says something he shouldn't," she resolved.

Her fears proved groundless. When she entered the parlor both men rose and Mr. Rogers said:

"Duffy here dropped in to see you. We've been having a chat, and I've just discovered he's a Democrat."

"Father, you don't have to shout so—I'm right here in the room." And then to Father Duffy she smiled a greeting and made an apology. "Jesse gets to talk so loudly down at the railroad. You know, he's connected with the

Reading, and they have to shout above the noise of those engine whistles."

"Indeed, I should have known your husband was a railroad man. There's something about us that makes a kind of brotherhood, I suppose. I was a railroader before ever I turned priest, and I say we are a hail-fellow-well-met crowd."

The priest received a slap on the back that would have floored the average man. "You don't tell me, Duffy, that you're a Democrat and a railroad man to boot! You're surely a man after my own heart."

"Yes, I was also on the Reading. Long before I entered the priesthood, and I still thrill to the sound of wheels clicking over switch points. I was a brakeman on the Pottsville Division. My father before me was a canalman. He never forgave me entirely for deserting to the railroads." He turned toward his hostess as they all seated themselves and explained: "Canalmen hated railroaders, you see, and I tell you it was a pretty serious day in the family when I insisted on taking my little tin lunch pail and reporting to the yards for work. My good old father, may God bless his soul, took it as a personal defection."

Mr. Rogers looked appraisingly toward his wife; his tongue licked around his lips. He reached into a hip pocket and brought out a plug of almost black tobacco and held it toward the priest. "I never knew a railroad man to refuse a chew," he announced in jovial thunder.

"Indeed, no." Father Duffy's smooth round face took on the cherubic expression of a little boy about to receive some forbidden candy. He bit off a corner of the plug and began chewing with such gusto that his blue eyes were almost hidden beneath the bunched cheek muscles.

Mr. Rogers also took a chew, and kicked out the spittoon from its hiding place under the whatnot. His face held a grin of malicious satisfaction as he spat into it with unerring aim. One of Mrs. Rogers' rules, established many years before, provided that his chewing must be done outside; the spittoon received houseroom only for the use of guests. Now he felt that he regained face in thus defying his wife, while he could suffer no aftermath of recrimination. He rehearsed mentally the exact inflection with which he would say, later, "Why, Gussie, the man was your guest, so I had to be hospitable." No— "so I *had* to be." . . . That was better.

Meanwhile, Father Duffy continued with his railroad reminiscences. "Yes, it was a great life—and it will never be the same again. The building of our railroads was a great and glorious chapter in our history. It's too bad they fell into the hands of commercial pirates. There is one solace, however—their money will never bring them the respect of their countrymen. I'm sure the names of Vanderbilt and Gould will carry such opprobrium to future generations of Americans that they will never be spoken except in loathing and detestation." The priest sighed. "Well, I'm afraid there are some bad days ahead for railroad workers. We're in for bad times, worse than any we have had so far. The rule of greed has replaced the rule of brotherhood, of Christian good-fellowship."

The priest's quid extended his ruddy, smooth-shaven cheek, and he shifted it to an easier position on the other side. "The conditions here in Kensington, in this very parish, are pitiful indeed, but they are nothing to the hunger and poverty up the state, through my own anthracite coal regions."

"Don't you think things will be better now they've rounded up the Molly Maguires?" Mr. Rogers asked. "Lawlessness and murder made the mine-owners disinclined to continue developing their properties."

The priest shook his head. "That's the attitude the political leaders subscribe to. I'm not so sure. If there has been piracy in the railroads, there's been worse on the part of the mine operators, and they control the police and the courts. It is hard for otherwise defenseless men not to turn to force when other courses fail. While I do not defend violence and murder, I can understand the human frailty of those who founded a secret organization of terrorism to protect themselves from the avarice and cruelties of their employers.

"I am glad to see the passing of the Mollies, but I wish it had not been through the instrumentality of the Pinkertons." The priest gave a mirthless laugh and shrugged his shoulders. "While I think the Church needs priests like myself who have been workingmen, and understand their needs, it places me at times in a peculiar position. I can't help feeling that MacParland—the detective, you'll recall, who joined the society and took part in its affairs—is a kind of modern Judas who betrayed his comrades for a paltry hire."

Mr. Rogers blew out his whiskers. "It's strange to hear you take that attitude. I've always thought of the Molly Maguires as nothing but cutthroats and murderers."

"So they are. So they are. And they will pay the penalty for it, sure enough. But they were driven to murder by the desperateness of their position. In the same dock with those poor deluded souls should be indicted, tried, and convicted those godless men of wealth whose avarice forced their crimes upon them."

Mrs. Rogers listened with bored disapproval while she tried to give the impression of being intensely interested in the priest's discourse. Her black eyes, birdlike, seemed to be waiting to pounce on each worm of fact as it was uttered, although actually she deplored the subjects men

100

picked for discussion. She was surprised at, and disappointed in, Father Duffy. Underneath his suave, quiet manner, his courteous burred voice, was another plebeian like her husband—one who chewed, and looked back with pleasure on those dreadful days when he had been a railroad man. She had saved up in a kind of mental chatelaine all sorts of oddments, little proofs of piety for which she sought approbation, minor problems to be related for the priest's solution. It was aggravating to have Father monopolizing an entirely different kind of conversation. And amazing that both men seemed to enjoy each other's company so much.

She retired to the kitchen to supervise the preparation of tea, and the men were almost unaware of her withdrawal. A little later, when Mary bore in a huge tray that seemed too weighted down with food for her to manage, Father Duffy was still deep in dire predictions for the future. He was calling Mr. Rogers "Rogers," just as his host, with Quaker persistence, called him "Duffy," and the priest relished the feeling that for the moment he was a man among men, and not, as he was so often forced to believe, a churchman set apart from them.

"I tell you, Rogers, all these employers' organizations that have been started, with their blacklists and writs of injunction, will lead to such an outbreak of violence as the country has not yet seen. One place it will hit hardest is with the railroads—take my word for it. So long as men have hope for an orderly and legal adjustment of their wrongs they'll not resort to violence. When that hope is gone, watch out!"

"You put a good case, Duffy. You should talk with my next-door neighbor, Sol Peale. He's a member of the Knights of Labor. But I think workingmen understand it's the politicians, and not their employers, who are the cause of their troubles. Employer and employee are in the same boat. In my own case, my salary has just been reduced, but how can I object when I know the railroad's income has been cut almost in half?"

The priest snorted impatiently. He had forgotten the carefully imposed restraint of his voice, and was shouting now in tones only less in volume than those of his host.

"Rogers, Rogers! Wake up, man! It's the employers make and own the legislators and politicians. Remember the Ames case, with its wholesale buying of votes, and the Crédit Mobilier—practically giving away millions in stocks for legislative protection."

Both men noisily disposed of their quids and dug greedily into the heaped-up cookies and cakes, the little sandwiches hastily prepared. Underneath their surface smoothness and whiteness, the priest's hands still revealed, in bunched muscles and spread palms, the years of toil they had known, although Mrs. Rogers was now engaged in excusing to herself his unsuspected crudities. "The saintly man realizes the only way to appeal to Father is through his baser instincts," she reasoned to herself, "and in spite of all the pain it must cause him, he is willing to make any sacrifice to win Father as a friend." She felt better able to endure the discussion when she thought of it as the priest's subtle method of winning her husband's regard.

"There's nothing like tea, and these cakes are delicious," Father Duffy pronounced.

Mrs. Rogers colored prettily, and began apologies, but they were lost in the din of her husband's protests. He took a full cup of the hot liquid and downed it in a single draft before announcing:

"I can't stand the stuff. There's no body to it—give me coffee any time. There's a man's drink. A railroad man's drink. How you can drink tea is beyond me!"

But Father Duffy only grinned at the comment. "You forget, Rogers, it's seldom I see the men on my parish calls, and discussions with the womenfolk seem better washed down with the lighter beverage."

"I'm surprised to see a real man like yourself following such a namby-pamby profession. It must be a comedown, after railroading."

"A matter of conviction, Rogers. Our good Lord was a workingman, and so were His Apostles and Disciples. Common fellows, they were, fishermen and carpenters and so on. By far too many of the clergy have lost touch with the needs of these good people, as they themselves are shot from school and college to the seminary and the priesthood. We need men like myself. I became convinced of that, and there was nothing I could do about it, much as I hated to give up the feel of wind and cinders in my face."

"As a Quaker, I can understand that. It's one of our principles to follow our individual conscience, and do what it tells us to. In my own case, it's taken me away from the Meeting. In yours, it led you into your Church."

Father Duffy helped himself to a second quid and settled back in his chair. "I know too little about the Quakers, I'm afraid. When I heard that one was husband and father to four good Catholic women, I was curious to meet him. I must say you differ from my expectations."

Mr. Rogers roared, and slapped his guest on the knee. "By the Lord Harry, Duffy, I know what you mean. I'm no solemn-faced, thee-and-thou drygoods clerk, or sober banker counting seven-per-cents in queer-looking clothes, but I'm still a Quaker, I'll have you know. They were real he-men once, and there are plenty of them left. They were pioneers, colonists, soldiers, seafaring men. I come from a line of sea captains myself. They believed in one thing in common, the power and goodness of the human soul and the bestiality and uselessness of war and the use of force. They wouldn't raise a hand in anger, but they were contentious enough, and fearless in both advancing and defending what they believed in.

"They've fallen on evil days, I think, with this tread-quietly-and-speak-softly business. They were more responsible than any other single group for the war, but few of them ever fought in it. They've turned inward, and wait for the spirit to move them. I say you have to possess a spirit before it can move. Well, I have spirit, and it tells me the present trend is wrong. I'm in favor of being personally strong and fearless, but mild as a people, while they've become milksops as individuals and militant as a group. It doesn't make sense."

"I'm afraid I've been taken in by the current phase," the priest admitted, but his host still had more to say.

"Of course, marrying Gussie out of Meeting changed me, undoubtedly. It set me apart, sort of, so that I could look at Quakers with the eye of an outsider. I could see, suddenly, that we had shunted ourselves off on a siding for almost a hundred years. I'm convinced, though, we'll get back on the main line some day, and then watch our smoke! You fellows depend too much on externals, churches, priests, sacraments, vestments, and creeds. The real Quaker places his trust in the power of his own inner soul, that is close to being part of God Himself."

Mrs. Rogers hovered in the hallway during this discussion, and after the priest made his farewell, she gave her own version of it to Mary. "Imagine, arguing with a priest! I'm surprised Father Duffy ever put up with him."

"It was wonderful they got along so good, I say." Mary munched on leftover sandwiches. "They are two fine men, and they took to each other, and if you ask me, ma'am, I'd let it go at that."

Mrs. Rogers nodded. Yes, it would be a shame to undo all Father Duffy's work. Mary was right, she would let it go at that. Mr. Rogers was rather disappointed, if anything, when nothing further was said about the visit, or about the tobacco-chewing episode, even after he passed judgment on their visitor at supper that evening.

"That man Duffy is a fine fellow—enjoyed talking to him. He may be misled in his religion, but at any rate his politics are sound."

Chapter 3

ON THE second of February, Mr. Rogers was awakened from his morning nap by an excited wife. Through all the years during which he had witnessed her passions, excitements, tantrums, and kindred emotional outbursts, he had never seen her so agitated.

"Jesse, you will have to get up quickly, and do something. Zena arrives in New York tomorrow. A letter just came this minute, and she's been on the high seas a week or more."

"In New York? Tomorrow? Without letting us know? Of all the giddy, irresponsible females, you two girls would take the cake."

Mrs. Rogers shook her head impatiently. "There must have been some misunderstanding; perhaps a letter went astray. She seems to think I ought to be expecting her, that's plain enough." She read from the perfumed sheet in her hand: " 'We sail from Havre on the eighteenth of this month, on the La France, of the French Line, and expect to arrive in New York on the third of February.' She goes on and says, 'I am so anxious to see your dear face looking for me, at the dock, and to meet the handsome husband you've written about so much.'"

Rising from bed, Mr. Rogers pulled in his stomach until his chest swelled. "You've been boasting about me," he observed, complacently, but his wife wailed:

"Oh, Jesse, think fast. I'll have to leave for New York today, if there is a train I can make. I wouldn't for anything miss welcoming Zena to America. My only sister, and I have not seen her for many years—the constant companion of my childhood." She began to cry, very softly, while her husband stood by in abashed silence. "It was the three of us, she and I and my dear father, against the world. We were inseparable, like—like . . ."

Mr. Rogers guffawed. "May I suggest ham and eggs?" Then, before his wife could think of a sufficiently cutting retort he went on: "This isn't getting us to New York, Gussie. Get packed, while I tell the girls. . . . We'll all go to greet your sister, and make an expedition of it. I shall tell Lucius to harness the phaeton, so I can drive down and arrange for several days' leave. By the time you are ready, I'll be back, with a hack in tow to take us to the station. Look smart, now!"

"That's wonderful, Father. It's been years since we've been in New York—of course, in my girlhood it was different—but the expense, Jesse? Can we afford it?"

"We'll go over and back on passes, of course. There's only the cost of hotel and meals—I know of several respectable but modest establishments. It won't be like the Astor, where I suppose you and my dear father-in-law always stayed. . . . But now to get the children started." Mr. Rogers walked to the head of the stairs and yelled: "Zenie, Julia! You, Henry and Gene, get yourselves ready! We're all going to New York to meet your Aunt Zena." He outdid himself with a last blast, "*We're all going to New York, so get ready, all of you.*"

2

Mrs. Rogers felt gratified with the appearance of her family. Ensconced in one of Mr. Pullman's new parlor cars, they all remarked that it was exactly like a parlor, with lovely red carpet, and mirrors, and hangings at the windows, and heavily upholstered chairs. "All we need is the piano and the whatnot, to be right at home." They were ushered into the car as if they were traveling royalty, she thought complacently. They were given seats all together, at one end of the car, and the conductor stopped every little while to inquire if they were comfortable.

All that Mrs. Rogers had to do was to swing her chair slightly on its pedestal to keep her whole brood under surveillance. She nodded approval as she surveyed them. Her husband wore a new high hat of gray felt. It was of stylish shape, and extremely becoming. It gave him an air of importance, she thought, that a derby could never achieve. And his beard was handsome. It was so long and curly, and with such rich golden lights in it. His suit was equally distinguished, and set off by the handsome massive gold watch and chain he had inherited from his father.

The watch was much in evidence, for he spent almost the whole of the trip into Jersey City comparing the actual time of arrival at the various stations with the timetable. When the train made a stop on schedule he shouted in triumph, as if he and the engineer were together responsible. When the train ran late he snorted with anger. "A minute, a full sixty seconds behind time! No wonder the railroads lose money! Our freight trains may not look so fancy, but they wouldn't tolerate lateness, I can tell you."

Teresina sat in the chair across the aisle from her mother, so that she appeared to be framed in the window. She wore her good bonnet, a pert little magenta creation, cradled like a small boat in the upsurging sea of her elaborate coiffure. Its sail was a curled tip of ostrich, and its banners the streamers of velvet ribbon that fell to her neck. Mrs. Rogers had trouble deciding which enhanced the other, the hat or its wearer. At any rate, the ensemble was perfect. "I know Zena will be ravished when she sees my Zenie, and proud she's named after her," she thought.

Julia also looked better than usual; her cheeks had more color. She sat directly in front of Mrs. Rogers, and spent most of the journey gazing out of the window. The mother said to herself: "The child is pretty, when she doesn't look so sallow." As she watched her daughter's flushed cheeks, her thoughts ran on. "She's excited, I suppose, at the prospect of seeing her aunt again. After all, Zena was very good to her, even if she didn't take advantage of it."

Even the twins aroused a reluctant admiration, with their sparkling eyes and glowing, ruddy faces, but this did not last long. Her complacency, and the growing annoyance of the other passengers with Mr. Rogers' passion for exactitude, were soon interrupted by an interlude in which both Henry and Georgina participated.

They had begun a crude game of hockey, using as the puck one of the neat, flat little cuspidors Mr. Pullman provided for his guests. It glided over the smooth carpet as if the floor were of ice. The twins sat out of the range of Mrs. Rogers' vision, and kicked the cuspidor back and forth. At first the game had no point, and then it became a contest to see who could give the makeshift puck sufficient speed so that the opponent would fail to block it.

Henry won, with an unfortunately hard shot that Georgina missed entirely. It sent the receptacle careening the full length of the car, dribbling its burden of nicotined effluvia along the way. This put an end to the game; the whole family sat abashed while the Negro porter cleaned up the mess as best he could. Then both parents took turns at scolding the culprits. Mr. Rogers promised retribution with the cat-o'-nine-tails the moment of their return home. Mrs. Rogers called the twins unnatural children and washed her hands of them. Julia and Teresina blushed with shame, and tried to pretend they were not a part of the family, but their mother defeated this purpose by holding them up as models. "Look at your sisters!" she cried. "There is deportment for you. The idea of acting so scandalously, and before other people, too!"

Gradually the tumult subsided, and by the time the train reached Jersey City the little incident was forgotten and only the delights of the journey remained fresh in their minds.

The ferry provided another diversion for the twins. Excepting for narrow aisles at the sides for pedestrians, it was filled to the gate with all kinds of vehicles; two-wheeled carts and four-wheeled wagons, heavy drays and light carriages. The cart and dray horses were tremendous beasts, with long, shaggy fetlocks and bulging muscles at rump and shoulder. These were quiet as the vessel moved from its pier, but the higher-spirited carriage horses had to be held in check by their drivers. In spite of tightly held reins and a continuous chorus of soothing cries, they shied, pranced, and kicked, until Henry saw promise of real entertainment.

He moved close to a fractious horse, and made a noise

109

imitating the buzz of a large and malignant bee. It was a school trick that involved no change in the facial muscles, and so avoided detection. Suddenly the animal pricked up its ears and moved sideways, to tangle with the shafts of a butcher's cart, the driver of which immediately began a tirade directed at the elderly gentleman who held the reins of the frantic horse.

The noise caught Mrs. Rogers' attention, and her suspicions were aroused when she saw her son standing so close to the scene of trouble. Although he looked on with interest, his face appeared so innocent that she allowed her misgivings to be lulled. A moment later there was another commotion, farther down the line of vehicles, and it was Georgina who stood near by. By the time the ferry reached midstream, every horse on board was infected with the fear of buzzing insects, in spite of all the efforts of carters, draymen, and coachmen to quiet them. Even the foot passengers in the side aisles became conscious of the turmoil, and more than a little apprehensive.

Only the Rogers twins seemed unaffected. They were too unconcerned, their mother decided. "Something is riling those horses, and my bet is it's Henry," she told herself, and edged quietly through the crowd until she stood immediately behind him. There was an angry buzz, and she looked around, apprehensively. It occurred again, and a light dawned. Henry was making that virulent hum! No wonder the horses were excited! She reached out, caught him by the ear, and pulled him after her to the shelter of the cabin. "Now you stay here while I get that other imp. The idea of such behavior!"

She did not try to catch Georgina red-handed, so that young lady screamed in protest when she was suddenly seized and pulled away. Much to the distress of all three, they stayed confined in the cabin, the twins as prisoners and their mother as jailer, until the vessel made fast to the slip. Mrs. Rogers reflected that at least a stampede of the horses and the possibility of a greater tragedy had been averted. . . .

Mr. Rogers procured two hansoms for the family. In the first he installed Teresina with the twins, on the theory that the oldest daughter might be a restraining influence. Julia rode with his wife and himself in the second. The hotel he had chosen was far uptown, the Broadway, at the thoroughfare of the same name and Forty-second Street—a peaceful spot out of the hubbub and din of downtown traffic.

The hansoms left the ferry slip at a good gait. It was dusk, and a strong, cold March wind blew down the river. Although they were protected somewhat by the folding front doors of the cab, their faces were stung and reddened. After the first burst of speed, the horses slowed to a dispirited walk, which irritated Mr. Rogers extremely. He opened the little door above them, to shout to the cabby on his lofty perch outside: "Say, can't you make this old crowbait move any faster than this? We haven't eaten yet, and I'm getting hungry!" When this produced no results, he clicked at the horse himself, again without avail.

"If you would go to a hotel miles away from everything, practically out in the country, I'm sure it's not the horse's fault," Mrs. Rogers remarked. "We only get over to New York once in a coon's age, and you insist on staying at a place as dull as Philadelphia."

"I thought it would be more quiet out there. One of the men from the railroad goes there, and he says you can sleep perfectly. Out of the bustle, you know."

"Quiet!" Mrs. Rogers screamed above the noise of steel-tired wheels over Belgian blocks. "Quiet! Anybody from Philadelphia ought to be fed up on quiet, I'd say."

"It wouldn't be too far if this horse would move a little faster, and right now I'm getting hungry," Mr. Rogers grumbled, but in due time they reached the hotel. The cabbies were paid off after a long and loud argument that ended in Father's favor, according to his story afterward. The family left him bickering at the curbing, and when he rejoined them in the lobby, he shouted triumphantly: "By Harry, if anyone thinks they can skin a Philadelphia Quaker they have another thought coming! I gave those bandits what-for, I tell you!"

The Broadway proved to be a comfortable hostelry. They engaged a suite of rooms consisting of two bed chambers and a sitting room. They were all tastefully furnished, although the sitting room, with walnut furniture upholstered in horsehair and a lovely collection of framed prints and mottoes, appealed the most to Mrs. Rogers. While the bellboy made up fires in the fireplaces, as usual in strange surroundings, Mr. Rogers tested the bed. He bounced up and down until the sturdy piece of furniture seemed in danger of breaking, it creaked so loudly. When the fires began to blaze merrily the rooms did look homelike. After the boy had gone, Mr. Rogers lit all the gas jets in the imposing chandelier, a luxury he rarely allowed himself at home. "Might as well have all the light you need when we're not paying extra for it."

It was arranged that their parents should occupy one of the rooms, and the girls the other, while Henry was to have a cot which would be set up in the sitting room. As the clerk had informed them, there was a women's bathroom located on the floor above, and one for the men on the floor below—a comfortable and satisfactory arrangement, all agreed after making use of these conveniences.

"Come, let's go out and eat!" Mr. Rogers shouted. "But

remember, I'm like the fellow in the song, I have but fifty cents." He cocked his high hat over his right ear while his face took on its most devilish expression. After marshaling the family into the hall and locking the door, he marched down the narrow passage singing this favorite ditty of his. In spite of an obbligato of objections, of "Pet, not here, you'll disturb everyone," and similar dissuasions, he continued the song of the unfortunate young man who had invited the wrong girl to lunch with him, and the twins joined in behind him, shouting the chorus:

She said she wasn't hungry, but this is what she ate—
  A dozen raw, a plate of slaw, some chicken and some roast,
Asparagus and applesauce, and soft-shelled crabs on toast,
  A big box stew, and crackers too, her appetite was immense;
When she called for more I nearly fell on the floor,
     As I had but fifty cents.

Chapter 4

IN THE morning Julia solved the cause of the misunderstanding over her aunt's arrival. Mrs. Rogers got out the first letter, just to reassure herself, and showed it to her.

"There it is, as clear as can be—'. . . the *La France* is quite fashionable, and there is a sailing fits in with my plans, so unless you hear further, I shall see your dear face'—Your aunt always loved me—'I shall see your dear face about March second.' See, there it is, 'three-two,' the figures are as plain!"

"Oh, Mother, how silly! You should have shown me the letter in the first place. It says 'three-two' right enough, but don't you remember, Continentals always write the day first, and then the month? It's the third of February!

You've been misled by that stupid Americanism of putting the month down first."

"Well, I never! . . . Now don't say anything to your father about this, Julia, or we will never hear the end of it. He will do nothing but preach about the correctness of the American way, and he'll torture poor Zena with ill-timed jokes about her heathen habits. As for dates, we'd never have a chance to get one right again, he'd deliberately mix us up with them!"

The French Line pier was Number 59 on the North River, so the Rogerses took the belt-line horsecars, arriving in time to see a large vessel, still in midstream, which was pointed out as *La France*. It was imposing in size, of almost five thousand tons, and Mr. Rogers, who had vast stores of misinformation regarding ships, proceeded to explain the theory and operation of the screw, and the obvious advantages of the paddle wheel as a means of propulsion. The last time he had seen an ocean liner was on the *Great Eastern's* first trip. That vessel was by far the largest ever built, with five or six funnels and as many masts for sails. According to him, it had been a grand sight, with paddles churning and sails set, and he proceeded to compare it with *La France*, much to the disadvantage of the latter.

The pier was cold, with the damp, pervading chill peculiar to the New York water front, and Mrs. Rogers and the girls shivered in their heavy cloth coats, quilted dresses, and plentiful petticoats. At another time, Mr. Rogers also would have complained of the cold, but as his wife announced that she was gradually freezing, he took the attitude of being the robust and hearty man of the outdoors, and blustered about with coat open, boasting to all and sundry that he couldn't understand why anybody should be cold on such a perfect day.

Meanwhile *La France* was shoved toward her berth by tugs that worried her like a pack of terriers herding a reluctant cow. The sudden deep bellow of her whistle announced her angry protest at the treatment she was receiving. As the black hull ranged alongside, Mrs. Rogers gazed upward, scanning eagerly the faces of the passengers along the rail. Finally she announced with disappointment:

"I don't see her. I don't see her anywhere. I hope she's not ill."

Julia spoke in a flat voice that held no enthusiasm. "Why, there she is, Mama. Right opposite, with the purple bonnet."

"I declare you are the most aggravating child. Why didn't you tell me? Now point her out to me again, quickly."

"I thought you saw her, that's why I didn't speak. There she is—don't you see? With the purple bonnet. She's next to the man with the blond beard—the mutton chops." Julia believed that it was a grievous social error to point, and she attempted to indicate her aunt's position by a stiff nod of her head.

Impatiently her mother burst out: "Good heavens, girl, I haven't seen my sister for twenty-five years, and I'm starving for sight of her! Point her out to me quickly."

Julia pointed upward, hesitatingly. "There she is—there, Mama. Can't you see? Next to that good-looking blond man with the mutton chops."

"That old woman! You can't mean her! Why, she's a hag! You never told me she looked like that—my dear Zena, who used to be so beautiful."

"She looks the same as she did two years ago. I told you when I came home she wasn't beautiful, but you wouldn't listen."

Mr. Rogers was also busy looking for his sister-in-law. "I see her!" he shouted. "There's a family resemblance, Gussie. That's her, all right, with the feather in her bonnet—a darn fine-looking woman, if you ask me."

The ship was slowly warped along the pier, taking Aunt Zena from their view, and because of the crowd they were unable to follow. They waited impatiently for the placing of the gangplank and the discharge of the passengers. It was a slow process, attended with much shouting of orders in French, and Mr. Rogers viewed the whole operation with scorn.

"These Frenchies don't know how to handle things at all. No system—nothing but confusion and more confusion. Did you ever hear such outlandish gibberish in your life as all that shouting back and forth? Like a lot of monkeys, that's what they are. If I was in the steamship business I'd run it like the railroads. The boats would have to come in on scheduled time. You know what the schedule for this ship says? 'Expected arrival, February third.' No hour—not even sure it would get here then." He examined his watch. "It's nine-seventeen now. I'd say, 'Due nine-seventeen A.M.,' and I'd make them stick to the minute, too, and no shilly-shallying."

During this running commentary, a steady stream of passengers descended the gangplank, and then a commotion more furious than any preceding it came from the vessel and could be heard on the pier. A strident voice began screaming what sounded like curses, in French, and Mrs. Rogers exclaimed: "That's her! That's Zena! I'd know her voice anywhere—it hasn't changed."

Julia also recognized the screams, and began to tremble from nervousness. Her father appeared to be deep in thought. What seemed to be the last of the line of passengers had now descended, and the pier filled with groups

116

engaged in emotional reunion, or the reclaiming of baggage which had been chuted down from some place aft. Now the gangway began to empty out covered wicker chests and Saratoga trunks, portmanteaus and bags. Each piece of the luggage was followed by adjurations in French from the same piercing voice. Mr. Rogers for the first time in his life took cognizance of Julia's knowledge of French without adverse comment. He nudged his daughter, and whispered loudly:

"What's she saying all the time, up there? Can you make it out?"

"She's a wicked woman, Papa—really wicked. She's telling the porters to be careful of her trunks and things or she'll have them discharged. And she's calling them names, too."

Mr. Rogers thought: "Perhaps it is just as well that Gussie's sister is going to stay at a hotel. Something tells me she'd be a little hot to handle."

A woman in black hat and coat, so typically the French maid there was no mistaking her vocation, walked through the gaping hole in the ship's side that was the gangway. The unseen voice followed her as she began the descent of the gangplank, and the maid kept answering in a monosyllable quite as loud. She used only the word "Oui," but it was said with a variety of inflection and emphasis that made her answers perfectly understandable to Mr. Rogers. "My French is coming along," he thought. "She's telling that harridan up there not to worry, she'll take care of everything. 'I'll attend to all those things you're telling me about,' she's saying, and you know she will, too."

Now came the blond young man with mutton chops. He proved to be quite tall and extremely broad, and Julia, watching him, felt a sudden stab at her heart while Teresina wondered to herself: "That can't be Aunt Zena's nephew! He is much too large for a Frenchman. But if he is her nephew, and he must be, he's certainly handsome."

The young man in question was evidently holding some kind of animal on a leash, but the side of the gangplank prevented them from seeing what it was. Another porter made his appearance, with a small trunk balanced on his shoulders. Mr. Rogers gazed after him apprehensively as the man added the trunk to the huge pile of luggage on the pier over which the maid was now standing guard. Then another maid came through the gangway, carrying a handbag of black leather, and then Aunt Zena herself, the ostrich plume in her bonnet shaking in agitation, but with a satisfied look on her face at a job well done. Her disembarkation had been carried through successfully!

As the Rogerses pressed forward to greet her, there was an excited yapping of dog, and between the feet of the onlookers they could see two elongated creatures of sorrel color. Mrs. Rogers could restrain herself no longer. She began to scream, in hysterical fashion, "Zena! . . . Zena! . . . cara mia!" while she pushed her way by main force through the remnants of the crowd. Even the pier of the French Line had never before been the scene of so dramatic a reunion. Aunt Zena responded to her cry with a torrent of mixed French, English, and Italian. She threw her hands over her head so suddenly that they pushed askew the flamboyant purple bonnet. "Tina! My dear, my only!" She collided with one of the porters and gave him a shove, upsetting the poor man over a bag. The sisters embraced, and as Zena was the taller, it seemed as if Mrs. Rogers would surely be smothered against her formidable bosom. The shouts, screams, shrieks, and cries of rapturous greetings continued for a full five minutes, to

118

change into an equally voluble but less intense period of mutual appraisement.

"My darling little cabbage, I should never have known you, never. I looked everywhere, and I can tell you, I was disappointed. I spotted Julia, of course. Who could forget that prissy little face? I'm sorry to say that, Tina, but you might as well know what I think of her. . . . And you've got so dumpy—and gray hair . . . Thank God I don't have a single one yet."

Mrs. Rogers was talking as rapidly. "It's ridiculous, of course, not to allow for the passing of time. When Julia pointed you out, I couldn't believe my eyes—you used to be so regal, so beautiful, so gorgeous. . . . Do you remember?"

As a good railroad man, Mr. Rogers recognized danger signals, so he stepped forward and broke in, with a more courtly bow than he had ever before essayed in his lifetime. "Of course this is my dear sister. . . . I'm Jesse. Welcome to God's own country!"

Aunt Zena turned on a different brand of emotion. It was a compound of allure, affection, surprise, and admiration. She threw her head up and sideways in an attitude that might have been called coy in a smaller, less dynamic person.

"Well, Jesse," she said. "Why, you are much more handsome than I expected, even after all of Augustina's rapturous descriptions." Her voice had lost entirely its strident quality and took on a throbbing seductiveness. Combined with her accent, her intonation and mannerisms, it made, so Mr. Rogers thought, a very charming effect. He bowed again, as elaborately as the first time, in recognition of the compliment, and added one of his own. "I've heard so often of the second of the Borelli beauties.

. . . To my great amazement the realization exceeds all my anticipations."

A slow smile of thanks for his gallantry rewarded him. Except in Mrs. Rogers' eyes, blinded by a remembrance of the girl she had known, there was no doubt Teresina Lascalles was still a handsome woman for her years, in spite of an inclination to stoutness. She was dark, much darker than her sister, and more Italian-looking. A faint mustache that lined her upper lip for some reason did not detract from her appearance, nor did the large rings of violet shadow beneath her eyes. The first gave added mobility to her mouth, and enhanced the color of her lips, the second added depth and poignance of expression. Both sisters had a birdlike quality, but where Mrs. Rogers might have been compared to a particularly pert sparrow, Zena resembled the hawk or the eagle.

During the exchange between her sister and her husband, Mrs. Rogers tapped her foot impatiently. "There's no need for Jesse to fall over himself, kowtowing to Zena," she thought. "Especially after all the things he's said about her generosities."

Aunt Zena measured the six feet of Mr. Rogers' brawny two-hundred-pound frame. With a sudden theatrical gliding motion, she threw her arms about him, while her voice palpitated. "I must have a kiss from my handsome brother-in-law!"

Mr. Rogers was not a bit abashed while the terrific smack was planted on his lips, nor afterward. His whole expression reflected his thought—"She's a stunner—and fire. . . . Make no mistake about that."

At the same time Mrs. Rogers was thinking: "Really, there are limits to the things even a sister should be allowed to do, but Zena was always like that, looking out for the main chance to get a man, even if he was her own sister's husband." Her voice took on an acid edge as she said: "There are other members of the family beside my husband. This is Zenie, your namesake."

As Teresina stepped forward, determined to make a conquest of her aunt to further her own schemes, she also gave an exhibition of demonstrative affection. She hugged her aunt and gushed: "My dear Aunt Zena, I've loved you so many years, and now to actually see you! I can hardly stand the exquisite pain." She kissed her aunt on the cheek, and then, as if overwhelmed by her love, kissed her even more fervently on the other cheek. Aunt Zena was touched. Tears started in her eyes and ran unaffectedly down her cheeks. "My dear child. My dear child. How I have waited for this moment! You know I feel as if you were my own daughter. Indeed I do."

Mrs. Rogers looked on approvingly, and her husband in astonishment. He had never before seen his oldest daughter so apparently agitated by her feelings, and he thought, "My God, that woman's got something that draws you out, for a fact." Mrs. Rogers was thinking, at the same moment, "Well, thank goodness Zenie knows how to play her cards to hook Zena."

Aunt Zena went on: "Sweet child, and you are quite pretty, too. I can't say you are as handsome as I was at your age, but you might be if you were dressed properly. What you need, my dear, is some good clothes, and I propose to get them for you. We'll go on a shopping trip in the morning, and then you can throw these things away. Augustina never had any real taste with clothes. Imagine such a ridiculous bonnet, with that tiny tip of feather! You shall have a new one, with a whole plume, the best that money can buy—I promise you." She was suddenly conscious that she still had duties to perform. "Name of God," she cried, "the luggage! I must attend

121

to it, if you'll excuse me. I wouldn't leave a single piece of it out of my sight over here—especially with wild Indians roaming around everywhere. When I was here before things were still civilized, to some extent at least. Imagine allowing those savages to get out of hand—but what can you expect in a republic?"

She was gone before anyone could refute these astounding statements, and the family followed more slowly toward the pile of luggage, where Aunt Zena was already screaming in French to the maids, while they seemed to be answering quite as loudly. The handsome young man with the mutton-chop whiskers stood by in bored amusement, holding the leash of the two misshapen dogs, whose sad expression seemed caused by realization of their unfortunate conformation.

Mrs. Rogers nudged her husband and said: "Pet, what in the name of heaven are those animals? They're not dogs, are they?"

"I believe they are the breed known as dash-hounds, and are even more homely than I suspected from the descriptions I have read. It's a breed of dog the English Prince Consort is supposed to admire, and I can't say he shows much taste."

When Aunt Zena returned she made profuse apologies. "That luggage! You know they wanted to take it away somewhere to put ashore, and I told them a thing or two. 'Every last stick goes ashore with me under my eyes, or not at all,' I said—and—oh, you haven't met Philippe."

She called across the pier, "Philippe, my dear, do come over!" The young man approached, still leading the dogs, and she introduced him: "This is my nephew, Philippe Lascalles—my husband's brother's son, you know. He's half French and half English. His mother was one of the . . ."

122

Philippe interrupted, speaking in a pleasant, drawling manner, and including the whole family in a very fetching smile. "Come, Zena, I'm anxious to meet your American relatives, and I am sure they don't give a sou for my pedigree."

Aunt Zena drew herself up to her full height and proclaimed: "This is my darling sister Tina. We spent a happy girlhood together. My, do you remember the times we had? It's too bad those days are over. . . . And this is her husband. . . . You must call him Jesse. I feel as if I'd known you for years, and I can call you Jesse, can't I?"

Mr. Rogers beamed and boomed, "Of course, Zena, of course."

"And this is my favorite niece, Teresina. . . . Teresina, my favorite nephew, Philippe Lascalles. I hope you two will become very good friends."

Teresina dropped her eyes modestly and then lifted them, as if to turn the full light of her beauty upon him. He gave a short bow and another of his pleasant smiles, but meanwhile had engaged himself in greeting Mr. Rogers. "Jove, I'm happy to meet you, sir," he said, shaking hands heartily. The two men were of equal height and breadth, and looked not unlike, with high foreheads, straight noses, gray-blue eyes, and curling blond hair, although Mr. Rogers was somewhat more corpulent. Had their beards been cut in the same style, the resemblance might have been quite startling.

Philippe went on: "I say, sir, what a pair of shoulders you have, if you don't mind me remarking about them. I wager you are an oarsman."

Mr. Rogers, who had been in a small boat but twice in his life, looked down modestly and said, with perfect truth, "Oh, I did a little rowing in my youth."

"I knew it, sir. You can't fool me on oarsmen—there is nothing like rowing for body-building."

Aunt Zena explained: "Philippe was a blue, or a green, or something at Cambridge." Then she went on hurriedly, to complete the introductions: "And this is Julia, and I suppose these are the twins, Henry and Georgina. My, Henry, what a big, strong and fine-looking young man you have become—quite a younger edition of your father, I'll be bound.

"Now last, but not least, I want you to meet Fortune and François." She dove down and caught up the dachshunds, one under each arm. "Aren't they beauties? Aren't they charming?" She poked the two wet-nosed melancholy faces close to Mr. Rogers'. "Your new Uncle Jesse—don't you have a kiss for him, darlings?" Before he could shy away, two tongues dribbling saliva painted wet streaks across his cheek and nose just above the line of his beard. "What darlings! See, they love you already. I knew they would.

"But what are we standing here for, waiting? It is bitter in this drafty place, and your American climate is atrocious anyhow. Simply atrocious!

"Philippe dear, do go and get some hackneys, and try to pick cabbies that don't look like rascals, if you can find them. I must say I never saw more villainous-looking people than your American working class—simply villainous.

"And tell them we are going to the Astor. Perhaps you'd better write it down on slips of paper for them, so there is no mistake.

"Jesse, you and the family will stay with me, of course."

"We came over yesterday, and we are already most comfortably situated in a quiet, peaceful location."

"Oh, indeed? I am disappointed. At what hotel?"

"The Broadway. It is quite far uptown, out of the din of traffic."

Aunt Zena shook her head. "The Broadway? I never heard of it, so it can't be much. I can't leave my own relatives at such a place. You might be murdered in your beds—I wouldn't sleep. No, you will go with us to the Astor. I can't say I expect much there, but it has a good reputation, at least.

"Come on, everything is settled. You'll go with us now, and this afternoon you and Philippe can get your luggage from that other awful place, wherever it is."

Mrs. Rogers looked expectantly toward her husband, but if she anticipated his usual vociferous objections to plans other than his own she was disappointed. "Zena knows how to manage people," she thought. "She just tells them what to do, and then acts as if they were going to do it, but some day she will come against a Tartar in Father."

Almost hesitatingly, Mr. Rogers ventured a suggestion. "You don't need to have hacks carry your trunks and things. Just leave them there on the pier, and send the whole kit and caboodle by dray."

"I wouldn't think of it. Not in this awful country. The things I have couldn't be replaced with money—particularly over here—and I propose to keep them under my eyes as much as I can. Now, Philippe, get some porters and begin loading up. I shall send a maid with each of the first two cabs, and then Jesse. I know you won't mind riding alone to the hotel. And then you, Philippe, and then Henry. I think you're quite big enough to prevent anyone from stealing your aunt's possessions from right under her eyes. . . . These republican countries! France is almost as bad now, I assure you, although we are spared the Indians, scalping people.

"Julia, you and your mother in the next, and I shall ride

with Teresina. Now let's see. . . . Georgina, I think you can safely travel alone—only a fiend would attack a girl of your years—and you can take the dogs with you, for protection."

Georgina, who had already fallen in love with the two queer little monstrosities, immediately gave a squeal of pleasure, and knelt down to pet them.

"Now that's eight. . . . We'll have to send one hackney alone. Pack the servants' luggage in it, and put it between you and Jesse, Philippe, and tell them to stay in line." Like a commanding general, she continued to shout orders as the luggage was reloaded, the great purple plume in her bonnet waving and bobbing as she admonished, cajoled, scolded, and threatened the porters and cabbies, her maids and relatives. "On to the Astor!" was her battle cry, and soon the parade of cabs, with whips cracking, horses prancing, and cabbies shouting, began their crosstown march.

2

Dinner at Delmonico's! It was awesome to a frugal Philadelphia Quaker to watch the unconcern with which Teresina Lascalles spent money. After individually and collectively damning the cab-drivers, she had given them tips so out of all proportion to their services that Mr. Rogers had remonstrated. She had replied that it was not for what they *did*, but a reward for their honesty in delivering her belongings intact when they might have made way with all of them, and cut their throats in the bargain. At the hotel, she had got a room and sitting room for himself and Gussie, separate rooms for each of the children, a suite for Philippe, and another for herself with a large extra room she called a salon. She had even insisted upon a private bath!

126

Then her persuasive abilities! The clerk in the hotel office questioned the propriety of having the dogs, Fortune and François, in her rooms, and she responded with a scene that quickly ended with the clerk's apology.

In a short time the animals were ensconced on pillows in the salon, and the room itself was transformed. Mr. Rogers was astonished to learn that four of the trunks contained nothing but knickknacks and photographs, and these now sat on easels, hung, or were placed about in thick profusion on every available space of wall, shelf, or table top.

And now they were to dine at Delmonico's, the whole family. His sister-in-law had given the order quite casually. In the midst of rearranging certain of the photographs and portraits, she had asked: "Where shall we dine tonight? Do you think the children would enjoy Delmonico's? It's quite good, I believe, for America."

This constant disparagement of things American Mr. Rogers could not understand. Everyone knew it was a better country than France, which had been badly licked by an army of nothing but Germans just a few years ago. He intended to reason with Zena later, but at the moment he allowed it to pass, and instead began to object to the expensiveness of Delmonico's for so large a party.

Zena waved her hand to show how little the cost mattered. "I'll send Philippe down to reserve a room, and we will have a nice quiet family dinner." And thus it had been settled.

As Gussie was napping, the twins were out walking the dachshunds, and the girls were presumably in their rooms, he and Zena had the salon to themselves, and a change in her manner made it become a very intimate room indeed. She picked up one of the photographs, a large portrait beautifully tinted and ornately framed, that stood on an easel by a table. Looking at it with a languishing gaze, she exclaimed: "Ah, poor Jacques! You don't know how lonely a woman can be, Jesse, when she loses the man she loves. When Jacques died the world ended for me."

Mr. Rogers nodded in sorrowful agreement. "So that is your late husband. He was a fine-looking man."

"My husband? Why, what an idea, Jesse! What gave it to you? Philippe has been dead for years and years. I doubt that I have a picture of him. He was one of those creatures one wants to forget as soon as possible—a gouty, disagreeable old man. No, Jacques was my grand passion. His death devastated me. He was an officer in the army. Just think, he survived Sedan with not a scratch, and then was killed in the rioting of the Commune! How I have hated the masses since, for murdering him. I have no great admiration for Thiers, but I did enjoy it when he shot down thousands of them. . . . I tell you, life hasn't been the same since." She kissed the photograph with great dramatic fervor, and assumed an attitude on the settee close to his chair. "Ah, Jesse, if I could find a man like you—handsome, strong, but complaisant to a woman's little whims—a successful man of affairs, and yet not so successful that his business would take his time away from me. If I could find a man like that, I might be saved an unhappy middle age."

It was difficult to refrain from offering himself to so noble a cause, and Mr. Rogers h-hru-u-umped several times to indicate the depth of his feelings without making any commitment. There was something about Zena that overwhelmed one. He withdrew a handkerchief and sopped the perspiration from his forehead.

He was saved by the entrance of his wife, refreshed by her nap. She and Zena began to chat; he walked around, nervously, examining pictures. They were all of men!

Short and tall, stout and thin, young and elderly, with the utmost variety of beard and features. A surprising number of them were of the military, and several might have been ambassadors, or other functionaries, from the decorations they wore. An astounding woman! His curiosity might have prompted him to further inspection of the portraits, done in so many different mediums, but he turned away when his wife said, impatiently:

"Jesse, do come and sit down instead of walking around like a hen on a hot griddle. I declare, you make me nervous."

3

With the exception of Mr. Rogers, the whole family allowed Aunt Zena to order for them. He felt it was time for him to assert himself, and when she began to order in French what appeared to be an extremely complicated meal, he announced:

"Not for me, Zena. I prefer simple fare. Meat and potatoes, I say. If they have a nice rib of beef that is good and rare, you can order a slice for me, and none of your fancy fixings."

Aunt Zena was amused, and gave a high, tinkling laugh apparently reserved for public occasions. "My dear Jesse, how droll! Of course you shall have meat and potatoes— practically raw beef, if you wish it."

Later, during the meal, when he looked around at the others' plates and saw the lovely quail, bursting fat and oven-gilded to a golden brown, and afterward the thick tenderloins sauced with wine and mushrooms, that Aunt Zena had ordered for them, he regretted his insistence upon his ordinary fare. He had the expression of a small boy who is not allowed a dessert that the rest of the family are eating.

Notwithstanding, he could not forbear another show of independent action, this time over the matter of wine for the twins. While it was being decanted, he restrained the waiter who moved to fill the children's glasses. "I think the twins are too young for wine," he announced, but his sister-in-law overruled him. "Nonsense, Jesse, a little wine never hurt anybody. Why, we used to drink wine like water when we were children, didn't we, Tina, and it never hurt us. Fill them up, garçon!"·

Julia had wine too, which may have partially explained her flashing eyes and spirited manner. She sat at the left of Philippe Lascalles, while Teresina sat at his right, and her conversation and appearance were so animated that she succeeded in capturing his attention for a good deal more than half of the time. Teresina, who was exercising every wile to be as charming as possible, although inwardly raging at the presumption of her sister, was at one disadvantage. She did not speak French, and Julia turned naturally to that language to make inquiries regarding the present life of Paris and to renew her remembrance of things Parisian. Her own life in Paris, which she had so detested, suddenly became a glorious, golden experience to be shared with Philippe.

Both Mrs. Rogers and her sister viewed Julia's animation with surprise, the former to think, "Julia is setting her cap for that young man, and if Zenie doesn't watch out she'll get him, too. When I get Zena alone I shall have to find out what his prospects are, although from what she said at the pier this morning, I'm sure she picked him out for Zenie, and you can depend on Zena to be practical."

Her sister thought somewhat differently. "Look at that little beast Julia, throwing herself at Philippe. She never once looked so alive all the time she was with me. Then she'd look at me with a holier-than-thou expression for which I could have shaken her well.

"She is pretty, though, in a way, when she wants to be —if she wasn't so skinny, and had less frumpy clothes. Well, fair play, say I, and it's Philippe's money in the family I care about, and marriage to a saint might be good for him. . . . She shall have a fair chance at him, so far as clothes go, although I'll be bound I hadn't intended to waste money outfitting her."

Julia surprised her parents in another way. She ate every bit of the hearty dinner with a gusto quite different from her usual picking. The truth was that one moment had changed her outlook on life completely, and that was the second she had first beheld Philippe framed in the cavernous opening of the gangway, looking about him, so she thought, like a modern Columbus seeking a new world to conquer.

All of the emotion which had grown to adult force now found a center in this young man so much like her father in appearance, but lacking the loud boisterousness of manner which had so often disturbed her in the past. She slept little that night, going over the happenings of the day, repeating the details of their conversation during dinner, and enjoying in anticipation hoped-for intimacies on the morrow.

She determined on one thing. She also must have new clothes, for of course Zenie was after Philippe too—that was evident at dinner. She would have to do as her sister had done, play up to her aunt. Although she really didn't think about it, she was no longer afraid of Aunt Zena. On the contrary, she felt affection for her for bringing Philippe into her life.

Chapter 5

IN THE morning Julia tried to make up her mind how best to invite inclusion in her aunt's shopping tour. She shrank from attempting anything so obvious as Teresina's method. If Aunt Zena couldn't see that Zenie was just making up to her, it was just because she didn't want to, she thought.

During breakfast, a light repast of eggs and sausages, with fried potatoes and little pancakes—most delicious things—for the womenfolks, and a more substantial steak, with quantities of boiled potatoes, for the men, she considered the problem, and as yet found no answer. When her aunt said in matter-of-fact tones, as if all of her future did not depend on it: "Julia, I know you are not much concerned with appearances, but if you think you could do with a new rig you might as well come along," she could hardly believe her ears.

"Oh, I do. Indeed I do, Aunt Zena—and thank you so much for including me."

To imagine that she didn't care about appearances! Or that new clothes were not of the utmost importance! For so long Julia had had dinned into her ears the inadequacy of her hundred-and-thirty-pound figure and the dark sallowness of her skin that she was quite convinced her only hope of winning Philippe lay in miraculous new garments which would conceal the omissions of nature and create an illusion of more ample bust and hip than she actually possessed. Alas! there was little to be done with her dark skin, except as bright colors might enhance it.

She was sorry that she had not made better use of her opportunities to acquire naturally the roundnesses she had been nagged into believing men admired. She regretted each meal at which she had been bored with the food, each snack and luncheon she had returned untouched. As she accepted her aunt's invitation she made a promise to herself that some day not far distant the requisite flesh and bone should replace a false framework of hair, whalebone, and cambric.

They started out right after breakfast, in a stylish rig Aunt Zena had hired for her New York use. It was a landau, drawn by a beautiful pair of bay roans, and complete with a liveried coachman. For shopping, Aunt Zena had chosen to wear a most gorgeous creation that made her seem even larger than she was. Teresina was quick to compliment her aunt. "What a lovely dress, Aunt Zena! It is handsome—quite the most elegant I have ever seen."

While Julia regretted that she had not thought of the compliment first, Aunt Zena looked down at herself complacently. "Do you really like it, child?" She smoothed the dress with a stout, much-ringed hand. "It was extremely expensive material. I bought it in Paris, of course. You couldn't get goods of that quality here. Perhaps it was extravagant of me, but when I saw this glorious color, I couldn't resist it."

"Like a deep magenta, isn't it?" Teresina inquired. "I've never seen anything quite so brilliant."

"It's the new shade—solferino, they call it, from some place in Italy. I suppose it appeals to my Latin blood."

By this time the morning traffic was at its height. None of the girls had driven through New York during business hours, and they reacted to the ride according to their natures. Teresina sat back with an air that imitated her aunt's, and imagined that *she* had married a tremendously wealthy husband, and this was her landau, and the horses were part of her large and pure-blooded stable. In spite of these enjoyable reveries, she was annoyed when a carriage passed with a footman sitting on the box by the coachman. Aunt Zena didn't have a footman! Perhaps she couldn't afford one! She wondered if Philippe's fortune was great enough to provide her with the ostentatious luxury of a useless servant, to sit so straight beside the coachman. She must, at all costs, she must have a footman, and in the most elegant livery.

While Teresina thus daydreamed, Julia watched the passing throngs with a feeling of wonder that out of all the people in the world she had found the only man she could possibly care for. She compared him with the men in the passing carriages. There were none as handsome. Then she was frightened. In all this traffic, surrounded by multitudes of strange people, something might happen to her or, of more seriousness, to him.

Aunt Zena watched her niece, thinking: "Well, a year or so certainly has made a difference in that child. She is positively radiant. She's fallen in love—that's what it is. I know, because I always feel inside like she is looking, when I get in love. . . . I wonder if it will ever happen to me again." She sighed, and called up to the coachman, in a louder voice than necessary, "Alphonse, do be careful, we don't want an accident."

Georgina was frankly enjoying everything, and her head seemed on a swivel, she had to swing it about so quickly to take in all the sights. It was not far to Stewart's great new store, about which they had all heard, but the jam of drays, carts, and vans, of carriages and rigs of various sorts, not to mention the fleets of Broadway stages, so retarded them that they were a full half-hour in reaching the magnificent new building between Ninth and Tenth streets. It was a whole block long, and they swung into Ninth Street to leave the plebeian world of carts, vans, and stages behind. Here there were nothing but elegant equipages with mettlesome horses, carriages so handsome even Aunt Zena was impressed.

As they dismounted at the entrance, she gave instructions to the coachman. "And don't forget, Alphonse—be on the watch for us constantly. I hate so to be kept waiting for my carriage."

As the coachman had a very Irish look and spoke with a brogue, Georgina burst out: "Aunt Zena, how funny— an Irishman named Alphonse! Whoever heard of such a thing?"

Aunt Zena was marshaling her charges for an assault on the treasures of New York's merchant prince, Alexander T. Stewart, but she also smiled at the incongruity of the name.

"The coachman I've had for years in Paris was called Alphonse, and I couldn't bother learning a new name. When I hired this rascal, I said, 'I don't care what your name is; from now on it's Alphonse—take it or leave it.' . . . And now we shall want to get some dress materials first. Lead the way, Teresina, until I can make inquiries."

They had a busy morning, searching through bolts of dress goods, swatches of samples, lengths of draped remnants, through braids, embroideries, and buttons, through taffetas and failles, brocades, silks, louisines and foulards. These were for dresses to be made up later, in Philadelphia. They got new corsets, Madame Foy's, of the latest and most fashionable style that threw the body forward into the popular Grecian bend, and a complete supply of underthings, drawers, camisoles, and a variety of petticoats, of linen, flannel, and heavily whaleboned cambric.

When Aunt Zena shopped, the whole store seemed to turn in order to wait upon her. She carried on the purchase of several items at once. She bought only one quality, the best, and proceeded to bargain for each article in a manner quite foreign to Mr. Stewart's suave attendants. In spite of many protestations of their one-price policy,

135

she effected all kinds of concessions—forced them to admit the slightest flaws, depreciated the quality of everything, and made her own memoranda of the prices.

They bought ready-made dresses for immediate use, and spent hours longer, surrounded by dressmakers, measuring for the necessary alterations. Here again Aunt Zena argued over each projected change, and revealed a knowledge of their craft that won the grudging respect of all the dressmakers. Even Teresina was affected by the grand manner of their shopping, and was awed, with the others, into complete agreement with all their aunt's decisions. She was fitted for a street dress of plum-colored silk, the skirt trimmed with ruffles and plaiting. To this was added a bonnet of similar color, set off with blush roses. It was the consensus of the store staff that the effect was fetching, and even Aunt Zena nodded her head in approval. For evening, they chose an embroidered magenta silk cut in the new princess style, which revealed to perfection Zenie's flowing lines.

Julia's dress was of elephant-colored silk and plaid camel's hair, with an underskirt trimmed with plaitings. She also was allowed a bonnet. Georgina had to be satisfied with a hat, as being more in keeping with her tender years. For her first real dress, they picked a light-blue silk with a bodice of striped blue and white grenadine. It was so plentifully decorated with fringe and lace, with plaitings, puffs, and ruffles, that her aunt declared, "Indeed, Georgina, my dear, you look like a delicious French bonbon—quite good enough to eat, in fact."

Once the serious items of purchasing were over, their aunt relaxed her sternness. She laughed, joked, and spent three or four times as much as she had saved by her bargainings on useless little gifts ranging from cut-glass perfume bottles to sets of braided-hair jewelry. This latter purchase occasioned more amusement, as she had hair snipped to make each of them a memento, and then insisted in making sure there was not a single gray hair among the black ones. The girls all chose to have their aunt's hair made into earrings, and when the orders were given, she burst out: "That gives all of you mementos, but what about me? You've had me shorn, and now it is my turn. From you, Teresina, enough hair for a nice bracelet—I need a new one, anyway—and a brooch from you, Julia, and that spun gold of yours, child, shall make me earrings." To the clerk, she added: "And I want long earrings, understand? Double length—triple length—something you can see, and not hidden away under one's coiffure."

It was wonderful how much fun Aunt Zena could be! Julia's memories of her were so different that it was hard to reconcile them with this boisterous, generous woman. She seemed more like Mother now. With the same zest for living, and she could laugh as heartily over the simplest pleasures.

2

After they completed their shopping, Aunt Zena suggested luncheon. "It's well in the afternoon, and I'm sure you are all starving. There is nothing like shopping for the appetite." They went to a French restaurant, the Café Martin, which seemed restful and homelike to Aunt Zena, and the others, even Julia, enjoyed its Parisian atmosphere. It was quite late when they returned to the Astor House, tired and happy. While the girls bubbled over with descriptions of all the new finery, their aunt said:

"I tell you, Augustina, I envy you your daughters. It is years since I felt as young as I did in their company, and they are all sweet girls." When the subjects of this dis-

137

cussion retired from the salon, she continued with her confidences. "I'm afraid Teresina will always be my favorite,
but I have changed my mind about Julia. I suppose it was
just a phase she was going through made her appear so
odious. Though she is on the quiet side, she's a nice girl,
underneath everything.

"Now the one I would watch, if you don't mind my
saying so, is Georgina. There's a little minx if there ever
was one. She'll be pretty as a picture, though, in her new
clothes. I couldn't have got anything in Paris more becoming, and it suits her to a T."

"I'm afraid you spent a great deal on them," Mrs.
Rogers objected. "You know, in a place like Philadelphia
clothes mean so little, because there are so few opportunities to wear them. You can envy me my daughters, Zena,
but you don't know what it means to bury yourself in one
place, and such a place, all your life."

"Why, Tina! Philadelphia will be the center of the
world this summer. There has never been anything on a
scale to approach the Centennial. They will need clothes
—and I had as much fun buying them as they will have
wearing them. You know, it's not having money I like,
it's the spending of it, and knowing there's more where
that came from."

"Well, this summer, perhaps, but that's no compensa-
tion for all the years I've thrown away in the awful place."

"With a man as handsome as Jesse, I'm amazed at you.
He fascinates me—so big, so strong, so virile. Ah, if I
could only have met a real life partner! . . . You know,
Augustina, I'm fifty, and nothing but a wasted life to show."

"You're fifty-five if a day, Teresina Borelli, though I declare I don't know why you should want to pull the wool
over my eyes. You were only eight years older than I."

138

Aunt Zena screamed: "Eight years! How can you have the effrontery . . ."

"All right, Zena, we mustn't quarrel—over ages, anyway, but you did exasperate me. You were talking about a real life partner, and I'm sure if you had one you'd be good and tired of him. You wouldn't put up with the best man alive for long." Mrs. Rogers waved a hand, to indicate all the pictures about the salon. "You would have been bored to death as soon as you found out he always ate the same things for breakfast, and made the same remarks at dinner. In two months you would have tired of him, and frankly, I have been bored myself, for years. I'd give anything to have had your life, your opportunities; to know hundreds of men."

"Not hundreds, Tina! Really, you exaggerate. I admit I have known a few, but it is an empty life. I assure you it is. I would gladly give it up to have a home, lovely children, and an adorable husband who worshiped me." Teresina Lascalles twisted her head archly and wagged a finger at her sister. "I don't mind telling you, my dear, your husband fascinates me. I have never met a man in my whole life whose nearness gives me such a thrill."

"And that reminds me of something else." Mrs. Rogers' voice took on an extremely sharp quality. "I know you from of old, Zena, and you had better keep your hands off my husband. I didn't like the way you kissed him the other day, and your adjectives are much too enthusiastic."

Teresina laughed in a superior tone. "As jealous as ever! My, the fights we used to have over men, do you remember? And how we used to disturb poor Father? You were like a little wildcat when you'd go for me, and he would pull you off. It was just unfortunate men couldn't resist me, nor I them, for that matter. I venture it was a good thing I wasn't around when you met your Jesse, but now, my dear! It's absurd! And besides, you are married." She la-la-ed, and walked to the pier glass which embellished one side of the salon with a travesty of a younger woman's assured stride.

Mrs. Rogers' face flushed, and her eyes narrowed. "She hasn't changed. She can make one as furious as ever," she thought. "I'd tell her a thing or two, but it would be terrible to fight with her the second day we see each other; though if she sets her cap for Jesse I'll scratch her eyes out."

Teresina Lascalles stood before the ornately framed mirror, to admire the effect of the solferino-colored dress before changing it for her new gabrielle. There was a distant expression in her eyes, and her upper front teeth, still beautiful and little yellowed by the years, bit into her lower lip.

"You know, Tina, something tells me I shall enjoy Philadelphia. It's a strange city, even as I remember it years ago—it's so dull, and so complacent about it. Perhaps I could do something to wake things up. Instead of staying at a hotel, as I planned, I shall visit with you. Philippe will have to locate out near Fairmount Park, at any rate, to be near the Exposition, and Céleste, who is quite along in years, and safe, can do for him. There will only be my other maid and myself."

Mrs. Rogers, taken by surprise, was caught between two emotions. Many times she had offered her sister this hospitality, never dreaming it would ever be accepted, and she couldn't very well withdraw now. On the other hand, Teresina was up to something—she remembered that faraway look, and she had forebodings. She stammered:

"Why, Zena, I'm delighted, of course, but we live so simply—not in the style you are used to—and we've no friends but the most ordinary people. I assure you, ice cream and cake of an evening is a dissipation."

"Nonsense, I can get along perfectly well, and it will be like old times. Now not a word—it's settled. Though of course you must allow me to pay you for accommodating me."

3

Mr. Rogers and Henry returned from their walk a few minutes later. The boy ran over and kissed his aunt on the cheek, and she gave him a pleased hug in return. Mr. Rogers brought with him the boisterousness of March winds, and a vitality that dissipated the atmosphere of the gallery of lost lovers in which the women were seated.

"By the Lord Harry, it's wonderful outside! We took a long tramp down to Canal Street, and over to the new bridge to Brooklyn. It isn't near finished yet, but you never saw such columns in your life. It is a bold attempt to conquer space, but I fear it is doomed to failure. They will never get a roadway suspended from those cables, mark my words. The force of the wind is too great. It will crumple the masonry as if it was an edifice of cards. Remember what I say, and see if I'm not right."

Mrs. Rogers sighed. "You might as well know it, Zena— Jesse is a prophet of ruins. Since I have known him, he's predicted nothing but the most dire calamities, none of which ever happen. . . . Now, Henry, run and get washed —you're a sight. . . . Jesse will never realize people wouldn't put up a bridge like that if it wasn't going to work. That's just sense. But I've something important to tell you, Father, when you get done about the Brooklyn Bridge. Zena is going to stay with us over the summer. I explained to her about our simple life."

"Grand—we keep the pigs in the parlor. I suppose she

told you, but we'll do our best to keep them out of your bedroom." Mr. Rogers' face beamed in genuine pleasure. "I felt all along it wasn't right for my wife's only sister to put up at a hotel while we had a place for her. And don't believe a word of what Gussie says about our simple life. We set the best table in Kensington. There's meat and potatoes every day, except when we have herring. There's no herring in the world as good as those smoked within a few squares of our home. Welcome, I say—welcome!" The photographs shivered in their frames, and Zena thrilled all over again to the vitality of her brother-in-law. Among the Parisian gentlemen, the diplomatic functionaries, the naval and military men she had known Teresina Lascalles had never met a man so completely male as this one. "Gussie is a fool if she's bored with him," she thought.

"And as for horses," Mr. Rogers went on, "we've the best horse in Kensington, bar none. I'd wager anything on Mr. Quinby!"

Philippe appeared, to give a recital of his day, spent in consular and customs offices. "Your Exposition is supposed to open in May. We have so little time to attend to things, but instead of helping, your officials seem to take pleasure in making things difficult for us. It is most annoying."

"It's the Administration!" Mr. Rogers shouted. "I suppose the officials you spoke to all wore bright-red shirts?"

Philippe looked up in surprise. "Why, no, I don't believe they did—I noticed nothing extraordinary, except the quantities of tobacco they were chewing."

"Red shirts, every last one of them. You just didn't notice!" Mr. Rogers shouted in glee.

When Philippe appeared puzzled, but too polite to inquire further, Mrs. Rogers explained: "Don't pay any attention to Father, Mr. Lascalles. It's his idea of a joke, that's all. Since the war, ex-soldiers who go into politics do nothing but boast about all the engagements they were in, and how they bled for the Union, and it's called 'waving the bloody shirt.' I'm not at all sure they are any worse than the men who didn't fight and didn't get wounded, and who are on the other side, and never get elected."

"The Republicans in this country . . ." Mr. Rogers began his usual tirade on the evils of the Administration, when Zena broke in.

"Republicans, bah! I feel as you do, Jesse. I think they are odious. Under the Empire, life in France was delightful—everything so gay, the court and all—and now it is all gone. You know, I lost a very dear friend during the war."

"I know, Jacques—you showed me his picture!" Mr. Rogers cried out.

"Not at all, Jesse. Not at all. *He* came after the war. . . . But as I was saying, today the Monarchists dare not show their heads, and the Republicans have everything their own way, as they do here. I am glad to learn you are a sympathizer with the anti-Republicans. What do they call themselves? And whom would they enthrone? Your great General Grant?"

Mr. Rogers laughed until the tears ran from his eyes, and he had to hold in his stomach from the pain. "Ho-ho-ha—the anti-Republican party would make Grant king if they could! He's had two terms as President already, and they'll try for a third, mark my words. When any President in these United States gets a third term it will be the end of democracy. See if I am not right!"

Aunt Zena and Philippe appeared bewildered, and Mr. Rogers continued to roar with laughter. Finally his wife said: "La, Zena, I don't pretend to bother about politics, but I'll try to explain, as Jesse is so busy making fun of you.

143

There are only two parties in this country that matter, and for the life of me I've never been able to understand what the difference between them is, except that the Republicans always get elected, and the Democrats never. There's no thought of monarchy at all. The Republicans insist they are democratic, and the Democrats say they are for the Republic, and there you are.

"But there is one thing I know—from now on there will never be a political discussion in our house—and we have too many of them, I assure you—without Father's bringing up your little gaffe."

Mr. Rogers was still too overcome with laughter to do more than nod his head weakly in assent. There was a commotion in the hall, and the sound of scampering feet. The dachshunds raced into the salon, their little bodies twisting and cavorting in glee. Aunt Zena picked them up and kissed each of them in turn.

"Philippe, I miss it when you're not here to give the dogs their walk. Denise had them out, but I suspect they got very little exercise with her. Jesse, aren't they little darlings? Don't you love them?" The animals sat with mouths open and tongues hanging, as if awaiting the verdict.

Mr. Rogers smiled fatuously. "Why, of course I like them. They are lovable little brutes."

"Brutes? The idea, Jesse! Now it's very important that I know for sure whether or no you like these two little darlings."

"Of course I do. I am very fond of animals of all sorts. Nothing could separate me from my horse Total Eclipse. There's a bond between us.". . . He paused long enough to indicate chains of iron, "And they like me. There's never been a dog that I couldn't win."

Aunt Zena shooed the dachshunds from her lap. "Now

144

run to your uncle," she commanded. "We shall see how good you are at winning affection."

Mr. Rogers put down a large, hairy paw, and the dogs slithered over to him. In an extreme of proof he picked them up and balanced them uncomfortably, one on each knee.

"There! You do like them—and they like you. Jesse, I can't tell you how glad I am. It's been worrying me."

Mrs. Rogers looked askance at her sister. "Now what in the world is Zena up to? She's getting Father into something. I know that, if he doesn't," she thought as he carefully placed the dogs back on the floor, and they ran to their accustomed places on the pillows.

The conversation turned to plans for the coming week, fittings for dresses and plays to be seen. Mr. Rogers cleared his throat importantly. "Unfortunately, I am a man of business. The railroad can't wait for the fitting of dresses. I shall have to return to Philadelphia in the morning."

Aunt Zena pouted. "So soon, Jesse? Can't you tell the old railroad to wait a week or so? Why, I had hoped we'd have a high old time together in New York."

"Indeed, there is nothing would appeal to me more. It's a change for Gussie and the girls—and for me also, I can't deny that, but I have to go back. Things pile up while I'm away." He gave the impression of a railroad's practically ceasing operations awaiting his return. "Mary and Martha can attend to my few and simple wants. Our family retainers, you know," he explained to Zena.

"Well, if that's the case, let's have a theater party tonight, instead of later in the week. What would you like to see?" Aunt Zena asked.

"Oh dear, Zena—I just haven't been able to keep up with the theater. The last play we saw was *Saratoga*, and

145

it seems years ago, although it's only one or two. It was at the Arch Street, and I think it was really wonderful."

"At any rate, it was American," Mr. Rogers vociferated, "American people doing American things, instead of this Frenchy or la-di-da English stuff."

"Of course, everyone knows France is the leader in the drama, and personally I can't think of anything over here worth writing a play about. It requires culture, refined situations, for play subjects. They'd be too dull, just about ordinary people and things. . . . Philippe, have you investigated the theatrical fare as yet?"

"Not especially, Zena, but there are several good things, I know. Fanny Davenport is starring in something at Wallack's—no, it is at Daly's, I'm sure—and *The Two Orphans* is at the Union Square. I'm sorry, but I suspect both plays are from the French. However, Davenport is practically an American, though I believe she's English by birth, and Kate Claxton, who stars in *The Two Orphans*, is, I know. She plays the part of the blind orphan, and I'm told she gives a poignant and heart-rending performance." Philippe himself was somewhat bored with plays, however soul-searching, after the London and Paris seasons, and had intended to suggest Madison Square Garden. Barnum's Great Roman Hippodrome, holding forth there, aroused his interest as a fresh kind of entertainment, but Mr. Rogers interrupted him to settle the discussion.

"*The Two Orphans* it is!" he roared. The title and the description both appealed to his sentimental nature. "A blind girl—it sounds most pathetic. *The Two Orphans* for me. French or no, there's nothing like something good and sorrowful to watch when you want entertainment."

Chapter 6

*I*T WAS too bad the new dresses were not yet finished. Julia wondered if praying would hasten the alterations, but it would take a miracle to have hers ready for the theater party, and she debated whether it was altogether right to ask God for a miracle for such a frivolous reason. Why had she worn such a somber dress to New York? Black, of all things, when she knew perfectly well it made her appear sallow. Until she met Philippe she had been too stupid, she decided. A touch of color was what she needed—a touch of color. . . .

She had an inspiration. That piece of red ribbon her mother had given her! She had never used it, and Teresina had borrowed it. The startling cherry-colored velvet would be just the thing. She would make it into a series of little bows, to wear at her throat. She knew her sister had brought it with her to New York, so she dashed into the next room and began a hurried search through her belongings. There it was—and more beautiful than she had remembered. To think that she hadn't cared about it at all! For the next hour she was engaged in embellishing her dress with the ribbon. Her slender fingers, deft from lacemaking, experimented with half a dozen different ideas until she found one that suited her.

It had been an inspiration. She gazed into the mirror with an expression of rapt awe. For the first time in her life she had a realization of her own potentiality for beauty, which she ascribed, wrongly of course, to the cherry-colored ribbon. She was at that moment truly beautiful, and the knowledge did not inspire her to vanity, but to a feeling of deep thankfulness.

If Philippe would only notice, she hoped, but of course Zenie would also be there, and she did not feel beautiful enough to compete with her sister in that attribute alone. She determined to cultivate an inner charm as well. When Zenie was imperious toward Philippe, she would be gracious and sweet. When Zenie was cold and distant, she would be warm and sympathetic. When Zenie was demanding, she would be sacrificing.

Her thoughts were interrupted by the entrance of Teresina herself, who called from the doorway: "Have you seen that piece of red ribbon? I want to tie it in my hair tonight, and I've looked high and low for it." Then she noticed the little velvet bows Julia had made. "So, you took it—you stole my piece of ribbon. I might have known!"

"Why, Zenie, how can you say such a thing? It's my ribbon, and when I thought of using it, I just looked in your room."

"*Your ribbon!* You gave that ribbon to me, and I intend to have it!" Teresina's voice was furious. "You're a little sneak, that's what you are. Stealing it out of my things!"

"I didn't give it to you at all, and you know it. You asked if you could wear it and I said to go ahead, but this old black dress of mine looked so dead I got it to give a touch of color."

"Yes, and I know why, too! Well, listen here, Julia Rogers—you won't have a chance, because I've made up my mind to Philippe myself, so there!" Teresina began a highly dramatic performance of her own. "He's the first man who ever interested me, and the only one I shall ever love. You might as well forget him. . . . And I want that ribbon, and I intend to have it."

By this time, Teresina was screaming, and she walked toward Julia as if to tear the bows right off her dress. Julia backed away and said quietly, although fearfully:

148

"Don't you touch me. It's mine, and I intend to keep it, and besides I think you're acting very foolishly. What if Philippe hears you screaming like that? His room is just down the hall."

Before Teresina could reply to this suggestion their mother came in. "What in the world is all this hullabaloo?"

Teresina decided that tears would avail her more with her mother than temper, so she began to sob. "Julia stole a ribbon I was going to wear tonight, and won't give it back."

Mrs. Rogers turned from one to the other of her daughters. "Well, it took a man to bring Julia out," she thought, "and Zenie could melt any heart but mine—I know that girl's tantrums too well. She does look beautiful, laughing or crying, but it won't get her anything this time."

She spoke sharply. "Stole that piece of velvet ribbon? I gave it to Julia myself. It was real cheap, down to Levy's on Second Street, and I thought it would give a touch of color to her—she looks so sallow sometimes—and if she gave it to you, she'd no business to, after I bought it for her." After this somewhat illogical reasoning, Mrs. Rogers went on: "Besides, you look perfect as you are, Zenie— another stitch on that dress would spoil it. Now run on and get ready, and hurry, too. We don't want to keep your aunt waiting."

She left them in time to intercept the twins in a particularly devilish bit of ingenuity. They had been left alone in the salon with the dogs, and conceived the idea, suggested by their shape, of tying them, nose to tail, around the table legs. Unfortunately for them, neither Fortune nor François entered into the spirit of the play, and at the moment Mrs. Rogers entered, the animals were resisting vigorously Henry's attempt at one table leg, and Georgina's at another, to fasten a loop around their tails and tie it to their collars. She quickly ended this project of decorating table legs with circlets of dachshund, and after the twins were dispersed to their rooms to dress, sighed and shook her head, and then confided to the photographs: "It keeps a body on the jump with this family, between Latin temperament and Quaker devilishness—and I declare, I don't know which is the worst!"

2

Philippe Lascalles dressed before the wardrobe mirror in his room, but his thoughts were more concerned with his aunt and her nieces than with his own reflection. "It's just like Zena to be so obvious about those girls," he thought. "She can't abide seeing me remain a bachelor." He examined the tip of the winged collar he had just put on after a considerable struggle with a too heavily starched buttonhole. Damn the thing—it was rough, and right at the tenderest point of his neck. These American laundresses were worse than English ones. It took a good French *blanchisseuse* to launder linens properly.

It was natural enough, he supposed, for Zena to want him to marry into her family—after the irritation of the collar, Philippe returned to his former train of thought. And the girls were both charming, if extremely provincial. One might think the elder, Zena's namesake, was the reigning Parisian beauty, the hauteur she affected, instead of being merely a product of the backwoods of America. The other girl, the younger one, was a naïve little thing, and always quite overcome in his presence, but she was also rather pretty. Thank God Zena had taken them in hand and was getting them new clothes. American women certainly did not know how to dress!

Well, of one thing he was assured, a pleasant summer. He was glad he had accepted the commission with the Centennial—and perhaps, who knew, he might end up by marrying one of the sisters. A man should marry sometime, and a provincial American might be more amusing in the long run than a bored and overcultured Parisian. He suspected the girls were not too well provided with money, but it was reasonable to suppose that his aunt would provide either of them with a dot. Not that money meant a great deal—his own fortune was ample—it was merely the French side of his ancestry asserting its practicality. He shrugged his shoulders. In due time he supposed he would know where his interests really lay. He remembered some verse—"How happy I could be with either, were t'other dear charmer away"—and felt a pride at his own cleverness for the aptness of the quotation.

He carefully tied a wide silk cravat of rich, dark purple, and arranged and secured its folds with a coral-mounted gold pin. He combed out his beard, and examined the effect with an appraising eye. Were mutton chops really his style of whisker? They gave his face breadth, and a substantial, bankerlike appearance, but as he weighed a good fifteen stone, did he need to look more substantial? This matter of a beard! As a very young man, he had tried a Vandyke for a little while, and then changed to an imperial. Since the fall of the Empire, during the time he had gone to live in England with his mother's people, he had affected Dundrearys, until he read the play and discovered that Lord Dundreary was a comic character, a crude satire on the English. Why should men pattern the style of their beard or mustache after a comedian, a buffoon? He had them transformed immediately into mutton chops, which he had been wearing for over a year. He had a strong chin, which this style revealed to advantage, but very soon he would have to settle finally on a beard that would be identified with him for his whole life—one couldn't go on changing one's principal feature continually, and he couldn't imagine wearing mutton chops during eternity.

He shook his head at the glass, and frowned in concentration. Of course, he could follow the growing English fashion and become clean-shaven, but women liked beards, they were so masculine, and besides, he didn't wish to look like a priest. The whole Gallic side of his nature rebelled at the thought of a naked, hairless face. No, he had to make his decision—he was twenty-five, and it couldn't wait much longer. He would grow a full beard, like the girls' father. Jove, there was a man for you! He commanded respect. His hirsute appendage would be impressive without figure or face behind it, and with Mr. Rogers' bulk ("He must weigh two stone more than I do," he thought) it was irresistible.

Yes, he would grow a full beard. He made up his mind about that as he gave a last touch to his carefully combed curly hair. He had the size to carry it off, as Mr. Rogers had. Of course, one of your little men should be careful in attempting a full beard. There was always the danger, in such cases, that the beard would overshadow its wearer in importance.

With the self-satisfied look of a man with his mind made up, Philippe walked into the salon to find all of them waiting for him.

"I declare, Philippe, it takes you longer to primp than it does the girls," his aunt complained. "I was just going to send for you."

Philippe made his apologies for keeping them waiting. His eyes, meanwhile, were busy reappraising the girls. The younger one was even prettier than he had thought. She had more color than he had noticed before. But what in the world was that silly little bit of ribbon she had put on her dress? She had worn the same clothes the night before, and it hadn't been there then, he was sure.

His aunt said, "Philippe, supposing you take the girls by hansom, and the rest of us will go in the carriage."

Mr. Rogers interrupted to say: "Why, it's only half a dozen squares to the theater, and your namby-pamby New York squares, at that. What anybody would want to ride that distance for I can't see. As for me, I shall walk, and I'll be waiting at the theater for you."

3

When Julia awoke in the morning, the events of the previous night were like nothing but a dream, and she had to concentrate to remember enough tangible incidents to prove to herself that she had not dreamt it all. Everything had actually happened! She lay in bed with the covers tucked under her chin and watched the maid remake the fire in the fireplace. "This is so much more pleasant than getting up in a cold room at home," she thought. It was the first time she had ever allowed herself really to enjoy the comforts around her. Then, as the fire began to crackle, she recalled once more the delight of sitting next Philippe in the theater. She could remember nothing of the play itself except the sweet plaintiveness of Kate Claxton's voice as the blind orphan, and the fact that she had cried when the others cried, reveling in the pleasure of melancholy.

No, her mind was not occupied with anything that had been said, or with the plot of the performance, but with her own feelings—the sensation of riding beside Philippe in the hansom, and gazing at the bright lights of Broadway.

The prodigal use of gas to make a world so bright the stars seemed merely faint reflections. The sensation of walking beside Philippe under the flaming gaslight of the theater entrance. The sensation of sitting beside him in the warm darkness of the auditorium.

In all of these pleasurable remembrances there was no acceptance of the fact that Teresina had been hanging on Philippe's other arm, interrupting their talk with inane observations. That night, and also in her memory of it, Philippe existed for her alone.

But here she was, lying in bed daydreaming when she should be having breakfast with the others! Father was taking the train back to Philadelphia, and if she didn't hurry, he would be gone before she could say good-by. She jumped from bed, ran across the cool floor to the pleasant warmth of the fireplace, and hurried with her dressing. She was the last to reach the salon, and a large rasher of ham and eggs and potatoes had already been left in front of her plate.

Aunt Zena said: "Well, Julia, you did sleep! I told them not to call you, as you needed the rest, and I ordered a substantial breakfast for you. A young girl needs plenty of food."

Julia murmured her thanks, and looked around the table. There was no sign of Philippe. To her distress, she soon learned that he had already breakfasted and had gone to attend to more of the interminable business of the French exhibit at the Centennial. She attacked the ham, and when the waiter returned Aunt Zena, presiding in a handsomely brocaded house dress, ordered more of everything for her. She accepted without a murmur. Being in love was so good for the appetite!

Her father coughed impatiently, and pushed back his chair. He did not feel altogether comfortable having meals served in the hotel room in this fashion. It smacked of the sybaritic, and it had affected his eating. Downstairs in the dining room, he could have ordered three or four helpings without the uncomfortable knowledge that the waiter had to convey the food so far from the kitchen. But it was pleasant, and almost like home, to be able to eat breakfast in the circle of one's family, without onlookers. This was curious about hotel life: it was supposed to relieve the monotony of home by providing a more luxurious existence, and yet the privileges which were intended to convey this sense of luxury were the homelike things. As he had been doing every five minutes for the last half-hour, he announced again his immediate departure.

"I'm off, Mother. It would be an extremely bad example for me, of all people, to have to dash for the train."

"Why, Father, there's a good hour before the ferry leaves, and it's but a ten-minute ride to the slip. You will have ages to wait."

Mr. Rogers wiped his mouth with a voluminous linen napkin, and then folded it very carefully and laid it beside his plate.

"Pet, you mustn't fold your napkin like that when you're away. What will the waiter think?"

"Think? The waiter? What about?" Mr. Rogers included all of them in his stare of bewilderment, actual or assumed.

"To fold your napkin so carefully is a sign of bad breeding."

"Breeding? May I ask since when the orderly arrangement of anything has become bad breeding?"

"Why, the waiter will think we use napkins over and over again at home, to save laundering. You are supposed to crumple them and leave them carelessly by the plate, to show you don't care about expense. Isn't that so, Zena?"

Mr. Rogers roared with laughter. "Gussie, the ideas people get! I do care about expense, and we do use our napkins over at home. I've had the same napkin ring for more than twenty years, as you very well know. Why should I wish the waiter to think me anything but a frugal and saving man who husbands his resources?"

Aunt Zena went to his help. "Indeed, in France it's quite the thing to save one's napkin. The French are thrifty folk. I remember, though, dear Father's teaching us it was the fashion over here for people to pretend a certain carelessness about small money matters."

"At any rate, my napkin stays folded, and that's that. Let the waiters think what they will!" Mr. Rogers thundered. "I'm off, and I'll see you all later, when you are good and homesick for Kensington." He was well kissed by everyone. For the first time in Mrs. Rogers' life she would be away from him for more than one night, and she suddenly burst out crying at the thought.

"Father, I think we shall come tomorrow, after the girls have their fittings. I can't see you alone in that house with nobody to look after you but that crazy old Irish woman."

He blew his nose violently, to conceal his own emotion, but insisted again: "Now, Mother, you've been talking about New York for years. Promise you won't come home until you have your fill of it."

Aunt Zena sailed toward him with both arms held wide open, the train of the house dress sweeping over the carpet like a wake curling up behind her. She hugged him tightly and kissed him on both cheeks.

"Jesse, my dear, you shall have your family back very soon, I assure you. They couldn't stay away from anyone so lovable. And you know, I'll be in your family also, for the whole summer."

The twins swarmed on him, and he encircled each of them with an arm, lifting them clear from the floor. Teresina exhibited the most control. She said, "Good-by, Father," and gave him a cool kiss which missed his cheek altogether and was implanted instead on his beard.

It was Julia, however, who surprised him, and whose farewell touched him the most. He had never felt that she really loved him, but now she also threw her arms about him and, speaking tenderly, said, "Good-by, Papa. It seems so long until we shall see you again."

The various emotional responses of the family to their parting affected Mr. Rogers' sentimental nature to such an extent that he walked to the ferry, crossed the river, waited for the train to be made up, and traveled halfway to Trenton before the glow wore off. He then felt a necessity to unburden himself of his feelings. He made friends with the conductor and told him all about his journey.

"I'm Rogers, of the Reading," he began, and a background of mutual acquaintances and experiences was soon established. "Just been over to New York for a few days with the family," he confided. "Left 'em over there. My wife's sister just came over from Europe and we met her. The wife and children are staying over for a few days. I have three daughters, stunning girls, and a boy who's a young rascal—chip off the old block."

The conductor nodded his head, and then told about his own family. They were not very interesting, Mr. Rogers thought, and he became rather bored, as there was still a great deal he felt compelled to relate about his own children.

When the train stopped at Trenton, where it waited for some time to connect with a local, he strolled up the platform to the locomotive. After looking it over with a highly professional eye, he spoke to the engineer, engaged in oiling the bearings with a long-spouted can.

"I'm Rogers, of the Reading freight department. Just been over to New York and left the family there."

The engineer also had children, and the train was three minutes late when it started on the run down the Delaware Valley toward Philadelphia.

Chapter 7

WHILE the parting with his family had been touching, Mr. Rogers looked forward to having the house to himself. There were many inhibitions under which he ordinarily suffered, or felt that he did, and these he intended to disregard. The first day he was at home alone was quite up to expectations. He reveled in a sensation of freedom. Upon his return to work he had determined to attack a great mass of detail which he was sure would be awaiting him, and planned to catch up within a week. To his surprise, he found the accumulation of way bills, invoices, and correspondence dissipated in one night of furious effort.

A little rest from work once in a while may be good for one, he decided. In an age when no one took regular vacations, this was heresy, not only to accepted ideas, but to his own oft-repeated pronouncements. Until the occasion of this trip to New York, he boasted that his years of labor had been uninterrupted by a single day's absence for illness or pleasure. Now he began to agree with an idea he had hitherto rejected. A few pioneering souls were advocating summer vacations, and Mr. Rogers' principal objection, that one could never catch up with the time lost, he had now disproved.

He returned home in the morning with a feeling of great accomplishment. Martha had prepared a breakfast for him quite as large as she regularly cooked for the whole family, and he kept Mary busy hobbling in and out from the kitchen, refilling his plate. Not that Mary minded in the least.

"Sure, it's good to see the mister's face again," she confided to Martha, with a happy, toothless grin, "and a pleasure to watch him down the vittles."

After breakfast he napped, and then was plied by the indulgent servants with a dinner that would have foundered a lesser man.

He disobeyed the first taboo when he appeared at the table collarless, and in carpet slippers. Then, the *Philadelphia Press* clutched in one hand, and in the other *Harper's Weekly*, to which he subscribed because of Thomas Nast's cartoons, he retired to the parlor. Here he proceeded in earnest to upset the conventions of the household. He placed his armchair by the large black parlor stove, in which a slow fire burned. Then he arranged the cricket at a comfortable distance, to serve as a footrest, brought out the spittoon, and bit off a chew of plug tobacco that was even larger than his usual nightly quid at the freight office. With cheek thus happily distended, he prepared to read the papers undisturbed by any of the usual family harassments.

It was a glorious afternoon, an orgy of unrepented sinning, and Mr. Rogers looked forward to a succession of them. He read the paper with more thoroughness and deliberation than had ever before been allowed him. The news, most of it, was unpleasant. Complacently told stories of political corruption, of the numbers dying from hunger in the industrial centers, of the Indian wars.

This Indian trouble was serious. The Government had issued an ultimatum to the Sioux to return to their reservation, and they had refused. Now they were on a rampage, and so far, Sitting Bull and his followers had set at naught the attempts of a whole army to bring them to bay. Mr. Rogers' sympathies were with the Indians. The poor savages had been misused, lied to, and betrayed. "I wonder if a nation as a whole must answer sometime for its misdeeds," he asked himself. "If so, the good Lord has some heavy penalties to exact from us, in His good time. This so-called Christian nation has certainly set a bad example to the heathen world," he ruminated, spitting with deadly accuracy into the overrefined parlor cuspidor that offered a target less than a quarter the size of the great brass receptacle in his office.

Finally, he laid down the Philadelphia paper, and turned to *Harper's Weekly* and the Nast cartoon. Thomas Nast, the little German boy who had come to America! There were few of its native sons who had done so much for it. The power of the cartoon in his hands had overthrown a tyrant and exposed villainies that orations, sermons, and editorials had failed to touch. While Mr. Rogers was a Democrat, he had followed with glee and approbation Nast's long and bitter campaign which had resulted in the defeat of the Tweed Ring in New York. It was a pet remark of his that America needed a dozen Nasts to pick out the decay in its life. The nation was like a giant oak tree, apparently strong, but rotted within.

Liberal foreigners, coming to America for refuge, had the perspective natives lacked. There was Carl Schurz, for instance—the magazine carried an article about his activities in Missouri—another German, by the way, whose example and political astuteness were doing much to heal the sores left by the war.

Seldom enough Mr. Rogers enjoyed the repose necessary for such elevating and satisfying thought. He had to shout aloud: "Bachelor's hall! Freedom from contentious females—by Christopher, there is nothing like it." The roar brought in Mary, anxious as to the cause, and eager to be of assistance. "In the name of God, is there something happened?" she asked, her faded eyes peering into the parlor from the doorway.

It took him some time to quiet the old woman's apprehensions, and by then he had become restless. He slippered around the house, searching for an occupation, and ended up in the fourth-floor front room opposite Julia's, which was used as a storeroom. Here was a harvest! Mixed in with all kinds of discarded household impedimenta were many remains of the days of Rogers glory when ships bearing the name had, to use his mental phrasing, scoured the seven seas and entered every clime. There was the figurehead from the first *Sally Rogers*, checked and cracked, discolored and disfigured. It had been through the many vicissitudes of the Rogers family. It was wrong, terribly wrong, for it to end its days forgotten, neglected, discarded and disgraced—Mr. Rogers ran to adjectives— and he decided then and there to have the figure, a crude representation of a buxom woman in Quaker garb, repaired, repainted, and given a place of honor in the garden, both as decoration and as a reminder of better days. There were also a number of crayon pictures of various of the Rogers vessels. The *Jedediah Rogers* plowing through cottony seas, and the *Sally* herself sailing with all her sails set into a bank of ominous cloud.

He shook his head, and tsk-tsked. What in the world was Mother thinking of, to relegate these works of art, these family heirlooms, to this Sargasso Sea, where all the jetsam from years of living had floated with the action of some mysterious current, there to rot, and eventually sink to the ash bin? He dusted off the frames and glasses, determined upon an immediate rescue. "I'll find a suitable place for these, where they can be enjoyed by the family," he decided mentally. He spent the rest of the afternoon until it was time to get ready for work lugging the crayons downstairs. He was faced with a new problem, which he had not anticipated. There was not sufficient room on any wall to hang even one of the Rogers fleet! Each foot of space seemed taken up with a picture of some kind. He ranged through hall and dining room, and everywhere it was the same. For the first time in years he noticed engravings, waxworks, and mottoes that had been hanging in the same spot for so long the eye had tired of recording their presence.

It seemed a pity, a great pity, not to be able to display all one's possessions, but there was nothing else to do—a choice had to be made, and a pair of Landseers, Rosa Bonheur's horses, and that old favorite "The Lovers' Parting" were relegated to the storeroom, along with some less choice pieces.

Mary shook her head dolefully when she retailed the news to Martha. "Wait till *she* sees 'em. There'll be hell to pay from *her*. The mister's tastes may run to ships, but *she* fancies horses, or animals of some sort. The mister's gettin' himself in for something, but I might as well keep me own trap shut."

The next afternoon, when a similar routine lacked the savor of the initial escapade, Mr. Rogers took Total Eclipse for a short workout, and the third day he was frankly bored, and wandered around the house, as Mary put it: "Like a

162

poor lost soul he is, without the childern and the missus around, to liven things up like."

Then Father Duffy, through one of those channels of information open to neighborhood clergymen and doctors, learned that Mr. Rogers was alone. He called the following day and was met with a boisterous greeting such as few of his parishioners would have dared.

"Well, sand my rails, if it isn't Duffy!" Mr. Rogers roared, his growing boredom forgotten in genuine pleasure at seeing the priest. "None of the praying members of the family are around this afternoon, but if you'd enjoy a chew of black strap with an old reprobate, come in."

"I'd dare the Devil himself for a chew," Father Duffy laughed, "and I stopped in especially because a man needs to be free of females once in a while, and I heard you were enjoying that privilege." His broad, ruddy, smooth-shaven face took on a comical, pleading expression, as if he was asking to share the bliss of Mr. Rogers' bachelor state.

"Come, Duffy, you can't pull the wool over my eyes. It isn't to escape the womenfolk you stopped in to see me, but to talk railroading. So come in, and we'll chew the rag for a while."

"Not forgetting your well-flavored plug." The priest grinned as he followed into the parlor. After the third day of slippered ease, Mr. Rogers had reverted to his habitual dress, and wore collar, tie, and shoes as he would have done with his wife at home, so the only symbol remaining of his play in the cat's absence was the favored position of the spittoon. The men took chairs on opposite sides of its convenience to enjoy Lady Nicotine's supremest pleasure.

After exhausting the whole subject of the moving of freight, as was inevitable the talk turned to politics and the affairs of the nation. As usual, Mr. Rogers was not at all reluctant to blare forth his own views, and generally Father Duffy agreed with them, several times going so far as to say, "That is a point that never occurred to me, Rogers, and it is well taken." Had the priest's interest been less genuine than it actually was, he would still have earned the friendship of his host with this statement. The supremest flattery was this, not only to say, "I agree with you," but to add, "I never thought of it in that way before."

When they left the broader problems, Reconstruction, Indian affairs, and the currency question, and turned to the immediate future and the growing undercurrent of feeling between labor and capital, they began to disagree, until the priest shouted:

"You're a strange man, Rogers! The things that are far away from you, and concern you only in an impersonal way, you judge with astounding good sense. In fact, your conception of big principles far surpasses my own in power, but you're blind as a bat about things right under your eyes. You say we are just recovering from our troubles, and I say we are just coming to them. Another year like this one will see the railroads bankrupt—unless they lower wages tremendously, and workingmen can't subsist on less than they are getting now. You will see violence and disorder, and it is only the beginning. The greed of our financiers and businessmen, which is leading toward this catastrophe, is completely at variance with the principles of Christian teaching. And yet, to do you credit, most of my fellow clerics feel pretty much as you do. I'm borrowing trouble, they say.

"Then there is the feeling we have no right to champion political or economic reforms, if for no reason but to keep the Protestants from jumping on our necks. I say we are living in an age of economic injustice, and the priests and clergy, regardless of creed, every mother's son of us, should be shouting the fact to high heaven. What good does it do for me to dispense the little charities I have at my disposal when I know it's like spreading salve on a malignant tumor which should be cut out?"

Father Duffy slammed an open palm on the marble top of the parlor table as if to emphasize his words. "I feel in my bones that this will be a critical year. There is still time to build a great nation on the Christian principle of the brotherhood of man, but let the feeling of class hatred once burst out in violence, and fires will be lighted that a hundred years won't dampen."

Mr. Rogers waved his hand airily. "You've heard a few of the hotheads talking. We have some in our company. If they don't like the way the railroad treats them, why don't they leave it? It's a free country! No, they go on working, and kicking—and I'm opposed to the labor-union idea. It sticks in my throat to think that I might have to join some union, although I didn't want to, in order to get a job. The right to work without let or hindrance from anyone is a free man's prerogative."

The priest shifted his quid and spat as accurately as Mr. Rogers, who had added emphasis to his argument with a resounding splash.

"The concomitant to that argument is the right to starve in a society oversupplied with labor. I see you agree with the ideas advanced by my noted colleague of another faith, Henry Ward Beecher. I tell you, I don't think a clergyman has ever been guilty of greater disservices to the people of a country than has our Brooklyn friend. He is, I think, a minister of Mammon, not of God."

This was a moment for a real peroration, and Mr. Rogers rose to his feet to make the most of it. He lowered his chin, pressing his beard against his waistcoat, and searched in the caverns of his chest for its deepest tones.

"I think you are wrong, Duffy. I think Beecher is wrong. I don't hold with religious groups of any sort mixing in political issues. They mean well, but they have no balance, I say.

"I'm a Quaker, myself, and I'll die a Quaker. If you have any illusions about converting me, you can forget them—but it's years since I've been to Meeting. The Quakers went back on their principles to take active part in a struggle to free the slaves that could only lead to fratricidal war. All the high-sounding speeches in the world about freedom and liberty won't change the fact that it cost Great Britain but a few pounds, relatively, to buy the freedom of its West Indian slaves, while we desolated a nation and caused years of suffering that are not yet over."

Father Duffy sighed, and held out his hand. "You're convincing in argument, Rogers—there must be some Irish blood in you—and it has been a pleasure chatting with you this afternoon. More of a pleasure than you can know, for you're a man I can speak with frankly, which is a boon to someone in my position. As for Quaker or Catholic, who knows? I'll say this to you, my friend: You can take the horsecars at the corner, or walk over to Fifth Street. You may prefer one route or the other, but if you stay on long enough you'll get to Frankford either way."

Mr. Rogers shouted: "An appropriate simile, I must say, but better suited for comparisons with the Methodists or Presbyterians than with Friends. Either Catholic or Protestant may ride in comfort to their destination, but Quakers get there by shanks' mare."

2

"So, a week was long enough for them!" Mr. Rogers nodded to himself, and read the paragraph in the letter

166

over again. "Mary, they'll be home tomorrow!" he shouted, as if Mary were still in the kitchen instead of at his elbow. "After all these years of fussing about New York and its pleasures, a week is enough for them. I tell you, Mary, New York is all right as a place to go for a visit—all the horses and traffic, the theaters and the gaslight making the night into day—but for living in, I pick Kensington any day."

"Sure, the house hasn't seemed like itself without a commotion going on." Mary shook her head and chewed on her gums. "There's something about the missus keeps things livened up."

"Livened up—I'll say she does. Mrs. Rogers is a wonderful woman, Mary. We have to be patient with her at times, as she's high-strung."

"There's none better—none better," Mary agreed. "Will you be having more hot cakes, to go with the coffee you ain't drunk?"

Mr. Rogers sat back with a frown of concentration, and examined with the eye of a connoisseur the stack of cakes that had just been placed before him. "Mary, I have on my plate one of the master creations of the culinary art. There is nothing can tease my palate and provide at the same time a substantial fullness to the stomach like a few stacks of Martha's flannel cakes."

Mary closed her eyes and grinned, her smile so wide it almost bisected her face. "Martha will be glad for those words, Mr. Rogers. She does pride herself on her hot cakes."

The master of the house assumed a heavily playful attitude of mock seriousness. "Mary, that is the second time you have miscalled this dish. Hot cakes are thin, pallid concoctions with no substance, no solidity, and I despise them. These are genuine flannel cakes, and should be called such. Notice their thickness, nigh a full half-inch—and light, with each one of them a golden brown color.

"And above all, note that crepelike texture of the surface." He ran a heavy forefinger over the cake. "If that were an ordinary pancake, it would be smooth and shiny from the too great application of concentrated heat, or the effect of the sheet iron—I've never determined exactly what causes the unfortunate effect.

"Now consider flannel cakes—they are made on a heavy cast-iron griddle which distributes the heat evenly, and the result is a surface such as these possess—brown, you will observe, but velvety—a quality which earned for them the name they're known by. In the future, Mary, I hope you understand . . ."

The old woman had been standing in a pleased befuddlement. Mr. Rogers' language, the long words, the intonation, always intoxicated her with its rhythm and spirit. Generally she understood nothing of the meaning of his discourses, but this time she was able to interrupt, pertly:

"It's flannel cakes, sir, and I'll tell Martha, so she knows. It would be a sin to be a-makin' them and thinkin' they was only the regular kind—and you'll be havin' more, I take it."

"An astute woman!" Mr. Rogers shouted, clapping the poor, arthritic old creature around the waist so that she staggered under the force of the salute to her sagacity. The mister was certainly in fine fettle, she thought, and she also was happy in the morning's news.

She limped out to tell Martha, but the cook shut her off. "I heard it as soon as you did—almost bored holes in my eardrums, he did; you'd think a body was deef." When she returned with a new ration of flannel cakes, Mr. Rogers said:

"Mary, I've determined on a surprise for Mrs. Rogers.

Up in the storeroom is a beautiful figurehead from my father's first ship. Why it has been languishing up there all these years I don't know—probably placed there temporarily, and forgotten. I've decided to have it erected in the garden, as a decoration. It will be infinitely more appropriate than a cast-iron stag such as she has been coaxing me for."

Mary nodded. "It might be real pretty sitting out there —a touch of decoration like—but would *she* like it?"

"I'm going to surprise her with it! Lucius and I will set it up this afternoon, and we'll paint it as well, if there's time enough. Won't Mother enjoy it when she gets home?" Mr. Rogers slapped his knee. "I know where it will go, too—just the spot—in front of the pool Henry dug a year or so ago."

Apprehension dawned in Mary's faded eyes. "Maybe you'd better wait and see what the missus says—she gets some funny ideas about doin' things."

"Nonsense, Mary, she'll be delighted. Why, that figure is a work of art—worth a dozen iron stags or cast-iron dogs. It was hewn out of a solid log by an ancestor of mine a hundred years ago, and piloted the first Rogers vessel to fortune. . . . When you're finished with the breakfast, dust it off good, and after I have my nap, Lucius and I will place it in the garden." Mr. Rogers' face lighted in anticipation. "I can just see Gussie now when she catches sight of it. I tell you, Mary, it was providential that I found it."

Mary was still dubious as she gathered up the dishes, and the soiled china rattled in her nervous hands as she conveyed it to the kitchen. The cook glanced at her sharply, distressed by her obvious concern. "What's the matter, Mary? Was them last cakes heavy? If they was . . ."

"Whisht, it's worse than heavy cakes. We'll be in for it tomorrow when the missus gets home."

Martha turned from the range and placed both hands on her ample hips. "What's he up to? Tell me quick!"

"There's a statue like, a figure of a witch, I think it is, up in the storeroom. 'Twas in front of one of the Rogers boats, he says. He's settin' it up in the garden this afternoon"—Mary's voice took on an inflection of the broadest sarcasm—"to surprise the missus."

"Surprise the missus! She'll eat his head off. She hates the mention of the word ship. Did you tell him what he was getting in for?"

Mary shrugged her shoulders in resignation. "Try to tell a man anything, especially that man. Pigheaded as they come, he is. There'll be a surprise all right, but he's the one that'll get it."

The cook pushed the griddle to the back of the range, and pressed her lips together. "And up to a minute ago I was sort of anticipatin' *her* comin' home. Worse fool me—there'll be hell to pay, and we'll all catch it."

Chapter 8

THIS was the platform for the New York train. Mr. Rogers again reassured himself that it was not yet late, and peered up the track, past signal lights and switch houses, as if to evoke the train from the sooty air.

A distant plume of smoke, funnel-shaped, like a cyclone driving toward the city, the rhythmic chatter of pistons and the clank of drivers, and the New York express slipped by. He almost jumped with impatience. He strode along the cars, gazing in vain for the familiar faces of his family. "By God, just like them to miss the train," he thought, and then he saw the twins, waving from the baggage car. The

170

baggage car? What in the world were they doing back there? He hurried along, and almost ran down Julia and Teresina. He hadn't recognized them! There was no time to comment on their appearance in the new finery, for Julia hurried him on, in great agitation.

"You better go and help, Papa. Mama and the twins are back in the baggage car." She called after him, "I wanted to stay with her, but she wouldn't allow it, because of the new clothes."

"What could Gussie be thinking of, traveling in the baggage car?" he asked himself again. The answer was quickly forthcoming. An agitated Mrs. Rogers appeared, apparently pulled along by the two dachshunds, and followed by the twins. For a moment he was amused by the dogs. "Even the Creator had to be in a humorous mood once in a while, but this time his jest misfired," he thought. As they seemingly recognized him and pulled his way, he remembered that Zena was not supposed to accompany her. "What in the world is Mother doing with those animals? This needs looking into."

The dogs wiggled and scampered on the pathetic stumps that served them for legs, and Mrs. Rogers, disheveled and distraught, called:

"Jesse, we've had the most awful time! I want you to take it up with the railroad first thing tomorrow."

"Why, my dear, what was the matter? What is the meaning of these animals? Are you keeping them for your sister?"

Mrs. Rogers put her hand to her breast, as if to get her breath. "Oh, Pet, don't rush me! Do you know where I have been, all the way from New York? In that awful baggage car. The conductor, an odious man, wouldn't allow Fortune and François to ride in the parlor car, and I couldn't leave them in the baggage car alone. They

171

would have been simply frightened to death, in a strange land and all, and not understanding the language. Zena would have been furious, right after she gave them to me."

"Good God, woman," Mr. Rogers cried out, "you can't stand there and tell me that those monstrosities, those animated sausages, those caricatures of dogdom, are ours! I won't have it. Give them back."

"Jesse, don't begin now. I've been sitting on a trunk for two hours—the hardest trunk I have ever experienced—while that train jolted and swayed. I'm sure I'm black and blue where I sit down."

Mr. Rogers, whose humor was not to be overcome by any occurrence, however serious to him, shouted: "It sounds interesting, my dear; I'll make an inspection as soon as we're home!"

"Now, Jesse, behave yourself. If you could have seen me balancing on that trunk, and these poor animals, so frightened we had to take turns holding them, the twins and I . . ."

"What I want to know about is those animals—Fortune and François, bah! You can't even pronounce their names. We don't want them. Give them back. Give them back, I say!"

"Why, Jesse, you assured Zena that you loved those dogs. You even sat like an indulgent father with one on each knee, and looking pleased as Punch about it."

"But we have a dog, and a whole litter of puppies."

"A stable dog, Jesse—these are house pets. Zena bought them for us especially. They are all the rage in Europe she tells me, and they are darling, affectionate little creatures, indeed they are. They know me already." She looked down at them and crooned, "Fortune darling— François." The little dogs began to bark frantically, and she continued, "You see, Jesse . . ."

172

"But I don't want dogs in the house. The place for dogs is in the stable, or outside. We'll be falling over these creatures—one of us will end up with a broken leg. They'll misbehave in the parlor. . . . If I must say so, your sister can think of the damnedest things to buy with her money."

Mrs. Rogers' face puckered, and she injected a throaty sob into her voice. "I must say, Father, I didn't expect a welcome like this—away from you a whole week, and there you stand, in front of all these people, obviously in a temper. What will they think? And what am I to think? Quarreling with me in public, and then cursing me. Come, children, let's hurry away from here, I'm too ashamed."

People did look around curiously, although most of the onlookers, hearing the sound but not the separate words, probably assumed that Mr. Rogers' voice was that of the train announcer. It reached unparalleled volume as he shouted in an extreme of exasperation: "Woman, I am not quarreling with you! I am not cursing you—I am merely . . ." She was already far down the platform, and there sat the luggage, just as it had been lifted from the train. Realizing the ineffectiveness of further words, he signaled for a porter, and followed toward the cab rank.

By the time their horse began to clip-clop over the Belgian blocks toward home, Mrs. Rogers was in command of the situation. In a firm voice, she said:

"Now, Jesse, there's been enough of this foolishness. We have the dogs, and you will learn to like them. You can't blame this on Zena—she knows how fond I am of animals, but she was afraid you mightn't like them, and took the greatest pains to discover what your feelings were. If you had to make a chump of yourself in front of her, I can't help it. I told her you wouldn't like them, and she told me off, I can tell you. She remembered every word you said about them." Mrs. Rogers laughed in pretended un-

173

controllable mirth. "I shall never forget your silly expression, Fortune on one knee and François on the other, and all three of you grinning, with your tongues hanging out."

Mr. Rogers sat in glum silence. He forgot all his happy anticipations of the moment when his own surprise would be enjoyed by his home-coming spouse. When they had unloaded, got inside, and received Mary's rapturous welcome, he did say, in plaintive tones:

"At least, Gussie, humor me in one thing. I can't call those creatures by their present names. I can't even pronounce them right. Let's get good dog names for them, Rex and Rover, or Sport and Spot—but Fortoon and Franzwah— It's impossible."

The subjects of the discussion sniffed at various interesting details of their new home, and then seated themselves in front of their new master and looked up at him with most solemn and intent expressions. Frowns creased their foreheads as if they had a real understanding of what was being said, and feared the worst.

Mrs. Rogers said: "Look at them, Jesse. They're the most intelligent things. They know we are talking about them, and they're worried."

"Worried? They're sulky, and moody. 'Dash-hounds,' a good name for them. 'Double dash-hounds,' I'd call them."

At this, one of the dogs put up its head and gave a long, plaintive howl, while the other one sat by, more dejected than ever. Mr. Rogers' humor got the better of him again as he slapped a hand on his knee. "By Christopher, I have it! He's singing—he's Sankey. And the other one is more moody than ever—he's Moody. Moody and Sankey it is!"

"Those awful evangelists! Pet, how can you—and they're

174

Protestants, too," Mrs. Rogers objected, but her husband, roaring with laughter, shouted: "It's too late! They are named. Moody and Sankey it is."

Mrs. Rogers might have continued her protests, but the twins, who had entered the parlor in time to hear their father's pronouncement, joined in. "Moody and Sankey—just the names for them—Moody and Sankey— and there's Sankey, singing again!"

In spite of winning out in the renaming of the dachshunds, Mr. Rogers never really accepted their presence in the house, and they joined the French clock and the spindly-legged chairs as object lessons in misapplied generosity, although during the time of his sister-in-law's visit he did refrain from carping about them.

The servants awaited with dire apprehension the moment when their mistress would notice the change in pictures and learn of the erection of the figurehead in the garden. The excitement of the home-coming and the difficulty over the dachshunds delayed the time of discovery, but it came, and Mary began murmuring "Hail Mary's" in the hope of tempering the blast. Mrs. Rogers looked up to rest her eyes on the noble expression of a stag with spreading antlers, and saw instead a ship, the brig *Increase Rogers*, sailing majestically across the parlor wall.

Mr. Rogers, noticing the fixity of her gaze and its focal point, began enthusiastically: "Isn't it beautiful, Gussie? And there's another, over there, and look at these in the hall. I got them down to surprise you. They are really artistic—more colorful than those dead-looking old prints."

"Why, Jesse, you've been working real hard to surprise me," Mrs. Rogers began, in a choked voice, and her husband bustled over to the window, importantly. "Look out here, and see what I've done. Talk about your iron statuary—there is real hand-carved work that will knock your eye out."

There was no storm. Mrs. Rogers threw up her hands in a gesture which might have been dismay or surprise, and which her husband chose to think the latter. "La, Father, you are the beatingest man," she said in a voice rich with feeling, and her tone compensated him for the effort more than a longer but less heartfelt expression of her surprise might have done. Gratified with the success of his venture, he promptly forgot about the whole thing, and never noticed that within the week the "Stag at Bay" and Rosa Bonheur's horses were all back in their rightful places and the Rogers ships returned to the storeroom.

Mrs. Rogers waited another week to arrange for the permanent withdrawal of the good woman Sally Rogers to the loft of the stable. "If he ever thinks about it, which he won't, I can tell him it fell over, and I forgot to mention it," she decided.

PART - - - THREE

❧ ❧ ❧

March to July

❧ ❧ ❧

1876

". . . Striding through the confusion,
By thud of machinery and shrill steam-whistle undismay'd
Bluff'd not a bit by drain-pipe, gasometers, artificial fertilizers,
Smiling and pleased, with palpable intent to stay."

—WALT WHITMAN.

Chapter 1　　　　*M*ARCH came in "like a lion" with the worst storm of the winter. It was late in the afternoon, and still snowing heavily, when Henry pushed open the back door, ran across the shed, and through the kitchen, leaving behind him a watery track of melted snow. Martha had left early and Mary, who slept in, was finishing up her work. She had just scrubbed the kitchen floor and blacked the range against the morning.

"Holy Mary! Was there ever such a child!" she complained, hobbling quickly to the sink for the floorcloth. Painfully she got down on hands and knees and crawled along the path he had taken, wiping before her as she went, and grumbling aloud the while. "A body's work is never over in this house, I declare! If it isn't the missus herself, bad cess to her, it's the young devils."

She wiped clear up to the shed door and then, with the doorknob to hang to, she slowly pulled herself erect and gave a sigh of mingled pain and relief. Her work was labor lost, for Henry came running back, his mother close behind him, and the snow melting from his boots and clothes tracked the floor again.

Mary threw down the floorcloth and angrily faced her mistress. "There are limits, ma'am," she began, but Mrs. Rogers cut her off quickly.

"Oh, drat the floor, Mary. Leave it go. Mr. Quinby's down in his stall and he seems real sick, Henry says. He might have wiped off his feet in the shed, but he didn't . . ."

179

"I did, Mother—I did wipe them, but the way it was snowing outside, I would have had to brush off as well, and I didn't take the time." While Henry made this explanation, Mary was trying to help Mrs. Rogers into an old coat kept ordinarily behind the kitchen door for such emergencies.

"For heaven's sake don't jitter so. Hold the sleeve steady for a moment until I get my arm in." Mrs. Rogers' arm was short, and the sleeve of her dress too tight for ready movement. The combination didn't help her temper, and her voice was sharp as she issued instructions while making futile jabs for the coat sleeve. "Now, Mary, don't you dare come out to the stable in this storm. I know how newsy you are, and with all the other troubles I have, I don't want a sick old woman on my hands as well.

"Put the draft on the range again and get the fire up. . . . You better get some water heated, too, I may need it. That horse would have to get sick a night like this, with Father at work and Lucius home, and I doubt if Henry could get to Dr. Pepper's house, the way the snow is coming down."

Mrs. Rogers continued to shout orders as she followed Henry out through the shed: ". . . And you'd better get Gene down to help me. Don't bother Zenie or Julia. Neither of them is worth a whoop in the stable."

Outside, she kept close behind her son. He was already taller than she was, and helped to break the wind a bit. He held the lantern before him, to light the path through the garden, and she shouted over the wind in provoked tones, "Henry, for the land's sake hold that lantern so I can see too!"

In a moment they were covered with driving flakes, the snow lying on the waves and tight curls of Mrs. Rogers' hair so that her head looked as if sculptured from white

180

stone. It took the combined strength of mother and son to open the stable door, and as they stepped into the pleasant animal warmth, it blew shut, catapulting them into the stable. As she rubbed her hip, Mrs. Rogers cautioned, sharply, "Henry, mind the lantern!" And then, "Heavens, child, can't you hold it up, so I can see?"

The yellow rays picked out the stalls, the hames hanging like blank faces, the carriage harness gleaming with brasswork, held aloft by rope and pulleys, pitchforks and rakes in a corner, an open bag of grain, and the eyes of the animals, shining yellow or green from the shadows with which everything else was a part.

There was an air of expectancy in the stable. Total Eclipse thrashed nervously in his stall and whinnied when Mrs. Rogers came toward him. Nellie hurried forward and looked up with large and questioning brown eyes, as if trying to learn from her mistress the cause of her friend's strange behavior. The puppies, all six of them, moved at her heels, creeping along with bellies close to the straw instead of scampering and playing as they usually did. They were growing fast and had become polka-dotted beauties which at another time she would have been unable to resist.

Henry hung the lantern on a bracket on the side of Mr. Quinby's stall, and Mrs. Rogers dropped into the straw by his side. She felt the sweating neck and hot muzzle, and the slight quiver that she knew was Mr. Quinby's acknowledgment of her presence. All the masks, the little attitudes, poses, and pretenses that were hers, dropped away, and she was just a frightened woman beside her friend who was in great danger. Her mouth fell open a little, and her lips twisted with her anguish. "Henry, he's going to die. I know he's going to die."

It was hard to move in the coat, and as she worked her-

181

self out of it, like a snake shedding its skin, Henry, for the first time that he could remember, heard his mother sobbing. The horse lay so still his rich chestnut coat seemed but an enrichment of the shadows, and then, over his mother's shoulder, Henry watched the animal's sides begin to heave. He could see the swollen abdomen and the pain-flared nostrils, and watched as she ran a hand over the swollen place. It was like a child's white, chubby hand against the deep russet smoothness of the stretching hide. She talked partly to herself and partly to the horse. "Mr. Quinby, my dear, my precious—you'll have to get up, whether you want to or not. Come now, and try it." She gave little tugs at the halter and then took the broken halter rope and pulled on it. "Come up, Mr. Quinby!" The horse's neck muscles strained and he pawed frantically with his front feet. In a moment he gave up the effort, and her voice took on a harsh tone of command. "Henry, you will have to help me. We must get this animal on his feet, or he's gone, sure. When I say the word, pull on his head as hard as you can while I touch him with the whip." Henry moved into the stall, slipping and sliding on the straw as he evaded Mr. Quinby's hoofs, quiet now, but likely to begin kicking when the colic pains began again. He took the halter firmly, and his mother commanded, "When I give him the whip, pull as hard as you can." He nodded, and made sure of his hold on the worn leather while she got a carriage whip.

Now her voice was the demanding horsewoman's. "Mr. Quinby, sir, up, up, up—up with you. Pull, Henry, pull, p-u-l-l." She cracked the whip in the air, and then let the horse have it, a stinging bite on the rump that brought up a spot of hair as it bit into the hide and into her own heart. Mr. Quinby struggled with all the strength he could muster. His hoofs beat an irregular tattoo against the side of the stall, and pawed and slid on the straw-strewn board floor, but neither whip nor boy was enough to bring him to his feet.

There was a blast of cold air that made the flame flicker in the lantern, and they heard the bang of the stable door. In spite of his exertion, Henry smiled as he pictured Gene slammed in the rear by the stable door, as they had been. In a moment her wet, excited face was peering into the stall, and she began hurried explanations. "I couldn't get in. I couldn't get the door open, account of the wind— that's why I've been so long—till there was a lull."

"For the land's sake, shut up, Gene. Mr. Quinby is awfully sick. It's the colic, and we can't get him on his feet. I'm trying to think what to do."

"I'll harness up Total Eclipse and go for Dr. Pepper," Henry offered eagerly.

Mrs. Rogers shook her head. "It's too far. It's 'most two miles each way. You would never make it on such a night."

"I could take the sleigh."

"In this deep snow? Don't aggravate me. You'd have Total Eclipse foundered."

Georgina suggested: "There's a veterinary on Lehigh Avenue. He's not so far. Maybe we could get him."

In the meantime, Mrs. Rogers had made up her mind what to do, and she shook the suggestion away. Laudanum —that was it. To deaden the pain and quiet the horse. There should be part of a bottle around. "Henry, go look where the horse liniment is. There's a bottle of laudanum there as well. Bring it quickly. And, Gene, do you think you can make it back to the house and fetch me some hot water? Hot as you can. If you can't get the door open, kick on it and we'll hear. Hurry now!"

No sooner were the children gone than the spastic pains

began again. Mrs. Rogers could almost see the colicky gas force out the abdomen walls, and from a feeling of uselessness, she began to cry again, softly. "The laudanum will quiet you, if it's about. I know it's good for the colic. And don't think I wouldn't have sent Henry out for that doctor on Lehigh Avenue—though he is a strange veterinary, and God knows I don't want strangers treating you —but he couldn't get back in time, if he'd come at all, and I need the children to help me.". . . She went on in this way, talking in a low monotone, as if Mr. Quinby were a person who understood every word, while she performed a number of little tasks to make him more comfortable. She forked down some fresh straw, spread it about, and made it into a kind of pillow. She rubbed the sweat from his neck and sides and placed a blanket about his shoulders. When Henry came with the bottle, she clutched for it. "Thank God, there's laudanum! It will ease the pain."

He shook his head. "The bottle's empty—there's nothing in it."

Mrs. Rogers went into a mercurial rage. "Damn that no-good darky! I bet he's been taking it home to quiet those black brats of his when they cry. I know there was a good quarter of the bottle left the last time I looked at it." Then anxiety for the horse again softened her. "I have it," she exclaimed, suddenly, "the soothing syrup!" She seized Henry's arm. "Run upstairs to the medicine closet—on the bottom shelf, in the back, is a bottle of Mrs. Winslow's Soothing Syrup. I've had it since you twins were little, and I came across it just the other day. I was going to throw it out, and the good God stayed my hand. If it will soothe babies, it'll quiet horses, if you give enough.

"Run, now, and bring it, and maybe you can help your sister back with that hot water. That good-for-nothing Mary must be taking all night to heat it up." Mrs. Rogers went back to her patient. There seemed nothing further she could do for him for the moment, so she lay by him, along his back, with her arms around his neck, as if to help him bear the terrible, rending pain of the colic spasm.

The pain continued uninterruptedly until the children returned, covered with snow. Georgina held the large tea-kettle of steaming water while her mother took the bottle of soothing syrup from Henry. "Practically full." She nodded with a feeling of satisfaction. Now the dose! "It will take half a bottle at any rate, and maybe that won't be enough. Should I try to give him the hot water first, or after the syrup?" She felt less helpless, now that there were things she could do, and she quickly decided upon their order. She dispatched Henry for quart bottles—"There'll be empty ones around the stable somewhere"—and when he came back with two of them Georgina filled them with hot water. "Pour it slowly, to keep the glass from cracking," her mother cautioned. She inserted the neck of one of the bottles between Mr. Quinby's clamped jaws, and upended it so the hot water gurgled down his throat. He choked and thrashed the harder, but when the bottle was empty she gave him the second. "Henry, can't you see he needs his head held? Do I have to do everything?"

The spasm seemed to lessen slightly, but Mr. Quinby's abdomen had swollen to new proportions, and while Georgina held the lantern close, Mrs. Rogers pressed gently around the distended area. "It stands to reason the poor animal can't put up with that long—the gas will push against his heart and it'll be all over with him. If he wasn't more than human he'd have been gone before now," she said. Doubts assailed her. Perhaps she should have sent the children for Dr. Pepper or the other veterinarian, what did it matter? What did anything matter beside the saving of Mr. Quinby? She tried to remember if there was a saint one could pray to for the healing of horses, but she could only think of St. Luke the Beloved Physician. Well, why not? As she took the bottle of Mrs. Winslow's Soothing Syrup and poured a good half of it into some hot water in one of the larger bottles, a whole stream of prayers ascended to heaven.

An hour later, Mr. Quinby was still alive, and resting a trifle easier, and Mrs. Rogers gave thanks to St. Luke, although she was worried that the soothing syrup was all gone, and that as yet the horse had broken no wind to ease the terrible pressure that distended his belly.

"Gene, you might as well go to bed," she ordered, "and your brother will stay up with me. How is the weather out? Is it any better?"

Henry shook his head. "No, and there are drifts. I'd have tried to get through before, but I know I couldn't make it now." Mrs. Rogers nodded her head. She had expected no less. "Well, Gene, run along, anyhow, and get some sleep."

But Georgina stayed on, and in a little while, in spite of St. Luke and Mrs. Winslow, a new colic spasm began. The three knelt and watched anxiously. There seemed nothing further they could do, and before their eyes they could watch the gas from the colic distend the hide of the suffering animal until it seemed ready to burst like a balloon.

Then, as Mrs. Rogers told many times afterward, St. Luke did come to her aid. She would never have thought of such a thing; she had never even heard of its being done. "Henry, you and Gene run back to the house. Run, mind you, and bring the pointed butcher knife. Not the broad one, the pointed one—the boning knife. Tell Mary to sharpen it up if it isn't keen already, and bring me some more hot water—boiling, this time."

The children looked at their mother as if she had suddenly gone demented. "Run now," she screamed, "instead of standing there looking at me with your mouths open! And make sure the knife is sharp, you hear?" They ran, and Georgina said: "Henry, what do you suppose Mother wants with that knife? Did you ever see her look like that before?"

"I don't know, but we'd better get back with it quick!" Henry shouted back, and then added as an afterthought, "If we don't, she'll skin us alive with it."

When they told Mary they wanted the knife, she rubbed her eyes sleepily, and then, when the words registered, she was startled completely awake. "In the name of God, what for? If the woman's gone daft it's no more than I've been expecting, and that's the truth." But she rummaged through the drawer of Martha's table until she found the knife, and then tried the edge on her thumb. "Be careful of it, now. It's the special one Martha uses for sticking fowl, and she'll be mad enough if it comes back broke."

The twins paid no attention to the old woman's warnings, but hurriedly refilled the teakettle and set off once more for the stable. When they came in, their mother was listening to Mr. Quinby's breathing with much concern. It was evident to all of them that he was struggling to breathe at all, and each painfully caught gasp brought a momentary feeling of relief that he had not yet gone.

Mrs. Rogers compressed her lips. "Gene, take his head and hold it down. Sit on him if you have to, but keep him down—I think he's too weak to struggle. You, Henry, hold that lantern close, and don't shake. I have to see what I'm doing."

The children sprang to their duties, but watched their mother's actions with apprehension. She seemed to be in a trancelike state. At the same time, her face had never looked so hard and determined, so resolute, as now. She was feeling all over Mr. Quinby, who was so quiet he seemed already gone. Then she held her left hand against the bloated hide, as if to mark a vital spot. With awed eyes they saw her nod suddenly, as if satisfied with some decision she had made. She reached for the knife. . . .

The impulse of both children was to stay her hand as she raised the weapon. Georgina thought frantically: "Mother's decided to put him out of his misery. . . . She loves Mr. Quinby so she can't stand to see him suffer any longer." Neither child could move as the knife raised, poised for a moment, and descended with all of Mrs. Rogers' strength behind it. The horrified Georgina gave a little whimper of pain and terror as she saw the point pierce the hide and drive home to the handle in the horse's vitals.

For a moment nothing happened, and then, as their mother attempted to withdraw the blade, there was a hiss of escaping gas, which changed, as it gathered force, into a shrill whine. There was little blood as Mrs. Rogers gently bathed the wound with the hot water poured directly from the teakettle. Miraculously the diaphragm collapsed like a punctured balloon, although the foul, colicky air still bubbled through the mingled blood and water of the cut.

Mrs. Rogers began to cry in a high-pitched, hysterical fashion, and then she stopped and spoke in calm, subdued tones:

"Henry, run and get the brandy in the house—I should have thought of it, but I didn't. If I've fainted before you get back, don't either of you be frightened. Just give me

188

a little, and then force some into Mr. Quinby too. It will help him."

He dashed off, but his mother did not faint. When he returned, Georgina was supporting her. She was still kneeling by Mr. Quinby. The perspiration was starting on her forehead, and she was trembling violently. She took a long drink of the brandy, then motioned toward the horse, watching approvingly as the twins forced his teeth open and poured the rest of the bottle bit by bit down his throat.

"Well, no sense in my behaving like that—and before the children, too. I'm ashamed of myself," Mrs. Rogers said to herself. She jumped to her feet, shook the bits of straw from her clothes, and tried ineffectually to repair the damage done her hair. She turned again toward her patient, quite confident of his recovery. In a few moments the animal's breathing became normal, and gradually his muzzle cooled. Mr. Quinby was saved, there seemed no doubt of it, but the trio decided to sit up and watch him for the rest of the night.

2

It was still dark when Mr. Rogers left the Philadelphia & Reading yards. In spite of the storm, the night had been an easy one. Nothing had gone wrong, and there had been comparatively little freight to move. It had stopped snowing after midnight and, with the fickleness Philadelphians were so proud of, the weather had definitely changed and was becoming warmer. There were drifts, but they were easily circumvented, and he reached home about his usual hour, with the winter sky just graying into morning. He was in fine fettle, and hungry for breakfast. As he usually did when it snowed, he walked around the house plowing through the soft drifts, to

189

remove his damp clothes in the shed. He was surprised to see a dim flicker of light through the stable window, and walked back to investigate. The path the children had made to and from the house had blown over, and he was framing in his mind a sufficiently stern criticism for whoever had been careless enough to leave a lighted lantern in the stable.

When he pulled open the stable door, he saw that the lantern was not in its usual place, but by Mr. Quinby's stall. There an unusual sight met his eyes. Mr. Quinby slept gently, while Georgina lay with her head pillowed against his throat and her hair forming a golden blanket over the strong neck. His wife and son slept in the straw at the horse's back, an old coat covering the boy. His eyes took in the assortment of bottles, the teakettle, the bloody knife and the wound on the horse's side, and he reconstructed the night's happenings.

It brought a new sense of pride in this family of his, a pride such as he had never known before. "By God, there's a woman for you!" he thought. He was about to give out a blast of sound, to arouse the sleepers, and then he had a new thought, given him, perhaps, by the Dalmatian's action. Nellie and the puppies chose this moment to return to their accustomed quarters in a corner of Mr. Quinby's stall. They curled up together and dozed peacefully off. Mr. Rogers laughed silently in his beard, as if enjoying a huge secret joke. He took off his heavy felt boots and overcoat. Tiptoeing over to the sleigh, he removed the buffalo robes, one of which he placed over Georgina; with the other he blanketed his wife and son. Next, he put out the lantern, and like a huge bear prepared to hibernate gently crawled under the robe next to his wife.

For a little while he lay thus, with his beard outside,

mingling with the matted hair of the buffalo hide, and just a shade lighter in color. He was enjoying his joke hugely. "I'll lie here watching them until they wake up," he thought, "then I'll shout, and surprise them." He ran over in his mind all sorts of wild and extravagant tricks to play on them, but he felt too tired now to put any of them in action.

The rest of the story was begun many times by Martha, during the ensuing days. "I was late getting here, what with the snow and all," the cook's account began, "and the house was like a morgue, with the fires still banked and no sign of the family at all, and the mister not there, bellowing like a bull for his breakfast.

"I goes into the kitchen, and there's the gas jets still lit, though it's broad daylight, and the range out cold with the draft on full. Burnt out, it was, and no wonder. And there's Mary, fast asleep by the cold range, a-makin' mush as she's snorin', and shiverin' the while. I shakes her, but she don't wake up at first, and then when she does, she jumps up thinkin' I'm the missus. Did I give her a start! Well, she tells me about Mr. Quinby being sick, and that the family must have gone to bed and forgot her in the dither. So up we trots to *their* room, but the bed ain't been slept in, nor Miss Gene's either. And Miss Zenie a-sleepin' away, looking pretty as a picture. She wouldn't wake up on Judgment Day unless someone called her.

"Well, out we heads for the stable . . ." Here it became Mary's habit to continue the recital. She had a greater gift for the dramatic than the phlegmatic Martha, and salted her tale with varying remarks and incidents.

"Out through the snow we goes, and it up to our knees in places, and me with nothin' but an old shawl over me shoulders.

"There's the mister's footprints, leading to the stable, large as life and twice as natural, as they say. We shouts, but there's no answer, so in we goes, and what a sight! There's the whole family of 'em sleepin' in the straw with the creatures, like the Holy Family, no less, and the mister with his whiskers blowing up each time he snored, and the missus like a pretty little doll beside him, and Miss Gene like a saint, with her goldie hair about her, the rays of the sun catchin' it up in a halo, like."

At this point, Mrs. Rogers always interrupted sharply. "Come off, Mary, if ever there was an imp it's Gene, although she did help that night, I'll be bound, and so did Henry, for that matter." She would stop for a moment, and toss her head, before continuing:

"I felt Mary yanking at my arm, and there's Father, fast asleep in the straw beside me. I knew right away what he'd been up to, so I turned the tables. I slipped out of the robe and woke the children with my hand over their mouths, so they wouldn't make a noise on waking, and out we sneaked, and Father didn't wake up until dinnertime." This drew a laugh, and then she went on: "When Dr. Pepper came he said I did the only thing could have saved Mr. Quinby, so there! It shows what prayer can do, I say. I tell you, St. Luke came to me that night and told me his blessed self that cutting Mr. Quinby open would let the gas out and relieve the pressure that was killing him."

During this part of the story, when Mr. Rogers was present he always began to look a little sheepish at the thought of sleeping with the horse until past noontime. His joke had certainly rebounded on him! But when St. Luke was mentioned, he couldn't be restrained any longer. "St. Luke!" he would shout. "St. Luke be blowed! No one cured that horse but Gussie." And then, facetiously,

"Mrs. Rogers did the job, I say—unless Mrs. Winslow helped, with her Soothing Syrup—good for horses or babies!"

Chapter 2   THE SNOWSTORM, to be forever remembered by Mr. Quinby's colic, was succeeded by a thaw that started rivulets of dirty snow water across the uneven brick pavements. These gray trickles formed gutter rivulets which soon became raging torrents foaming along the curbing. Sewers overflowed and backed up, and the torrents became noxious floods which marooned on street corners the unfortunate pedestrians who had to be abroad. Walking became a problem in navigation across wide and treacherous oceans of chocolate-colored liquid.

They were treacherous not only because of their depth, but also on account of their deceptive appearance. Slush and unmelted snow floated on the top, creating many times an illusion of solidity that was dissipated only when one's foot plunged ankle-deep into the cold tide.

The condition of the streets aroused the inventive minds of the Rogers males. With great labor and some ingeniousness, Henry attached to his shoes low stilts made of short pieces of wood he found in the stable. With these he was able to stand in the middle of a deep, slush-covered pool and give the impression that his feet rested on the surface of snow and ice that was still solidly frozen. It was an invention that provided considerable diversion for the twins when they perfected the technique of their deception. Henry stood by the curb until someone drew near. Then he moved out into the street, pausing when the flood reached his soles. At this moment Georgina, an exceptionally sweet expression on her face, called to him, and he turned to engage in a pretended discussion with her. Meanwhile their victim, observing the security of Henry's foothold, confidently stepped off the curb, to be doubly shocked, by the icy water and by the sudden jeers of the innocent-appearing youngsters, into realization of the trick played on him.

Mr. Rogers' brainstorm, which he explained at the dinner table, was of a different sort, and designed not for entertainment but for its utilitarian possibilities. Unlike Henry's idea, however, it never got to the working stage. Apropos of nothing that had been said before, he suddenly announced, with a most portentous expression:

"The yearly freshets on the Nile are, I am told, a great boon to the farmers who live along its banks. The brown flood spreads over their fields and gives them new richness. . . . Now I propose we should use the experience of the poor heathen Egyptian farmer to our own advantage."

Except for Mrs. Rogers, the rest of the family went on with their soup, too used to their parent's vagaries to express any surprise at his statement. She said: "Why, Jesse! What in the world started you on Egypt?"

He waved a hand in the general direction of the front street. "Mother, have you looked at that rich flood which fills Richmond Street without getting some idea for utilizing it? Where is your imagination, woman?"

"La, do eat up your soup before it gets cold. It won't do you any good to worry about the water; it won't flood into the cellar, not unless it gets a lot worse."

"Madam, that street in front of our house is full of gold —liquid gold. Do you realize that is nothing but manure, in an aqueous state? Calculate, if you will, the number of vans, carts, drays, the sleighs, the carriages and rigs, that

194

pass daily; multiply them by the hours this snowfall has lasted, and realize that each steed has contributed its share to that wealth we would spurn."

As Mr. Rogers warmed to an idea, he was apt to become dramatic in presenting it. He wiped his hands down the front of the napkin protecting his beard, and shouted, "Liquid gold, I say!" in a voice that gained, at last, the attention of everyone. "And I seem to be the only person in this house with the wit and imagination to put it to use." He looked about him with a belligerent air, as if expecting to be heckled, but as the family merely continued to stare at him, he went on:

"What I propose to do is to devise a pump that will lift that flood of almost pure fertilizer, and deposit it in a rich, life-giving stream on our garden, so it will bloom like an oasis of the Egyptian desert. . . . Who knows what tremendous cabbages, fat onions, prolific potatoes, mammoth beans . . ."

He paused, awaiting a response, but the children returned to their food without comment, and Mrs. Rogers chose to ignore the whole idea. Gradually, after a few grumbles at the lack of appreciation his family displayed, he subsided, and noisily finished his own serving. The grand plan was never again mentioned.

In a few days the last patches of dirty snow disappeared and Mr. Rogers' energies began to be consumed by worry that spring might not arrive in due course. The first week of March was over and there had not been a single robin. He was impatient with a season that seemed definitely on the way, and completely refused to countenance any argument that he was anticipating too early the arrival of the feathered harbinger.

"Good grief, Jesse, the snow is hardly off the streets from the worst storm of the winter; we can have a blizzard yet, like as not, and the poor birds would freeze." Mrs. Rogers repeated some variation of this disquisition every year. "We never have robins before Easter—we just never have them."

The statement aroused a barrage of argument. Mr. Rogers marshaled all kinds of instances, which he believed implicitly as soon as he invented them, of whole flocks of robins that in years past had descended upon Kensington as early as February. It was decidedly contrary that this year they should be so delayed. He was impatient for spring, as later he would be testy if summer were not early, and as last fall the winter had been too slow in coming.

Spring did seem to be in the air, and on several occasions Mr. Rogers went riding on Total Eclipse. It was a brave sight to see him mounted on the big black. The horse was built like one of the Clydesdales that pulled the drays of the warehouses on Front Street, but he dwarfed to normal saddle-horse proportions in comparison to his rider.

It was after one of these rides that the incident of the barrel wagon occurred which helped to decide Henry's future. Mr. Rogers left the stable at a canter, and returned at a gallop. Not that he forced the horse for the whole afternoon. On the contrary, his rides along the pleasant country roads that spread fanwise beyond Kensington were all taken at Total Eclipse's regular swaying walk. The start and finish represented merely an effect in which horse and man concurred. Indeed, the black was a consummate actor, and always made a last, rearing prance right at the stable door. His eyes appeared wild, and showed their whites in a manner quite foreign to their usual brown-velvet benignity, while his nostrils distended and revealed fiery red membrane when he snorted. Once the show was over, he returned to his stall as mild-mannered as ever.

With the famed inconstancy of Philadelphia weather, the day had turned not springlike, but midsummerish, and the ride proved hot and dusty. Instead of returning directly to the stable, as he usually did, Mr. Rogers stopped at Paddy Guirk's for refreshment. Tying the horse to the hitching post in front of the saloon, he entered and ordered beer. It was no minor feat to drink from the massive handled schooner without straining the brew through his beard, and he approached the task in a leisurely manner.

The pleasant calm of a Philadelphia late afternoon was suddenly broken by hoarse shouts of anger, followed by shrieks and wild cries that had a familiar sound. Still clutching his schooner of beer, Mr. Rogers rushed to the door and watched a sight to which he responded first with curiosity, and then with more mixed feelings. A cooperage wagon, drawn by a single tired-looking horse, was approaching so slowly that its wheels seemed to poise on each cobble before rolling over. Its driver walked alongside with head uplifted, shouting furious threats at what appeared to be a load of empty barrels. These were arranged so that they lay on their sides at a slight cant, making a high pyramid which seemed disproportionate to the size of the wagon and the apparent strength of the horse. Mr. Rogers laughed aloud. "It's a wonder one of those nosy women in Henry Bergh's society isn't after him, with a load like that," he observed.

Then he realized the true cause of the driver's anger. A flushed, excited face appeared in the round, shaded cavity of one of the highest barrels. It was Gene—impossible not to recognize those blond braids. The driver shouted, "Come down out of there, you devils, come down, I say, or I'll skin the pair of you!"

Georgina called down, "Get me if you can—get me if you can!"

197

"Come down out of there! You'll get them barrels rolling, and it'll be the death of you," the driver warned, more frantic than ever.

The tired horse stopped in front of the saloon, so that Mr. Rogers could see his favorite daughter climb from one barrel to the next with childish disregard for the state of her dress.

Another voice began to jeer, and a second head poked out from the top of another barrel. It was Henry, of course. His father laughed. "Those youngsters are chips off the old block," he announced to an empty barroom. "Hard to know what they will be up to next." Lifting the schooner carefully, he took a long draft of beer, and then guffawed at a new antic of the twins. The driver made a desperate effort to climb the side of his load, but the children were out of their hiding places in an instant and scurrying to the very top of the pyramid. Georgina capered about in an excited dance, and threatened: "You better not come up! We'll roll a barrel down on you if you come higher."

Gradually Mr. Rogers' amusement was replaced by another emotion. "By Harry, this is no way for a full-grown girl to be carrying on," he told himself. "And as for Henry, that imp, I'll have to give him another hiding." His decision came at about the same moment he finished his beer, and he placed the schooner on the bar with an angry thump, determined to end the scene and punish the offenders. He was stayed at the door by Georgina's voice, shrieking to her brother. Her sharp eyes had just noticed Total Eclipse hitched to the post, and she cried: "Henry—Father's horse! We'd better beat it, quick, or he'll see us!"

Careless of the continued shouts of the driver, hoarse now with exasperation and overexertion, Henry called back: "Gosh, what's the use, Gene? He's been watching us. He must be in Paddy's now, watching through the door. We might as well get down and face it."

This would have been the moment to show himself, but Mr. Rogers delayed long enough to hear his daughter's reply. "Nonsense, Henry, don't be silly. If Father saw us, he'd have stopped us right away. He's no sneak, I tell you, he comes out with things. He wouldn't stand in Paddy's watching us without yelling. Come on—let's run." She climbed down the side of the load of barrels like a squirrel, evaded the driver's clutch, and streaked up the street with Henry close behind her.

Mr. Rogers' face was red. He had been sneaking on them! He had stood there enjoying their antics, instead of putting a stop to them. And now he couldn't punish them for it—that would be a confession. His peculiar sense of fairness decided: "I'll forget the whole episode, but the very next time I catch either of them doing anything, by the Lord Harry I'll lick them twice as hard as I would otherwise."

As he mounted Total Eclipse to begin the homeward gallop, on which both horse and man entered with such enjoyment, he also decided to himself: "I'll have to do something about Henry. It's months since he was expelled, and I've let the boy run wild. I suppose his mother would like to get him into one of her schools, but I think it's about time he went to work and made a career for himself."

Later, when the matter was discussed with his wife, she was surprisingly indifferent. "I'm sure, Jesse, I am not going to share now the responsibility of Henry's upbringing. He's spoiled beyond anything I can do for him."

"Oh, it isn't that he's really spoiled. He's very much like I was at his age, full of animal spirits. I've been too easy with him, that's all. I had a father less tolerant than

199

I am. When I didn't behave I got licked within an inch of my life."

Mrs. Rogers pressed her lips together. "I never noticed that it made a perfect man of you, and I do know that the surest way to spoil a horse is to beat it so severely it shies from you, as my poor father used to say before he passed away."

"Gussie, spare me his nuggets of wisdom. I'm concerned at the moment about the welfare of our son, and not whisperings from the tomb."

As was often the case, a scene in the household was averted by the makings of another. From the third floor could be heard a violent quarrel in which Georgina and Teresina seemed to be the participants. Mr. Rogers blustered toward the door, on the way to put an end to the din, but his wife spoke up sharply. "Now, Jesse, you handle Henry, and I'll settle the girls."

He thumped downstairs dutifully enough, and it was the last ever said about Henry's going back to school. Mr. Rogers began a campaign to find a place for him, which was not at all an easy task. Most businesses were cutting down in the number of their help instead of taking on new people, but he continued hopeful. As he explained to Henry in a father-to-son chat he had with him on the subject:

"Your chance will come one of these days. I'll find you a place that is filled now with an older, more expensive man. Then it will be up to us to prove that you could do the work for less money. That's business, son—the man who does the most for the least money gets ahead. He gets the jobs. That is a lesson you will have to learn." He nodded his head, and beamed in delight at the simplicity of it all. "The man who gives the most value for the money sells the goods."

Georgina also presented a problem which increasingly annoyed her father, because it began to disturb his comfort. The twin was his favorite, and she was growing prettier and prettier, with a healthy, sanguine color that intensified or paled according to her emotions. Her hair was naturally curly, and made a thousand little ringlets across a high, smooth forehead. Her eyes were the same gray-blue as his own. She was a healthy, high-spirited tomboy, but she was maturing rapidly, and an increasingly large number of adolescent youths sought her company. Of these, she favored young Al Naylor, Harry's brother. Al was very dark, like Harry, with skin of an almost coppery color and straight black hair, but here the resemblance ceased. In features and temperament, in thought, sympathies, and expression, he differed completely. He was fun-loving and intense in his manner, and had earned the displeasure of his family by refusing to be awed, or even pleased, by his brother's meteoric rise in politics.

Although he was considerably older than Georgina, she began to imagine herself desperately in love with him. It was an infatuation which no one else in the family took seriously, and it did not prevent a host of other youths from making their bids for her favor. More than ever before, the Rogers house became a gathering point for all the youth of the neighborhood. It was this that aroused her father to protest to his wife.

"By the Lord Harry, we not only have to put up with dash-hounds under foot, but there's a whole raft of puppies in the parlor as well, courting Gene."

"I wish you wouldn't say things like that, Father. Gene is much too young to think of being courted, and all she can think about right now is Al Naylor. She'll never marry him, of course, if I can help it. He has no money, and he can't hold a job after they find out the ideas he has—always talking about the rights of working people, and Socialism and things, instead of trying to get ahead and amount to something, like Harry. . . . No, there's safety in numbers, I say, and as long as there is a whole houseful of boys hanging around after Georgina we haven't much to fear. I only worry when she and young Naylor are moping some place alone."

Mr. Rogers tried to consider all this very carefully, and he put on an expression of grave concentration, but actually his wife's remarks seemed only an evasion of his just complaint. It was so hard to keep in mind that the twins were growing up—and that caused a parenthesis of thought, Henry hadn't found a post yet, nor wouldn't, he supposed, unless he was jogged along a bit.

"Young people of this day and age," he began an oration familiar to generations of mothers, "aren't like when I was a boy. We didn't sit around a parlor with a girl, choking to death in our collars and with hair plastered down with grease—they are travesties of youth, and damned annoying underfoot. We did things. We went out. We skated, and rode, and went on picnics. Young people had fun those days. Now they just sit in someone's parlor and indulge in inane conversation. By Harry, Mother, I don't know what the world is coming to, and I'm sick and tired of pimply skin and fuzzy faces. I never had pimples—and I shaved, until I was man enough to grow a proper beard."

"Well, you don't need to worry about Gene so much right now," Mrs. Rogers interrupted with assurance. "The trouble is going to be later, when Zena gets here. Neither of the girls is thinking much about entertaining right now, because they both have their caps set for Zena's nephew, but when *he* comes, they'll be wanting the parlor to entertain *him*. I always said we should have had a house with an extra sitting room, and now you can see my reason for it."

"Woman, what, I would like to know, what are the rights of parents, anyway? You forget I enjoy the parlor myself. Where can I sit and read? Where can we spend a quiet evening together if not by our own fireside? And what you say about Zena's nephew surprises me. I never noticed that either of the girls paid much attention to him. You never told me. Did they say something—confide in you?" As Mrs. Rogers shook her head impatiently, he went on complacently, "As for his part, he spent a lot more time talking to me than he did to the girls."

"Yes—because you hung around all the time, and he is a polite young man. What could he do, tell you to chase yourself? You might as well realize it, you have three daughters, and they are all of marriageable age, although Gene can wait a while. But Zenie can't! Another year or so and she will be an old maid. A girl who waits until she is past twenty to marry is taking a risk, I'm telling you —though I'm not worried about Zenie, really. With her looks, and her practical mind, she'll do well eventually, I'm certain. That's another thing. They not only need husbands, I intend to make sure they fall in love with men of means instead of the other kind. Because I've had to scrimp and save all my married life, I want my girls to have a little happiness."

Mr. Rogers snorted. He blew in his beard, puffed out his lips, rumbled in his chest, and made other noises preparatory to vocal expostulation, but his wife gave him no opportunity. She continued with shrewish vigor and pertinacity to press home to him his failings as a father.

"It's up to you to get out of the way when you see either

203

of the girls alone with an eligible young man. In these days, when times are so difficult and the future uncertain, a man is a fool to think of marriage if he can get out of it, and it's hard enough for our girls—though there are no more beautiful in Kensington—it's hard enough for them to make a catch without your complicating matters all the time."

Mr. Rogers, who had begun the discussion with a mistaken feeling that he was the injured party, that his rights had been trespassed upon, found it difficult to rearrange his mental processes under this criticism of himself and his actions. Again he was given no opportunity to reply as, womanlike, his wife began to relate past defections.

"You want to enjoy the parlor. You want to sit and read. What about your daughters, and their future? You made things difficult enough for Zenie last winter, when she was entertaining Harry Naylor and Gus Palmer. Not that Gus is so much—I'm not at all sure he'll ever amount to anything—but you didn't need to sing your ribald songs with him all the time. You sang 'One Fishball' until I thought I'd die, with poor Zenie sitting there. . . .

"And politics with Harry. . . . There's a man with a future. A girl will rarely get a more desirable prospect. He may even be President some day, and every last time he called on Zenie you talked politics. What girl cares about politics, anyhow? Certainly not Zenie. But there she was —and Harry such a cold fish he'll never be an easy one to land."

She paused for breath, and Mr. Rogers seized the opportunity to shout: "Cease your harangue! I've had enough of it. You talk about men as if they were nothing but fish about to be hooked. I'll not be a party to that kind of angling, I tell you now." At this moment, his sense of humor reasserted itself, and he lowered his voice to a pleasant thunder, inquiring with a smirk, "If that's your attitude, I suppose you thought I was a pretty fine-looking trout in the stream, the day I first swam under your eye?"

But Mrs. Rogers was in no mood for fun, especially of so complacent a variety. She bent her head forward and impaled her husband with rapierlike glances from flashing black eyes.

"What I thought and what I got were two different things!" she cried. "You know what you are? A big, fat, sluggish old carp, content to live in a dead old ditch like this, and wallow around in the mud! I'm telling you, Jesse Rogers."

No, something had gone wrong with his attempt at a protest, radically wrong. He turned from the tirade and walked quietly toward the stairs, still trying to understand how a reasonable complaint against manifest discomfort had boomeranged so disconcertingly. He consoled himself with the thought "Mother doesn't mean what she says" and shook his head. "I suppose that's always the case with high-strung women."

Chapter 3

THE NEWS of the second postponement of Aunt Zena's coming to Philadelphia arrived at breakfast time. Mr. Rogers had already retired for his morning nap, but Mrs. Rogers read a paragraph from the letter to the girls. " 'Philippe is still so occupied here in New York, I hesitate to leave him to *his own devices.*' " She pursed her lips. "She's got 'his own devices' underlined. You know what she means, girls. Your aunt is looking out for your interests."

Teresina shot a venomous glance at Julia, who kept her eyes on her plate, heaped with links of smoked sausage and buttered mashed potatoes, while their mother read on: " 'The poor boy is worn out every day, after coping with your *stupid* officials. They have no efficiency. They never seem to get anything *done*, like our French ones. We plan now to be in Philadelphia the Monday after Easter. The French exhibit simply *must* be ready for the Centennial opening, Philippe says.' "

As she was dreading the presence of her sister in the house, and this was another reprieve, she could not help feeling relief. At the same time she sympathized with the girls, both of them so eager to try their skill at charming the most acceptable young man they were likely ever to meet. She stuffed the letter in her belt, behind her chatelaine. Well, it was too bad, in a way, that Zena wouldn't be with them for Easter. It would have been nice to drive into town for mass at St. Joseph's, the oldest church in Philadelphia. It was typical of Mrs. Rogers that she didn't count in this reckoning the numerous older Protestant churches in the city, nor realize that to her sister, from an older France, St. Joseph's, less than two centuries old, would seem comparatively modern, and its squat red-brick exterior and plastered and wainscoted walls decidedly ugly. "Zena would enjoy St. Joseph's," she thought. "It's so old, and quaint-looking, too. And it's beautiful on Easter morning, with the flowers and all."

Her thoughts ran on. "It will give me a little time, still, until she gets here. Once she arrives, the whole house will be disrupted, though if Zena tries to boss things, I'll sit on her. It's awful to think that way about my own sister, but she is certainly someone you can love better from a distance. On the other hand, she is generous. She spent a small fortune on the girls' clothes. I should be looking forward to her coming, I suppose, and feel ashamed of myself for not."

The girls finished breakfast and went to their rooms, Teresina to read Elizabeth Wetherell's *Daisy*, which she had been trying to finish for months, Julia and Georgina to indulge in that supremest of feminine pleasures, the rearranging of their wardrobes. It was a new experience to both of them, this business of unpacking bureau drawers and closets and reassembling their contents. New in the case of Julia because until the advent of Philippe she had no interest in clothes, and to Georgina because she had never before owned anything except remade or altered dresses of her sisters', which had not seemed worthy of so much attention.

Mrs. Rogers supervised the preparations for dinner, which were already under way, and then hurried toward the stable to rout out Lucius and get him started on the garden. It was early, of course, to start planting, but she believed in being forehanded about everything, and prided herself particularly on having the earliest vegetables in the neighborhood.

The dachshunds followed at her heels like twin shadows. She had become so used to them that she never turned or moved without first looking to avoid stepping on their stout little bodies. The names Jesse had chosen for them seemed singularly appropriate—even she had to admit that, although the popular evangelists were themselves distasteful to her, with their spectacles and cheap revival music. Be that as it may, Moody, who was growing to be slightly the larger dog, continued to look like a believer in hell-fire and damnation, with worried creases on his solemn little face. Sankey, on the other hand, seemed to have accepted his lowly condition and to make the best of it. He still indulged in the highly pitched howl which first gained them their new names—much to Mr. Rogers' exasperation, as a favorite occasion for this vocal display was during the rendition by himself of any of his favorite ballads.

Mrs. Rogers had completely opened her heart to the grotesque little creatures, and they lived there, secure in her affection, with the horses and Nellie. Perhaps they helped to fill the vacancy left by the sale of Nellie's puppies, which with one exception had all gone to new homes.

As the dachshunds followed, with their funny rolling stride, she hurried down the garden path. Her eyes strayed approvingly to the deep lemon-yellow smear of a row of daffodils, but she was intent on trying to catch Lucius napping, and did not linger. She had planned the words with which she expected to startle him from a stolen slumber, and was disappointed to find him busily engaged in grooming Mr. Quinby. As a result, her voice was sharper than usual, and poor Lucius ran over in his mind his acts of the last few days, trying to guess the reason for her tone.

"Come, Lucius! Inside a day like this, grooming the horses? Keep that for rainy days—the garden is just waiting for attention. I want it all turned up—immediately, mind you. And work the old manure well into the soil. And don't go just dabbing in the dirt, either. I want you to dig at least a foot deep."

Lucius sprang toward the garden tools in the corner, as if to indicate that this hasty action was an earnest of the pace at which his mistress's instructions would be carried out, but she stopped him sharply. "You needn't begin yet. Wait until I've looked over the stable with you. There are probably a dozen things you've let go." She examined the carriage, and found the dark-blue lacquer needed cleaning, and the floor dusting. The harness was drying out for lack of oil, and its buckles and fittings were dull. "I want them polished, mind you, so every buckle shines. When

208

we go to church Sunday I don't want to be ashamed of our rig, as I usually am."

Lucius thought, "My, the old lady is in a huff today, sure thing," and he decided to postpone a request he had intended to make.

The sleigh had not been covered with its canvas for the summer. One of the horse collars needed patching. The stable itself was in a state, and the stalls needed revarnishing. "I declare, I don't know why I put up with you, Lucius, and I don't see how you got hold of a good girl like Louisa for a wife." Mrs. Rogers had been saying this to him for so many years that it made absolutely no impression, but it gave her a great deal of satisfaction. She returned to the house, followed by the patter of Moody and Sankey, and thought: "Well, I certainly gave him what-for! Maybe I'll get things done for a little while— and that reminds me, I'll have to get down to see Louisa's youngsters soon, and see that they are getting fed properly."

Mrs. Rogers was in the grip of one of those moods which possessed her every so often, when her mind raced with plans and projects, and as she completed one, or gave directions for its doing, she thought of another, and continued in that way until she was exhausted, when the family and servants could sigh with relief and rest from the terrific pace she had imposed.

There must be something for someone else to do! She thought of Teresina, but gave up the idea immediately. Zenie was too useless. It was a waste of effort even to suggest that she do something. She would agree, of course, and promise completion of any task, but that would be the end of it. Her mind fastened on her son. The boy hadn't found work yet, nor had he tried, she was certain. All that talk of Jesse's! Well, if he wasn't to grow into a lazy good-for-nothing she would have to do something about it.

She bustled through the house to the stairway, and called, "Henry! . . . Henry! . . . Come down this minute!" There was no answer. "Probably he's at some corner, loafing," she thought. "If I'd had the raising of that boy he would have amounted to something." She opened the front door, and was pleasantly surprised to see him playing ball with Al Naylor.

"Henry, come here this minute!" she called in a tone of voice that brought immediate obedience. Her plan took form as she began to act upon it. "I know where I'll send him," she thought. "He was one of my most persistent admirers." When her son followed her inside, she said: "Run upstairs and get dressed. Get washed first—and I mean washed—and your hair combed, instead of all tousled the way it is, and your shoes blacked. All around—do you hear me? When you come down, I'm going to send you out for a job. You've been around here loafing entirely too long."

Finally, after two or three trips for further cleaning, Henry presented himself in a condition that met his mother's approval. "Now listen sharp to what I tell you. You go to Mr. Madeira's office. He's on Fifth Street, close to Walnut, and he is in the coal business. Mr. William Madeira—remember? He is a very nice man, and you needn't be afraid of him, but don't be flip, either.

"If you see him right off, tell him you're Augustina Repetto's son, and he'll be quite agreeable to you, I'm sure." She stopped a moment and sighed. "I threw him over for your father, and I've regretted it ever since, but that's neither here nor there. If you see Mr. Madeira's clerk, be very straightforward and gentlemanly, but at the same time make him think he is dirt under your feet, and just say you want to see Mr. Madeira, without any reasons. Now a lot depends how you do this, Henry. Your whole future, perhaps, and you'd better not make any mistakes, or I'll flay you myself when you get home.

"You tell Mr. Madeira that your mother was anxious for you to get a business training under him, and she sent you to him especially, and you don't care whether you get any wages or not—do you understand?"

"But, Mother, if I work, it seems I ought to get some pay," Henry began to protest, but his mother broke in impatiently.

"Of course you'll get paid. You just say that—it sounds better. I always found Billy Madeira a generous man, and I'm sure he hasn't changed, though it's over twenty years since I've seen him. Be gone with you now, and when you get home, I expect to hear from you that you're in the coal business."

She watched his retreating figure as he walked purposefully down Richmond Street. "He'll get it too. . . . Billy will like him, right off," she mused. "He's getting his father's good looks and figure, and with my gumption behind him, he may amount to something."

2

Henry returned to the house just before one-five P.M., the time fixed by his father to be aroused from his nap, so Mrs. Rogers had no opportunity to question him about the details of his visit, although his beaming face apprised her of its success.

"You better not tell Father I sent you to Mr. Madeira," she warned. "There's no knowing how he would take it, and what he doesn't know won't hurt him."

Mr. Rogers made his appearance at one-twenty-six, on

211

schedule. He came downstairs prepared to grouse about the French clock, which had been spared for some days, but his purpose was forgotten with the announcement of Henry's good fortune. He accepted the news as a tribute to his own sagacity, and dinner was delayed as he pontificated:

"What did I tell you, Henry? There is always room in the old U.S.A. for a young man who will give more value than anyone else. I hope you followed my advice, and told your new employer you would work for less than he pays at present?"

Henry looked up innocently. "I told him I would work for nothing, just to be with him to learn the business."

"By the Lord Harry, that was smart—the Quaker coming out in you, my boy. Supposing you do work a few months for nothing? In that time you can make yourself indispensable. Go there early and stay late, after everyone else has left. It won't be long before you will be getting a salary, I tell you."

"Oh, I'm getting a salary right away, and a good one, too—two dollars a week, to begin with."

"Two dollars! Do you hear that, Gussie? Excellent wages for a mere boy. There's many a clerk in the railroad who doesn't make a whole lot more. And the coal business is a good one, too. Everyone needs coal, even if they can't afford to have it." He seated himself, tucked his napkin into his collar so that it protected his beard, and proceeded with equal enthusiasm to talk and eat at the same time. "You see what my advice has done for Henry," he boasted. "This, my son, disproves all the theories of lazy malcontents who say the day of opportunity is past. I say the man who wants work can get it."

Mrs. Rogers allowed her husband to enlarge upon his share in procuring the position for Henry. She ate quietly, and with the affected daintiness she used at times. She was quite willing to forgo her share of credit, but it was exasperating to look forward to a future during which this incident would be regularly trotted out and exhibited as proof of his unerring wisdom. She would have to agree with his future statements, or put an end to them now. It was a hard decision to make, but she resolutely controlled herself as he called upon her for approbation.

"Mother, here is proof of what I say. There is nothing so helpful to youth as the seasoned advice of a father with years of business experience."

She merely shrugged her shoulders, and remarked, "La, Father, at any rate he will be doing something, and not hanging around the house, or getting into devilment." She was pleased, however, at Henry's circumspection, and the fact created a new bond between mother and son. Later, she asked him for more details about his adventure. "And how was Mr. Madeira?" she questioned eagerly.

"Oh, he's a nice old man. He looked grouchy, but when I spoke to him, just like you said, he was pretty nice."

"An old man! He's not a day older than your father." Mrs. Rogers dropped her head, coyly. "He used to have the loveliest hair, almost black, and curly. Reminded me of your dear Grandfather Borelli, he was so handsome."

"Well, he doesn't have it now," Henry asserted stoutly. "He's little, and baldheaded—shiny bald. Dad doesn't look any older than he ever did, does he?"

"He hasn't changed much, and that's the truth," Mrs. Rogers agreed complacently. "But I've been doing for him for over twenty years, and Bill Madeira has been a bachelor. When I turned him down, he swore he'd never get married." She forgot that Henry stood before her, and thought back to the difficulty of the decision (as she recalled it). Ships or coal, it had been, and in the early fifties coal had seemed a chancy commodity, with so much wood available. On the other hand, ships—solid oak planks, pine decks, and great full sails . . .

Well, she had been wrong, and she had had to scrimp and save instead of being able to enjoy life, like Zena, with a new lover whenever it suited her. Thoughts of her sister caused her to tighten her lips. "If Zena so much as looks at Jesse, I'll tell her off," she said to herself. "If she wants a man so badly, why doesn't she get one of her own?"

Henry interrupted her train of thought, and left this last question unanswered. "He asked about you, though, and said he didn't think I looked much like you. . . . He said to come in and see him sometime, when you're in town."

She looked up, startled. "What? Oh, Mr. Madeira? Well, when in the world would I have the time? With this family to take care of!" Mrs. Rogers felt pleased with herself. The coal business for Henry, and Billy Madeira had not forgotten her! But the boy mustn't get any notions! He stood there grinning at her, and it was time to tell him off. "Once Mr. Madeira finds out how shiftless and useless you are . . ." she began sharply, but Henry, his elation unaffected by his mother's changed tone, raced out to find Al and continue their game of ball.

Chapter 4

EASTER, that grand day on which new dresses and bonnets could be displayed in church before the other parish women, this year had little interest for Teresina Rogers, although her handsome New York clothes excited envious looks that at another time would have carried her to a seventh heaven of happiness. To the women of Kensington, the joy of resurrection was generally limited to the miraculous transformation of dead, somber winter garments into the vivid new life of spring finery, and it was indicative of Teresina's mental state, due to the frequent postponements of Philippe's coming, that she derived no pleasure from it.

Julia was happier in the admiring glances she received. They helped to bolster a confidence in herself that needed additional propping with each passing week that separated her from Philippe.

Easter Sunday was a beautiful day, so warm and sunny, and it was lovely driving home in the carriage, with Lucius at the reins. Everyone remarked at the lateness of Easter —the sixteenth of April, imagine—and a friendly argument arose as they tried to recall a past Easter that had been later in the year, other fair Easters, and inclement ones. Julia sat back in her seat, dreamily enjoying the fragrance of her corsage, made that morning by her mother from early garden blooms.

If neither girl enjoyed the holiday to the full because it lacked Philippe's presence, their mother felt only a respite at her sister's nonarrival. Now Zena was due tomorrow, and Mrs. Rogers' premonitions of disaster became stronger. The family mood, however, was one of anticlimax, and it persisted all day. Mary and Martha had dyed eggs with beet juice, coffee, and a variety of other home-contrived coloring materials, and these were admired and then eaten.

In the afternoon they joined the parade of carriages on Broad Street, Mr. Rogers showing off a completely recovered Mr. Quinby. Again pleasure was lessened by worry that there might be another postponement, and there was general relief when night came without any last-minute telegram.

Aunt Zena and Philippe actually did arrive with no further delays. Mr. Rogers met them at the station with the carriage, and even Mr. Quinby, pawing impatiently, realized the importance of the errand. Mr. Rogers had timed his arrival nicely. He had no more than a half-hour to wait, and was just beginning to feel impatient, and worried lest the railroad might fail him on this crucial day. After all his boasting to Zena, suppose the train was late!

His fears were groundless; the train puffed in on time, and Zena, flanked by her maids, greeted him from the steps of the parlor car. As he had observed before, she was a fine figure of a woman, and her embraces were as lusty as his own.

"My, Jesse, we meet once more! Although I have seen so little of you, I feel we have known each other for years. But you are so much handsomer—Tina never really prepared me—and so terrifically strong! You overwhelm me all over again."

This obvious flattery was accepted with an expansive smile and a dashing bow. It was seldom that Mr. Rogers wanted for words, but Zena left him speechless. The appearance of her luggage saved him, and he bustled off to attend to it. By this time, Aunt Zena had begun to accept the idea that Americans were not as villainous as they looked, and that although they were Republicans, the spirit of red revolution had somewhat abated. Also she had learned that while the papers were filled with stories of the Indian wars, the savages were themselves well removed from Philadelphia and New York. She therefore assented willingly to Mr. Rogers' proposal to have her luggage transported to Kensington by van.

Philippe, whose hearty handshake came after the end of his aunt's long and fervid greeting, had already arranged by correspondence for his accommodation. He was to stay at the Globe, the tremendous new hotel which had been built opposite the Exposition grounds. After it was agreed that he would repair to the Rogers home for dinner, he departed for West Philadelphia by hackney, accompanied by Céleste, the older maid, while Mr. Rogers and Zena drove toward Kensington with Denise, the younger maid, alone with the jewel case in the back seat of the carriage.

Mr. Rogers acted as announcer of points of interest; to the accompaniment of the steady, rhythmic clop of Mr. Quinby's pace he gave his companion, as well as the pedestrians on the sidewalks, a description and a history of each landmark. He was proud of Philadelphia, with its narrow streets, red-brick houses and pavements, and well-scrubbed white steps at the doors. "The city of homes, by Harry," he proclaimed to all and sundry on Arch Street. He pointed out the shopping and theatrical section on Eighth Street—"Even New York hasn't much on our shops"—and the beautiful park of Franklin Square, surrounded by the large comfortable homes of the well-to-do. "I don't believe in Paris you would find a nicer park—with greener grass."

Zena held to his arm. "The grass is green, beautifully green," she murmured, while her thoughts were turned toward her sister. Such beautiful children—and such a husband. Why hadn't she ever met a man like this, who could sweep her off her feet, make her forget practical considerations?

Instead of turning up Second Street, Mr. Rogers drove over to the river, explaining the fascination it had for him. "Up this way is where the Rogers fleet used to come in. I suppose shipowning blood still runs in my veins, for there's nothing I like better than the sight of a vessel outward bound."

It was a noble river, the Delaware, however marred by piers and warehouses, lofty masts and smoking funnels, all the gear and paraphernalia of shipping. Zena was really

217

moved, and her voice shook as she observed the grandeur of the flood.

"I don't think you appreciate your rivers. In Europe they are prized for their beauty as much as their utility, and everything is done to make them as handsome as possible. Here in America people are so practical. This bank should be a well-paved, wide avenue instead of a rutty, uncared-for street, and elegant homes should line it, to take advantage of the vista. Imagine, all this filth and squalor beside the majesty of that stream!"

"Oh, I don't know. We are a practical people, as you say. All the elegant houses in the world wouldn't send a single ship across the Atlantic. We admire a beauty of our own. For instance, the bow of that ship yonder, overshadowing the street, is more beautiful than a wide avenue, and pays higher dividends, too."

Zena was not disposed to argue. It was much nicer to sit back in the comfortable upholstery of the carriage and be overwhelmed by her brother-in-law's voice and presence. "Oh, you businessmen," she breathed, and he felt like a combination of Jim Fisk and old Commodore Vanderbilt himself. He had never met a woman who set him up so! He clicked to Mr. Quinby, and found an outlet for his exhilaration in the speed with which the horse raced toward home over the last broad stretch of East Girard Avenue.

2

Dinner that evening was one that the family recalled with the greatest pleasure for years afterward. A midday meal was out of the question, so for this occasion of welcoming Aunt Zena and Philippe to Philadelphia, Mr. Rogers slept in the afternoon and dinner was set for its old hour.

218

Mrs. Rogers and the servants worked all day preparing the meal. It was to be a typically Philadelphia repast, and more elaborate than the hostess usually attempted. April was the last of the "R" months, so there could still be oysters, and a whole bag of them had been shucked and were "fattening" in the shed. There was to be pepper pot, and the long sheets of creamy white tripe were cleaned and boiled, ready to be diced along with the necessary potatoes and onions. Snapping turtles had been bought at a yard on Kensington Avenue, and Mrs. Rogers butchered the creatures and removed the flesh from their shells, because both Mary and Martha professed to be frightened of the reptiles and their savage beaks.

She also prepared the hors d'œuvres with an artistry equal to that of the finest chef. She arranged tempting, dainty strips of herring, cut from the fattest of the delicately smoked fish for which Kensington was famous. She took cottage cheese, "schmierkäse," as it was called by the old Pennsylvania Dutch farmer who sold it in the Spring Garden market. This she rolled in little balls and sprinkled with paprika. There were deviled eggs flavored with mustard. Recourse was had to the stock of various condiments which stood in jars in the cellar, and the platters were completed with pickled Jerusalem artichoke—dug last fall from the tangle of them at the foot of the garden—and the tiny pearl onions that were her special pride.

Of course, as it was in the Easter season, the pièce de résistance was ham—and such a ham! All the markets had been scoured to procure one of sufficient size, and cured and hickory-smoked to Mrs. Rogers' satisfaction. It was to be baked and sauced after a recipe she had inherited from her father. The sauce had a basis of white wine, and was garnished with sultana raisins. When the preparations were completed, and Mrs. Rogers felt that she could safely join the family, she gave last-minute instructions to both servants.

"Mind, now, the snapper must have plenty of sherry, and don't put it in till the very last moment. And you understand the courses? If you make a mistake, either of you, out you go, and I'll get servants I can depend on. After the hors d'œuvres—those things on the platters—serve the oysters, and then the peppery pot, and mind it *is* to be piping hot! I wager Zena never tasted anything better than good peppery pot—and then the scrapple. I never heard of anyone's having scrapple for dinner, but it's delicious, and I intend to serve it as a kind of entree. I want the slices cut thin and uniform, mind you, Mary. None of your ordinary Irish slapdash business." She turned a warning glance on the old woman. "They're to be rolled in bread crumbs and dropped in the fat when it's good and hot."

Martha, who had prepared the typical Philadelphia dish in this way for many years, answered with a series of bored "Yes, mums," but she looked rather startled when her mistress said, "And just put one slice in the center of each plate, and a spoonful of apple butter on top."

"Apple butter on the scrapple, mum?" she questioned.

"Yes, it will be real tasty that way, I know." She thought for a minute. "There ought to be something to set off the dish a little. I know—doilies. Put one of those little round doilies Miss Julia made—you know the ones I mean—put one of them on each plate, and then the scrapple on it, right in the center, and mind it is good and brown, but not burnt and not greasy—and then a dab of apple butter, and don't smear it."

Martha shook her head slowly, and thought, "The missus is goin' raving crazy over this sister of hers," but the action was interpreted as assurance that the scrapple would be right.

"Then the snapper, and then the ham, and then the ice cream. . . . And mind you, Mary, if you dare to steal so much as a taste until we've all eaten, I'll know about it. . . . And don't serve the coffee until last, no matter how much Father bellows for it beforetimes. My sister is used to the very best, and I intend to show her this once that we know how things ought to be done, even if we don't always do them."

The meal went off quite as well as planned, without a single hitch. Zena exclaimed in delight at everything. The artistic arrangement of the hors d'œuvres overwhelmed her, and earned the warmest praise from Mr. Rogers, who was in the most expansive mood possible. The cottage cheese was new to Zena, as were the pickled artichoke roots. The oysters were wonderfully thick and fat, and better than the meager little shellfish of Europe; the family called for them again and again from a seemingly inexhaustible supply.

Philippe was astounded at the richness of the fare. Excepting for the famous, and also expensive, restaurants like Delmonico's, he had found American food sadly lacking in imagination and variety. The piquant flavors of the hors d'œuvres and the lusciousness of the oysters had already sharpened his appetite and increased his amiability until it was second only to his host's. "Jove, what oysters!" he cried after his plate had been refilled with the third half-dozen by the excited Mary, who accepted each compliment to the food as a personal commendation.

Mr. Rogers guessed the kind of soup before he had eaten the last of his oysters. He suddenly lifted his head and sniffed, and a beatific expression transfigured his face. "Peppery pot, by the Lord Harry—real Philadelphia peppery pot!" he shouted. "Wait until you taste this, Zena—nothing like it in France, I swear."

Aunt Zena entered into the gustatory spirit of the occasion. The dishes were so different! They piqued a bored and jaded appetite, and she pronounced the pepper pot delicious.

"Downtown, and in parts of Kensington as well, for that matter, men come around through the streets selling peppery pot," Mr. Rogers explained between spoonfuls. "They have a peculiar cry." He began an imitation of the well-known long-drawn-out cry of the pepper-pot sellers, standing up to do so. "Pe-e-e-epp'ry-y-y-y *pot,* pi-i-ipi-i-ing *hot.*" He repeated the cry several times, lifting his head so that his beard jutted out aggressively, and allowing his voice to float heavenward. Because of the power of his lungs, he would have been certain of success in the pepper-pot field, although in the dining room the effort was somewhat hard on eardrums. He was roundly applauded, and launched into a dissertation, with appropriate imitations, on the cries of other Philadelphia street venders, of the past and the present.

At another time, Mrs. Rogers would have been annoyed by an interruption to a carefully planned meal, but she realized that the performance which her husband now began served several purposes besides that of entertainment. The size and elaborateness of the meal was a severe strain on the facilities of the kitchen, and the delay allowed Martha to catch up. Also, the fun and interest the guests of honor found in the show gave them a chance to recuperate for further assaults upon a long and heavy meal.

As Mr. Rogers progressed with his imitations, they became more ambitious. He walked all the way around the table, with back bent over and one shoulder depressed, pretending to carry clothes props while he sang out "Clo-o-o-o-'es pra-a-*aps*." He trundled an imaginary wagon as the fish 'n' chips man. An appreciative audience listened as he ran through a long repertoire. He was, in turn, the old-clothes man and the catfish peddler, the deviled crab and horseradish venders, as he cracked the plaster with their time-honored and distinctive cries. Aunt Zena was crying real tears of amusement, while Philippe shouted "Bravo!" over and over. The twins were convulsed, Teresina smiled, and Julia clapped frantic applause. Mary forgot entirely to remove the pepper-pot plates, and stood watching while she thought, "Ain't *he* a one—*ain't* he a one!"

Mrs. Rogers sat back, enjoying the success of her undertaking and the pleasure everyone was having in the antics of her husband. "I declare, Jesse is a case," she told herself.

She also noticed that the attentions of her daughters toward their male guest were having an effect. His stiff English conventionality and surface Gallic gallantry were giving way to a perfectly natural animation. Yes, both daughters were making headway, and she was quite as satisfied with them as with her culinary achievements. There was no doubt about it, Julia was gaining weight now that she was eating heartily, and Teresina had need to look to her laurels.

The entree, Mrs. Rogers' inspirational combination of scrapple and apple butter, was hailed as a work of genius. "Really, it should receive a name in French, and be entered in culinary literature," Philippe proposed when he was told that this combination of two Philadelphia products was of Mrs. Rogers' invention. "But what would be the French for scrapple?"

When everyone confessed ignorance, Mr. Rogers shouted: "At least we can give it a foreign-sounding name —if a good American one, which suits me, won't do for posterity. How about 'panhaus'? That's what the countryfolk upstate call it."

"Capital! 'Panhaus à l'Augustina' sounds excellent to me," Philippe rejoined. "I shall inscribe a letter to the Academy at once, and describe the new masterpiece and its official title."

The stewed turtle met with quite as much acclaim. It was a purely Kensingtonian dish, little known in other parts of Philadelphia. Aunt Zena delivered an opinion that it was immeasurably better than any other turtle dish she had ever eaten, with one exception, some green turtle they had tasted, years ago, in New Orleans.

"Don't you remember, Tina? Father took us to an old French place. We were traveling incognito at the time, but Father divulged his title, and they made the most extravagant fuss over us—and prepared this perfectly heavenly dish. I can't say it was better than this, but it was as good."

Mrs. Rogers recalled the incident perfectly, and embroidered on the remembrance a pattern of accompanying incident that made the poor nobleman's wanderings with his marriageable daughters seem like a most romantic odyssey.

While everything in the dining room continued in the best possible mood, trouble developed in the kitchen which was not to be completely dissipated during the length of Aunt Teresina's stay. Denise, her only maid since Céleste had been detailed to care for Philippe, was a dumpy woman of about fifty, and extremely conscious of her rights as a free Frenchwoman.

She entered the kitchen and took the chair from under the cook's table. Martha eschewed chairs while she was working, as a matter of principle ("How a body can cook, sittin' down, beats me"), but she was annoyed to see another woman, also a servant, occupy it while she was busy. Furthermore, although Denise did not speak English, she knew another language which all women understand—the Esperanto of the lifted eyebrow, the sneer that masquerades as a smile, the stare of disapproval, and the shrug of disdain.

Martha did not cook in the French fashion, so every operation was commented upon in this silent but expressive medium, and long before the ham was served Martha was in such a rage that the clattering of her utensils became audible in the dining room.

Mrs. Rogers understood the meaning of the noise, but was unaware of its cause. "Martha's in a pet about something," she thought, even as she accepted further tributes to her meal with her politest, most gratified smile. "Martha's in a pet, and heaven knows why. She seemed as interested as I was in having the dinner, and now, because it's a little more work than she bargained for, she's gone cantankerous."

The family was spared a violent eruption which might have marred an otherwise perfect meal when the cook discovered that Denise could not understand her. She used as a safety valve for her mounting anger an almost continuous commentary accompanied by the forceful movement of pots and pans.

"What does she think *she* is?" (Bang of roasting pan) "She's no better than us, and sittin' there on my chair like a queen on a throne—and a foreigner at that!" (Furious beating of mixing spoon against iron bowl) "She might at least turn in and offer to help a bit, even if I wouldn't have her messin' her dirty French hands in my things, but no, there she sits, and us workin' like troopers!"

For odd moments she forgot her plaints, when Mary, in high glee, reported in a stage whisper the triumphant progress of the meal. "Tender as a woman's heart, the mister said the ham was." Her whisper hissed between her bare gums like escaping steam, and a moment later, when there was time to be more confidential: "Young master Philip—I calls him Philip, and none of your fille-e-p —if he eats another bit he'll burst. Well, he won't be eatin' ice cream, that's sure, and it'll mean so much more for *us* if *she* ain't in a mean mood, and decides to save it."

The crowning satisfaction for Martha was when Mary, like an archconspirator, whispered in her ear: "The missus's sister asked for the receipt for the sauce with them white raisins in it, and the missus says, real biggity, 'You'll have to ask Martha,' she says. 'It's a prize receipt, but she might let you have it,' she says."

These pleasant tidings caused Martha's frown to relax, but in a moment she would be cutting across Denise's black, supercilious stare with another remark, aimed at the hurrying Mary. "Did you hear *her* sniff, then? Who does she think she is, sniffing at the way I do things? Let me tell you, she wouldn't last the week, working with the missus. Let her try and put up with *her* for twenty years, and she'd have something to sniff about. She'd be out on her ear before the end of the week."

After the family had finished, and had retired to the parlor for the pleasant digestion of their repast, the servants had their own feast in the kitchen. First of all, Martha put aside a portion of ham, a good quantity of the turtle stew, and a very small amount of ice cream—she shared Mary's passion for this latter delicacy, and allowed this to influence her judgment. These represented reasonable leftovers, which Mrs. Rogers would be sure to check. Everything that remained, and there was plenty, was set out in dish, platter, and tureen to be eaten. Denise was not backward in joining Martha and Mary as they helped themselves.

226

As they had hoped, there was plenty of ice cream. The Frenchwoman had no liking for this purely American dish, and watched in amazement and disdain as the other women engaged in a race to see who could consume the greater quantity of the snowy pile heaped up before them. In spite of their efforts, and they were valiant, there was still a quantity of food left over. At this juncture Lucius arrived, as nonchalantly as if he had not been waiting outside for this very moment. While both Mary and Martha pretended a tremendous disdain for him, and for Negroes in general, he was quickly dispatched with peppery pot, ham, and turtle enough for all his family.

"And not a word out of you to the missus. She'd be having fits if she knew I was giving you any of her victuals. And have the dishes back by morning, you thieving black rascal." Martha actually had no ill feeling toward the Negro, and always received his willing aid, but it was part of convention, inspired probably by years of "Uncle Tom" on the stage and in the printed word, that made her talk like a more beneficent than usual slave overseer—just as from a like habit she used her own kind of pigeon English to the Chinese laundryman. Certainly her tone or words aroused no animosity in Lucius, who ducked and grinned as she arranged the heaped-up dishes in an old market basket.

Chapter 5

PHILIPPE had to get on with his task. It seemed to him that all his time was spent in the Custom House. It was irritating that it required more time to clear the display under his charge, and transport it from New York to the Centennial grounds, than was needed for the whole voyage from France. He had talked to other exhibitors, and they were also angry and distressed at the methods and attitude of the American customs officials. There seemed to be a conspiracy afoot to prevent the Centennial from opening.

In the same hotel with him lived the members of the staff of the German exhibit. Philippe had made friends with his erstwhile enemies, and found them congenial and delightful fellows. They even discussed the battle of Sedan without rancor, but any mention of the battle of the Port of New York brought congested faces, angry words, and new accounts of the hungry insistence of the Treasury Department officials on taxes or bribes. Of course all the difficulty stemmed from the policy of the high tariff. It was a selfish and insular policy, they agreed. What would happen to trade and commerce if every nation erected around itself this barrier to normal business? Philippe could look into the future a little way, and see a world of separated, angry peoples, each shut in behind such restrictions.

Philippe was sure that eventually, if it were not checked, this new and vicious method of doing business would quicken the pace of wars and ill feeling between nations—right here and now, what incentive was there for any of the manufacturing countries of Europe to show their wares to America, when it would be almost impossible to sell anything here afterward? His thoughts continued in this vein as he prepared a fastidious toilet in preparation for another attempt at browbeating, cajoling, or bribing the customs officials. He gave himself over to a mood of irascible contemplation.

He hated Americans, and America. It was the people, though, more than the country. They were so smug about their republican institutions that were rotten with graft until they stank with corruption. They had no culture, and prided themselves on the lack of it. They were completely ignorant of the European civilization which they affected to despise. Their financial system was a shambles, and still they talked of the good old U.S. dollar. Imagine the time lost, and the annoyance, in checking and verifying every single banknote before accepting it, to be certain it was not a counterfeit or an issue from a bank that had long since failed! And yet Americans scorned the methods of European banking and currency.

In his mental survey of the country's faults Philippe next turned to the difficulty of adjusting the daily fluctuations of the dollar in terms of gold. He arranged his cravat with the necessary billowing folds of material, and impaled it with his pin of carved coral, while he considered this problem. Every time he spent a fifty-cent note—and such notes, crumpled, worn, filthily dirty, and carrying heaven alone knew what diseases—he had to make a mental calculation as to its value. Was his dollar that morning worth eighty-seven or eighty-nine cents? For his own pocket money he gave up making these calculations, but for his official expenditures they were important, and irritating.

He examined his beard carefully. It was in an amorphous state, a transitional period. For the moment he wondered if he had been wise to decide upon a change of style. The golden stubble that now covered his chin and cheeks beyond the line of his mutton chops was not yet long enough to give much indication of what the future effect might be, and meanwhile it was distressing to Philippe's complacency as a well-groomed man to appear in public barbered in a fashion that was no fashion at all. There was a flaw in the glass of his mirror, and he made various contortions to get a full and unobstructed reflection of his face.

That was another thing—no first-class hotel should have

a mirror like that. He felt most uncomfortable in this tremendous but impersonal and poorly run hostelry. As soon as he was done with those interminable custom matters he intended to find a respectable house near the Centennial grounds and go in residence. With Céleste to care for him, he should be able to manage without another servant. The hotel was another example of the way Americans did things. They had a passion for bigness, and little regard for quality or artistry. Everyone boasted that this hotel, the Globe, had a thousand rooms. It was a tremendous conception, a whole city under one roof, but the purpose of a hotel, to offer comfortable and homelike quarters, was defeated by its size.

The Centennial was to be the biggest exhibition ever held, and the newspapers made much of the fact that the Corliss engine which would furnish the power was the largest ever attempted. There was much disappointment when plans for a Main Building to cover more floor space than had ever before been placed under a single roof were given up for practical reasons. Quickly the boastful American mind adjusted itself, and the Main Building became the biggest *exhibition* building ever erected.

This passion for size extended to all kinds of things, Philippe found. Even urchins on the street seemed to take a special pride in a waterfall somewhere on the boundary with Canada, simply because it was, they claimed, the largest in the world. It came into the most casual conversations. Mr. Rogers had mentioned it, the other night at dinner. "You mustn't go home until you see Niagara Falls" —that was the name, Niagara Falls—"They're the largest falls in the world."

Philippe caught himself smiling as he remembered this. He could forgive Mr. Rogers his Americanisms, he was such a genuine person, robust and hearty, with an over-developed sense of humor, perhaps, but he could be keen at times, and discerning. He was the only American Philippe had met who could see other than his own side of a question. This tremendous partisanship was another characteristic that annoyed and distressed him. It made the most ordinary conversations difficult. To anyone who had led a life similar to his own, dividing his time between England and the Continent, this narrowness of viewpoint was particularly disconcerting. He realized there was nothing all black, or all white, in European politics, but here sympathies determined the logic of history in most confusing fashion. Americans as a people sympathized with the French, partly because they had lost the war, and he suspected also because in the process the Empire had been succeeded by the Republic and there was a fellow feeling of democracy. He was amazed, however, to discover that over here everyone looked upon Germany as the aggressor and seemed to have no realization at all that the war had been due to the unhappy (and unwise, as it turned out) desire of the Emperor to recoup his fortunes and his reputation after the fiasco of his Mexican adventure with Maximilian.

They were simple people, these Americans, vulgar beyond his imaginings, with their constant tobacco-chewing and spitting, their boasting, their certainty that they were always in the right in any discussion, personal or national. But the American women were beautiful!

Following this more pleasant train of thought, Philippe left the hotel and caught a horsecar bound for the city. He did not notice that the progress of the vehicle was less speedy than the six miles an hour which was so boastfully advertised. Instead, he gave himself over to a consideration of the Rogers girls. They were beautiful. He believed he favored Teresina a trifle. She had a better figure, and she wore her clothes with an air. She was preposterously confident of herself for anyone who had never seen Paris, or even London. But, Philippe admitted while his feet dug in the straw of the horsecar floor to escape the spring chill still in the air, she would be a sensation on the Continent. New countries bred women with a freshness and a vitality that more than compensated for their lack of savoir-faire. Yes, it would be something worth striving for, to assault the maidenly bastions of Teresina Rogers, and have them leveled before his attack.

He understood already that he could never hope to dominate Teresina. There would always be one last inward fortress which would be impregnable. For a complete surrender he would do better to look to Julia. She was tender, quivering, passionate—and these qualities gave to her face an expression of charm her older sister lacked. If he were to accept Julia as his wife, he could reasonably expect life-long fidelity, subserviency to his wishes, and all the pleasure of compliant surrender. She was not so nobly proportioned as her sister, of course. Philippe was inclined to think of the female form in terms of bust, waist, and hips. There was little difference in the slenderness of the sisters' waists, but considerable in the other essentials.

On the other hand, Julia was several years younger. Perhaps Teresina's form was only a promise of what hers might yet be. . . . It was a difficult decision, in any case.

Philippe's practical nature asserted itself. He must have a talk with Zena, and see what preference she might have. And there was also the matter of a dot. While his own resources were ample, and little affected by the war, the increase of fortune through marriage was a very foundation stone of a strong civilization.

Although he had been a good hour on the way, he was surprised to see the noble steps and the simple, strong columns of the Custom House. As he rose from his seat he thought how well some provincial architect had caught the Grecian spirit, and then, as the horses slowed from a trot to a walk and the driver applied his brake lever, he sighed at the thought of having to brave again the rude Philadelphia officialdom.

2

Philippe had little opportunity to see his aunt, much less talk with her, until the very day before the Centennial opened. By this time he had given up all hope of having the French exhibit in readiness. He had lost to the U.S. Treasury Department! Furthermore, he had convinced himself that the American public was less interested in models of government buildings and products of the quarry and mine—which made up so much of the French governmental display—than it was in the most intimate or bizarre exhibits, or in those which appealed purely because of their size. "Show Americans the largest cow in the world and they would flock to see it," he thought bitterly.

He had lost all enthusiasm for his undertaking. The beautifully made models that would have entranced Frenchmen by the hour had been rudely appraised by officials. He had met nothing but obstacles and delays. Now that he knew definitely that it would be impossible to be ready in time, he arranged to meet Aunt Zena for the afternoon. She had some shopping to do, and he accompanied her through a city transformed within the last few days. Gay buntings hung everywhere, in every conceivable kind of arrangement, scalloped, rosetted, draped, or wound on façades, cornices, pillars, and standards. Hawkers crowded each other selling pennants of the city, lead badges of the Liberty Bell, maps, reduced prints of the cyclorama, and copies of the *Centennial March* written by the great Wagner, the *Centennial Hymn* composed by Whittier, the *Centennial Cantata* by Sidney Lanier.

The horse railroad down Chestnut Street was choked with traffic, and the pavements were filled with pedestrians so cosmopolitan in appearance one might imagine it was Paris. Aunt Zena entered fully into the festive spirit. While Philippe loved and enjoyed his aunt, he was always a little embarrassed by her exuberance. She waved frantically with her parasol at a passing corps of the Boston cadets, and shouted "*Vive la France!*" when someone displayed a French flag.

It proved too crowded for the carriage, and Lucius was dispatched to a livery stable, to pick them up at a later hour on less-congested Broad Street.

As they made their way up Chestnut Street, Aunt Zena adopted all the Italian and French mannerisms which would identify her as one of the visitors, and she used her nephew as a foil for arch glances, pretended reproaches, and simulated coquettish pouts and laughter, but all the time her black eyes were engaged in picking from the throng and appraising the qualities of the men who might appeal to her. There were many in uniform, Army officers, State Fencibles, members of the City Troop, officers of the National Guard. There were also a number of distinguished gentlemen in high felt hats, Prince Albert coats, and with varied and engaging styles of beard, who aroused her interest.

Philippe protested that his aunt's dress was entirely too handsome to be exposed to the throngs. Although her clothes were at times inclined to flamboyance, this street dress of alternating wide stripes of black and cerise was quite in the mode, and most stylish, Philippe thought. Aunt Zena shrugged away his objections. She had worn it several times before, and it did not matter. Besides, it was

234

comfortable for walking, as it had a comparatively short train, and although it did sweep along a considerable portion of the accumulated rubbish on the pavement, that was only the natural discomfort of dresses in general.

Philippe was amused by his aunt's flirtatious nature. Whenever a particularly fascinating gentleman or officer passed, there was a suddenly accelerated tempo to her walk, her conversation became more sprightly, and there was always some object in a shop window to be indicated with her parasol, and enthused about. Her shopping was not of a very serious nature. She bought all kinds of little trinkets, most of them expensive, to take back for the girls. Philippe deplored her taste in these, but knew better than to object. She glanced up at him suddenly, and remarked: "Philippe, my dear, I haven't seen you wearing a thing but that carved coral pin in your cravat, and it's hateful! Don't you have any others?"

Philippe instinctively fingered the pin. "Why, I always thought you liked it, Zena. You bought it for me yourself, long ago, don't you remember?"

"Of course I remember. I got it for you at a very tragic moment in my life—one that I'd rather forget. I bought it because it was like one a friend had—at least I thought he was a friend, but he betrayed me in the most odious manner." Aunt Zena's eyes filled with tears, and Philippe looked around in distress for a place to retire with her, but she shook her head. "No, no—I'm perfectly all right. But there's a jeweler here. I insist on buying you another pin immediately." They turned in at Caldwell's, just above Ninth Street, and in a little while emerged again, the coral pin relegated to Philippe's pocket, and a handsome large agate, at least an inch in diameter, nestling in the silken folds of his cravat. Aunt Zena was jubilant over the purchase. "This is so much more interesting. Did you notice the moss actually caught in the stone, Philippe? How infinitely more beautiful the handwork of nature than the mere craftsmanship of man!"

This elegantly phrased thought appealed to her, and she was also filled with satisfaction, and a little awe, that something so poetic and so profound should have occurred to her.

They had a late luncheon at the La Pierre House at Broad and Chestnut streets. Because of the noble breadth of Broad Street, and the nearness of the governmental buildings under construction where Market crossed it, the city this far west was almost as busy as nearer the center of things, around Eighth and Ninth streets. Indeed, both thought that Broad Street had more the character of a European city thoroughfare, especially with the beautiful Moorish domes of the recently built Alhambra Palace visible to the south.

At luncheon, Philippe was not long in broaching the matter uppermost in his thoughts. "Zena, I must confess to a serious interest in your nieces," he began, rubbing his hand over the new growth of beard on his chin.

Aunt Zena finished the claret in her glass in one draft, and motioned to the waiter to refill it. She gave a coy laugh, as if she were being proposed to. "Philippe, this is so sudden. I had no idea you gave either of the demure little dears a thought. Don't you think they are both too young to think of marriage?"

Philippe grinned. His aunt was delightful—a little on the vulgar side, and a little overfond of men perhaps, but delightful all the same. Not that the scandals concerning her had ever disturbed him. He had enjoyed the reflected glory of being the nephew of the notorious Countess Lascalles—and had profited from it. And she was certainly most understanding at a time like this.

"Oh, come now, Zena, you watched over me in New York like a hen over a lone chick, and I'm sure you didn't dispense with Céleste just so she would be able to take care of my laundry. I'm certain she makes a daily report to you on everything I do, and the hours I come in. Unless I misread the signs, it's the nieces you have in mind. You've made no effort to secure me for yourself."

It was Aunt Zena's turn to smile. "No, I know my own limitations. I must restrain myself to young men of forty or so. And you have behaved perfectly, my boy. Nothing has been reported to me which would give me a single gray hair. You have all the exemplary qualities of my late husband's family."

Philippe toyed with his own wineglass. "Joking aside, Zena, I am truly falling in love with your nieces. In many ways they are very much alike, you know, and I think it is the qualities in them that remind me of you that enamor me."

"Ah, my dear boy," Aunt Zena sighed, "why couldn't you have lived just one generation earlier, so I might have married you instead of your uncle?"

"You can picture the quandary I'm in. I hardly know how to direct my affections. Each fair niece has so much to commend her . . ."

"You don't know how happy you make me, Philippe. I've always hoped the Lascalles fortune would be reunited, and you and my nieces, my dear and only sister's children, would naturally be the ones to inherit my share. . . . Oh, I know what you are getting at well enough, and it is one of the qualities I admire in you, although I've been inclined myself to fall in love first and think of practical things later."

"My dear Aunt, if family traditions serve me rightly, you assured yourself of the future first, and then, when it was no longer a concern, you could allow love to take its course as frequently as you wished."

"Father—I wish you had known him, Philippe, he was a sage and good man, an Italian nobleman and all that the name implies—Father impressed upon us daughters the difficulties of impecunious young females in a man's world. . . . But enough of all this fencing. They are both attractive girls, and either one of them can make you happy, I am sure. I must confess Julia used to be a stick, but since she's seen you she has changed. That girl is in love with you, Philippe—really in love."

Philippe found himself slightly embarrassed, but a little complacent as well. He readjusted his new tie pin, which did not yet sit comfortably, and waited for his aunt to continue.

"Of course, Teresina is a stunner. She is almost exactly my image when I was her age. I had a little more fire, perhaps—and then of course I wasn't raised in such a dreary city. But Teresina would be a stunner anywhere, even in Paris. Then, too, she's my namesake, and I don't think I'm being unfair when I say I should prefer you to get her.

"On the other hand, I admire grit, and if I know Julia, she'll make a fight. You'll be fought over, Philippe, and you may end up by getting the girl with the strongest will, instead of the one you choose. I'll say this to you. I'll be quite generous with either girl in the matter of a dowry. My poor sister married a fine man—I've already learned to love Jesse dearly—but she's had a hard time of it financially. I've helped her out frequently with articles for the home, and furniture, and I had Julia educated, and for any dowry at all they would have to look to me, of course. And I'll come through. . . . Suppose we leave it at that."

238

This conversation Philippe reduced to its simplest terms. His aunt preferred her namesake, and the practical French part of his nature determined that there was no sense in losing further time. Besides, there were a couple of other suitors in the offing. There was the young medical student he had met, a nice fellow but not a rival to be feared. On the other hand, he had heard considerable mention of a young but prominent official, a state senator or something of the sort—he might be dangerous. It was unwise to be too self-assured where a fickle beauty was concerned. He decided then and there to accompany Aunt Zena back to Kensington and make an immediate engagement with Teresina for the theater or the concert—or perhaps the tableaux, which he had seen advertised and praised so extensively.

Chapter 6

THE PLEASANT rhythm of raindrops on the tin roof overhead had lulled Julia into a state of half-awakeness in which she realized that this was an important morning, but for some time the significance of the rain itself escaped her. But this was an important day! The day the Centennial opened, and they had tickets to hear the President make the opening speech and see the Emperor and Empress of Brazil. Now the weather would spoil it all!

She lay back in her cot and came close to crying. Things had not been going so well. Philippe had taken Zenie to the concert without her, and also had invited Zenie to view the great picture of "The Siege of Paris," in the Coliseum outside the Centennial grounds. And now for this to happen! It was no consolation to reflect that the rain would fall on everyone alike. It was a purely personal disaster.

She got up and dressed to the melancholy sound. When at last she descended to the dining room for breakfast, she was surprised to find the spirits of the others undaunted by the weather. Her father, who had sworn a hundred times that wild horses would not drag him to see the President, was already consulting his watch and planning a number of tentative schedules for the five-mile trip from Kensington to Fairmount Park. One timetable was based on using Mr. Quinby. A second provided for the substitution of Total Eclipse, a slower horse, but better able to stand a long day without attention. A third schedule provided for using hackneys.

Mr. Rogers sat at the table, his beard completely swathed in a napkin, and shouted, "Gussie, how long do you imagine it would take one of those hackney crowbaits to get over there?"

A flustered Mrs. Rogers stuck her head in at the door. "For the land sakes, Pet, this isn't the railroad. We'll leave in plenty of time, and no fussing and fuming if we don't stick to your old schedules."

He was undaunted, and with complete disregard for his napkin, shoved food in the general direction of his mouth with one hand while he computed theoretical passages of time with the other. Everyone else had breakfasted, and Mrs. Rogers, observing that Julia had not even dressed for the occasion, called to her:

"Good heavens, child! Dreaming up in that attic of yours again! I must move you down to the second floor when Zena goes, where I can keep my eye on you."

"It's raining—I didn't think we'd go in the rain."

"What? Your father wouldn't miss seeing President Grant for anything. He's hated him so all these years, I think he'd go just to hiss at him. Besides, it's clearing up."

"No, it isn't—it's still raining; I can hear it plainly."

"Tut, child, I just looked outside at the sky, and I ought to know. There's a big patch of blue showing right now. As your dear grandfather that you never knew used to say, 'If there's a patch of blue as big as a Dutchman's breeches, it will clear,' and this is bigger, many times bigger, I assure you."

Mr. Rogers snorted. "The rubbish with which your parent of blessed memory filled your head! And how did he proceed to measure the Dutchman's article of apparel, may I ask?"

At another time, Mrs. Rogers would have responded angrily to this remark and there would have been a scene in the making, but she chose to ignore it, and chided Julia all over again for her lateness.

In the end, Julia's tardiness worked to her advantage. The family had two sets of tickets in opposite sections of the stands. Harry Naylor had sent four tickets to Teresina, with a message that they were in a favored position, among Philadelphia and Pennsylvania officials with whom he himself would be seated in his senatorial capacity. Philippe had also received four tickets, and three of the family were to sit with him. These were in the part reserved for foreign exhibitors. It was here Teresina intended to sit, to be at Philippe's side, but Mr. Rogers planned otherwise. "We can't all go in the carriage, that's certain, so I'll take Teresina and the twins with me. They are all ready, and we'll leave now in a hackney. As soon as Julia is dressed, Lucius can drive you over behind Mr. Quinby. Now let me see —it's eight-thirteen now. Crowbait or no crowbait, we should be there by nine-thirty. It's up to you to hurry that darky along, Mother, and get off by eight-fifty."

Mrs. Rogers threw her hands in the air, and her curls

shook in agitation. "Jesse, if you insist on saying 'eight-fifty' when you mean quarter of nine or something, you might as well hold your breath. I can't add and subtract that fast, and that is all there is to it. Besides, I won't be rushed. I'll get there as soon as I can, and if I don't hear President Grant, from what you say I haven't missed much."

Teresina realized the futility of crossing her father, but her thoughts were wicked as they set out by hired coach. It was giving Julia an advantage of which that sneak of a sister would make the most.

Meanwhile, Mrs. Rogers had an idea. "You know, Zena, I think Father clean forgot they are running trains from Richmond Street station right into the Centennial grounds. . . . What do you say we have Lucius drive us there, instead of all the way to West Philadelphia? It will save Mr. Quinby, and I think it will be much more comfortable, besides."

Her planning was more successful than her husband's. The West Philadelphia roads were deep in mud from the rain, and the hackney mired twice en route, so that Mr. Rogers and the children missed the great Richard Wagner march, and the entrance of the President and his party. The train, which did not depart until nine, deposited Julia, her mother, and her aunt on the grounds well in advance of the whole ceremony.

It made a gay sight for old-fashioned Philadelphia, the many-colored pennants, the marching Guardsmen, the display of bunting, and the multitude of people. Above all, the multitude of people, of the most varied types, from turbaned Orientals to rough gold-miners just in from the West.

They couldn't pick out Mr. Rogers and the other children, although even Aunt Zena kept an eager watch for

242

the towering form of her brother-in-law, and Mrs. Rogers expected at any moment to see the twins disrupt the ceremony. The crowd was terrific! Only Aunt Zena's imposing appearance enabled them to reach their own seats. She wore her purple velvet dress, with bonnet and feather to match, and the throng opened before her as if she were the Brazilian Empress herself.

Philippe found them, and, oh, the pleasure for Julia to have him next to her without Zenie on the opposite side! She almost swooned with delight. They were alone at last. Not one of the hundred thousand people around them counted at all.

As for Mrs. Rogers, she intended to remind her husband that her prognostication concerning the weather had been correct. It had stopped raining completely—that proved her father's teaching. In matters of weather, Dutchmen's breeches were important, and Jesse would have to admit it!

2

Mr. Rogers twisted around on his chair impatiently, and strained to hear what was being said. Finally, to an accompaniment of angry sh-sh's all around him, he declaimed:

"If I was making a speech, I'd open my mouth good and wide and say what I have to say, instead of reading it from a paper. Did Daniel Webster sneak out penciled notes when *he* spoke? Did Patrick Henry mumble in his beard as he read his immortal words from a paper chit? They did not! They stood on their own two feet and orated! *By the Lord Harry, I can't hear!*"

No one else in that tremendous audience heard more clearly than Mr. Rogers, but the rest listened with better grace. In fact, many of the politicians surrounding them— confreres of Harry Naylor, who waved from a little distance

243

—seemed relieved that they could not hear what was said. Nevertheless, they glanced reproachfully as Mr. Rogers bellowed his complaints. Teresina was mortified, and when he became louder than usual, she jabbed at him with an ineffectual elbow.

The twins spent their time debating whether the ordinary-looking man in black could really be the Emperor of Brazil. The Emperor of Brazil! What a romantic name! That couldn't be the fabulous Dom Pedro!

Of course that was the Empress, in her handsome lavender silk, white satin bonnet, and lace shawl. She looked her part! It was too bad the Emperor hadn't worn a crown, one set with rubies, or emeralds, to make him look less like a greengrocer.

Between speeches there was music. Theodore Thomas's orchestra was a Philadelphia institution, with a hall up on Master Street, and because it was theirs, the local people thought it was the best in the world. They sat back complacently, as if to say, "Now let these poor strangers hear some really good music!"

Alas, though Mr. Thomas directed frantically and the bows scraped in unison and the cellists did their stately dance by their instruments, the music could not compete with the impatient rustle of the tremendous audience.

"I like a brass band," Mr. Rogers announced to the world, and added the irrefutable argument, "You can hear it!"

As he and his children arrived late, he did not see the President enter, and tried to pick him from among the large group on the platform. Had he taken ill at the last moment? Surely he wouldn't be late otherwise, on so important an occasion—unless the Presidential party had mired in the mud. This thought occasioned a smile. General Grant and his party had been mired in the mud for a long time!

244

Gradually realization came. Among all those important-looking, if pompous and self-satisfied, individuals there sat a seedy, graying, ineffectual-appearing man who spoke from time to time to the heavy gentleman at his side. That man was the President! His beard looked moth-eaten, and he had a worried air. It was natural he should be worried, with his Secretary of War but recently indicted, and his friends and relatives involved in scandals that might at any moment drag him into disgrace. This was the man the populace loved! What queer people the American public choose for their heroes! No man in the history of the country had made so many mistakes as this President, but he still commanded the wholehearted support of a majority of the voters of the country.

Now that Mr. Rogers saw Ulysses S. Grant, instead of hating him, as he had done for so long, he felt merely an overwhelming pity. This was the poor, weak vessel into which the American people had poured their affection! This was the man so lacking in imagination that he could allow the youthful blood of America to be wasted like water on a dozen battlefields without realizing the enormity of his crimes, or fearing their consequences. And this prodigality of others' blood had made a hero of him. The hero of the war! Who was the hero, he who directed, or those who charged? Now that he saw the man, Mr. Rogers knew. "Butcher Grant," his men had called him—from the depths of his Quaker heritage he loathed what the man stood for. But he realized now that any man who accepts the responsibility of the deaths of his fellows meets a day of reckoning. President Grant paid no attention to the delirious applause that greeted him when at last he stood up; as he spoke a few words—also from a paper, held in trembling fingers—his eyes looked beyond the crowds, into a private hell of his own.

245

The Centennial was declared open, although none could hear the words of the Chief Executive, and four thousand officials and dignitaries joined the line behind the President and Mrs. Grant, Dom Pedro and his Empress, and walked toward the Main Building and the great engine. The largest engine in the world, to power the largest exhibition that had ever been held, in the greatest country that had ever been! As the President threw the lever that started the towering steam engine, it was a truly symbolic action to begin the second hundred years of the nation.

"Well, Zenie, I'm hungry. Let's get a snack to eat," Mr. Rogers proposed, after the ceremony of starting the engine had been duly watched. They tramped through the mud from one refreshment stand to another. Sold out! "Not even a dish of ice cream?" Mr. Rogers asked plaintively, and received a shake of the head in answer. He would have received little consolation, probably, in learning that at that moment the President and the Emperor were engaged in the same vain quest. The first day of the Centennial had been a sellout!

3

It was almost as thrilling to read about the Centennial in the newspapers as to have been there. Of Philadelphia's eighteen papers, the *Press* had by far the most comprehensive accounts, Mr. Rogers thought. It reported the ceremonies from all kinds of viewpoints, masculine and feminine, lay and clerical; from inside and outside the grounds. There were human-interest stories, and the tale of the fire engine that got caught in the mud while answering a call in the grounds—some untutored visitor had pulled the fire alarm by mistake. There was much of the doings of the Emperor and Empress, and how truly democratic they really were in spite of their titles, and how their beautiful Brazilian ladies in waiting curtsied when they passed. In fact, each Lord, Lady, Duke, Count, or Prince who had attended the opening day, or who could be mentioned in connection with it, came in for recognition.

Mr. Rogers, who read the paper aloud to the assembled family, expressed disapproval for this catering to aristocracy and nobility by a series of grunts and the refusal to mention their names. Ordinarily neither his wife nor the children cared very much about the newspaper, but this morning they listened with close attention, for they knew it would be hours before their husband and father would relinquish it, and they did want to know all the things that had happened which they had been unable to see. It was most annoying when he read, "Lord and Lady Hoity-toity . . . hu-u-u-rmph . . . of the English Legation, came from Washington . . ." But all of his listeners knew there was no use in interrupting.

Aunt Zena joined them. She had been quite tired by the excitement of the previous day, and Denise had taken breakfast up to her. Mr. Rogers scrambled to his feet in a gesture of politeness he rarely bothered about. "I've been reading to the family the remarks of the press regarding the inauguration of the Centennial yesterday. Perhaps you would also care to listen?"

"Why, Jesse, I would love to. You read beautifully— with such expression." Aunt Zena, in a house dress and corsets less constricted than her usual ones, subsided comfortably into the chair nearest her brother-in-law.

It was strange to have been there, among all that multitude, and then to learn of so many occurrences of which they knew nothing. The difficulty over admissions, for instance. The Commissioners in charge had insisted that nothing would be accepted for admission but a fifty-cent note. The couple who tendered a dollar bill and the man who presented two twenty-five-cent notes were alike denied entrance, and referred to the special booths set up for change-making. Rather than brave the long lines waiting at the windows of these places, many patronized the speculators who sold fifty-cent notes at a handsome premium. Several near-riots had resulted among the disgruntled throng.

The Rogerses had missed this annoyance because of their complimentary tickets, and were inclined to feel smug about the matter. As enjoyers of special privilege they sided with the officials who had denied it to others.

Then the counting mechanism at the turnstiles had broken down. This gave the newspapers a chance to claim that at least a quarter of a million people must have been in the audience to hear the President. In another section of the paper was an interview with General Grant himself, in which he gave it as his opinion that there were seventy or eighty thousand present, but this was ascribed to his own modesty. The looseness in mathematics annoyed Mr. Rogers excessively.

"There was bad management somewhere, and I know what the difficulty was. The Republicans counted admissions the way they count votes, by fraud and deception. I can't wait until November, when the whole thieving crew will be swept from office."

After he finished reading through it, the family agreed that the most interesting piece in the paper was that written by Colonel Forney, the editor.[1] His article described a dream in which an old man came to his editorial chair in the *Press* office at Seventh and Chestnut streets. The visitor had lived a hundred years into the future, instead

[1] *Philadelphia Press*, May 11, 1876.

of into the past, and he described the history of the next century, to May 10, 1976, in considerable and engaging detail.

"Ha! This is good!" Mr. Rogers shouted. "You can't beat Colonel Forney for running a clever newspaper. Listen to this.

"He predicts the Mexicans will apply for admission into the Union by 1880, and that three years later Canada will follow. I wouldn't be surprised if he were right, either. And listen—when Queen Victoria dies, Great Britain is going to become a republic, with the Prince of Wales as the first President. What an imagination! I tell you, I'd like to put this paper away for a hundred years, and see how close it hits the nail on the head. Not far off, I predict."

"I declare, that doesn't interest me so much," Mrs. Rogers interrupted. "They got rid of the Emperor in France, and we live just the same here as we've always done. . . . And I don't see what good Mexico is—nothing but a lot of Indians."

But Aunt Zena was dismayed. "Another republic in England! What is the world coming to? Next Russia will be losing the Czar!"

Mr. Rogers (and Colonel Forney) reassured her. "No, Zena, that is one country you won't have to worry about. No revolution there. Perhaps you will go there to live. The Czar will be as strongly entrenched as ever. In fact, he is the only monarch who will still rule."

Aunt Zena pursed her lips and nodded. "I'm glad of that, anyway. And it proves what I've always said. In Russia they know how to handle the rabble. The Napoleons always catered to the working people, and what did it get them?"

Mr. Rogers read on a couple of lines, mumbling the

249

words in his beard and then repeating the gist of them aloud. He shook his head. "Here's something I don't hold with, but Forney was always a lady's man. He says there'll be a woman President in nineteen hundred, when women get the right to vote. Women voting, bah!"

The idea of voting herself would never have occurred to Mrs. Rogers, but she resented her husband's tone and observed acidly: "I've listened to you complain for twenty years or more what a mess men have made of things. Women couldn't do worse, and they might do a lot better —so there!"

It was an issue better avoided, and Mr. Rogers went on: "We are to have four colored states, South Carolina, Mississippi, Louisiana, and Alabama, where all the freed Negroes will live, and their schools and institutions will be amongst the best in the country, and renowned through the whole world."

At this juncture, Moody and Sankey, recently fed by Mary, romped into the parlor with their peculiar seesaw gallop, and made the rounds of the family, sniffing at feet and ankles, until they reached Georgina, seated on her favorite article of furniture, the cricket. They jumped up immediately, one to each side of her, on the velvet-upholstered seat. At another time, Mr. Rogers would have used the occasion to reprove the dogs, but he was enjoying the audience of his interested family too much to make a digression. Then he read a paragraph which caused him to really explode—with laughter, and not indignation, but the volume of noise was comparable, and the blast sent the little animals scurrying.

"Talk about the devil and he is sure to appear." It was quickly evident his quotation was not altogether apropos, but no one questioned it. "Listen to this—Moody and Sankey, the evangelists, are going to China and will convert so many of the heathen to Methodism there will be as many Christians in that benighted land as there are followers of the heathen joss." He shook his head admiringly. "He's thought of everything, and he closes with this interesting scientific note. The Keeley motor proves a complete success. For your information, Zena, the company backing it has offices in Philadelphia. I've always insisted it is a marvelous invention, and this verifies my judgment. It runs without the use of steam, or other power, through some alchemy of air and water. If the editor is right, and I believe he is, it would make a good investment. He says here that in the century to come it will be adapted to uses as diverse as running the trains and heating houses without the use of coal."

Mrs. Rogers looked disturbed. "Good grief, and just when I got Henry into the coal business! You might know something like this would happen." The words were out— she stopped aghast. She felt only relief when her husband gave her a reproving glance, and pontificated:

"It will be years until the Keeley motor reaches this stage of refinement. When I suggested to Henry that coal was a profitable business for him to enter, I made the decision because there are kinks in the perpetual motion machine— with which I am familiar—and it will be some time before they are all ironed out."

To divert his attention from the unfortunate subject, Mrs. Rogers spoke up effusively. "Gene has been practicing the *Centennial Cantata*, Father. She plays it real pretty, and I think this is a good time for us all to hear her. Run to the piano and play it for us, child."

Ordinarily Georgina would have required no coaxing to perform—she shared her father's love for an audience—but this morning she was obstinate. "Oh, Mother, I don't feel like it, and besides, I don't play it good enough."

251

"Nonsense, you play it beautifully. I heard you—and you sang the words, too. They are extremely elegant and poetic."

Georgina was obdurate. "I just don't feel like playing."

"If she doesn't feel like playing, let her alone. I'm sure she will favor us some other time," Mr. Rogers suggested, but by now his wife had worked herself into a temper in which the original reason for her request no longer mattered. She was angry at being crossed. "Gene is a most obstinate child," she thought, while her voice took on a strained quality which the family had long since come to recognize and fear. Aloud she said:

"Here we spend fifty cents every week for music lessons for that girl, and a whole fortune besides for pieces, and she won't play for us. No one would ever know she could play. You would think money grew on trees, the way it is wasted around here on ungrateful children."

As a matter of fact, the house was often filled with the noise of Georgina's banging, but no one attempted to controvert Mrs. Rogers in such a mood. Aunt Zena, who feared her sister's wrathy moments as much as anyone, avoided a further scene by adding her plea to her mother's. "Now, Gene," she coaxed pleasantly, "do play for your father, and for me too—I would love to hear you sing, and later in the day I want you to come up to my room. I have a gift for you I bought when I was shopping the other day."

This came dangerously close to bribing one of the children to be good, which was against Mr. Rogers' principles. However, he raised no objection as Georgina, with further apologies of a face-saving nature, descended on the piano, moved to each side the lamp brackets that graced its front, lifted the lid, adjusted and readjusted the square, red-plush-covered stool, and attacked full tilt the cantata they had heard the day before. The applause meant not only tribute

252

to Georgina's playing, but insistence that her qualms were out of place and her rendition perfect. It was so gratifying, in fact, that she required no further persuasion to sing the words, which she ranged through in credible fashion, particularly the exciting and highly melodramatic chorus:

> Mayflower, Mayflower, slowly hither flying,
>   Trembling westward o'er yon balking sea,
> Hearts within "Farewell, dear England," sighing;
>   Winds without "But dear in vain" replying,
> Gray-lipped waves about thee shouted, crying,
>   "No, it shall not be!"

The last lines, beginning "Gray-lipped waves," she sang at the very top of her voice, as befitting a marine tempest, and accompanied herself with thunderous chords. It was very well received indeed, although Mr. Rogers, who preferred simpler and more intimate and personal pathos in his songs, felt forced to add, "It's very stirring, I'll be bound, but by Christopher, I'd like to know what it means!"

Chapter 7

*L*IKE everything else connected with the Centennial, Philadelphia's span-new theater, the Alhambra Palace, was late in getting finished, and did not open its doors until weeks after the scheduled time. Teresina received invitations to the first night from all three of her suitors. Gus she refused flatly. She put off Henry Naylor with an ambiguous "We'll see, and besides, Father says it will never open, the rate it's going." Philippe she accepted.

After several disappointments, the event was to take place tonight. The formal opening was to be made by the Mayor,

253

so Teresina decided to wear the evening dress her aunt had purchased in New York, and which she had been saving for an occasion. She also wheedled her doting relative into lending her Denise. The maid, who was ordinarily sulky and distant with the Rogers family, responded enthusiastically to this drafting of her services. Her Gallic love of beauty and clothes saw an opportunity to wed the two in a perfect match.

Teresina was glad she had all new underthings, for she would have been embarrassed to have had the maid view the coarse but practical garments that had served her well enough before her aunt's coming. The gas burners were at their bluest, to give the maximum of light, and she felt a little nervous and testy as she washed, preparatory to calling the Frenchwoman. She consoled herself with the thought that Philippe was courting her quite assiduously. He spent almost every evening at the house, and had taken her out a number of times, to the tableaux, to a concert, and twice to the minstrels, of which he proved inordinately fond.

"Poor Julia," she thought, "the silly little goose had a nerve to think she could get him away from me. . . . Well, she knows better by this time. He's hardly looked at her for weeks. She's mad as hops about it, too, but the little sneak doesn't let on. She just tries to look sweet and angelic—and it takes more than an angel to get a man like Philippe. I know how to handle him. I never allow him to presume for a single moment that I'm interested. I've mentioned Harry Naylor to him often enough so he knows he's not the only pebble on the beach. All he'd have to do is whistle, and *she* would fall in his arms, but not me."

Evenings were still inclined to be cool, although it was late May, and Teresina pulled on the elegant combed lisle underwear her aunt had purchased for her. Her modesty rebelled at being seen completely nude in the presence of the servant, but the close-fitting knit garments enhanced her figure, if anything, and she still felt qualms as she called for her.

Denise's frank, openly admiring remarks actually caused her to blush, but the maid assisted with her drawers as if she had not noticed. These were Teresina's special pride, by far the loveliest she had ever had. They were of sheerest lawn, trimmed with lace inserts and ruffles, while dainty red ribbons ran under the insertions and tied in bows at the side.

Her corsets carried a similar trimming of lace. They had the new straight-front effect, which was just coming in style, and it required all of Denise's strength, and her own fortitude, to get them laced to the degree of slimness she wished to achieve. As Teresina's hips were already of fashionable proportions, it required no more than a narrow pad of horsehair—one of the so-called figure-improvers— to add the necessary bustle effect to the rear elevation. A short flannel petticoat for warmth, and another whaleboned one to form a foundation for her dress, the donning of a delicate underchemise also trimmed with red ribbons, and she was ready for the final ordeal of putting on the dress. First of all, she examined her reflection in the mirror, twisting herself as she did so, to make sure there were no wrinkles or bumps that were not supposed to be there. The eagle-eyed Denise found several which she had missed, and repeated over and over in French words that would have gratified Teresina had she understood them: "Mademoiselle is beautiful. Mademoiselle is chic. Mademoiselle ravishes one." In her own way, Denise could be extremely sentimental, and now she thought: "Oh, if Monsieur Philippe could only see this little pigeon now. He would be beyond restraint. He would eat her up so—pouf!"

Suddenly, Denise stopped in the midst of her duties and, with a secretive gesture, departed like a conspirator. Teresina heard her footsteps go along the hall, and in a moment return, with others keeping pace behind them. She had run to summon Aunt Zena, of course, but that was not all. After her aunt had screamed with delight, "Zenie, you are absolutely the most beautiful thing I have ever laid eyes on!" and then had critically examined the cut and quality of the various garments for which her money had paid, she said:

"Oh—I have a little surprise for you. Some trifles I picked up the other day. Get them, Denise."

Evidently the gifts had been hidden outside the door, awaiting this moment, for the maid was back in a second with two packages, which she handed to Teresina. "Stockings and garters," Teresina thought, feeling the shapes of the packages, but she opened them with pretended excitement, allowing her fingers to tremble as she picked at the cords. Aunt Zena really enjoyed the moment, and felt an urge to take the packages herself and undo them.

"Oh, Zenie, do hurry—I'm so excited to know how you like them. They are just little things I picked up the other day, but I do want you to think they are pretty."

Wrappings off, the first package disclosed a pair of most elaborate garters. They were of crimson plush surrounded with lace and fastened with bows of crimson silk ribbon. They were beautiful! Teresina could visualize them high on the unattainable reaches of her creamy-skinned thighs. They would never be seen, of course, but they would contribute to that sense of complete beauty—a beauty of more than surface depth—that appeals to the woman who worships at the shrine of her own perfection. She showed her pleasure by hugging her aunt furiously, although she was pushed back sternly.

256

"Now, my dear, you mustn't disarrange your things—and look at what I got to go with them."

The stockings were long, sheer lisle of a white just less flawless than that of Teresina's skin, and they were beautifully embroidered with a pattern of butterflies, crimson butterflies, winging their way upward. Aunt Zena was very satisfied with her purchases—not that their cost mattered, or the things themselves; what she had bought was the pleasure of giving, and this she had received.

"I remembered your underclothes were all set off with red ribbons," she explained. "With your dark coloring, it suits you, too."

She stayed on, helping with the dress. This was the silk in the new elephant shade. It had a heart-shaped décolletage that revealed more than a hint of the plump fullness, the creamy velvet quality of Teresina's bosom, although the extremity of the style was tempered by a ruching of orchid. The orchid note was continued in a tasteful row of flounces that were caught in the back with a huge orchid bow. The effect was stunning, and Aunt Zena kissed her namesake on both cheeks while tears of joy ran down her own.

"Now I mustn't disturb you. Philippe will be here any minute, and I know he will be entranced when he sees you."

Teresina maintained the pose of girlish excitement and sweet gratitude until Aunt Zena left with Denise, when she was again her cool and calculating self. If the dress really created such an effect, perhaps tonight would be an auspicious time to lead Philippe on to the point of proposal. He was interested in her, that was certain. To strengthen her conviction, she recounted the times they had been out together as if they were beads on a rosary. Considering the short while he had been in Philadelphia, they formed a long string. There could be no doubt of it

257

—he was serious; it was not just gallantry, or loneliness. Teresina reassured herself. Silly! Of course he was serious —and there was no time like the present to make certain of him.

2

Despite the objections of Mr. Rogers, who insisted that his own horses never had as much exercise as they needed, Philippe appeared with a hired rig, a sporty two-seated outfit, with a lean horse that lacked some of Mr. Quinby's good looks and even gait, but was quite as fast and knowledgeable. They raced downtown, threading their way through the unusual traffic without lessening their dangerous pace, and made the four-mile trip in less than three-quarters of an hour. Teresina protested several times that the horse's speed was blowing her to bits, but her cheeks were blooming and her manner was pleasantly animated by the thrill of the ride. They left the rig at the livery where Philippe kept it and walked to the theater, but a few steps away. It was far enough for him to reappraise his companion's beauty. She was wearing a new cloth dolman over her shoulders, and a bonnet of the same material as her dress perched in the high sweep of her coiffure. It was an adorable bonnet, held in place less by the streamers that tied under her chin than by discreetly used hatpins— and he was sure there would be no one else as attractive in the audience. How could there be, when in all of his travels she was the most ravishing creature he had ever met?

Broad Street was a glorious sight. Following the custom which had been inaugurated on New Year's Eve, upon the suggestion of Mayor Stokely, gaslights blazed in the front rooms of private homes and office buildings so that their glare could be seen through the unshuttered and unshaded windows and the whole thoroughfare sparkled with the brilliance of a new firmament. Beautifully gowned women and their escorts, many of them in uniform, directed their steps toward the new theater, with its glorious Oriental domes and minarets. The exotic edifice drew exclamations of admiration from everyone. Teresina held Philippe's arm a little tighter, so he could feel her weight, and gave him the full benefit of a languid glance.

"Look, Philippe—it is like a building of fairyland, done in lacy embroidery against the purple velvet of the sky."

It was a creditable description. Philippe followed the meaning behind the somewhat mixed and hazy metaphor, and decided his beauty had brains as well as good looks.

"Is it moonlight that makes the front of the theater appear so dazzling?" she asked, innocently. Men always took such pleasure in explaining things.

Philippe pointed out to her the location of the calcium lights, artfully concealed so that they were not readily noticeable, and detailed the whole method by which ordinary lime was made to give such brilliance.

"Ah, Philippe," Teresina whispered, "wouldn't it be marvelous to see the world—the places where buildings like this line the streets?"

"But we are seeing it tonight. You forget, we are going around the world in eighty days, and the whole journey will be done in two hours! We shall surpass Mr. Verne's wildest imaginings."

Teresina rewarded the pleasantry with a bell-like tinkle of laughter. "Of course, Philippe—I had quite forgotten the name of the drama we are to . . ."

Philippe interrupted to add an afterthought: "But eighty days is much too little time for us, isn't it? We should need a lifetime."

It was the most encouraging speech so far. Teresina lowered her head prettily, and glanced sideways at him

259

through her lashes. It was an answer that allowed further advances without making a commitment.

Within the auditorium of the theater there was a decorous buzz of conversation. The highly ornamented plasterwork, in imitation of the Moorish style, was not quite finished in places, and there were other signs of the hasty exit of the workmen but a short time before. The brilliance of the gathering and the richness of the decorations made these deficiencies pass almost unnoticed. There was no doubt about it, the Karalfy Brothers' new Alhambra Palace was the most beautiful theater in the city.

Jules Verne's masterpiece proved as exotic as the playhouse. Philippe, as a veteran playgoer used to the most expert French and English theaters, found the acting somewhat amateurish, and the staging and direction showed the effects of hurried preparations. Teresina enjoyed it completely. The melodramatic adventures of the eighty-day journey proved to be a series of spectacles, which passed like a kaleidoscope before her eyes.

Almost as entertaining as the play itself, and providing the proper moral tone to the melodrama, was the appearance between the acts of the Westminster Abbey Choir, which sang a number of choral pieces. In addition to the music they provided, the choir had the effect of drowning out completely the backstage shouts, hammering, and shufflings of feet necessary to the change of scenery.

Philippe suggested they spend an intermission in the beautiful Oriental garden in the rear of the theater, which was one of its features. Graveled paths wound between potted palms and ferns, while here and there a table and chairs discreetly invited the theatergoer. Most of these were already filled, but he easily found places, and gave an order to one of the hurrying waiters. In a few minutes they were sipping wine in what seemed to be wholly tropical surroundings. The clear, boyish voices of the choir, deeply involved in the *Centennial Cantata*, floated out through the open doors, while overhead it required little imagination to transform the balmy Philadelphia May skies into those over less prosaic alien shores.

One of the prettiest features of the garden, which Teresina especially admired, was the use of colored glass shades on the gaslights. They were shaped like hemispheres, open at the top, and sparkled like giant jewels in the evening sky —priceless hangings of emeralds, rubies, and sapphires. In the center was a large open space, and this, Philippe informed her, was to be the site of the fountains, which were not yet erected although they had been extravagantly advertised. "They are to be fountains of living water," he explained, "at least, so the announcement runs," but neither he nor Teresina questioned the meaning of the adjective.

After the performance was over, which was not until past ten o'clock, although it had begun promptly at eight, the horse seemed unwilling to turn toward Kensington. "Let us give him his head," Philippe suggested, and the sagacious animal, from its long experience in livery, turned toward Fairmount Park. It set off at its regular good clip, which grew slower and slower until it came to a complete halt, and proceeded to forage from the bushes lining a lane to the rear of Belmont Mansion.

The excitement of the evening, and the influence of the moon, Teresina would have averred, caused her to lose her head. What would Philippe think of her? She was behaving shamelessly! His kisses did, in fact, stir her deeply. She had been kissed before—the shamefaced, embarrassed touches of kissing games and quick, furtive embraces, hasty pecks, from Gus and other youths. But Philippe was a man—and a Frenchman. If this went on, she would lack the will to put an end to it.

The desperateness of her struggle convinced Philippe of her innocence, and his proposal followed. It was long, and couched in poetic terms, the kind of proposal a girl can remember for years afterward and repeat to herself almost word for word. Philippe painted a glowing picture, which he believed in himself as he heard the words issue from his lips. They would embark together upon a lifetime of bliss in which one spectacle would succeed another—spectacles much more vivid and satisfying than those they had seen tonight. He touched briefly and in good taste upon his wealth. It meant nothing to him except as it would bring adornments, comforts, and pleasures to Teresina. He rhapsodized about her flawless beauty, a face that Da Vinci might have painted, and a form with the perfection of a Greek statue. When finally he said:

"Teresina, dear, I humbly ask, will you do me the favor of marriage?" she was too overwhelmed with feeling to answer. Instead, she bent her head so that the tip of her bonnet tangled in his beard, and her ear, pressing against his chest, heard the beating of his heart while she murmured, "Philippe—dear, dear Philippe."

It was an acceptance that revealed to him the depth of her emotions, and he felt pleased that the choice of his language had so aroused her. It was a tribute to his eloquence. He resolved that he would never forget the poignance, the very accents, of her whispered pronunciation of his name, the sound muffled by his Prince Albert coat.

The drive home was a delirium of bliss. Well after eleven o'clock, all of Philadelphia was naturally in bed, although an occasional street light illumined their way. There was no sound but the trot of their horse as it sped

262

eastward through empty streets. No sound but the ring of steel on cobble—and the pounding of their own hearts.

Teresina did not dare trust herself to more than a hasty good-by. Philippe unlocked the front door for her, then crushed dolman, elephant-colored dress, flannel petticoats, Mme. Foy's corset, and the adorable creature palpitating beneath it all in an embrace that almost robbed her of the strength to push him away and close the door upon her importunate lover.

Mrs. Rogers, watching the scene from the busybody at her window (the contrivance of mirrors served more than one purpose), nodded her head approvingly. Something had transpired between Philippe and Zenie, but her daughter was keeping her head. . . . There was nothing so helpful to young maidenhood as a mother's stern training. She listened for the light quick run of Teresina's footsteps on the stairs. The sound was muffled by the stair carpet, but a mother had sensitive hearing at a time like this. She could even hear the rustle of the heavy silk dress down the hall. Down the hall, and past her own bedroom! Where in the world was she going? There was a distant, discreet knock. Of course—trust Zenie to know how to work things! She was confiding in her aunt. Fresh from her lover's arms, palpitating with the news, she would be surpassingly lovely, and Zena would be delighted! It was a subtle kind of flattery her sister would love—and it certainly wouldn't do the young pair any harm in a financial way.

Mrs. Rogers returned to bed, gently allowing her weight to fill the familiar hollows, so she wouldn't waken Jesse, who was sleeping tranquilly—"boiling mush," as she called it—except when he twitched his head slightly as an occasional hair from his beard tickled him. This was the time to appraise a husband. Her features remained inscrutable

263

as she studied his, but when she finally turned off the gas cock, she admitted to herself that there were compensations to marriage and a family. For the first time in years she felt pity for her sister.

Chapter 8   *M*RS. ROGERS waited all the next morning for Teresina to confide in her. She was certain the previous evening had been an important one and also that Zena already shared the secret. It was all very well for Teresina to have gone to her the night before—that was merely knowing on which side your bread was buttered—but it was infuriating to think that her sister was now the possessor of information to which she herself was by right entitled. Every time she saw her oldest daughter she favored her with a sharp, inquiring glance, and a manner designed to encourage her to speak, but to no avail. What was more provoking, Zena kept to her room, and Denise took her breakfast on a tray. "The most important moment in my own daughter's life, and she has said not a word to me, her own mother, about it," Mrs. Rogers said to herself.

A suspicion entered her mind, but she rejected it as unworthy of Teresina. Still, it was just possible. Philippe was a man of the world, and Teresina an inexperienced girl who might have been dazzled into who knew what indiscretions. No—it was impossible. Mrs. Rogers was certain her daughter would not have allowed the embrace she had observed through the busybody unless it had been preceded by a declaration and an acceptance. But why didn't the girl speak up? As her mother, she was entitled to a complete account of the whole incident, and not Zena,

264

still lolling upstairs in bed like a great lady while she herself had the cares of a whole family on her shoulders.

It was Zena who finally spilled the beans, and in such a way as to contribute to the mother's feeling of injury. The whole family was seated at the table and dinner had begun on scheduled time before she made her appearance. The unforgivable sin of lateness at mealtimes was overlooked by Mr. Rogers in her case, probably because he would have been worn out in remonstrating at a daily occurrence. There was no doubt about it, Zena had a lamentable disregard for time.

She burst into the dining room in a house dress that was a confection of baby-blue silk ribbons and lace ruffles, and cried:

"Don't get up, Jesse, I beg of you! Aren't you simply overwhelmed at the news?" Mrs. Rogers' lips set grimly while her husband looked up with a blank stare.

"News? News? Has something happened I should have been told about, and haven't been?"

Before Aunt Zena could explain, Teresina spoke up, languidly, as if stating a fact which all of them should have expected and accepted as a conclusion without any announcement by herself.

"Philippe proposed to me last evening, and I have accepted."

"Well, I never! It seems to me I should have known about this," Mrs. Rogers couldn't help complaining, while Aunt Zena showed her confusion by scolding:

"Why, Zenie, do you mean to tell me you haven't broken the news to your father and mother until now? What a thoughtless girl!" Then, complacently, "She came running to my room last night, to tell me the first thing."

Mr. Rogers was elated and surprised. "Well, who would have thought of Zenie marrying Philippe? What happened

265

to the state senator? I thought he was the favorite suitor."

The womenfolk gave him a pitying glance—except Julia, who went on eating mechanically, just as if the world hadn't come to an end for her. She looked over at her sister, gazing calmly across the table. How could she have hoped to make an impression on Philippe in competition with Zenie? She had been an extremely vain and silly girl to believe there was the least chance for her. During the remainder of the meal, while the rest of the family chatted excitedly she retreated within herself, and tried to decide just what she would do. Some gesture of finality was needed. She might retire to a secluded spot and find solace with the birds. This was a conclusion that sounded too much like the chorus from a popular song. She might pine away into consumption, or she could leave the world and enter a convent—one of the orders that would enforce the strictest seclusion. That would be a real act of renunciation. Something done for love. . . .

Her mother's sharp reminder disturbed her reverie. "How do you expect to keep up your strength if you don't eat? I declare you make me nervous picking at your food that way. . . . Jesse, put a couple more of those potatoes on the child's plate, and another piece of the lamb."

Julia made no objection, but as she ate this further generous helping, she pondered upon the futility of it. What did it matter now whether she weighed a hundred and thirty pounds or a hundred and fifty, the goal she had set herself no longer ago than yesterday? She waited until the meal was finally over—no use risking her mother's displeasure, and further reproof, by missing the dessert. As soon as she could do so afterward, she rose, conscious of her mother's eyes following her, and left the dining room. The last words she heard were a reiteration by her father

266

for the fifth or sixth time that he was completely bowled over by the announcement.

She climbed to her room. The fourth floor seemed at once too far away to ever reach, and the most desirable refuge possible, if she could make it. She had to cry, and the tears wouldn't wait. Sobs began choking her before she reached the third-floor hallway. At least Zenie would never know how much she was suffering. She threw herself face downward on her cot and abandoned herself completely to tears.

This was one time her mother allowed her that luxury without interruption. It was hours later before she tiptoed into the room and placed a gentle hand on her disconsolate daughter's shoulder.

"Come, Julia. There's no man alive worth more than one good cry. I've brought up a little dish of soup for you. It's good and rich, and you'll feel better for it, I know."

2

Augustus Palmer, M.D. Or should he call himself Augustus L. Palmer? L. for Lincoln, or C. for Caesar? How would C. Augustus Palmer, M.D., sound? He shook his head. That wouldn't do, definitely. Gus had been christened with only one name, and he sadly felt the need of at least a middle initial. This might even prove to be a professional handicap. He tried to visualize his name in the printed letters of a doctor's sign. He pictured his whole future office and residence. It would be a house very much like the Rogers', and in one of the front windows downstairs would be the discreet little sign DR. AU-GUSTUS PALMER—and if anyone didn't like the absence of an initial he could go hang!

He and Zenie would have to begin in a small way, of

course. They couldn't expect to have as large a home as her parents right away. That would be the goal they would set themselves. Four stories, with a brick front—or it might even be serpentine, the beautiful green stone that was so handsome, and in such favor with people of means. Of course they wouldn't live in Kensington, but in a more fashionable section of the city. Perhaps on Franklin Square, or over on Spruce Street, near the old hospital. He didn't intend to have a house in the middle of the row, either. There should be a large side yard, and in it the most elaborate cast-iron fountain that money could buy. Its jet would be running continually, except in freezing weather, and nasturtiums should flourish at its base. They would have four horses, two for Zenie, spirited animals, yet gentle, and a good fast team for himself, for making calls. The famous Dr. Palmer!

He knew the kind of practice he intended to have. He would be a baby doctor, specialize in the care of them and their mothers. Too many children died in coming into the world, and during their first year. Even in a civilized community like Philadelphia, modern knowledge had not yet succeeded in overcoming ignorance and all kinds of prejudices and superstitions. To these he intended to give battle. As Gus made this resolve, his chin became firmer than ever. Yes, indeed, they would come to him for their babies, white and black, Protestant and Catholic. He would devote his life just to that one field. How could a doctor busy with general practice keep up to date in a subject so tremendously broad in scope as that of obstetrics? People were inclined to laugh at the idea that a pregnant woman needed a doctor's care, needed more than special corsets, perhaps. He would disabuse them of that, some day. He'd have corsets discarded entirely, along with all the prudish ideas that restricted the mind as they did the body.

These plans and resolves sustained Gus until he reached the Rogers doorstep, and then all his old doubts returned to assail him. He could be persistent and masterful enough in everything else, but sight of Teresina turned his knees to water and his resolutions to thin air. He ran over again all the arguments he planned to use with Zenie, the dreams for the future which a few minutes before had seemed almost as substantial as the accomplishment would some day prove to be. He spurred himself on. This time he would be masterful. He would allow her no chance to refuse him. Now was the time! He pulled the bell so hard and firmly that he could hear its tinkle from clear out in the kitchen. When finally the door was opened, after what seemed an interminable wait, it was Julia who let him in, and not Zenie, as he had hoped.

At first he thought Julia was ill, and then he realized that she had been crying recently, although she smiled bravely enough as she invited him to enter. He looked around the parlor, crowded with all the familiar things he knew so well. Julia stood aside as he asked the question uppermost in his mind.

"Where's Zenie? I'd hoped she would come to the graduation exercises the other night, but she didn't."

Julia smiled unhappily. "So now I suppose you are a full-fledged doctor! When do you hang out your shingle?"

"I wish I could, but I'm going into a hospital first, for a couple of years."

"My, it takes forever to become a doctor, doesn't it?"

"Oh, the time will go by quickly enough," Gus answered, carelessly. He wondered what had so upset Julia. She picked nervously with her fingers at the braided decorations on her dress, and seemed completely distraught. Finally he asked again, "Is Zenie out somewhere?"

Julia took a breath like a swimmer about to plunge into

269

unknown waters. "She's in town, shopping with Aunt Zena. They should have been back hours ago, but my aunt has no regard for time. . . . Gus, perhaps I shouldn't tell you. I should let Zenie tell you herself, but she can be so blunt. She doesn't mean to be unkind, really, it's simply that she is thoughtless. . . . I know how fond of her you are, and I don't want to see you hurt." She paused a moment, while Gus glanced at her curiously, still completely unaware of what was to come. "Zenie has become engaged to Philippe Lascalles. They are to be married in the fall, I believe." Julia reached out her hand, and placed it lightly on Gus's sleeve, but he seemed to take the news more easily than she had anticipated.

Zenie was going to marry Lascalles, that big, broad-shouldered chap who was some kind of a cousin of hers. Philippe Lascalles—Zenie. Teresina Lascalles, and not Zenie Palmer. Well, why shouldn't she, if she wanted to? He couldn't blame her. After all, what was he? Little more than a medical student. Teresina Lascalles! She would never, never be Zenie Palmer—Mrs. Dr. Palmer. He was conscious that Julia was looking at him compassionately. Her eyes were large, and almost as dark as her mother's. They resembled Zenie's as well, although they were softer; Zenie's eyes had a regal, demanding look that Gus adored.

Gus felt no pain at the moment, and no shock. He was like a man who had lost an arm by the sudden blow of a sword. In a day or so it would hurt without ceasing, but for that moment the blade itself provided a merciful anesthesia. He smiled at Julia and rose. "I guess I'll be getting along, and tell Zenie for me I wish her happiness. I won't wait for her right now—another time."

It was still several hours before sunset, the beginning of a long summer evening, but Gus was unaware of its beauty.

270

To Julia, watching him, he seemed to walk like a somnam-
bulist. She stood in the doorway until he passed out of
sight down the street, and she went back into the house
again, still undecided whether or not she had made a mistake in telling him.

3

"The spell is past, the dream is o'er." He had sung the
words so often, and they had never had a real meaning to
him before. "And though we meet, we love no more."
The tune began to hammer through his brain, the first
throbbing realization that he had indeed lost a part of himself. "And though we meet, we love no more." But he
would go on loving! Soon Zenie would forget him. She
would go to France, probably, where Lascalles came from,
and he would never see her again. The dream was indeed
o'er.

More than ever before in his life, Gus wanted a piano,
so that he could pour out his sorrow in song. He began to
walk around the square toward Paddy Guirk's. It was a
long time since he had been there. That had been after
a spat with Zenie, and he had tried to forget his unhappiness by drinking. It hadn't worked; he had only made a
fool of himself. He remembered arguing with Mr. Rogers
afterward, right out on the sidewalk. Zenie's father had
been pretty decent toward him then, and had taken his
behavior in good part. He had no intention of repeating
that performance! He did want to be alone, and play, and
that was a place where no one would ask questions. He
pushed open the short swinging door, and nodded to the
old Irishman.

"Hello, Paddy, I'll have a beer, if you please, and do
you mind if I strum away at your piano for a while? I'm
in a singing mood."

Paddy Guirk made an expansive gesture with his arm, indicating that the instrument, as well as everything else in the establishment, was at his command. Gus turned to the piano, ran his fingers lightly over the keys, and began to hum one of Zenie's father's favorite songs. How many times he had played it in that household, which would now be denied to him forevermore! In a moment his voice lifted, and he was unaware that all the corner hangers-on were dropping in by twos and threes to listen:

> Oh, who does not love Kitty Clyde,
> That sunny-eyed, rosy-cheeked lass
>   With a sweet dimpled chin
> That looks roguish as sin
>   With always a smile as you pass.

Chapter 9

DESPITE Teresina's betrothal to Zena's nephew, Mrs. Rogers resented more and more the presence of her sister in the house. She had anticipated some difficulties, but she had completely failed to imagine to what extent her sister's personality would come to dominate a household that, in Mrs. Rogers' language, "had run along smoothly for years." Zena liked to sleep late in the morning, while Mrs. Rogers preferred to be up early and, like a good housekeeper, have the morning chores finished well in advance of the preparation of the midday dinner. But Zena hated to breakfast alone, so the meal had become more and more tardy, until now it was rare indeed for the breakfast dishes to be disposed of before the dinner ones. The arrangement of chairs in the dining room was altered because Zena objected to being under the scrutiny of Grandfather Rogers during mealtimes. The parlor was hardly recognizable, for it had been made into a veritable Turkish harem, or as Jesse called it, "the seraglio." As a result of the Centennial, Zena, along with the rest of America except Mrs. Rogers, had become enthused over inlaid teak furniture, pierced brass work, varicolored lanterns, Oriental scimitars and shields, and vivid red and yellow curtains.

Shortly after the announcement of Teresina's engagement to Philippe, Mrs. Rogers returned home after some shopping to find the parlor done over in this fashion, complete with canopied hangings which created an impression that the room did not have four straight and solid walls, but was a tent of some desert potentate—and there was Zena, pleased as Punch, waiting in anticipation of her surprised pleasure. "But where is the other furniture?" she managed to ask, when finally she recovered from a shock which rendered her momentarily speechless.

"Oh, those old things! . . . I gave them to the man who brought the new furniture. They were worn out anyway, and he looked needy. Tina, doesn't the room give an entrancing effect? Look at this furniture—the inlays are genuine mother-of-pearl and silver, all done by hand."

In place of the old horsehair sofa, a broad divan heaped with pillows filled the whole end of the room, and Jesse's favorite chair had been replaced with a type of contrivance she was unable to recognize. "It's a Turkish rocker, dear. I wanted something big and substantial for Jesse, and he will love it, I know."

One thing to be thankful for, Zena had not disposed of the little vases, figurines and bronzes, the fancy dishes and souvenirs, which decorated the room. Each piece had a tremendous value in her eyes, from years of cherishing or from association with some event, and the loss of a single one would have been a real calamity.

273

Mrs. Rogers' gaze fastened on a peculiar jar of unusual shape. She surmised it was some kind of gas fixture because of a flexible hose which extended from it, but Zena, noticing the direction of her glance, hurried breathlessly along.

"You can't guess what that is, but Jesse will like it, I know. It is especially for him. I hope it will make him give up chewing. He says he can't smoke because it is too dry on his throat, but this would fix that. It's a water pipe, a narghile, as we call it in Turkey. I learned a lot of Turkish once. I had a dear friend who was a Turk. Quite civilized, and not at all the kind of person you'd think from reading about them in the papers."

It had been too late to do anything about it. The old furniture was gone and the new was there—and it was impossible to argue with Zena anyway. Furthermore, Mrs. Rogers read *Harper's Bazaar* enough to know that the Turkish corner was fast becoming a necessity in every modern house. She had dreaded Jesse's reaction, though, certain that he would never forgive the loss of his chair.

And that made her angry all over again, in retrospect. He had been pleased, and not at all put out. He tested the Turkish rocker by teetering back and forth on it until she thought she must scream. Furthermore, all the children liked the room, and in her innermost being, Mrs. Rogers herself admitted that it had a handsome and exotic flavor. She was so unreasonable that this also angered her. Furthermore, Zenie and Philippe found in the sensuous luxuriousness of the Turkish room an atmosphere akin to that in which their affections had first sprung into bloom.

As Mrs. Rogers pursued her bitter thoughts, she reflected: "That is the trouble with Zena. She does all kinds of things for people without consulting them. She's so generous and impulsive, and if you do anything but thank her after some outrageous purchase, her feelings would be irreparably hurt." The matter of Zena's generosities had been for twenty years a source of dissension in the family, but with Zena at a distance, Mrs. Rogers had found her gifts welcome and a source of great pleasure, while Jesse inveighed against them. Take the French clock, for instance. She had always thought the Venus de Milo looked most handsome with the time set in her vitals, and Jesse had made life miserable about it. Since her sister's arrival, however, only her first gift, the adorable Moody and Sankey reposing now one at each side of her chair, met with her approval, while to her husband, the dash-hounds, as he always called them, were anathema.

It was provoking that everything else the exuberant Zena toted in the front door, every silly, trifling purchase, met with Jesse's complete approval. Jesse never tired of that German music box, and the antics of the bird that fluttered automatically on its top. Almost the first thing he did after his morning nap was to wind up the box, and he beamed like a delighted child as the wooden bird sang its trite, mechanical note.

And the fountain! All of Philadelphia had gone fountain-mad. Of course the fountains at the Centennial were responsible, and the great hydraulic display in the huge reservoir built to the rear of Machinery Hall. Every concert park was advertising as the principal attraction cascades of some sort, and a dozen projects were on foot for the building of permanent fountains in memory of one or another notable person or event.

Fountains were all right in their place, but not in the home. Had Mrs. Rogers known what was in that package that Lucius brought in so gingerly while a beaming Zena followed, she would have put her foot down then and there, and announced to her sister that enough was enough. She was being driven insane by that fountain! She had heard of the water torture to which Chinamen were subjected, and she understood for the first time the fiendishness of the device. The Automatic Crystal Fountain, as it was called, now occupied a special table Zena had purchased for it, and sat in the front of the hall, next to the clothes rack. It was not connected to any water supply at all, and by means that seemed little short of magical, spouted a slender column of water which fell back with a pleasant sound into a metal basin, to be reused again and again. Everyone who saw it was enchanted. Mr. Rogers spent hours trying to fathom the mystery of its operation; the children could watch it play indefinitely; and every chance visitor remarked on it, and desired explanations of its principle.

But she had to live with it, and the constant tinkle of water proved more than she could stand. It had a most peculiar effect on her. She would forget the sound for a little while, then, hearing the noise of water dripping, would rush frantically from bath to kitchen, searching for a leak, to remember finally it was only the Automatic Crystal Fountain.

Mrs. Rogers never admitted, even to herself, the real reason for her growing animosity toward her sister. These were only the excuses she made for feeling as she did. What she had anticipated was now occurring before her eyes, but her pride would not allow her to acknowledge a fact which her feminine intuition cried aloud. Jesse and Zena were becoming too interested in each other for safety. . . . That was why he was complaisant about all her purchases. He almost jumped out of his chair when she entered the room. He called her "dear Zena" in accents no husband should use to a sister-in-law. As for Zena, she was continually doing little things: placing his slippers handy, adjusting a pillow behind his head, fixing his tie, or adjusting his coat—attentions that would have irritated him if anyone else had performed them.

Worst of all was Sunday mornings. Mrs. Rogers was regular in her weekly church attendance. She and the girls drove to mass in the carriage, and as there were always friends with whom to chat, or Father Duffy to consult, time sped rapidly. Mary and Martha attended an earlier mass, but also stayed to gossip. Henry, at his father's insistence, was going to a heathenish Quaker institution called "First Day School," whatever that meant. In other words, Mr. Rogers had the house to himself, and as he didn't work the night before, he made a pleasant, lazy morning of it.

Now Zena, the wretch, insisted that she had long ago given up church attendance. Mrs. Rogers was certain this was not so. It was purely a stratagem to be alone with Jesse. She was so sure of this that she had forgone church the week before, to keep her eye on them. Nothing had happened, and both culprits seemed unperturbed, which convinced her of the suspicions she entertained. Zena was up to her old tricks, and Jesse was nothing but putty in her fingers!

Mrs. Rogers' fingers stitched harder than ever at the crazy quilt with which she occupied her odd moments, her lips moving in rhythm to the passing of the needle through the varicolored materials. She was rapidly working herself into a temper. She hoped it would be one that would allow her to accuse Jesse to his face, and send Zena packing. She knew all the time she would do neither of these things— unless circumstances changed. She had no grounds whatsoever on which to base her suspicions, and the interests of the children demanded a continuance of her sister's friendship. If Zena got angry enough, she would be capable of anything!

It was insufferably hot. The unseasonable weather combined with her torrid imaginings until she felt like a human volcano that must erupt its fire and brimstone somewhere. Fortunately for her, there were always the servants. She took a last jab with her needle, and then secured it in the patchwork, which she folded over neatly and placed on her worktable. "I haven't seen hair nor hide of Mary for an hour," she said aloud. "She's hiding out some place, that's what, and I intend to find her right now, and give her what-for."

2

Mr. Rogers would have been surprised indeed to know the trend of his wife's thoughts. He liked Zena, that was natural. She was so like Gussie in her vitality, exuberance, and changing moods. In the long run of marriage it was not beauty of face or form, intelligence, wit, or cleverness that held a husband's interest, but variety of disposition, so that he was, in effect, married to a number of different persons who by chance occupied the same body, but who furnished nonetheless the change masculine nature requires.

At the moment he was engaged in repairing the grape arbors—spring and early summer always started him on these little tasks, most of which he never completed—and Zena sat near by in the shade of the vines, handing him tools when they were needed, and reminiscing meanwhile about her own life.

"It's hot. Devilish hot. We've never had a June like this in my life," Mr. Rogers remarked. He mopped his forehead with a handkerchief, rubbed a large grimy paw on the old trousers he saved for odd-jobbing, and thrust it behind him. "The pincers, Zena!"

She picked them up and handed them over with alacrity, never stopping the babble of her conversation. "Those were the good old days, Jesse. I shall never see them again.

278

I was a young widow then, and gentlemen were very kind to me. Fortunately I had plenty of money, so I wasn't beholden to anyone. . . . Oh, well, I suppose we must all grow old." She gave a deep sigh and took back the pincers, which were wordlessly held toward her while her companion tugged at a wire, and made use of a pruning knife, contorting his face and puffing as he hacked through a piece of dead vine.

"Nonsense!" he boomed. "Nonsense, Zena. You're not old—not as old as I am, and surely I'm not old."

"I spent that winter in Genoa—it's not far from where the Borellis came from. I tried to look up my father's people there, but they were all gone, and the ancestral home was in ruins . . . ru-u-iiins." Zena could be quite as dramatic as her sister, and she made this pronouncement in tones appropriate to a scene from *Hamlet*.

"Tch-tch," Mr. Rogers clicked, and drove home the commiseration by hammering against an old nailhead that had worked loose. Half the time he did not really listen to what Zena was saying. Nor did she care. It was impossible for her to sit quietly by. She *had* to talk. She enjoyed rattling on in this way—enjoyed it almost as much as she did the sweaty male presence of her brother-in-law.

Mrs. Rogers looked out at the scene from the shed window and said to herself: "Look at them. Look at the pair of them. He's dawdling over that grape arbor for nothing but an excuse, and she's right on top of him, of course. The duplicity of sisters! Here I am, working my fingers to the bone, and ready to die of heat prostration. Well, I suppose they don't want to be interrupted, but I have to get garden lettuce from the patch, and Don Juan and Lady Gay will have to put up with it."

She marched out with storm warnings flying. Her mouth

was set in a grim line, and her progress down through the garden was like the advance of an avenging fury. The lettuce bed was sown so there would always be young fresh greens available for salads, but the drouth had affected them to some extent, and Mrs. Rogers spent quite a time in filling her bowl, while her ears strained to catch the conversation. She could hear only an occasional request from Mr. Rogers. "The pincers again," a peremptory "Hammer!" "Not a word from Zena," she thought. "She shut up quick enough when I came around." When she had passed into the shed again, and slammed the door behind her with window-shivering force, Mr. Rogers gave a long low whistle. "Well! Did you notice Gussie? Now what in the world has put her in a tantrum like that?"

Zena, who knew perfectly well, thought to herself, "Augustina is as jealous as ever," but aloud she merely remarked: "I'm sure I don't know, Jesse. She *did* seem disturbed about something. A tiff with the servants, probably. They can be most provoking—especially in a country like this, where they think they are as good as you are. . . .

"Well, as I was saying, when I took this house near Genoa, a most charming man lived next door. Elegant and refined. We would have suited each other, I think, but he died very suddenly. I've always thought his daughter poisoned him—she didn't like me. . . .

"Here's a nail, Jesse—do you think it is long enough? . . . Yes, you have no idea of the things I've been through. Money isn't everything, I assure you."

Chapter 10

JULIA was concerned about Gus Palmer. He was so broken up by the announcement of Zena's engagement. In spite of all their arguments and the disdainful way in which she often treated him, and although he had met both Harry and Philippe on various occasions, he had always felt that in the end he would be the winner. He could not visualize a future that did not include Teresina as his wife. It was unthinkable to him that she could marry someone else, and their difficulties were to him merely the progress of true love.

In her attempts at comforting Gus, Julia found an escape from her own pain, although she gave up less easily than he did, and would not yet admit that all was lost. Whenever she thought of Philippe, which was practically all the time, she would console herself with the thought "Well, they are not married yet." But poor Gus was completely at loose ends. If he only had work to do, but he would not enter the hospital until fall. There was a letdown from studies, and a complete absence of ambition. No future seemed worth while to him that did not include Zenie.

Julia prevailed upon him to continue coming to the house, to visit her, and while he had formerly been a frequent caller, he now haunted it. There was a kind of pleasure in suffering the tortures of Tantalus, and he knew only Julia to whom he could confide. He also understood, in a way, how Teresina's engagement affected her sister. While she never gave confidences in return, the hidden bond of misery was there, and company made it more endurable.

They were seated on the Turkish divan. The glow of early evening still lighted the street, but the gloom of the "seraglio" was as intense as that in their hearts. The cause of their misery swept in, wearing an old house dress and not looking at all her best. She lighted the gas in the red-paned lamp—it enhanced the complexion—and glanced around the room to make sure it was in readiness to receive Philippe. Sight of the mournful couple first startled, then displeased, and finally angered her. Even if Gus was out of the running, she didn't want him to see her in old clothes. Besides, she didn't like him in the house incessantly; it made her uncomfortable. She lifted her chin in the air at Gus's timid "Hello, Zenie," and swept away in search of her mother. Mrs. Rogers was engaged in making notes for the next morning's marketing, but Teresina burst out:

"I wish you would do something, Mother. Julia has Gus here continually, just to spite me. I'm sure Philippe is wondering why someone I threw over my shoulder is still around all the time. He was here the night before last, and again tonight. It's sickening—just sickening."

"Good grief, Zenie, Gus is a nice boy, and he's terribly hurt. Not that I don't think Philippe is a better catch, mind you. But if Julia wants to cheer him up a little, I'm sure I can't refuse him the house when he's been coming here for years. He's practically one of the family."

"I don't like the way Julia acts with Philippe, either. You would think now we're engaged she would give up trying to land him, but no, she's at the door the first thing he rings. Instead of letting Mary go, there she sneaks off, ready to fawn all over him."

"Tosh. Pish and tosh. This is as good a time as any to tell you, Zenie—if you lose your fish it will be your own fault. I hold with making a man toe the line, but it doesn't do any good making him jump through hoops for you. He'll begin to feel like a monkey, and that will lead to monkey business." Mrs. Rogers ticked off the items on

282

her market list, but glanced sideways to observe the effect of her speech.

"I know how to handle Philippe, Julia or no Julia—although I'll settle her hash quick enough if she starts anything."

"If I were you, I'd set an early date for the wedding." Mrs. Rogers stood on tiptoe to look up into the big kitchen dresser. "Drat that Louisa! I'll need more soap tomorrow. I'm sure she takes cakes of it home with her. If I could catch her I'd put a stop to it quickly enough. . . . You haven't said when you plan to marry."

Teresina took on a tone of smug assurance. "We'll be married in November. Philippe's duties here will be over then, and we shall return to France for our wedding trip. He has suggested going to Egypt for the winter."

Mrs. Rogers sighed as she counted the bottles of bluing and ammonia, the boxes of starch and cakes of sand soap. "I was as sure of myself once as you are, young lady. I hope you don't have an awakening. I've been watching things. Julia goes to the door for Philippe because you are not dressed, and I can't have Mary trotting back and forth all the time. She'd never get her work done. What's more, you are not ready a half-hour later, most of the time, and someone has to entertain Philippe. He can't sit there like a bump on a log."

Teresina's chin went up again. "Philippe should be glad to wait for me. You yourself have told me over and over, the time to get the upper hand is at the beginning."

"The upper hand, yes—but it should be gloved in silk, not be a mailed fist. I can tell you, Zena, I think all that pother about that Algerian beauty at the Centennial was uncalled-for. Philippe was completely innocent, I'm sure. Can he help it if the most talked-of woman at the Exposition happens to have a booth next to his? Your aunt reported the whole thing to me. She says Philippe is very much hurt, and you surely know Zena has your interests at heart."

Although this evoked a sudden tantrum that startlingly resembled her own rages, Mrs. Rogers was completely unsympathetic and unmoved as Teresina burst into a tirade. "I don't care," she finished. "When I saw him ogling that wicked, heathen woman—caught him red-handed—I put an end to it quickly, I can tell you."

"Yes, and made a scene before all Philadelphia! I declare to goodness, child, Philippe has gone to your head, and I'm surprised at you. No man is going to put up with things like that. Just because Gus would follow you like a puppy no matter what you did, don't think Philippe will. I notice he didn't call last evening, and he must have confided in Zena for her to know all about it."

Teresina pouted and turned away. "Mother, I assure you I can handle Philippe in my own way, and he won't be spoiled like Father is."

Mrs. Rogers' voice rose. "Spoiled like your father is—I like that! Let me tell you, young lady, it hasn't been a question of spoiling your father. It's been a matter of making him fit to live with. I started off with a provincial bumpkin, and I made a gentleman of him, if I do say it myself. You are starting with a wealthy man of the world, who knew other women before you came along—and as long as he's French he'll know others. . . . So long as he just looks at Algerian women, let him look, I say. Now run and dress, and be ready for Philippe. Meet him at the door with a smile. It will spare you further argument with him—he's not crawling back, you'll find—and the generosity of a smile will be good business for you, young lady, take my advice on it."

As he drove over Richmond Street, Philippe decided to follow Aunt Zena's counsel and pretend that nothing had happened. If Teresina referred to the scene, however, he intended to state his feelings in no uncertain terms. He was still distressed, dismayed, and surprised at Teresina's behavior. She was usually so sweet, so charming and understanding. Of course, as Zena had explained to him, love, and the great restraints it imposed upon a girl infatuated with a man like himself, might easily cause her to be somewhat unbalanced at times. . . . Still, it revealed a side of her character he had not suspected.

One thing was certain, he did not want to spend the evening in the parlor. The close intimacy of the Turkish hangings and the divan where he had spent so many blissful hours in sweet communion with his love did not suit his present frame of mind. It would surely lead to a quarrel if he were alone with Zenie for the whole evening.

Here was the house. The horse came to a stop without a signal and he tied it to the cast-iron hitching post. He intended to persuade Zenie to go to the minstrels with him, so he didn't bother to take the beast around to the stable. In the few seconds still remaining before he would see her, he went over again the whole cause of their quarrel, and again convinced himself he was innocent.

There was a booth next to the French concession run by an Armenian or a Syrian, and his saleswoman was an unusually handsome girl who had gradually become an attraction of the Exposition. News of her beauty traveled by word of mouth in all the places of the city frequented by men, until she became a creature of legend, and the booth did an unprecedented business. Of course the women of Philadelphia came to hear of the girl, and made it a point to avoid her location when they were escorted, and to pass in jealous, appraising rage when they were alone.

It was impossible for Philippe not to notice the beautiful Algerian, as she came to be called, and he lessened the tedium of directing his own display, which needed no direction, by occasionally watching her. She was beautiful —not with the kind of beauty that Teresina possessed, indeed, by European standards she appeared rather coarse— but with a strange, alien loveliness that was still exciting. He was certain, though, that no serious interest in her had ever entered his thoughts.

One of the newspapers finally took notice of the furore, and rose to the defense of American womanhood in an article headlined THE BEAUTIFUL ALGERIAN:

Imagine a fair, white complexion and eyes of lustrous blackness, with eyelids penciled in the Eastern manner. A nose of perfect symmetry, a mouth small, but well-shaped, which when open discloses teeth like ivory.

While her beauty is surprisingly great, yet there is something wanting—that delicate and womanly kindliness of soul that denotes a refined nature and a noble heart. The nameless grace that distinguishes a true lady is lacking.

The bitter part of the whole affair was this: While he stood there, comparing the flesh-and-blood Algerian with his mental conception of Teresina, he agreed with all the newspaper said, and then his love arrived and displayed neither delicate and womanly kindliness nor the nameless grace that distinguishes a true lady. In the middle of the ensuing scene, he was conscious, moreover, that the Algerian—out of pity, he was sure—had the grace to withdraw.

They would go to the minstrels. The black-cork-faced comedians were the only entertainment he knew that could make him forget everything but their side-splitting jokes.

He took from the carriage seat two separate packages—he usually brought Whitman's chocolates to Teresina, as he had discovered she was fond of them, but Julia had talked about novels the other evening while he was waiting for her sister, and it seemed like a nice gesture to bring one for each girl. He walked over to the steps and climbed them slowly—it was beastly hot, he discovered, now that he was not cooled by the breeze from driving—and pulled the bell.

Julia answered it, with a slow but warm and welcoming smile that placed him at ease again, and he handed her one of the wrapped-up books. "I happened to see this, and thought you might enjoy it."

"Zenie isn't dressed yet, and I'm talking to Gus Palmer in the parlor. Do come in until she's ready."

Gus was a nice fellow, Philippe thought, and he enjoyed conversing with him. Until recently, he had entertained a vague idea that he had supplanted Gus with Teresina, but he came to the decision that the embryo doctor was more a friend of all the family than a suitor of a single member of it.

They discussed the latest trouble of the Centennial while Julia was eagerly turning the pages of her novel. As a graduate of medical school, ready to begin his internship, Gus could talk learnedly about the topic that was gradually taking precedence over all others.

"Of course, the heat is partly responsible, but the new germ theory is worth considering. It is now fairly well established that minute bodies, invisible to the naked eye, cause diseases like typhoid, for instance, and they probably flourish in tropical conditions such as we are now experiencing."

This sounded so different from the fun-loving Gus who sang to them of an evening that Julia felt proud of him.

287

She compared the two men. Philippe was tall, broad-shouldered, and easy-going. Although she was in love with him, she could recognize certain faults of character. He had no decided convictions, no ambition, no aim in life other than to enjoy the wealth he had inherited. Gus was more slender, but by no means frail in appearance. He had worked hard, and had planned his future. As they grew older, Philippe might grow fleshy, but Gus would always be spare. Philippe was a broadsword that would hack what he wanted from life, and Gus a rapier that would find just one vital spot.

How sad life had to be mixed up the way it was! Gus really loved Teresina; more than Philippe could ever do, of this she was certain. And she loved Philippe, knowing Gus was probably the finer man.

Perspiration poured from the faces of both men, and she thought of asking them to remove their coats and waistcoats. She was afraid, however, that this breach of modesty might be misunderstood, and forbore. She was sure her corsets were soaked clear through and would never dry out again, and both petticoats were undoubtedly perspiration-stained, but women could cope with the discomfort better than men and still give at least an illusion of coolness.

"I have been in Africa when it has been as hot," Philippe stated, "and the population was quite healthy. On the other hand, Paris had an epidemic several years ago during a comparatively cool spring. . . .

"I think it is unusualness of conditions that causes these outbreaks. Take the Centennial police force, for instance. I'm told its ranks have been decimated by dysentery and typhoid, and I'll tell you why. As the Exposition is a national venture, the Congressmen had the right of appointment, and from all over the Union these political hangers-on, totally unfitted for the work, have come here.

288

I imagine they had to take rooms in squalid neighborhoods, and they have succumbed to conditions they are not used to. Their relatives at home, learning of their sickness, tell others, and the whole Exposition is getting a bad name, which it doesn't really deserve."

Julia broke in to say: "Oh, I do like the book, Philippe. I understand Mrs. Alexander is a very popular author, although I have never read any of her books before—and the title, *Her Dearest Foe*, sounds most interesting. In three words it seems to contain so much Christian doctrine. Our foes should be dear to us, because they give us the opportunity to prove our own selves. . . . Does that sound too much like preaching, Philippe?"

"Indeed, no. It seems a highly elevating thought to me. One we could all heed." The pleasant three-sided conversation was ended when Teresina made her appearance. She was effusive in her greeting to Philippe, just as if nothing had happened, and managed to display her ring, an heirloom from Philippe's mother, so that it became by some art she alone understood the most noticeable thing about her. It was a boast to Gus, a warning to Julia, and a brand that she was his alone to her betrothed. She had barely had time to take the second book, which he now handed to her, and to note that he had made a similar gift to her sister, when Aunt Zena came in, so bubbling over with excitement that she quickly imparted it to the others.

"Philippe, will you run and help Lucius? I've just bought the most amazing and marvelous contraption. I'm just dying to see it again, and you will all be overwhelmed, I know. . . .

"Zenie, my dear, you're looking pale—love isn't agreeing with you! My, it's hot, isn't it? I haven't experienced weather like this since I was in Martinique, years ago—on official business, it was—well, practically, anyway. And Julia, child, hot weather becomes you.

"Gus, I want you to see this, particularly. As a man of science, I think you will be amazed."

"Indeed! It couldn't be more amazing than the automatic fountain," Julia broke in. "I still can't understand what makes it work."

"It's a principle of hydrodynamics . . ." Gus began, eager to prove himself truly the man of science, but he was interrupted by the return of Philippe, accompanied by Lucius. They struggled along bearing between them a good-sized crate. They held it while Aunt Zena considered its disposition.

"Here, put it here," she ordered, and then: "No, this room isn't long enough. The dining room! We'll have it set up on one end of the table."

Philippe interrupted. "But, Zena—Teresina and I are going out. I was just about to propose the minstrels to her when you came in."

"Minstrels? I should say not! Why, Philippe, I knew you'd be here, and that was one of the reasons I insisted on bringing this with me. . . . And I learned all about the operation of the machine myself. Imagine!"

"Machine? I might have known it was a machine. It's thunderation heavy. Zena, what in the world have you bought now?"

"Do as I say, Philippe. You are most aggravating. Into the dining room, and call Tina and Jesse. This is the most amazing thing you ever beheld, and they must see it. I was going to make you all wait, as a surprise. You can't even guess what I have—but you'll be even more excited if I tell you now. . . . It's a moving picture!"

The words were repeated in chorus, and Aunt Zena nodded her head violently. "That's right, a moving picture.

A moving picture—just as I said. I saw the announcement card in the newspaper, and it was every word true. I've seen it. Come, Philippe, and you, Lucius, hold up your end, don't let Mr. Philippe do all the work. . . . To the dining room!"

3

As the lights were turned up again, the whole group sat in an amazed silence that was broken by Mr. Rogers.

"By the Lord Harry, that is the most amazing and terrifying sight I have ever seen. And that reminds me, where is Lucius? Didn't he make all that commotion when it started? I know that darky—he ran. I bet he's hiding in the stable haymow this minute."

More than one of the audience had come close to following Lucius' example at first view of the gruesome sight, but terror and the darkness had held them. Now they felt a pleasant sense of white superiority, and could laugh at the colored man's defection. That relieved everyone, and an excited chatter began that completely repaid Aunt Zena for her efforts. Each one tried to talk louder than the other, to explain his own reactions. Of course, as Mr. Rogers could top them all, it ended with his description doing duty for all.

"The most ghastly sight I ever beheld! Zena, you should have prepared us for it. Those first slides you showed are similar to some I have seen, excepting these were clearer. The view of the Pantheon was particularly clear . . ."

"The Colosseum, Papa," Julia whispered.

"Of course, the Colosseum—the Pantheon is a smaller edifice—and then, when the picture of the skeleton flashed on the wall, I was startled, but not overwhelmed."

"Until it began to move!" Mrs. Rogers shrieked. "I

declare, I would have run like Lucius did, but my knees were weak."

"Move? It danced—it did a jig, right before our eyes." Mr. Rogers again took over, with a bellow. "And then, when it took off its grisly head and played ball with it— gruesome, I would call it." He had an idea. . . . "Zena, what do you say, can you show it again? All the way through?"

"Why, of course, Jesse, and then afterward I'll show how it works, so you can operate it yourself."

"Goodness, Zena, we'll be haunted by dancing skeletons forever," Mrs. Rogers objected, but her husband was busily explaining the rest of his idea. "We'll have the Peales over. . . . Gussie, knock on the wall for them. Julia, run down and get the Naylors. Gene is probably down there, and perhaps Henry is as well. Bring them up, but don't breathe a word what for. Just say it is something important—they'll come."

He roared with anticipatory laughter. "By Christopher, this will be good. We'll sit here and watch *them* get scared to death. Where are Mary and Martha? I wouldn't miss seeing Mary's face for a fortune when that skeleton begins juggling."

Mrs. Rogers shuddered. "Pet, don't mention it, please. It makes cold chills run down my spine. . . . Martha's gone home, and Mary is in bed. She had a hard day, so don't waken her. There's the Peales at the door—I'll let them in."

Philippe jumped to his feet. "Stay right there, Mother Rogers," he admonished, and hurried down the hall.

Mrs. Rogers looked after his tall, broad frame, which almost blocked the hallway, and said to herself: "My, Philippe has nice manners. . . . I wish Jesse would think to save me steps once in a while, instead of ordering me about."

The Peales came in, commenting about the heat. The signal through the wall was not unusual; they expected, as was often the case, that the Rogerses had made some ice cream and they were being invited to participate. They looked around questioningly when they beheld Aunt Zena standing like a soldier beside a contrivance that resembled nothing they had ever seen before. Their host was smiling at them, with a grin that was almost malevolent, for the recurring thought in his mind was "By Harry, I want to see Sol Peale's face when that skeleton begins to move!"

They were no more than seated when the twins trooped along, followed by Al and by Julia, who laughingly denied all their guesses as to the reason for the summons. No, it was not ice cream! They had the same thought as the Peales about the surprise in store.

"Ice cream—I could eat a quart, right now!" Georgina shouted, and Henry, very much the man since he was working and making his own pocket money, frowned and reproved her:

"Shut up, Gene, and don't act like a child. If it's ice cream there'll be plenty to go around. Mother always makes lots of it."

They also were surprised at Aunt Zena's pose, and their father's exuberance. He just couldn't keep still. He talked, sat down, jumped up again, laughed, tried to look serious, and then would slap his hand on his knee and guffaw. Henry whispered to his sister:

"Dad is up to something—look at him. He's like a cat that just ate the canary."

The gas jets were turned low, until all that could be seen was a vague ray illuminating the far wall. By this time, everyone knew what to expect—a new kind of magic lantern! Aunt Zena fussed with the apparatus, apologizing for her slowness in focusing it. Then she found the proper adjustment, and a circle of intense light was thrown on the wall. She had already developed a kind of patter to accompany the showing of the pictures, and she went through a half-dozen familiar views with appropriate explanations. As the Roman Colosseum slowly jerked out of the circle of light the shadow of a new slide edged across like the passage of an eclipse over the sun. A skeleton glared at them with sightless eyes. There was a slight pause, and some startled oh's, and the noise of Mr. Rogers' chair pushing back as he maneuvered for a better view of his guests' expressions. Then the miracle happened. With a slow swaying of the waist the skeleton began to dance! It was a moving picture, truly enough. Someone screamed, but Mr. Rogers broke the spell by roaring with laughter at the sight of Sol Peale's mouth suddenly dropping open, and this made the rest of the picture almost anticlimax. Sensation could go no further, and the audience sat in tense silence as the skeleton suddenly removed its own head and tossed it into the air with a rapid, erratic movement. When the picture finished, Mr. Rogers leaped to his feet and turned up the lights, amid the startled exclamations, the almost hysterical descriptions of their feelings, described anew by everyone.

All Mr. Peale could think of to say was the phrase "It's uncanny," which he repeated to anyone who would listen. Even Gus, the man of science, admitted the lifelike quality of the illusion, while Al Naylor predicted, stoutly:

"It's wonderful, all right, but this is only the beginning of something new and great. That skeleton was painted on glass or something. Some day they'll be doing the same kind of things with people, using photographs, I mean. Just imagine being able to see pictures of your family walking home from church, let's say. That would be something to marvel over—and it could be."

Everyone stood in embarrassed silence. Al always had the strangest ideas. He wasn't at all sensible, like his brother. Finally the group broke up when Mrs. Peale made the sage pronouncement, "My, my—what *is* the world coming to!"

Chapter 11   WHEN the news of Teresina's recent betrothal reached Harry Naylor, at Harrisburg, he accepted it more philosophically than Gus Palmer did. He retired to the privacy of the senate writing room, and while his fellow senators chewed, smoked, and told stories, he indited a letter that covered six pages of official stationery, in which he intimated that if Teresina had waited only a little while longer she might have had an offer of more importance than the one she had accepted.

Teresina had difficulty reading the tremendous flourishes that obscured the smaller script with which they entwined, but as the letter was signed "Your disconsolate and ob^{dt} serv^{nt}, Henry Longfellow Naylor (Senator, Pa.)," she kept it in a corner of her bureau drawer as a kind of food for her vanity. He enclosed with it a number of tickets for the reserved section of the stands for the Fourth of July celebration at Independence Hall, as an indication of his magnanimous feeling, but with one accord the family decided not to attend, even though it was announced that he would be one of the speakers.

"In this heat? Good gracious, no—not if a hundred Harry Naylors spoke," Mrs. Rogers said. "It's hot enough here, goodness knows, but in all that traffic, with all those people, it would be unbearable."

Aunt Zena agreed. "Besides, I don't hold with revolutions anyway, much less with celebrating one. I shiver to think what has happened to poor France. All the best people murdered, and the country run by riffraff."

Of course no one else agreed with her Royalist leanings, but it was useless to argue with Aunt Zena. For a time the family had almost convinced her that the Indians were not a menace, and that they would not descend on Kensington some night and murder them all in their beds, but since the Indian war now occupied so much attention in the papers, she insisted she was in deathly fear of meeting Sitting Bull in all his war paint, and the family had given up trying to argue her out of the notion.

"I propose we spend the Glorious Fourth in the pleasant repose of our own garden," said Mr. Rogers. "We shall have a party under the shade of the grape arbors. We'll take the automatic fountain out there, so its pleasant waters can cool the atmosphere. What do you say, Gussie? We'll make two freezers of ice cream. We'll have a picnic lunch, outdoors. We'll have speeches—and I'll deliver them. I can make the finest patriotic address you have ever heard . . ."

"God forbid," Mrs. Rogers interrupted. "I'm all in favor of a quiet little Fourth at home, but no patriotic orations from you, Jesse. They would quickly end up the way of all your speeches—the sins of the Republican party. I've heard about them until I'm sick of them."

"Now let's see who we can invite," Mr. Rogers went on, as if there had been no dissenting voice; and again his wife interrupted.

"Invite? We'll invite no one. You said a little family party, and I'm sticking to it. If we have people it will mean work, and it's too hot to do more than a body has to."

He looked crestfallen, his face appearing to bury itself in his beard. "A party doesn't seem right without at least one guest." He made a heavy bow toward Aunt Zena. "Of course we don't think of you as a guest. I was going to propose asking Duffy. I swear the poor fellow sees nothing but women most of the time, and he'd enjoy a little family gathering."

Aunt Zena looked up at him. "Duffy? Duffy? I suppose he is someone . . ."

"Jesse means Father Duffy. He refuses to call him 'Father,' and shames the poor man by insisting upon his chewing tobacco with him." Mrs. Rogers' tone was sharp, and she became more angry as she spoke. "And you make me sick, Jesse Rogers, with your condescending tone about inviting him. As if it was a good deed you were doing. Let me tell you, he is probably the most popular priest in Kensington, and there are plenty of people who feel honored to have him, any time he can come to see them. If you think he's lonely you can disabuse yourself of the idea. I will ask him to come, though, for he is good fun, and no trouble at all."

2

The Fourth brought no letup in the heat. During the morning Mr. Rogers walked over to the river, in the hope an errant breeze might follow the water, but the Delaware had a glassy look, undisturbed by the least ripple, and several brigs that would have ordinarily found their way upstream under their own sails either lay becalmed or were under tow by steam tugs. By the time he reached the house again he felt completely fagged out.

In the kitchen, Mary moved about with none of her

usual animation. Her lips were purple, and the perspiration poured down gutters formed by the wrinkles on her cheeks and chin. "I'm tuckered out for a fact," she whispered to him. Mr. Rogers sought out his wife, who was sewing on the second floor, and shouted to her:

"Gussie . . . *Gussie!* Mary is sick. I was just in the kitchen for a drink, and she looks like a ghost."

Mary? Mary sick? Suddenly the old woman was tremendously important to Mrs. Rogers. As important as her right hand. "I'm coming!" she shouted. "I guess it's the heat. It's enough to finish most anyone. . . . We better get her to bed immediately." She hurried downstairs thinking: "She must be sick for Jesse to notice. A body could be most dead before he'd see a thing wrong with them." Her thoughts took a new tack—"and the very day I let Martha off, because we were going to picnic!"

The old woman had completely collapsed on one of the kitchen chairs by the time they reached her. "Pet, we'll have to get her to her room, and I'll send Henry for the doctor."

"Leave it to me," Mr. Rogers boasted. He picked up the frail, limp creature while his wife warned, "Be careful, Jesse, and don't hurt yourself."

He almost tossed Mary into the air to show how very light she was. "Shucks, I could carry her up ten flights of stairs without even thinking of it." By the time he reached her own little room on the third floor he was panting, in spite of his boast, and was quite willing to deposit her on the bed. This was the first time he could remember having been in the old woman's room, and he felt a sense of shame for himself. Mary had been so much a part of the household for many years, but what did he really know about her? Here was her room! These four walls probably held a different Mary from the one who greeted him every

298

morning. A crucifix of vividly colored plaster hung over her cot, and a tiny flame burned on her bureau. Mr. Rogers abjured these symbols, and ordinarily would have refused them houseroom. At this moment they were sacred to him, not as religious articles, but because of the meaning they had for one soul.

Two daguerreotypes in velvet-covered frames hung on the wall. They were both of men. Was one of them a father—or a brother? Had Mary been married in that past out of which she had come to them, years ago? And by the way, how had they really treated her? Had her life with them been a happy one? Had they paid her as well as they should have? She had eaten the same food, shared the same roof, but had she also shared their love and affection? It was all right for him to say that he was fond of Mary, but had he ever really let Mary know of his feeling for her?

"Well, stop mooning, Jesse, and do something," Mrs. Rogers interrupted his thoughts. "I think it is nothing more than heat prostration, although that's bad enough, goodness knows. I've sent Henry for Dr. Morris—fortunately the boy isn't working today." As she talked she began to administer smelling salts from the familiar dark-green bottle, and then loosened Mary's garments. "Now you had better go, Pet. . . . I can manage all right, and if I know Mary, she'd be mortified if you helped me to put her to bed. When the doctor comes send him right up— and get the ice bag and fill it. There's one in the bathroom. Not the hot-water bottle, mind. You're so stupid about such things. The one with the wide mouth. I'll put it on her forehead. It can't do any harm, that's certain."

Once her husband was dispatched upon his errand, she undressed Mary quickly and efficiently. The poor bones and thin, wizened limbs were shocking. She was regretful for the times she had been annoyed by the old woman's slowness. How old was Mary, really? She began to handle her even more gently, and by the time Jesse returned with the ice bag—filled with hot water—Mary was between the sheets, and breathing a trifle easier.

"Was anyone ever so exasperating? You brought the ice bag all right, but it should have ice in it. Ice, do you hear?"

Mr. Rogers was mortified at his stupidity, although he attempted an excuse. "Right away, Gussie. I'll get it immediately, although I am sure I remember you saying something about hot water—I can still hear the words in my ears."

She called after him: "I said not the hot-water bottle— and bring some brandy, too. There's a bottle in the kitchen cupboard." Shaking her head, she returned to her patient. "I suppose now he'll fill the ice bag with brandy. . . . What a man!"

The brandy helped more than the ice. Mary opened her eyes, deep-sunken in her head, and began to apologize. "I'm sorry, ma'am, puttin' you to all this trouble. I'll be all right in a shake, and get on with them things for the picnic."

"Bother the picnic. You've been going too hard lately, and it's my fault, I suppose, but now you're to take it easy in bed today. From now on, if I forget myself and seem to drive you, just tell me off. . . . Jesse, there's the doorbell, and the doctor. Will you get him up here?"

As Mr. Rogers thumped downstairs, she went on: "Mary, tell me something, will you? I suppose I have been a hard mistress at times, but be honest with me. Do you regret having come to us, ever?"

"To you, ma'am? As full of life and fun as you are? That's what keeps an old body young, and that's a fact—

lots of life and a good time now and then . . . and we've
had a lot of good times, and some bad ones, when the
children were little . . ." Mary paused, and Mrs. Rogers
knew what she was thinking about—the time Raphael died.
Her voice was stronger as she continued: "If you're a little
quick-tempered once in a while, it's the Eyetalian blood in
your veins. We can't all be Irish, and take things sensibly
as they come along, I says."

They were interrupted by the approach of the doctor,
with Mr. Rogers. She was suddenly conscious that both
she and her servant were crying. Not because of what they
had said, but because of the unspoken things between them.
Quickly taking hold of herself, she spoke in her usual sharp
manner.

"Come, Mary, we're behaving like two old women, and
here's the doctor. . . . Dr. Morris, do come in. Here's
the only member of our family who never gets sick, so you
don't see much of her."

The doctor deposited his little black bag on the wash-
stand, and plucked at the fringe of beard that ran from
ear to ear under his chin. He was clean-shaven except for
this adornment, and it gave him the appearance, somehow,
of a pink-complexioned, beardless youth peering out from
behind a gray bush of whisker.

"Of course I know Mary. She's been treating me royally
for years, whenever I've been in to look at the rest of you.
She knows my fondness for tea, and there's always been a
pot of it for me." In his best bedside manner he bent over
and asked, "Now what seems to be the matter?"

"Mr. Rogers thought she wasn't looking so well. He
told me, and by the time we got down to her she had collapsed completely. He carried her upstairs, and I gave her
salts, and a touch of brandy, and the ice bag."

"H-m-m-m." The doctor took a thin blue wrist and felt

301

the pulse, while Mary's eyes peeked over the rims of their sockets at him. "Nothing but the heat, I think," he finally announced, jovially. "I'll give you a little tonic, and you had better rest for a few days."

The patient began to move quite wildly under her sheet. "Oh, I can't at all, with the picnic this afternoon, and Father Duffy coming. What will he be thinkin' of me?"

"Now, Mary, it's all right," Mrs. Rogers soothed, and she explained to the doctor: "It's so hot we decided to have no cooked meals today, and instead we are picnicking in the garden."

Mr. Rogers had an idea. "What do you think, Doctor? I carried Mary up here. It was no trouble at all—I hardly felt her weight. Would it be all right for me to carry her down again, and fix up a place under the arbor for her? It would be cooler there, and we're having ice cream, and she will be the guest of honor!"

"It won't hurt her, unless there is too much excitement."

"Excitement? There'll be no excitement. There won't be anyone but the family, and Duffy—an old reprobate of an ex-railway man, but a quiet soul. . . . Of course there won't be any excitement."

3

In her whole lifetime Mary had never eaten so much ice cream at one sitting. And the missus egging her on! And the mister . . . wasn't he a one! And Father Duffy cutting up and acting like a two-year-old! And the arguments he and the mister had—in a friendly way, of course. And Aunt Zena, the missus's sister—wasn't she a one!

And the "childern," as she always called them—Miss Zenie, grown up and engaged to a Frenchie . . . not that he didn't speak English perfect, but he was still a Frenchie, you could tell by his clothes, and his manners. Miss Zenie was a sharp one, at times, but you couldn't help loving someone you'd held in your arms as a baby—and changed diapers on, for that matter. Her two loves, Henry and Miss Gene! What fine grown young folks they had become!

And Miss Julia, who had been a queer stick of a child. . . . She had managed the whole picnic, so that the missus needn't hardly pick up a spoon. Of course it was plain as the nose on your face, she was playing up to Miss Zenie's young man, and Miss Zenie, the fool, her, instead of playing up too, she was having one of her spells.

It was a great, glorious, and wonderful afternoon in celebration of a great, glorious, and wonderful day. Most wonderful of all was to sit there in the middle of everything, without having to hurry around while your rheumatism made you limp—like being the missus herself, it was.

The mister made a speech and Father Duffy made another. A most unusual speech for Father Duffy, who was usually so full of fun. It had been quite a serious speech, and lots of it didn't make sense to Mary. . . .

All the others had been very much affected by what Father Duffy said. He had to leave immediately afterward, and the little picnic party broke up with his going. It was an unusual power he had displayed in ending an otherwise hilarious occasion upon a serious and inspirational note. It might have seemed a strange talk to give before that little family gathering, although not one of them thought it incongruous. It was as if Father Duffy were using them either to practice on, to perfect his thoughts for later delivery to a larger audience, or as a means of communication— as if they would, in effect, carry his message to the greater group for which it was intended.

Actually, although none of his listeners could know this, Father Duffy's talk was for himself and to himself. It was

303

an affirmation before witnesses. He had not appeared to be in a serious mood when he rose at the conclusion of Mr. Rogers' mock peroration. He was still chuckling at his host's prize gesture, when he had shouted, "Look at the blood on my undershirt, where it flowed at Gettysburg—I haven't washed it since!" He bowed slightly to Aunt Zena and to his hostess, and winked, deliberately winked, at Mary, and said, "Ladies," then glanced directly at Henry, "and gentlemen!"

Mr. Rogers' face took on an anticipatory grin. He always enjoyed a good speech, and he was sure that Duffy could deliver a humdinger. The priest's own grin faded and he took on a serious, benign expression.

"My good friends. I want to thank you for this afternoon. Not for the food, or the shade, or the fun, but for an example you have set which fixes my faith. How fitting that on this day your servant should be your honored guest. How fortunate I am to have taken part in paying homage to her."

"Duffy's thoughts have gone woolgathering," Mr. Rogers thought, the pause was so long before Father Duffy continued.

"One hundred years ago, in a lodginghouse in this city, a man reaffirmed the dignity and brotherhood of his fellows. His words were made the keystone upon which our country has been built. The stirring words of the Declaration of Independence have fired men's hearts. The spark lit there has burned low at times, and fitfully, but it has continued to burn.

"Here, beneath the vine of a kindly man and his wife, it is a clear, serene flame—a torch they will carry on to the future."

Father Duffy glanced around at all the little group, and

304

was visibly affected by their intense concentration. Mary was even crying, gently.

"A fratricidal conflict almost extinguished this flame—a new and more terrible sort of war is dampening it at this moment. It is a war of stocks and bonds, of machines and property, against the people. It is a remorseless war, fought with starvation, exposure, and disease. The banners of profits, graft, and corruption are already waving upon the ramparts of one army, and the other is raising its own standards. There have already been casualties in this war against the spirit of brotherhood. The wounded occupy hovels all around us here in Kensington—people who asked no more than their daily bread, clothing, fuel and education and shelter.

"As the servant of a Master who taught the unimportance of property, my own position is clear, and I want to re-affirm it. . . . During the coming century, so long as I may live, my stand will be with the people, opposed to the ranks of vested interest. There also will stand my Church. Some of its members may be misled, and where priests take the side of Mammon they will be doubly scorned, as enemies first, as traitors and turncoats second. But the Church will be on your side. In the end it will be there, for it could be nowhere else.

"It is my prayer, my fervent prayer, that a hundred years from now, under this same vine, a patriarch of the twentieth century, with his family and his manservants and his maidservants, may celebrate a second Centennial, knowing this enemy also is dead—assured that his neighbors are also celebrating because they too have their share of the fruit of the land."

PART - - - FOUR

❧ ❧ ❧

July to September

❧ ❧ ❧

1876

"We meet today, united, free,
And loyal to our land and Thee,
To thank Thee for the era done,
And trust Thee for the opening one."

—WHITTIER, "Centennial Hymn."

Chapter 1

THE NOTICES of John Wanamaker, the merchant who was one of the proprietors of Oak Hall, at Sixth and Market streets, reminded Mr. Rogers of a need for new garments of lighter weight than those he usually wore. "If this weather keeps up, we shall have to run around in sheets, as they did in Bible times," he observed to himself. Mr. Wanamaker had opened a new store on the site of the old Pennsylvania Station at Thirteenth Street, where Moody and Sankey had had their revival the preceding winter, and he was advertising a sale of men's clothing in his usual extravagant manner. Instead of returning directly home after work, Mr. Rogers caught a horsecar for downtown. It was the second day after the Fourth, and he passed the time of the slow journey soliloquizing over the pleasant holiday.

"There is nothing like a day spent in the bosom of one's family," he thought. A feeling of pity lingered for his sister-in-law, who had been denied such pleasure until now. Just imagine living in foreign lands most of one's life! Poor Zena—all at sixes and sevens. She was like the king in some fable he had read, who had never been able to find love and affection, though his coffers were filled with wealth. She deserved better, and in his present mood, Mr. Rogers would gladly have offered her real love from his inexhaustible supply of the commodity, but Gussie was so apt to misunderstand things that were done from the noblest motives.

309

He swung off the horsecar in approved railroading fashion, without waiting for the horses to come to a dead stop. Although it was barely nine o'clock, the heat was already oppressive. It seemed as if God was on the side of those who had opposed the Centennial. Philippe had said yesterday that the grounds were practically deserted under the glare of that blazing sun.

He thought with approval of his prospective son-in-law. A nice young fellow. Someone after his own heart, and not a namby-pamby. The kind of a driver a filly like Teresina needed. "She's got a hard mouth," he told himself, "and won't take kindly to the bit. She's like Gussie in that respect. It took expert horsemanship and a good, strong hand on the reins to break her in to double harness."

All the Market Street sidewalks were covered with metal canopies or canvas awnings, so one could walk in a kind of shaded cavern for whole squares, and from its comparative coolness look out on the wide street. Beyond a double row of railroad tracks the street was cobbled clear across the portion taken up by the horse railways with their double tracks. It made a really metropolitan scene, the heavy freight cars pulled along by their double teams of horses, and hurly-burly of streetcars drawn by hurrying steeds, hackneys eager for fares, rumbling drays, loaded vans, and occasional private carriages. Mr. Rogers took pride in being a citizen of the second largest city in a nation of forty-four million people.

His musings were suddenly interrupted by overhearing a newsboy's cry. The whole purport of his shout was unintelligible, but he caught the word "massacre" and was immediately sure he knew what had happened. There had been further trouble with the Turks! He hailed the boy in a display of the proper use of lung power. "A paper here . . . quickly!"

310

"Day, Express, Herald, Star, Telegraph, North American, Gazette, Inquirer, Press, Ledger, Record, Item, or Times?"

Mr. Rogers reflected that it was a good thing the evening papers were not yet out on the street, or a choice would have been even more difficult, but as the newsboy's whole stock did not consist of over half a dozen papers, he asked for the *Star*—one of the less popular—for the perverse reason of finding out what excuse the boy would make if he could not deliver. The child—Mr. Rogers envied him his bare feet and tattered trousers—slipped through his sheets, and held out a grimy hand to display the one with the proper title. As he paid for it and walked away, Mr. Rogers reflected that his psychology was probably wrong. He should have asked for one of the more popular papers, of which the boy was probably sold out!

His idle speculation was quickly forgotten as he opened the front page and read TRAGEDY ON THE LITTLE BIG HORN, and went on with the account, chewing his tobacco furiously in his excitement. General Custer and a whole detachment of his men had been killed! The account was a highly lurid one. The heroic commander, leading a detachment of cavalry, had recklessly charged into a whole army of Indians in encampment, and in the words of the *Star*, the brave General and his men had all been massacred on the spot by the fierce and bloodthirsty savages.

The action had occurred almost two weeks ago, it seemed, but so slowly did news travel on the Western prairies that the news had reached the telegraph lines only yesterday, through a scout who had escaped. The *Star* still could not believe the disaster was as great as first reports made it, but it pointed an editorial warning. This is what came of pampering the redskins!

Mr. Rogers lifted his head for a moment, and saw other men, as deeply engrossed in their papers as he was, angrily reading the bloodcurdling tidings. With heavy heart he resumed his walk toward the Wanamaker store at Thirteenth Street. He heard frequent expression of this anger at the foul deed of the Indians. This also saddened him; people were so quick to see the beam and miss entirely the mote! What should the poor savages have done when the wildly charging little army appeared in their midst, with muskets firing and sabers swishing? Should the Sioux have submitted to the foolhardy band and allowed themselves, and the women and children with them, to be shot down as they prepared the tribal meal? Instead they had repelled the invaders, and somewhere along that stream so strangely called the Little Big Horn, some two hundred men, youths from the East—from Philadelphia, perhaps— lay dead in strange, wild surroundings, they and their too sanguine commander.

To him it was a mockery of a day so recently celebrated. "Within a week of the hundredth anniversary of our own struggle for liberty," he mused, "there on the Little Big Horn a few thousand savages were engaged in the same unending conflict for freedom, and the country which a century ago announced its own birthright so proudly was now the aggressor!"

If the first hundred years could make so great a difference, Mr. Rogers speculated as to what the second century would bring. How nearly right had Colonel Forney been in his article on the Centennial inauguration? In his present mood, Mr. Rogers doubted that he had been right at all. We were a preponderantly Anglo-Saxon country, in which the soul of the pioneer and the tradesman mixed. Wasn't it more probable that we would begin the loathsome course of empire, once the savages were finally disposed of? There was Mexico to the south. We had already ventured once in that direction, and had come out with miles of mountainous desert clutched in our hands. There were islands to the southeast. Spain, England, and France held them. When would greed send us adventuring thither? And there was all the vast Pacific, filled with islands, a rich empire. Right at this moment we were negotiating a trade pact with the King of Hawaii. Might we not soon displace our little brothers entirely?

No, it was not a happy prospect. As Duffy, a priest, maybe, but a good scout nevertheless, worried about the effects of just ordinary business on his parishioners, Mr. Rogers worried about his country on a world scale. It was a world he knew little about, but he had inherited the Quaker gift of personalizing nations and peoples, and accepting their rights as the equal of his own. He knew also something of the brutalizing effects of conquest, the price of empire. The great Indian mutiny had occurred but a short time after the birth of Teresina. How many English lives had it cost? How many Indians had died for freedom? The price of empire was a heavy one, and it had to be paid many times. In the gaining, first of all, and in protecting it thereafter from other nations no less greedy. And those who paid the price rotted where they fell; others reaped the ill-gotten gains.

In what four corners of the world might Americans be dying within the next century, that this westward tide of empire might pursue its way? Suddenly, Mr. Rogers felt alone. Terribly alone. He was probably the only man in Philadelphia who read the tidings of Custer's misadventure and reacted to them as he did. He had to see people— talk to them, know that he was actually of them. It was a necessity, an immediate necessity.

He turned into the dark, inviting door of a saloon, where a half-dozen men in convivial mood hung on the bar. He ordered a lager, spit his quid into the gutter within the front rail, restrained his beard with his right hand as he lifted the handled glass with his left, and immersed both parched lips in the creamy foam. The brew was a heavy one, and the first glass made him feel less despondent. He signaled for a second glass while he listened to the loud-voiced conversation. It seemed that all the men hanging over the bar were experienced Indian-fighters, separated from their destiny by the accident of space. Any one of them could have ended the farce of armed resistance to the United States in less time than the present commanders had required to reach the present fiasco.

Mr. Rogers deplored the warlike tendencies of men who were not likely to have to fight, and with the third lager he enjoyed a thought: Suppose a recruiting officer were to enter the bar at this moment, and lay a hand on the shoulder of the potbellied businessman who was shouting, "They ought to kill the whole lot of them, men, women and children, and be done with them!" He laughed as the idea took hold, and the other men looked around at the interruption to their martial discourse. He could see the surprised look of little potbelly when he turned around at the recruiting officer's touch, and heard his stern command —"Come on, we need you. You start for the Black Hills at six this evening. We have heard about your boasting, so here is your chance."

The idea was engaging—put the firebrands in the armies of the world. Let them shoot it out, and scalp each other. The chances for peace afterward might be immeasurably improved. He left the bar and stepped into a brighter world outside. It was still hot, but a pleasant perspiration that began to ooze through his pores cooled him as it evaporated. Except that he had determined to visit the new Wanamaker store, he would have stopped at the old one, near Eighth Street. Why in thunderation did anyone want to build a store so far away from the center of things? He crossed the tangle of railroad tracks and switches by the old terminal at Eleventh Street, and became conscious of a rapid diminution of the sense of well-being the beer had inspired. He was feeling hot again. He needed just one more drink to keep the sweat moving.

He turned into the public room under the Bingham House, bothered anew by the thought that while life had been moving along so pleasantly for him, men were dying in battle on this very continent; men who were, in a sense, his representatives. Just what was his own responsibility in the matter? Everyone excepting himself thought the cause a just one. Would he be absolved by a higher Judge from the sin of going along with the others without protest?

When he emerged onto the street for a second time he realized that until this moment he had never understood the real purpose of barrooms. They were designed as repositories for melancholy thoughts! Here a child was selling flowers, wilted bouquets of roses and fern. He dug his hand into a pocket and found a ten-cent note, which he exchanged for the sad little display. A little farther on, a street hawker was crying the advantages of a new kind of potato-peeler. With almost miraculous speed the tuber was divested of its skin, which curled in an even ribbon over the hawker's hand. Wouldn't Martha find a tool like that of inestimable value, considering the quantities of potatoes they consumed? His Quaker shrewdness was not lulled by lager beer. The potato-peeler the hawker was using was good—he proved it over and over—but what about the ones in the boxes that he gave away for a mere twenty-five-cent note? Mr. Rogers determined on a purchase, on his own terms. He shouldered importantly through the group of prospective buyers, and stood with head up, so that his beard stuck forth at an aggressive angle. Finally,

315

after treating the hawker to this view of himself, warning that he was not to be readily buncombed, he spoke.

"Young man, are those knives you are selling the same as the one in your hand?"

The torrent of sound failed to halt the man in his demonstration, and a long curlycue of potato peel fell on his little table.

"All the same, exactly the same—and sold for the mere cost of the box and printing, twenty-five cents."

Mr. Rogers held forth a large hand. "May I see it, please, for a moment?" As the hawker seemed to hesitate, he calmly took the potato and the peeler and tried it for himself. It worked! Undoubtedly it worked. While his peelings were not quite as smooth and regular as the salesman's, they satisfied him. Several newcomers had gathered around the stand to watch him demonstrate, and it was evident they took the tall bearded man with the stiff felt hat on his head for the proprietor. One of them now questioned him belligerently. "Are you sure they'll work?"

Mr. Rogers smiled at him. "Certainly they will work. Can't you see me working this one?" The man was satisfied, and handed him a twenty-five-cent note, while he took a peeler from the boxes of them piled to the front of the stand. Mr. Rogers added another note to the stranger's, and presented them both.

"Here you are, sir. Here is the money for the one I sold for you in my own demonstration, and here is my own note—for this peeler, which I shall keep, as it works very well indeed."

The hawker responded very much as Mr. Rogers suspected he might. He angrily retorted, "Hey, you can't do that—that's my demonstrator."

Mr. Rogers had already pocketed the utensil, and eyed the young man sternly through cold gray eyes. "Do you intimate that there is a difference between the knife I have purchased and those on the counter there?"

"I want my peeler, and the hell with you!" the hawker shouted.

"And I'll settle your hash, young fellow—I'll find a policeman and inform on you." He started off, and when he felt he'd walked a reasonable distance, looked back, to see the hawker hurriedly folding his stand. Mr. Rogers chuckled to himself. He had made a good purchase, of that he was sure. He put the peeler in his other pocket, which reminded him that his bouquet was becoming more bedraggled by the minute, and at the same time it was a nuisance to carry. He became conscious of another fact: in the excitement of his altercation with the potato-peeler salesman he had turned east instead of west. He was back to Ninth Street already, and it was getting hotter by the minute. As he had already found a cure for his discomfort, he turned in at the first bar to refresh himself and make further plans.

"The deuce with walking back to Mr. Wanamaker's!" He would buy clothes at another time, when it was cooler. It seemed a shame to waste a morning in town, though— he would do some marketing. Things were always cheaper down at the wharves than they were out in Kensington. He held up a thick forefinger as a signal to the bartender. . . .

2

It was difficult, disembarking from the horsecar with so many packages, and the driver was facetious. "Take it easy, Kriss Kringle!" he shouted, much to the amusement of the other passengers. "It's quite a load you're taking home."

Exercising unusual restraint, Mr. Rogers decided to overlook the remark. Then a suspicion occurred to him—had there been a double meaning in what the driver had said about taking home a load? He turned around angrily, but by this time the speeding vehicle was halfway to the next corner. If the driver thought his head had been affected in the slightest by the couple of beers he had taken down by the ferry house after the completion of his marketing, he would have liked to disabuse him of the thought. Of course it was too late now, but he determined that no one else should get that false impression, and he walked very slowly, and with great care, over to the curb.

His bundles were not disposed properly, and once on the safety of the sidewalk, he eased them carefully to the bricks. He noted a slight injury to the candy box. The five pounds of bonbons he had purchased at an unbelievably low price had squashed somewhat from the pressure necessary to hold them under his arm. He determined to carry the sack of potatoes over his shoulder. They were the heaviest single item, and a half-bushel bag had been a problem to load and unload from the horsecar, but when Gussie heard what he had paid for them, she would agree it would have been foolish to pass them up.

The thought struck him that the burlap bag no longer seemed to contain a half-bushel. At first he wondered if there were not a hole in it, but an inspection proved it was sound. Then he recalled what had happened, and laughed jovially. "Of course! Imagine forgetting! I used them up demonstrating the potato-peeler!"

But not a full peck of potatoes? He calculated with great care just how many potatoes he could have peeled. Of course, there were a number of saloons in the vicinity of the markets, but he had not been in nearly all of them. Because of the heat, however, he had frequented several.

That reminded him! It was hot now—extremely hot.

Should he go up to Paddy's and have a beer, or go home
and divest himself of his packages first? He wisely decided
on the second course, and returned to a careful, measured
consideration of the problem of the missing potatoes.
Well, say he had peeled six for that first bartender, who
had been skeptical about it. No, he must have peeled
twice that many for him—no matter how deftly he'd made
the peelings, the man had not been satisfied that it was
quicker than an ordinary knife. He'd shown him! Even
if it had taken a dozen potatoes! Then, say a dozen multi-
plied by four—no, six or seven—stops; the business of assist-
ing bartenders in solving their potato problem had taken
a deuce of a lot of time.

Anyway, added up together, he'd used a lot of potatoes.
Too bad he hadn't brought them home with him. Martha
would have been saved a lot of potato-peeling. Oh, well,
what did a few potatoes matter? They were cheap as dirt,
and heavy to carry as well. He lightly threw the sack over
his shoulder—too lightly, for he knocked his hat askew in
the process. He felt his pocket to be sure his flowers were
safe. He picked up the paper bag of dried beans—country-
style beans, you just couldn't buy them in regular stores—
and the sack of rice imported directly from South Carolina.
One had to do something to help the struggling Southern
states. He tried to juggle the candy between the rice and
the beans, but it didn't work so well. There was nothing
for it but to put it under his arm again. One consolation,
the candies probably wouldn't squash any more than they
had already.

There was still one package not disposed of. What in
the world was it? Oh, yes, he recalled—that was glass, he
mustn't break it.

The sidewalk of Richmond Street was sadly in need of
repair. Mr. Rogers had never before realized the number

of depressions and ridges, broken and irregular bricks, and potholes where there were no bricks at all, that were ready to trap the unwary foot. It was a time for circumspect progress. He whispered a word of caution to himself. "Take it easy, Jesse, old boy. It's a hot day, and there is no hurry."

He managed so well that the neighbors who observed him thought only that it was an unusual sight for Mr. Rogers to carry home the marketing; his wife usually attended to it. Nonetheless, he breathed more easily when he reached his own front door. Here a new dilemma presented itself. Try in every way he could, it was totally impossible to free a hand to pull the doorbell, and he ended up by kicking smartly against the varnished door that was his wife's pride. As he waited impatiently to be admitted, he enjoyed in anticipation Gussie's delighted surprise at his marketing and gifts. It was a long time since he had brought her candy, courtship days since he had offered her roses, and so far as he could remember, there had never been an occasion when he had brought her both. A broad smile began to illumine his face, and it stayed bravely lit as his wife herself opened the door and greeted him.

"Where in the world have you been until five o'clock in the afternoon? You've had no sleep, you have to work tonight, and you come in looking like a ragpicker!"

This was hardly the way to be greeted, Mr. Rogers felt, but Gussie would be all the more apologetic when she saw his gifts. He followed her aggressive little figure down the hallway. Gussie always walked so thunderation fast—and the hall was ill-lit, he decided, as he stumbled twice in its length. "I've some potatoes here!" he shouted, and even to himself his voice sounded unnecessarily loud, so he re-

peated in a stage whisper, "I've some potatoes here, Gussie
—I better leave them in the kitchen."

One might have thought from this conspirator's tone
that he had stolen the vegetables, but even his wife did
not suspect him of this, although there was fire in her eye
as he unloaded his packages, and her foot tapped menac-
ingly against the table leg. He was too pleased with himself to notice. He delivered potatoes, beans, and rice like
a grocer selling his wares, and like a good salesman, he was
not put off by the discovery that he'd lost most of the
beans from a hole in the bag, or by Mrs. Rogers when she
protested:

"Ten pounds of rice! Good God, Jesse, when will we
use it? You won't touch rice, and you've always upheld
the children when they didn't want to eat it."

He caught himself shouting again. "By Harry, they'll
eat this!" and once more lowered his voice to a whisper as
he handed over the candy. The package was more than
slightly askew, and a thick pink syrup seemed to be leaking
from a corner of it. He was a little taken aback to see how
much his gift had suffered in transportation, and to cover
up an uncomfortable lull, he reached for the roses. As
they were none too fresh when he purchased them, early
in the morning, and as they had been clutched in his hand
or forced down in his pocket for the rest of the day, it was
understandable that Mrs. Rogers should not have recognized them for roses, but inexcusable for her to ask in a
tone of unmistakable sarcasm: "And what is this mess,
pray? Decayed beet tops?"

A man could come home with the best intentions in the
world, and this was the reception he received! Mr. Rogers
was becoming angry. He placed his last package on the
table, resolved not even to bother about explaining its

321

contents, but his spouse pounced upon it, and tore off the wrapper.

"Catarrhal Compound . . . asthma . . . bronchial obstructions . . . hacking coughs . . . night chills—who in the world is this for? May I ask who suffers from night chills around here?"

By this time, Mr. Rogers was on the defensive. He realized the fact, and it added to his sense of injustice, but he persevered in his attempt to control his temper.

"Now, Gussie, you yourself have often remarked about the unhealthfulness of the Philadelphia climate—the insal —insalubrity of its location between the rivers, so to speak. At any moment one of us may be stricken with catarrh, or asthma, or a disease of the respiratory organs. . . ." He began to recall the spiel of the man who had sold him the medicine, and he finished off in approved medicine-man style, holding the bottle aloft in one hand and pointing at it with the other, "And here—here is the sovereign remedy."

The effect was spoiled to some extent because not only had Mr. Rogers' hat been knocked crooked by the bag of potatoes, it had been deeply dented on the crown as well. At any rate, he failed utterly to move his wife to admit the wisdom of his purchase. The storm clouds were gathering, he could now discern, and he strove to head them off by a new stratagem. He would shame Gussie with the terrible news of the morning!

"Madam," he thundered, "do you know what has happened? The United States has just suffered a disastrous defeat at arms. Hundreds of soldiers, under the command of their intrepid leader, have fallen on the banks of the Little Big Horn!"

"If you mean Custer's charge, I read about it in the papers this morning, and I don't think it was important enough to excuse your coming home in this condition."

322

The woman was impossible. Who was master in this household? Who brought home the money? Who attempted the little, graceful things that made life easier and more pleasant? Whose efforts went for naught? It was with great difficulty that Mr. Rogers restrained these thoughts. He had one last ace-in-the-hole! If Gussie did not change her tune when she saw the potato-peeler, which had met the approbation of every bartender to whom he had demonstrated it—by Christopher, he would give her a piece of his mind! This was her last chance! He brought the marvelous appliance from his pocket, and held it up. "My dear, do you know what this is?" he asked with the air of a conjurer about to pull rabbits from a hat.

"Of course I do," Mrs. Rogers snapped. "It's a potato-peeler. Martha has been using one like it for years, and if you paid over ten cents for it you were cheated, so there."

What could you do with such a woman? He turned away sadly. He was not going to be tricked into a display of temper. He trod the dark hallway, and slowly ascended the stairs. In the morning, when Gussie was in a more reasonable frame of mind, he must speak to her about that stair carpet. It was very irregularly laid. He had tripped over it before, years ago. He recalled the occasion perfectly. Now he felt sorry for himself. To think what marriage had got him into—and there was his spouse, whom he had promised to love and to cherish, standing at the foot of the stairs, hurling untruths and vituperations at him!

He felt increasingly sorry for himself, and for solace, compared his lot with that of those poor boys who had lost their lives in defending the nation against the invader. . . . That didn't sound quite right, and yet he was certain he had remembered someone using those very words. The trouble was, he was sleepy, extremely sleepy. How was he to have known that Martha already had a potato-peeler?

In a way, that was proof in itself that the article had merit. He undressed and slipped heavily into bed, but before he gave over to deep slumber, a tear started in each eye—one for himself, and one for the heroes of the Little Big Horn.

3

Aunt Zena had gone for a walk a short time before Mr. Rogers' home-coming. Denise accompanied her for reasons of safety. No one knew what might happen, with the savages loose. Zena was very much disturbed by the news in the morning paper, and nothing her sister could say would convince her that the danger was several thousand miles away. She accepted the miles as figures in arithmetic, but she visualized the total as a distance comparable with that from Paris to Lyon, for instance . . . or from there to Sedan. Everyone had said the Germans could never occupy Paris. . . .

No, Philadelphia was unsafe, and first proof of the fact was the mystery of her brother-in-law. It was no mystery, really. Poor Jesse had been scalped—that unpleasant habit of removing the hair in which the Indians indulged. Her hope was that they had hacked off his beard, by mistake. Mrs. Rogers was also worried, and her sister's constantly recurring suggestions drove her frantic.

"For the last time, Zena—the Indians are on the other side of the continent. They have not captured Jesse, of that I am sure. Why don't you take a walk, or get Lucius to hitch up the carriage? The air would do you good."

The hazards of walking seemed less. The colored boy might venture too far in the enemy's direction, and Denise could hold her own in any company. They set out on a timorous promenade, and were returning to the Rogers home without incident when the sharp-eyed Denise noticed something on the pavement. She stopped and picked it up, and saw another ahead—and another.

With tense concentration, the two women followed a trail that seemed to blaze the very path they were following. There was no doubt it represented some kind of threat! They walked along, stooping every few moments and chattering excitedly in French. By the time they reached the Rogers doorstep both women were close to hysterics. The malevolent signs pointed directly to their doorway!

Mrs. Rogers had just finished cleaning up a sticky trail of pink syrup she had unwittingly made in carrying a box of bonbons to the garbage can when the bell rang. Mary was upstairs—she'd sent her up for an afternoon rest—and Martha was busy. She was hurrying to the door when a second frantic ringing began. "Is someone trying to pull that bell from its spring?" she wondered. Two wild-eyed females confronted her, neither of them capable of coherent speech.

"For the land sakes, Zena, what *has* happened? Don't talk so fast, and explain what Indians, and where you saw them."

There began a hysterical account of a mysterious trail they had followed, but before that could make sense, Denise gave a shriek and pointed to the floor. "There, madame—right into your own home the pathway leads." She stooped and picked something from the carpet, while Aunt Zena, with shaking hands, held out two little piles of similar objects.

"Beans—soup beans!" Mrs. Rogers shouted back, to make herself heard over the babble of French. "Of course they lead here, seeing they were in a bag Jesse had, and leaked out on the way home."

Chapter 2

IN THE intervals between her ordinary household occupations, and largely supplanting the work of mending clothes and altering them, stitching rag rugs, and working on a crazy quilt that had been in progress for years, Mrs. Rogers was devoting herself to plans for Teresina's wedding. Aunt Zena also had ideas for this occasion, although her sister pursed her lips and assumed an implacable attitude whenever they began a discussion of the subject.

"The one thing I intend to do for myself is run my own daughter's wedding," Mrs. Rogers declared to herself. "Zena's not content with coming over here and practically taking over the running of my household—she's got Martha and Mary following her around like slaves. Heaven only knows what goes on behind my back between her and Jesse, but I'll get to the bottom of that in the end. . . . Then there's that stick of a Denise to put up with. I declare the woman thinks she is even better than I am. I'll sit on her some day, even if my French *has* grown rusty."

Unpredictable as the weather, Mrs. Rogers' thoughts veered around to a different quarter. "I don't mind Zena buying the child things for her trousseau, if she wants to. After all, it was nice of her to send all the way to Paris for materials, just as if there wasn't goods a-plenty here in Philadelphia." She cooled herself with a small black fan her sister had sent her years before, and absent-mindedly scratched Sankey's ear after the dachshund had pulled himself up to receive the favor. "Goodness, I believe this is the hottest summer I have ever put in!" she interpolated, and continued a mental outline of her plans. "Let Zena buy all the clothes she wants to. I intend to have my own way about the wedding itself." She knew just what she wanted, a nice, quiet, dignified affair.

326

"I'm sure Philippe doesn't want anything too fancy. What man does? And Zenie will be guided by me. There will be our own friends, and perhaps some of Jesse's, from the railroad. As Father Duffy will marry her, I don't think Jesse will balk at going to church. They certainly seem to think a world of each other. He's a good man, too, and I suppose there *is* an awful lot of poverty in this parish, but I wish he wouldn't talk about it to Jesse all the time. When the two of them get together they're a caution. He just can't see his own daughter married and himself standing outside pouting, but he's just Quaker enough to do it, at that."

Fortunately, Mrs. Rogers' thoughts were her own. She could follow their tortuous course, although she would have had a difficult time explaining them to anyone else.

"As for making a splash, like Zena proposes, I'm against it. We're not in society, here in Kensington, and Zenie won't live here afterwards, so what is the use of too large an affair? A small one will be trouble and expense enough, even if Zena does foot most of the bills."

Much to her mother's surprise, Teresina did not side with her on the matter of the wedding. Nothing in connection with it could be too large for her. She and her aunt became conspirators, sneaking at all hours in and out of each other's rooms. These clandestine meetings usually began with a preamble by Aunt Zena—"Your mother won't approve of this, but if you think you'd like it, I'll do it for you"—from which point she would go on with some new, elaborate plan.

The major difficulty in the way of a large wedding, and one Mrs. Rogers had recognized from the beginning, lay in the limited circle of their friends. There were so few people they could invite, outside of a few neighbors. Mr. Rogers knew a great many wealthy and influential Quakers,

327

but he was on bad terms with most of them, and it was extremely unlikely they would attend a ceremony in a Catholic church even supposing he could be cajoled into inviting them. Teresina bewailed this fact continuously, and her aunt's assurances—"My, if you were only marrying in Paris, where I know so many people!"—did no good. Teresina had visions of a whole church full of her aunt's friends—elderly roués, all of them, following her with their eyes as she walked down the aisle. She had heard enough stories from Aunt Zena, in confidential moments, to know what to expect from *them*.

Her dissatisfaction made her continually petulant, and Philippe, who cared not at all for a wedding and would have traipsed off willingly enough and been married by the Mayor, was treated every evening to a long account of plans and difficulties. He consoled himself with the knowledge that a girl was always upset at such a time as this, and by holding before him the fact of Teresina's beauty. For she was beautiful. Wherever they went together, everyone's head turned to glance at her—and she was so unspoiled by it. She accepted the homage naturally and gracefully, very often making a wry face at him when a glance became too fervid, as if to say "Look, my dear, you see there is nothing I can do about it. People just will look in my direction!"

Over and over Philippe convinced himself that he truly loved his fiancée, and when he asked himself for proof of his passion, he always answered in the same way: "How can one help loving her? She is so stunningly beautiful." In spite of this, a tiny doubt persisted, which his argument did not answer. This he lulled into quiet by the ardor of his lovemaking. He had to convince not only Teresina of his affection, but also himself.

Since the night of their engagement, Teresina had repulsed all of Philippe's more ardent advances, or had evaded

328

being alone with him in any but the safest surroundings. She kept her lover not satisfied or content but hopeful and in attendance, with furtive, fleeting embraces, chaste kisses, and meaningful glances; with fluttery touches of her hand on his arm or shoulder and the apparently accidental proximity of a curl or a tendril of hair close to his lips. There existed a conspiracy, well understood by both parties to it, between Philippe and his hired horse, to gain again the seclusion of the roads near Belmont Mansion, but Teresina was not to be caught often, and when she was, all the art and passion of which Philippe was capable could not completely breach the wall of resistance she had erected within herself.

Truth to tell, Teresina had been shocked by the power of those first betrothal kisses. She alone knew how weak and complaisant they had made her, what little additional urging might have undone all the years of a mother's insistent teaching. It was a course of the strictest practicality that Mrs. Rogers taught her daughters. Neither sentiment nor passion had a part in it. Teresina had learned the lessons by rote, and believed in them utterly. Any display of familiarity before marriage, except certain allowable and carefully defined and listed exceptions, was not only sinful, but extremely bad business as well—this was the essence of her training, and it was ideally suited to keep uncontaminated anyone of Teresina's nature.

Nevertheless, Philippe's constant ardor, awkward though it might be to avoid, confirmed Teresina in the belief that he was head over heels in love with her. In spite of her mother's warnings, she displayed greater and ever greater confidence in her power over him. On the whole, it must be said, Philippe had a happy summer, while Zenie's own energies, taken up with plans for her future, allowed her no time to be too restless, or too dissatisfied, to be actually unhappy. It was only when her ideas were thwarted, or when jealousy disturbed her, that she made living intolerable, both for herself and for the family.

2

Early in August, after a torrential downpour, the long heat wave broke for a few days, and Philippe decided the welcome coolness offered an excellent opportunity to spend a whole afternoon with Teresina, and really cover the Exposition. He planned the excursion beforehand, to end with a dinner at the French restaurant—and a rest for coffee, in the afternoon, at the Turkish Café. While he was necessarily at the Centennial every day, he had not cared to visit the other buildings alone, and Zenie had not even been near Fairmount Park since the day she had created the scene over the beautiful Algerian, an occasion he was trying very hard to blot from his mind.

Yes, it was a delightful day. The asphalt paths, which had been sticky petroleum rivers, were hard again, and fit to walk on. The seared lawns and beds of wilted flowers had miraculously turned fresh and alive again. He left his exhibits of maps and models of railway stations and post offices, which no one visited anyhow, instructing his assistant about various unimportant tasks, and from the station on the grounds took the Reading train for Richmond, as the quickest way to reach Kensington. He walked over to the house, and as usual the door was answered by Julia, who had developed an ear for the sound and cadence of his footsteps. While it was most unexpected to have him call at this hour, she had heard his approach, and had begun the four-flight dash from her room in time to reach the door before Mary could hobble into the hallway.

Philippe had become so accustomed to this procedure

that he actually came to expect the door to be opened by Julia, and would have been surprised if Teresina had greeted him instead. Julia's face was flushed, and her breathing irregular. Even her smile was somewhat tremulous. In all this, she did not suffer in Philippe's eye. Accustomed to the cool poise Teresina always assumed, and her slightly disdainful air, he found her sister's naturalness a welcome change.

"I'll tell Zenie you're here," she promised, while her thoughts ran, "Imagine having to be told Philippe is here—the whole house is different when he comes in."

Philippe spread himself on the Turkish divan. He expected to have a considerable wait, as usual, and was surprised to hear the rustle of dresses almost immediately. The sound was accompanied by a strong fragrance of roses, and he smiled complacently. Teresina was making use of the scent he had given her.

Instead of his fiancée, however, it was Georgina who came in. She pretended surprise at seeing him there, but made no attempt to leave. Philippe straightened up, as if to rise, but she restrained him with her hand. "Don't get up on my account, please." And he was quite willing to allow himself to loll back again in the cushions.

He hardly knew Teresina's younger sister, he thought. While he had seen her any number of times, they had never talked together, and she always seemed to be in the company of a number of boys—generally with that intense youngster with the black hair. Al, his name was. Al—an unpleasant, unmusical kind of name.

Georgina, on the other hand, felt that she knew her prospective brother-in-law extremely well, although she had never conversed with him. She had studied him covertly on many occasions when he was barely aware of her presence. Those gray-blue eyes of hers that seemed to be look-

331

ing out on the world with a vague, innocent stare never missed a thing. For some time, Georgina had been watching the progress of romance. At first, since Gus had been saved the awful fate, from her point of view, of marrying Zenie, she was content to let events take their course. She disliked both her older sisters too much to go to the aid of either of them; but Julia had changed so much for the better that Georgina at last determined to enter the fray on her side.

"Hello, Philippe! My, you're early, aren't you?"

This was more of a conversation than Georgina had ever attempted with him before, and he sat up in polite attention, pushing the divan pillows behind him.

"Why, yes," he admitted, "yes, I am early for a fact. It is such a nice afternoon I thought your sister might like to go out to the Centennial with me. In all this time we haven't seen all of it together."

Georgina laughed, a childish kind of giggle, Philippe thought. "My goodness, I think you picked a bad day to come. What do you bet Zenie won't go?"

Taken back a little, Philippe indulged in his favorite gesture. He pulled at the new growth in his beard, which was assuming by this time fairly conventional proportions. "Why, indeed, Miss Georgina—"

"Call me Gene, like everybody else does," she prompted. "You won't bet, huh?"

Philippe began to be intrigued by her persistence, and laughed. "Why—oh—wait a minute. I wouldn't say that. I'm a sporting man, generally. Now what is the wager?"

Georgina explained very slowly and carefully. "I bet that Zenie won't go with you this afternoon. . . . Is fifty cents too much?"

"No—no, indeed. If I lose, I could stand fifty cents."

"Oh, you'll lose, all right. . . . So it's a bet, then?"

332

Philippe smiled, showing his white teeth under the reddish brown of his beard. "It's a bet! Now may I ask why you're so sure of winning?"

Georgina's vague stare changed to one of pleasant laughter, and Philippe was startled by her sudden resemblance to her father. "You're nice," she informed him. "I'm sorry I never bothered much with you before, but when I heard you were going to marry Zenie I wasn't interested."

This was too rich! Of all the enfants terribles! The child was the most natural thing he had ever met. Poor Philippe could not know that in the repertoire of both twins, guileless innocence had long been a favorite role, in which they were well versed. Georgina was studying the effect of each of her apparently spontaneous statements, and led from one to the other with no noticeable appearance of plan.

"Julia is an awful sissy, but at least she's human, but what anyone would want to marry Zenie for!"

Philippe was suddenly conscious that there was grave impropriety in discussing his fiancée with her youngest sister, but how could he have known the conversation would take this turn? "Come, you were telling me why I was going to lose my bet."

"Father says never to bet on a sure thing, it's not sportsmanlike, but, Philippe, you don't know how I needed fifty cents. If I tell you now, will you pay off like a gentleman?"

By this time, Philippe felt sure that he had been jockeyed into an intolerable situation. To all appearances, he was bribing Teresina's sister for illicit information which he didn't want. On the other hand, his honor as a sportsman was at stake! He held out a half-dollar note, and teased:

"You didn't say whether the bet was in gold or greenbacks, so I'm welching on you to that extent, but in return

333

I'll accept your word for it. You don't have to tell me a thing."

Georgina took the note and folded it very carefully, and Philippe could not help thinking again, "What a child she still is!"

Concentrating upon her role of guileless hoyden, Georgina made a sudden scamper toward the door. "Zenie won't be down," she assured him from that vantage point. "She's been fighting with Mother all morning about the wedding. She wants a splash that will throw waves of jealousy all over Kensington, and Mother has put her foot down. Is Zenie mad! She's so mad she could bite nails, and she looks a sight."

Philippe wondered desperately what to do to shut off this overgrown urchin, but she kept right on. "Let me tell you, Zenie Rogers in a temper is a whole lot worse than Mother, and when the pair of them get going . . ." Georgina left the effects of this contingency to the imagination, for she was gone. Philippe wiped his forehead with his handkerchief. He could hear steps approaching, and he needed to pull himself together.

Thank God, it wasn't that child back again. Julia's smile seemed unusually pleasant to him at that moment. He noticed also how easily and effortlessly she walked, and the deep, warm tones of her voice.

"I'm sorry, Philippe. Zenie wants you to excuse her this afternoon. She's not feeling well. In fact, not well enough to come down."

Involuntarily Philippe thought, "That young lady knew what she was talking about." Then he made excuses. . . . "She just wanted fifty cents, and made up that preposterous tale," but at the same time, in the back of his mind, a third chord beat—she had obviously told the truth. She was one of those too honest children that blurted out

334

everything she knew. There was nothing vindictive about her; it was purely lack of discretion. He must have presented an appearance of dismay, for Julia put a hand forward, involuntarily.

"Oh, Philippe, don't be too disappointed. Zenie can see you this evening, I'm sure. She isn't feeling well, I know, but a few hours' rest and she will recover."

It was disappointing, nevertheless, and the serpent's whispers of Georgina also had their effect. Philippe just didn't want to go back to West Philadelphia alone, and even Julia was looking at him compassionately. Impulsively he said:

"I know—why don't you come? You're not doing anything this afternoon, are you? And I'll take Teresina some other time."

Julia put her hand to her mouth. "Oh, I couldn't, Philippe—Teresina would be . . ." She started to say "furious" and caught herself. She intended to be scrupulously fair to her sister. She stopped a moment in what seemed to be further hesitation, and went on: "Oh, I don't think I should go. After all . . ."

"After all," Philippe insisted, "after all, you're Teresina's sister, and you are going to be my sister-in-law. There is certainly nothing improper in my taking you to the Centennial, do you think?"

"But Zenie . . ."

"I'm sure Teresina won't mind. How could she? She'll be delighted to have you go. I'm well enough acquainted with your sister by this time to know her generous nature."

Julia still appeared doubtful, and then made up her mind, as she had known all along she would do. "All right, Philippe—I'll go. I would really like very much to go. Wait just a second until I put on my bonnet." She turned and flew upstairs, and Philippe relaxed on the divan again. Unconsciously, he had come to think of waiting for someone in terms of Teresina, and he was pleasantly surprised to hear Julia's voice so soon. "All right, Philippe, I'm ready." The voice held an undercurrent of excitement, of urgency, that aroused a responsive chord in him, so that he also felt a sense of pleasurable anticipation, though actually Julia's concern was with the thought of getting away as quickly as possible, before Teresina realized what was happening and could make a scene.

Chapter 3   JULIA was so different from her older sister! When Philippe made a suggestion to Teresina, she pouted, and asked: "Why do you wish to do that? It doesn't sound very exciting," or "I don't think I want to, I have a headache." After a little coaxing, he usually had his way, and on these terms they had managed to enjoy most of the entertainment Philadelphia had to offer, although there were certain taboos. Teresina wouldn't go to variety theaters, which Philippe enjoyed, not even on the special ladies' nights. Nor could he prevail upon her to attend any of the entertainments or cafés at the Centennial along the row of temporary houses known as Shantytown. Immediately outside the gates, this section formed the first, abortive kind of Midway, and gained as much patronage from the fun-loving as the Centennial itself enjoyed from the more serious-minded. As it was also open in the evenings after the Exposition closed, he had suggested their coming a number of times, but it was one of the things Teresina felt a lady couldn't do, and she remained obdurate.

On the other hand, Julia was ready for anything at all.

He had only to make a suggestion and she caught it up eagerly, and her "Oh, Philippe, please let's!" gave the impression that she was begging him to do exactly the things he wanted, and that the whole adventure was just enough beyond the bounds of propriety for him to make the final decision, by which she would abide. Before the afternoon was over, he had exercised his ingenuity to make all kinds of outrageous and amusing suggestions, not one of which did she fail to take up enthusiastically, and subject to this special kind of pleading.

In the Japanese exhibit, which was by far the largest and most ambitious attempted by any foreign nation, they behaved like children before the demonstration of silk-growing, although fortunately none of the smiling little yellow people could understand their ribald remarks at the shapelessness of the women, and the queerness of their costumes, without any attempt at a civilized appearance of dress. Julia tittered. "You know, Philippe, I don't believe they even wear corsets. You would think they'd try to make something of themselves." The remark was risqué, of course, but Julia felt in a mood that made no allowance for consequences.

Quite without reason, they followed paths that landed them in unexpected places. . . . "I say, Julia, let's see where this walk goes, there's a regular little dell and copse on the way" and "Oh, Philippe, please let's."

Who would have set out on his own accord to see the Butter and Cheese exhibit, which occupied a building all by itself? Or the tombstones, carved from Vermont granite, in that state's little building? Philippe professed to be a connoisseur of wines, and a specialist on hock. As there were wine displays almost everywhere, he had plenty of opportunity to exercise his taste in this field, and Julia was prevailed upon quite readily to advance her own judgment in any particular choice. By mutual consent, they skipped Machinery Hall entirely, and made up for it by lingering in the beauty of the Horticultural exhibit, which they both pronounced the masterpiece of the whole Centennial. A tropical jungle had been transplanted and was growing under glass; birds sang strange, beautiful melodies from high in the palm trees. Philippe explained that most tropical birds actually could not sing. They possessed beautiful plumage, but had unpleasant, raucous voices. The birds in the horticultural display were mockingbirds from Texas and had been brought by ship directly to Philadelphia. Sad to relate, a storm arose on the way, and many of the feathered songsters had perished. They both waxed sentimental over the loss, and were doubly grateful for the song of the remaining birds.

They made a tour of the grounds by the little steam railway, and Philippe confessed that of all the thousands of people he saw in attendance at the Exposition, the ones who interested him most were the Westerners. There were plainsmen with high boots and guns at their hips, woodsmen in leather trousers and jackets who wore moccasins and walked with a loping stride. There were others in from working on the railroads being built across the central plains.

"They seem to be without womenfolk—and until I saw them, I never realized that this is still a pioneering country. With a population already equal to that of France, its possibilities are stupendous. I wouldn't be surprised if at some time not so far distant there would be close to a hundred million people in this one country—more than in any country in Europe."

For her part, Julia was most attracted by the Orientals, because they looked so alien in Quaker Philadelphia. There were the Persian fire-eaters, the Japanese attendants at their exhibit, patient Chinese workmen, and all the various kinds of men who wore turbans, classified by her as Hindus, and those wearing the fez, who to her were Turks. The English part of Philippe's nature caused him to make short shrift of this fancy for Easterners.

"They're a lot of dirty beggars, every one of them, and not to be trusted. Look at the way they behaved in India during the mutiny, right before your Civil War—and after all we had done for them."

The one slight discord in a perfect afternoon occurred when Julia exclaimed, "But, Philippe, you can't blame them for wanting to be free!"

As a former soldier, Philippe was interested in the armament displays, and they turned thither. The marvelous cannon of the Krupps struck awe to the heart of everyone who looked at them, although probably the Russian display of armament was even greater, and more remarkable.

"Mark my words," Philippe predicted, "Russia will be the next great European Power. She is already nibbling away at Turkey, and of course the French will throw in with her to get back at Germany. It will take a long time for us to recover from Sedan, but another thirty years or so, with Russia on our side—you will see, we will have our revenge."

It was disconcerting, in a way, this manner in which Philippe spoke now as an Englishman and again as a Frenchman, but as Julia knew nothing about European politics, and just walked along blithely nodding her head at everything he said, it didn't much matter. Finally, when they were both a little fed-up with the exhibition proper, Philippe made a proposal which he instinctively expected would be turned down. "What do you say we visit Shantytown?"

Julia merely caught his arm a little closer, and said, "Oh, Philippe, please let's!"

Circuses and dance halls. Variety shows and cabarets. Displays of freaks and games of chance and skill—all different from anything Julia had ever seen before, all tremendously exciting and teeming with people who lived, thought, and acted in ways quite unlike anything within her experience. It was a revelation of a new society which even spoke a strange language. A man stopped Philippe and said, "Say, cull—" and then made some further remark which she did not understand. What was a cull? Why hadn't she known that some people lived at a faster, giddier pace than that with which she was familiar?

Philippe was also enjoying himself, with an abandon he had not felt since student days. His companion was fun—he'd had an ever so much better time than he could have had with Teresina, he knew that. But they should be returning; the long summer day was rapidly yellowing to twilight.

All the way back to the Richmond station they relived the afternoon's pleasures, thereby enjoying them doubly. Julia, at least, began to experience a feeling of guilt. It was much later than she had expected to stay. Teresina probably had been having hysterics all afternoon, and there was no telling how her mother would take the escapade. Apparently Philippe did not realize the seriousness of his own defection—perhaps he did not care.

Julia determined to make an entrance that would give no hint of her feelings. When Mary opened the door she swept down the hall to the parlor entrance, with Philippe following. Aunt Zena was there alone, and Julia rushed up to her.

"Oh, we had the most wonderful time at the Centennial, this afternoon—didn't we, Philippe?"

"Indeed we did—by the Lord Harry, as Father Rogers says, we really saw things. . . . How's Teresina?"

"Well, I'm glad you children enjoyed yourselves. . . . Zenie still has a bad headache, though. I'm afraid you won't see your charming fiancée this evening, Philippe. She'll feel better when I tell her you called back, after she disappointed you today."

Philippe delayed his departure, and Julia watched her aunt closely. Would Philippe never go, so she could find out just how bad things really were? It seemed impossible that he could not sense his aunt's restraint. But then Philippe was a man. Like Papa, he never seemed to know what the women around him were thinking. Finally, he bowed in a mock military manner, clicking his heels together.

"Thank you, my future sister-in-law. Not even my dear betrothed could have given me greater pleasure by her company."

The door had barely shut behind him when Aunt Zena whispered ominously: "Well, young lady, you certainly started things. That sister of yours has behaved disgracefully, ever since you left. Even worse than your mother was at her age, and Tina could throw a mean tantrum, I assure you."

"Oh, I know—but Philippe urged me so, and after all, he is going to be in the family, and he was so disappointed when Zenie wouldn't go, I felt sorry for him."

"I think my precious niece made a fool of herself, and I'm almost ready to tell her so. I declare I never saw such goings-on, but you might have got home at a decent hour. It's after nine."

"It's all my fault. I was having such a good time, and Philippe is such perfect company I quite forgot the hour." She stuck out her chin aggressively. "I still don't think

341

Zenie is treating him right, and I'd like to tell her so—but now I'll run up and tell Mother I'm back."

"You won't need to, I heard you come in." Julia had been so intent on defense of her actions that she had not heard her mother's descent of the stairs. "I declare I don't know what I'd do without Mrs. Winslow's Soothing Syrup. It came in so good for Mr. Quinby I got another bottle of it, and I gave a triple dose to Zenie, so she's sleeping, but you better stay out of her way for a day or two, and as for Philippe, I feel sorry for him."

"When Zenie is in a more reasonable frame of mind, I intend to warn her that Philippe won't submit to browbeating," said Zena. "I've known him very well for a good many years. American men seem to respond to such treatment, and can be led around by women like whipped dogs. Englishmen get sullen and stubborn, but they remain honorable to their engagements, while Frenchmen begin to think of a way out. No amount of passionate regard keeps a Frenchman from being sensible." Aunt Zena began to laugh, the deep throaty chuckle she reserved for amusement at personal reminiscences. "Good grief, Tina, this whole business reminds me of that man we knew in Boston. Whatever was his name? You met him at a dance or something, and were insane whenever I so much as came in the room, for fear I'd snatch him."

Julia saw her mother's eyes narrow and her curls shake, and made a hurried exit—she had experienced enough excitement for one day.

2

Georgina waited at the corner for Henry to return from work. The bond between the twins was so strong that both of them looked forward to this daily rendezvous. On the way back to the house they exchanged news and planned the next day's activities. There was always a great deal to report, as the most trifling events were important to each of them. Tonight, when she was filled with real news, Georgina was on tenterhooks.

The appearance of her brother, swinging off the horsecar like any other businessman, filled her with pride. Just imagine, Henry in the coal business! Some day he would run the whole thing, and then he would be rich! She waved to him, in the new and ladylike manner he insisted upon as comporting with the dignity of being grown-up. Her face was flushed with excitement, and she began talking before his foot was on the pavement.

"I got another fifty cents today—and did Queen Zenie off, too. . . . I'll tell you about that afterward. That makes four dollars and eleven cents altogether, and you'll have another fifty cents out of your pay Saturday. We ought to be able to see the Centennial on all that money, don't you think?" She waited tensely for her brother's answer. They had been saving all summer to make an excursion free from the restraints imposed by parents.

Henry nodded importantly. "Besides, I've just had a promotion. I write a nice round, legible hand, Mr. Madeira says, and I'm going to write correspondence for him, beginning next week—and a whole dollar raise."

Wonderful news! It almost made Georgina forget her own tale of a full day's happenings. "Well, we've been having goings-on! Mother and Zenie had a fight this morning, over the wedding, and Zenie carried on high. She was in a state, I tell you! Then who comes but Philippe, right after dinner . . .

"But first, I forgot something. . . . I tried a drop or so, not much, of that perfume he gave Zenie, and the fight with Mother finished sooner than I thought it would— Mother just put her foot down, hard—and Zenie caught me helping myself. Well, you know her—but I paid her off."

Henry nodded his head at each veering of the course of this account, to show that he followed it, while his sister went on: "So when *he* came, I bet him Zenie wouldn't see him. You know how Zenie looks after she's been in a temper, and I knew she wouldn't dare show herself. That's where I got the half-dollar, on the bet.

"And that wasn't all, I put a flea in his ear as well. I told him Zenie was acting up—imagine her making such a fuss over a little scent. It wouldn't have knocked over at all if she hadn't startled me so. Then, to cap the climax, he takes Julia to the Centennial, and they haven't got back yet. I always hated Julia, Mother always saying, 'If you'd only be good, like *Ju-u-u-lia* is,' but she's crazy over Philippe, and it's sort of made her different. You should see her get downstairs when she hears him coming."

Henry laughed. That was the trouble with working, you missed the excitement of being at home! "What about Zenie now? I bet she's choking!"

"She can go ahead and choke, for all of me. From now on I'm on Julia's side, and between us, if we can't get Philippe . . ."

Such was the rapport between the twins that Henry already understood that Georgina had broken a bottle of Teresina's perfume, and his sister accepted it as a perfectly natural question when he asked what was uppermost in his mind. "Was it a big bottle of perfume got broke?"

"It wasn't big at all, and it didn't even smell very good. I hate roses anyway—'Otto of Roses,' funny name for a perfume—but you might of thought it was a quart of it, the fuss she made."

As Henry missed the family midday dinner, he had a hot meal saved for him in the kitchen. The twins walked down through the side yard, and in by the shed door. Henry was strangely quiet, and whistled tunelessly through his teeth. He was weighing the chances of success for his twin's project. It was not until they were seated at the kitchen table and Mary had loaded both their plates—the second heavy dinner of the day for Georgina—that he delivered his judgment.

"Well, you can try, Gene, but it's pretty hard to pry a man away from a girl as beautiful as Zenie is."

"Beautiful—that's all anyone talks about, how beautiful she is. Well, I don't think she's so beautiful. She's too dark, and sallow. I'm as beautiful as she is, any time, and I bet I could step right out now and get Philippe for myself, if I wanted him. I'd go after him. I wouldn't stand around mooning over him, the way Julia does."

"Have me two darlin's had enough to eat?" Mary broke in solicitously. Without waiting for a reply, she began to refill both plates with thick slices of pot roast of beef with horseradish, potatoes, and gravy. When they had finished their planning, well fortified with this additional provender, they walked toward the front of the house. Henry offered a final caution, born of his new experience as a man of the world:

"Don't do anything rash, Gene. Remember, your place is by the side of Al Naylor. He needs you!"

3

Unaware of Teresina's attitude toward yesterday's excursion, Philippe was in a happy mood as he gave his horse its head along the water front. While it was slightly farther than going across town, he had fallen into the habit of going to Kensington this way, for there was less traffic at most times, and the river smells of tar and ropes and warehouses reminded him of the sea, which in turn suggested his approaching return to France. In spite of the joy he had found in America, he was more than a little homesick, and the mere sight of a French or English sailing vessel, or a steamer from foreign ports, helped assuage this feeling. Tired from its first run, the horse had slowed to a trot, and Philippe was dreaming of the future when he was suddenly aroused by a hail. He reined in his horse instinctively, and looked over to see Georgina on the pavement, waving an extravagantly large parasol. "Well, young lady, aren't you a long way from home?"

Since yesterday's talk he had concluded that Georgina was a mere child, and not to be taken seriously. The effect of this was a new tone of condescension in his voice, which she did not miss.

"Oh, I'm so glad I saw you! I set out for a walk, and didn't notice how far I'd come. The heat and all has completely fagged me, I declare." Considering that she had been waiting at that particular corner for almost an hour, in the hope of intercepting Philippe, it required no great amount of acting to appear tired out. In another five minutes she would have given up, and started home. She got into the carriage meekly.

"You should be more careful when you go for a walk," Philippe chided her. "Besides, it's quite dangerous—a young girl unaccompanied in a neighborhood like this."

As Georgina had played and romped through this whole section for years, she did not take this warning very seriously, but gave a long sigh, and with her air of extreme innocence, remarked, "I suppose I shouldn't have—and I won't again, I assure you." Tears welled in her eyes, and her mouth quivered.

Philippe was instantly touched. "My dear child! What in the world is the matter? You seem most unhappy."

346

He allowed the horse to drop back to a walk. Georgina tried to look brave, and answered:

"Don't mind me, please, Philippe. It's nothing, really. I just had to get out of the house. Things are so unpleasant at home right now."

"Unpleasant? Why, it always seemed to me you lived in a most happy household. I've seen quite a lot of you all, you know. Come, tell me what's the matter."

Georgina thought, "My, isn't he taking it, hook, line and sinker!" She sighed again, lowered her head demurely, and said, "No, indeed—I just can't tell you."

Philippe insisted. "Of course you can. Why, I am practically one of the family."

"Oh, but I shouldn't. I'm sure things will come around all right, anyway."

Taking a light, bantering tone, Philippe coaxed, "Come now, honest confession is good for the soul—that's an old proverb my mother used to quote."

Georgina overacted a little, but it went unnoticed. "Surely you must have realized after you left yesterday that things in the house wouldn't be very pleasant."

"Oh, I'm beginning to see daylight. Your mother disapproves of gambling, and took you to task for our little bet. That phase of our wager hadn't occurred to me."

Wrinkling her nose in disdain at Philippe's slowness of comprehension, she assured him: "Oh, no—that was purely a private transaction, but you don't think Zenie would allow Julia to go to the fair with you yesterday without starting something, do you? You know, Philippe, that was pretty foolish. You let yourself in for something—and as for poor Julia!"

"Julia? Why, that is absurd. Teresina wouldn't object to my taking her yesterday. She was ill and couldn't go, and Julia is her own sister."

Georgina gave Philippe a glance in which compassion and pity mixed. "It's easy to see you don't know Zenie very well. She didn't only object, she had conniptions. She was in hysterics all afternoon, which is just another way of saying she was crazy mad—poor Mother got the brunt of that."

Philippe touched the horse with his whip, and the carriage lurched forward at a faster pace. "Good God, what a child!" he thought.

His companion waited a few seconds before continuing. "It's Julia I feel sorry for. She's worth two of Zenie. You should have been there this morning when Zenie tried to kill her."

In spite of his inward resolution not to listen to a single word of the child's chatter, Philippe looked up, startled. "Tried to kill her?"

"Please don't get excited, Philippe—she didn't succeed, of course. Mother and Aunt Zena struggled with her. It was dangerous, but once they got the hatpin away from her, she couldn't do anything. Julia had to promise, though, that she would never, never see you again."

"Georgina, I am convinced you are the most consummate . . ."

"Please call me Gene, Philippe, everybody else does," she interrupted, returning to her original, guileless manner.

"Gene, then. . . . Don't you know it's not nice for girls to tell such preposterous stories? I'm ashamed of you!"

Georgina thought: "All right, Mr. Philippe, go on talking to me as if I was six years old. See if I care!" Aloud, she retorted, as if she were being unjustly accused: "You asked me to tell you why I was so unhappy, and I have. I didn't want to at first—you don't need to believe me, but you'll see for yourself when you get to the house. You won't see Julia, because she promised not to even

348

leave her room while you are there—and Zenie won't mention about yesterday, because Aunt Zena made *her* promise she wouldn't. She'll be cold and polite. . . . And now if you'll stop the horse, please, I'd like to get out before we turn the corner."

"I think your story is made up out of whole cloth, and I shall tell your sister how you are behaving, but at least I will take you home."

"Indeed you won't," Georgina insisted. "I'll jump first. If Zenie saw me riding with you she'd scratch my eyes out, and don't think she wouldn't." She leaped agilely from the carriage. "Thanks for the ride, and I'm sorry I told you anything. I might have known you wouldn't believe me, but you'll see for yourself if I'm not right." She watched as Philippe clicked to the horse, and then hurried over toward the Naylor house. Henry would be waiting there, and she was eager to tell him of the success of her stratagem.

Chapter 4

OF ALL Mrs. Rogers' possessions, her greatest joy and pride was in the family carriage, a phaeton. It was a good-looking vehicle, made by the Cadwalader factory in Trenton, and the first duty of Lucius was its care. The varnish shone, and the brasswork was polished until it seemed to be alight with a fire of its own. The axles and the fifth wheel were greased to a nicety—adequate to prevent squeaking, not enough to cause an overflow onto the hubs and spokes. The harness was kept in impeccable condition with leather soap, the horses themselves were groomed daily.

On important occasions, the horse in use would also

349

have his mane and tail braided and tied with tasteful bits of ribbon, and Nellie, the Dalmatian coach dog, would trot along beneath the hind wheels. Then Lucius would wear the only good suit he owned, a semilivery purchased for him years ago, and hold the reins with a style quite different from his usual driving.

Mrs. Rogers reserved these extra touches for going to mass on Sunday mornings, for an occasional drive in Fairmount Park at a fashionable hour, and for infrequent calls on persons she did not know very well and wished to impress. When envious of another's good fortune, she was always able to console herself with the thought that at least no one had a finer horse and carriage.

Since her sister had been living with them, the phaeton had been put at her disposal. The horses were never worked as much as they should be, and they had agreed it would be wasteful for Zena to rent another carriage. Besides, since coming to the Rogers household she had been most generous in paying "her share" of the expenses, which was actually an amount more than twice the entire family outlay. These extra funds Mrs. Rogers kept in various hiding places of her own, and they were the source of a feeling of security, nest eggs against future contingencies.

In spite of these considerations, Mrs. Rogers' resentment toward her sister was increased because she used daily those extra touches on the carriage which Mrs. Rogers reserved for Sundays and special occasions. Sight of her own "rig," as she called it, instead of bringing the accustomed sparkle of delight to her eyes, aroused nothing but anger. "There she goes again, and with Nellie, I declare!" she would say to herself. "And Lucius in his best suit that we bought for him. There she goes, and me slaving away. Besides, I'm sure she allows Lucius to race Mr. Quinby. I know her—speed is what she is after, and it's not good for him in this hot weather."

The heat had indeed returned in full force, and Philadelphia baked under an intolerable sun, unlike anything the city had ever before experienced. The few days of relief which had led indirectly to the break between Teresina and Julia had done no more than provide a slight breathing space.

Mrs. Rogers' resentful mood was felt all over the house, and in the kitchen its effect was almost disastrous. Martha threatened to leave, and it required all Mary's persuasive powers to prevent her taking so rash a step. Since her illness, Mary had become a stanch champion of her mistress, who could do no wrong in her eyes. She was the only person in the family who believed in the duplicity of Aunt Zena, upon which Mrs. Rogers harped when she was angry. This despite the fact that the old woman had more money and better clothes than she had ever possessed in her life, owing to the open-handed generosity of their guest. Zena rarely went downtown, a frequent direction for her rides, that she did not come back with some remembrance for each of the servants.

Whatever Mary's feeling toward Zena, Lucius was her devoted slave. She had met all of his children, knew them by name, held and kissed the adorable fat brown babies, and played with the older ones. She also showered them with presents, most of which Lucius sold afterward for a quarter of their cost. The baby, little Jupiter, had received at least six blue dresses and caps, all of them tastefully decorated with embroidery or lace, and not particularly suited to an infant who spent most of his time crawling on the floor. Aunt Zena was later distressed to find one of the blue dresses adorning the next youngest child, a girl. She explained very carefully, to uncomprehending ears, the

351

absolute necessity of always dressing baby boys in blue, and girls in pink.

Aunt Zena's attention to Lucius and his family lacked that self-consciousness, restraint, and condescension which existed in the relationship of white Americans with their Negro neighbors and servants, and this, more than anything else, Lucius and his tribe felt and respected.

It was unfortunate that Zena, with all her generosities, and the impulsiveness and unselfishness of her nature, should have aroused, unwittingly and otherwise, so deep a resentment in her sister's breast. Not that this resentment was a constant thing. There were whole days when the relationship between the two women was perfect. They would sit together and sew—mending, or stitching on the crazy quilt—and talk and laugh over old times together, or over their separate adventures after marriage. Mrs. Rogers never tired of hearing about Zena's many love affairs, in furtherance of which she had traveled to many climes.

The temperaments of the sisters were very much alike. They were frank, robust in their humor, impulsive, and affectionate. They were also jealous, quick with their tempers, and suspicious of each other's motives. The most pleasant and amusing chat could turn, in the time of a single stitch, into a bitter argument. But these debates were like summer storms, noisy, accompanied with rapier-like flashes of lightning, and brief. In a little while the whole quarrel would be forgotten and they would be happily at work again.

These little spats did not rankle. The circumstances that relit the flames of Mrs. Rogers' resentment were connected with Zenie's wedding plans, attentions of any special nature which the family or servants paid her sister and evidence to her that she was being supplanted in their

352

regard, use of the carriage, and any accident or happening that left Zena alone in the company of her husband.

Considering that they were living in the same house, this last did not happen very often, and the circumstances were always most innocent, no matter how suspicious they appeared in Mrs. Rogers' jealous eyes. Zena had been flirting with men for so many years that her instinctive attitude, even with her brother-in-law, was flirtatious, or at least coquettish. It was part of her nervous reflexes that the mere proximity of a man made her reach out and touch him upon the slightest pretext, and indulge in long, provocative glances that actually had very little meaning.

Then Zena was outspoken in her regard for Mr. Rogers. The very qualities which his wife had pretended for years to dislike were those that appealed most to her sister, who had known enough and a-plenty of delightfully mannered and highly cultured men in her life. They had been decadent, overbred, and dilettante in the art they professed to know best. Her brother-in-law's handsome good looks, robust thunder of voice, and breadth of chest and shoulder, his whole overpowering masculinity, attracted her so much that she unconsciously heightened and exaggerated her touches and glances, all the little attitudes that twenty years ago or more had seemed delicate and girlish. In a middle-aged woman they were overcoy, and unnecessarily obvious. Obvious, that is, to everyone but Mr. Rogers, who seemed not to notice them.

This increased Mrs. Rogers' anger. If Jesse would only realize how he was being made up to! But no, it was all over his head. She had attempted to explain several times, and he had only gone off into roars of laughter.

"Why, Gussie, excepting for a little difference in size and feature, you and Zena are as alike in your natures as two Baldwin locomotives. Half the time when she gets pounding along the rails about the old days with dear Papa, I get mixed up in my mind and think it's you, I swear I do."

The comparison was not a very gracious one, but Mrs. Rogers had been treated to these railroad similes for too many years to cavil now at that part of his speech.

"Don't you tell me anything like that, Jesse Rogers. She had her hand on your arm, and I saw her. You don't mean to tell me I can't talk to men without pawing them."

"If she did, I never noticed. But what of it? You know Zena has had some sorrowful experiences in her life, and she likes to talk about them and get a little sympathy. Relieves her, I suppose. It would be nice if she could meet somebody that appealed to her and marry him."

Mrs. Rogers pursed her lips. "Zena is my only sister and I love her dearly, but I recognize her faults, and men are all of them. She wouldn't be satisfied with any husband of her own that ever lived. It's other women's husbands she's after, and I warn you, Jesse, if you ever try to take up with her I'll kill the pair of you."

"Bravo! Spoken like the daughter of a true Italian nobleman. Tell me, Gussie, what would be your choice of weapons, the stiletto or the pistol?"

"All right, you can make a joke of it, but if you don't see what is going on—poor blind fool of a man—I do, and there are limits, even to a sister's love."

It was to be supposed that this pent-up feeling—Mrs. Rogers couldn't ease the pressure by reproaching her sister when there was a perfectly reasonable answer to every one of her allegations—would sometime cause an eruption. When it came, it wreaked havoc with the hot ashes of hate, the engulfing flood of jealousy, and the poisonous gases of suspicion. A cataclysm of this nature requires a very small fault in the geologic structure through which to push its

354

way by overwhelming pressure. In the Rogers family, the weakness in the domestic strata proved to be the pair of dachshunds, Moody and Sankey. None of the other participants were less innocent than the dogs. It was an act of nature that no human power could have averted or hastened.

The weather was a contributing factor. Mr. Rogers had spent the morning trying to sleep, but the heat had made it impossible. Two more days would see the beginning of September, but Philadelphia weather, usually unpredictable, this summer had been such as to make accurate forecast simple. For most of July and all of August, the temperature continued fair and warmer—ever warmer. It was not to be wondered at that the master of the house repaired to the parlor in a mood quite unnatural to him. As he would have been the first to assert, he never got in a temper, was never difficult or unreasonable, could always be swayed by the least argument to a happy view of things.

He had put up with the presence of the "dash-hounds" for months and no one had heard a word of complaint, except occasionally a mild expletive when he fell over one of them, mistaking it for part of the floor coverings. Not more than twice he had sworn when one of them had deliberately tried to trip him on the stairs by running between his legs, and only slightly more often he had made veiled references to the stable as the place for animals, to inclusion of the dash-hound in the genus dog, to the taste of the Prince of Wales and Germans in general when it came to animals, to the uselessness of the dash-hound species and the complete unattractiveness of the breed in form, temperament, and habit. Beyond this, he had kept silent.

This noonday, after wretchedly tossing his two-hundred-pound bulk in a welter of soaked bedding and arising sleepless, it was too much to expect that Mr. Rogers would not register a slightly stronger protest against the animals than he had heretofore used when he descended to the parlor and found a large wet place in the center of the handsome Wilton rug for which he had paid out hard-earned money not over ten years earlier. Near the spot, suspiciously near, and yet seemingly unafraid of the consequences of his apparent crime, lay Sankey, of the mellifluous voice.

Mr. Rogers had pent-up emotions of his own, and this was a minor eruption, although at the time it seemed of considerable force. He heard footsteps descending the stairs, and quite naturally concluded they were those of his wife, so he delivered himself on the whole subject of the poor beasts, both of which had disappeared at the first burst of sound.

"These creatures have gone the limit. It's high time they were ground up into sausage meat, and as for me, I'd rather eat them than put up with their nuisances around the house." From this beginning, not entirely in his best vein, he went on to the animals' lamentable habits, and got down to their more intimate personal characteristics. "Look at them, look at the pair of them!" he declaimed. The exhortation was purely oratorical, for the benefit of Mrs. Rogers, who was, he supposed, already within earshot. "And you call *them* dogs—those caricatures of a noble animal, those sniffing, smelling, mess-making monstrosities. They're . . . they're . . . they're obscene, I can think of no other word for it—obscene. Genital organs on legs, that's what they are, and nothing else. Those damn dashhounds will have to go!"

Aunt Zena took the final pronouncement, delivered in full voice, from the very doorway to the parlor, and when Mr. Rogers, his peroration halted for lack of breath, finally

356

became aware of the identity of his audience, she was already dissolved in tears.

"Jesse, how can you? And I thought you loved the little dears so! You told me yourself . . ." Anguish was written large on her features, and although her subsequent emotional display may have been a play to the gallery of Mr. Rogers' sympathies, the original pained protest was from genuine love of the ill-proportioned pair. "It doesn't sound like you, indeed it doesn't, to talk of eating dogs—I suppose it's a habit you got from those awful Indians." She tottered across to the divan, and threw herself across its voluptuous length, to give way to bursts of convulsive sobbing. "No matter what I do for people, no one appreciates it. Surely, Jesse . . ."

The reproach was hidden by the pillows, but Mr. Rogers was already completely remorseful for his words. He wouldn't have spoken so to Zena for the world. He was a little angry with his wife that she hadn't been on hand, as she should have, when he indulged in remonstrance. The whole thing was a housekeeping matter; why had Zena come along at the wrong moment? With abashed features he moved over to the divan, and laid a hand on her shoulder. "Come, Zena . . . it's really nothing . . . a matter of fun, more than anything . . ."

"You said you'd eat them, those poor little . . ."

"A joke, a joke, believe me, my dear Zena. No one would think of harming either animal. I'm most attached to them. . . . I was provoked a trifle when I saw that spot on the rug, that was all."

"And that awful description. . . . It isn't like you, Jesse, it isn't." The sobbing began afresh, until it took both of Mr. Rogers' hands to soothe her. "You said they were nothing but . . ."

At the moment he had made the remark, Mr. Rogers

had thought it well put. Coming from feminine lips he feared its effect, and interrupted: "Please forget it, Zena. They are built a little heavy there, I meant nothing more." He seated himself on the divan beside his sister-in-law, and gently brought her up to a sitting position.

2

Mrs. Rogers was engaged in one of her frequent inspections of the stable and its occupants when she heard the distant sound of her husband's voice, raised in anger. "Let him roar. . . . If he thinks I'm going to come a-running he's very much mistaken," she told herself. At the moment, she was kneeling in the straw by Total Eclipse, examining a suspicious swelling on his leg. She had no intention of getting a spavined horse, if it could be helped. There seemed to be no cause for alarm in this case. She patted the black horse, and he turned his head to give her a melting look of understanding and affection.

The stable was cool as compared to the garden. The animals appeared to be entirely comfortable. Nellie, following around at her heels, was not even panting. It was a peaceful spot, intimate with the earth in a way nothing else in a city could be. "I think the good Lord was born in a stable because it's the one place human passions can't really intrude," Mrs. Rogers thought, and then realized time was passing, and the scheduled hour for dinner had almost arrived.

As she walked up the garden path toward the house, her elevated thought and the feeling of contentment the stable inspired were succeeded by a vague sense, a premonition, of disaster. And it concerned Mr. Rogers! "Zena is in there alone with him," she thought, "and I've a suspicion she's been up to something. I feel it in my bones." Her unhurried gait quickened, and she passed through the shed and kitchen intent on discovery.

The scene in the parlor exceeded all her wildest imaginings, and until, gradually, anger succeeded shock, she watched the progress of what seemed to be a most tender love passage.

Her husband and sister shared the divan, that unholy heathen article of furniture designed to further such dalliance as was going on here. They were seated close together—Jesse was actually embracing her, while his hand patted her farther shoulder. He was speaking in tones of the most moving nature.

"Why, Zena, please! . . . I had no idea you cared so deeply. It was a momentary outburst. I should have restrained myself. . . . I realize how shocking my words must have sounded."

"You did shock me, Jesse. . . . Tina has so often assured me of the affection . . ."

"It is true, but this was a momentary aberration—I spoke from impulse . . ."

"But when you mentioned . . ." Zena's head found a resting place against Mr. Rogers' chest, so that the eavesdropper could not hear the remainder of the sentence. But she had heard enough, she told herself. "Zena has led Jesse on until the poor fool lost his head and made an improper proposal to her. Now she's pretending to be shocked by it. . . . Well, I didn't come in from the stable any too soon." She made a lunge into the room, and its startled occupants sprang to their feet in attitudes she could only interpret as guilty ones.

"Well, this is a fine how-de-do! The minute my back is turned I find this kind of goings-on, right under my very nose." While her accusation included an apparently impossible feat of acrobatics, there was no misunderstanding

Mrs. Rogers' meaning, and now the flood of words seared and shriveled them. They were overwhelmed by accusation and drowned, finally, in a tide of jealousy.

Mr. Rogers attempted to halt the cataclysm. "Now look here, Gussie, you misunderstand things completely," he began, assuming an injured look.

"I heard you, and I guess I can believe my two eyes." This slight interruption in her tirade was no help at all, except to show the futility of further explanations. As Mrs. Rogers tired, Zena finally made an escape, and ran sobbing to her room.

Mr. Rogers remained slumped on the divan, in utter dejection, and did not even look up when eventually his wife left him. He first seemed to realize that he had survived when Mary came in carrying a large floorcloth. The old woman had lived through too many domestic discords to realize that this one was different, and she was continuing, as always, the placid round of her daily tasks.

"I declare, you give me a turn, sittin' there—for a fact you did." She painfully got down on hands and knees, and began to roll back the Wilton rug.

In a chastened whisper Mr. Rogers asked, "Mary, may I inquire what you are engaged in doing?"

"It's that fountain, the one works by itself, like. I was cleanin' it a bit ago, and me cloth caught somehow, and over went the whole shebang. I was waitin' for you and her and the missus, so I could clean up the water, but it's soaked in or dried up by itself."

3

Aunt Zena was packed in an hour—every photograph down from the walls of her room, all her dear bric-a-brac put away in its proper place, and her trunks, bags, hat-boxes, and cases filled and fastened, ready for carting away.

Mr. Rogers tried to dissuade her. "Tomorrow, when Gussie is in a more reasonable frame of mind, I'll explain the whole thing to her," he promised.

"No, Jesse, it's no use. The things she said to me will always hang like a sword between us. I never realized a sister of mine could have such vile thoughts in her head."

"It's nothing but the Italian temperament makes her rash at times. I'm sure you've said things in anger you have regretted later. . . . Believe me, it will all blow over. I can't see you leave here in an angry frame of mind."

"I'm not angry—indeed I'm not. I'm hurt, that's all, hurt to my very soul that my own sister could treat me this way." She stepped toward him with arms outspread. "Jesse, you are the only person in the world I have left. My sister has thrown me out, after grossly insulting me. Philippe is marrying. I am alone, completely alone in the world. . . . It is hard to face at my time of life."

Mr. Rogers comforted her as best he could, but she pushed him away. "No, no, Augustina will just make things harder for you, the more you take my part."

"Gussie be damned!" He found strength to attempt a feeble roar. The words bowled over his wife, waiting in her room at the other end of the hall to resume her histrionics at her sister's departure. "So that is the way Jesse feels—after a whole lifetime together, this . . ." She collapsed over her bed, sobbing weakly.

Mr. Rogers had Lucius bring round the carriage. That was the last, unkindest cut of all—her carriage. She looked down through the busybody, determined now to ignore both of them. There was that maid—she'd never had a chance to tell her off—looking as if all Kensington was dirt under her feet. And her sister, the snake in the grass, the . . .

Zena was really going—and after all these years, there had to be this final quarrel. After all, it was Zena's nature to be flirtatious, and Mr. Rogers was just a man. Could either of them help it if their natures had been too strong for them? To err was human, to forgive . . .

Hastily, Mrs. Rogers dried her eyes and ran toward the stairs. She just couldn't let Zena go this way. She heard the sound of the front door reopening, and her sister's voice shouting:

"Good-by, Augustina, I forgive you—forgive you for everything, but I'll never darken your door again."

Forgive *her*, would she? Of all the colossal nerve . . . She hesitated for a moment, then ran to the front window and threw it up in an angry frenzy. Forgive *her*, would she? She'd let her know a few things she'd forgotten to say before—let the neighbors hear, if they wanted to. But she was too late. . . . There went her rig, down the street —and Jesse driving! All right, if he preferred Zena to herself, that was his privilege. He'd made his bed, let him lie on it! Mrs. Rogers took hold of herself and walked down the hall like a little martinet, thinking: "Lucius has been getting careless with the garden. I'll have to root him out and get him at those weeds."

In the kitchen, the servants looked at each other in consternation. Excepting for Miss Gene, who had eaten a hurried meal in the kitchen, no one had appeared for dinner. The two older daughters had left the house early, but the mister, and the missus? Of course there had been a quarrel, a hot one, and Madame Lascalles had gone, along with the French maid they both hated. Aunt Zena had sent out a five-dollar note for each of them, but that hardly compensated for a good dinner ruined.

Martha banged her pots and pans as she gave expression

362

to her feelings. "I don't know what this house is coming to, when there's neither hair nor hide of the pair of them to eat their vittles."

4

Mr. Rogers prevailed upon his sister-in-law to stay at the Continental Hotel, at least overnight. "Besides, there are the girls. They will be brokenhearted if you depart without seeing them. How can I explain? And Philippe—surely you will want to say good-by to him?"

Before the world, Aunt Zena made a brave effort to be her old vivacious self, and after she had agreed to his urging, she indulged in all her little tricks of smiling and posturing, although much of the spontaneity was gone. She sailed into the Continental lobby, ordered Denise about, and directed the disposal of her luggage. Mr. Rogers appreciated courage, and patted her hand.

"I'll leave you now, but I won't say good-by. Don't take this too seriously, I beg of you, and I'll call on you in the morning, direct from work."

Mr. Quinby had never before been allowed to travel at so slow a gait when his master drove. He even stopped once, to forage at an overhanging leafy branch, and there was no impatient, commanding tug at the reins. Truth was, Mr. Rogers couldn't face going home. "Jealousy has been gnawing at Gussie's heart like a canker," he decided mentally. "It must be burned out completely, roots and all, or the foul cancer will eat in again and destroy us." What to do? That was the question he mulled over at length.

He could get drunk again. From the plains of sobriety he could look back upon the day of his great bender as though it were a mountain peak he had scaled right to the summit, but which he had no desire to attempt again.

He took a moment or two to try once more to decide for himself whether the episodes he remembered had actually occurred or were mere alcoholic chimeras. One thing he would say for Gussie, she had never since thrown up the day to him. Of course, he expected that sometime when she was very angry, and nothing else served, she would pick up the remembrance, out of a pile of such brickbats in the back yard of her mind, and hurl it at him. He only hoped that no one from the railroad had been watching while he demonstrated potato-peelers, either at the street corner or in subsequent bars.

No, definitely, this was a problem the solution of which required cool deliberation. It could not be attempted in one's cups. . . . He had an inspiration. Duffy—the very man. By God, he'd tell him the whole story right through from the beginning to the end. He was a regular fellow, and with understanding. Too bad he was a priest! On the other hand, that was the very reason he could be helpful now. Gussie would believe in him. By the Lord Harry, it was a capital idea! He clicked to the horse, which broke into a trot, and turned at the corner nearest the priest's church. In all the years he had lived in Kensington, he had studiously avoided the local Catholic church and never permitted it to make a record upon his mind. It simply did not exist for him. He could not have told whether it was made of brick or stone, or where its entrance was. The area it occupied was empty, a blind spot which he had purposely cultivated.

Now he drove by an edifice that was completely strange to him, and tried to decide how to go about calling upon his friend. There was a building next to the church, and yet evidently connected with it, that had the appearance of living quarters. He ascended the steps and knocked. An elderly nun answered. She had evidently been washing dishes, for her hands were still moist, and an apron and a towel were thrown over her shoulder. He looked up at her, thrust out his beard aggressively, and blustered, "Where can I find Duffy around here?"

"Duffy? Duffy, what Duffy would you be wantin'?" the Sister asked with a strong Irish accent. Instinctively, all of Mr. Rogers' antagonism toward the flood of Irish immigration was aroused, and he thought, "There ought to be a law against leaving them in," although he was ready enough at other times to fulminate at the callous cruelty of England toward her subject people, and to feel that the refugees from her tyrannies should be received with open arms. Now, in a combative mood, he answered, belligerently:

"Yes, Duffy . . . D-u-f-f-y—Duffy."

"Can you be meanin' Father Duffy?" The Sister, conscious of her red hands, rubbed them together nervously.

"He may be your father, but I misdoubt it. He's too young, I'd say, but he is certainly not mine. However, if he's around, I'd like to see him."

The Sister looked at her visitor askance. "Well, if it's Father Duffy you want to be seeing, come in. He's in his study."

Before anything further could be said, the priest himself appeared, and his voice reverberated down the hallway in a volume the Sister had never before heard him use. "Rogers—I thought it was you. I recognized your voice. Come in, man, and rest yourself in my shack here." The nun's expression as she gazed after the men was compounded of both curiosity and consternation. Not only was the visitor crazy, but good Father Duffy himself was behaving in a most unaccountable manner. What was the reason for it?

"It's good to be seeing you. I can't tell you how good."

Father Duffy wrung Mr. Rogers' hand. He grinned, that slow, charming smile Mr. Rogers had learned to like for its frankness. "You know, I want to tell you now, Rogers, I have never in my life enjoyed a day as much as I did the Fourth, with you and your family. It was indeed a glorious occasion. And how is dear old Mary, the guest of honor?"

In spite of his perturbation, Mr. Rogers also was forced to smile. By the Lord Harry, that had been a good day, and Mary *had* enjoyed it.

"She's quite recovered, and her old self. . . . But everything else is at sixes and sevens." He looked ruefully at the priest. "Duffy, if someone had told me that my home would be practically broken up within two months of last Fourth of July, I would have said he was crazy—but that is the case, and I want to talk to you about it."

Father Duffy looked seriously at his guest. No, of course Mr. Rogers was in earnest, and he should place him in the best mood possible.

"I have some good twist here in my desk. We'll be able to think more clearly on a good chew of it. I'm sorry it's not real railroad blackstrap, but at any rate, there is nothing to quiet a man's nerves like a good quid. Look at the cow—best nerves in the world." After helping himself generously, Father Duffy pushed a large brass spittoon between them. "The lights are all green, Rogers, and a straight, clear road ahead. Give her all the steam you want to—I'm listening."

In good railroad fashion, Mr. Rogers told the whole story, beginning at the very beginning. He told the history of the two sisters, of their Italian temperament. He explained them and excused them. He related Zena's generosities, the gift of the "dash-hounds" and their subsequent christening. Father Duffy laughed until tears came to his eyes.

366

"Rogers, if you ever get another horse of which you grow particularly fond, do me the favor of naming it Patrick Duffy. . . . I must stay ahead of the Methodists."

There is nothing for the telling of a tale, even a sad one, like a good audience, and Mr. Rogers rose to the occasion. In fact, he almost forgot he was asking for advice, he became so concerned with adding occasional flourishes to his yarn. When he recited his remarks anent the physical properties of the dachshunds, the priest almost swallowed his quid.

"I declare the first thing I noticed about those two beasts was that they seemed to be possessed of a relatively larger share of the old Adam than the rest of us, and that's a fact." When the recital was over, he turned serious again. "I think in many ways you are an astute man, Rogers—and in this case especially, I agree with you. Unless this is cleared up now, finally, you'll never hear the end of it. Man alive, what heartaches can start over something as trifling as a little spilled water on the floor!"

For a good fifteen minutes there was no sound but the slow, ruminative squish of teeth in tobacco, and the occasional splash of liquid against brass. "Rogers, don't go home—board your horse tonight at a good livery, not too near. Better yet, go to one of the smaller hotels—they'll put your horse up for you—the Bald Eagle, or the Black Bear on Third Street. I know both houses, and they have good stables. Dollars to doughnuts your good wife will be in to see me first thing in the morning. Send a messenger to let me know where you'll be, and I'll be in to see you later in the day."

"Not go home at all? Not all night?" The idea was unthinkable to Mr. Rogers. His home was the center of his universe, the hub from which all his thoughts radiated. Father Duffy laid a quieting hand on his sleeve.

"It is only one night, Rogers. Jealousy is a deep-seated disease, and it takes a stern remedy. Now away with you, man, before your wife catches you here. She might very well come in to see me this afternoon, although I think it will be after mass in the morning."

Chapter 5

As soon as her brother-in-law had left, Teresina Lascalles gave up all pretense of courage. She was so alone in the world! She could count on the devotion of Céleste and Denise, perhaps, but one never knew with servants. She felt, and looked, like a tired old woman as she took the steam elevator up to her apartment on the third floor. It was a sign of her mental state that she had accepted quarters so high above the street without a word of protest. Suppose a fire broke out? One couldn't count on this bird-in-a-cage contraption. Even the sound of the engine that operated it, the noise of cylinders and cogs and escaping steam, frightened her.

Denise and the luggage had gone up another way, and the maid was already engaged in setting out the most treasured of Zena's photographs and mementos. In a very short time the room looked quite homelike, and cheerful, and familiar. Her gallery of old lovers was a source of great satisfaction to her. It gave her a feeling of confidence in herself to look at the male faces she knew so well and think that they had once been conquests. In many cases her entire memory of the flesh-and-blood man she had known was blotted out completely by time, and he was only his daguerreotype in its ornate frame. When she thought of the officer she had accompanied to Martinique,

368

for instance, she called to mind the unchanging pose and sepia tints of his picture. He was "Edouard in the red plush frame," and not the stiff little martinet who had succumbed to her charms.

Once she was freed of corsets and tight shoes, and enjoying the comfort of ribbon bows and lacy frills, she began soberly to think, to plan.

There was no use being angry with Tina. Her younger sister had reason to be jealous, there was no gainsaying that. Teresina remembered with considerable satisfaction the times, long ago, when she had cut in on her sister's conquests. But she had made absolutely no headway at all with Jesse! He had been kindness itself, and sympathetic to a degree, but in love with her? She shook her head, regretfully.

Not that she had set out to capture Augustina's husband, she reminded herself, not at all. Still it hurt one's pride to think they had been in the same house for most of the summer and he had not once intimated that propinquity, or something, made her desirable in his eyes. In that way a Frenchman would have been more courteous, and yet it was that stupid, stolid faithfulness to Augustina that was one of Jesse's noblest traits. And did she twist him around her little finger! It was a pity and a shame to see a man so used by a scheming little creature like her sister. If *she* had married Jesse Rogers, he would have had his own way in everything. He would have been lord and master in fact. She would have been happy merely to serve him, to sit at his feet.

Teresina sighed. There was no use in her returning to the Rogers household. That was over! Some day Augustina would realize her mistake, and they would forgive each other, by mail. She never wanted to see her sister again. And not Jesse, either! She would make a clean break,

369

return to New York, and take the first ship to France. As she planned, hope revived. Somewhere in the world there must be someone who would not think of her merely as an old woman. . . .

What about Philippe? Zena shook her head. She had got her nephew into something, she feared. Her namesake was an artful, designing little wretch, and with her mother's temper. On the other hand, a man needn't expect beauty and a good disposition both, and he wouldn't value them properly if he got them. Look at her own case. She had been beautiful, and no one could say she had ever lost her temper with a man. Not often, at any rate, and what had it got her? Lonely at fifty. . . . Well, approximately fifty, anyway.

Nevertheless, she had a responsibility toward both her niece and her nephew, and as soon as she got back to Paris she would make arrangements to discharge it. She walked over to the little desk in the sitting room, and sat down heavily. She had some letters to write, and it was something she hated to do. Letters were so final, and could so often be misread. She pushed away the hotel stationery in distaste, and ordered Denise to get out her own, and her purple ink.

For the next hour she was busy, alternating furious writing, when her pen scratched and sputtered over the paper, with periods of concentration, when she bit on the penholder, and tried over aloud words, phrases, and whole sentences.

First there was a note to Céleste. That was quickly done, and dispatched by messenger immediately. She would need her maid for traveling, and Philippe could dispense with her now, she was certain.

Then a longer letter to Philippe, to go by mail. She didn't want him to get it until she had left. Then, hardest of all, the note for Jesse. She tore up three sheets of her best paper before it was done to her satisfaction. She instructed Denise: "We shall leave first thing in the morning. Céleste should be here early, to help you, and don't forget, I want this note left at the desk, but not until the last thing before we go." It was so important that Jesse should get her note, and understand. She almost wished things had worked out differently for her with him.

When Mr. Rogers called at the Continental Hotel in the morning, the clerk handed him a note heavily perfumed with the heady scent he recognized as Zena's favorite. He opened it with clumsy fingers and frowned at its contents:

DEAR JESSE: I *couldn't* bear the anguish of saying good-by, so I am taking the morning train to New York. I shall *never forget* you, nor your *understanding* and *sympathy* for a lone woman who needs a *true* friend.

The underlined words added a kind of special significance to the note, and he nodded his head sentimentally, then read on:

Say *good-by* to the children and the servants. I've left the latter *little* remembrances, and I will send the girls *something* from New York, and *dear* Henry who is like you must have been at his age. Tell Philippe I will see him this winter, and I am sorry not to *aid further* in the plans for his wedding. When I say I *fear* for his happiness I know you will understand. *Close* association with Teresina convinces me that while she has *my good looks*, her disposition is her *mother's*.

I shall take the first boat back to "la belle France."

Your *loving* sister
TERESINA

He felt truly sorry. He even considered going to New York himself. Zena would probably go to the Astor House. But then again, she might not. . . . He shook his head.

This was her wish. He supposed it was best to allow her to do as she had planned.

Mr. Rogers had a long day in front of him, and he utilized the walk from Ninth and Chestnut streets back to the hotel on Third Street in thinking over the whole matter of his relationship with his family. He was too easy with them, that was the trouble. Henry hadn't had a good licking for months, and Gene for an even longer time. The cat-o'-nine-tails hung neglected behind the shed door. Teresina had evidently got out of hand as well, according to Zena's letter. That came of Gussie's interference. There was no time in a girl's life that a good hiding wouldn't do more to correct her than all the talking to in the world. Julia was a probable exception to the rule. She was too good for her own good, and perversely, this disturbed him more than the wrongdoing of the others. Zenie must have acted up in her aunt's presence, perhaps while he was at work, or asleep. A good bit went on around the house that he didn't get to know about, particularly since he was on night work; and he resented it. When this business got settled with Gussie, he was going to demand a daily accounting of the actions of all of them.

He hadn't been firm enough—he took all the blame. Suppose he had insisted right off that he wouldn't have the "dash-hounds." For some reason, in spite of their complete vindication, poor Moody and Sankey still bore the onus for yesterday's trouble. He hadn't been firm enough, that was the thought his mind continually harped upon. Just see the mess his easy-going spirit had got them into. A strong hand was needed in a family, and in a country.

Turning from the domestic to the national field, he considered the happenings of recent weeks. There was hope in the fact that the Democrats had nominated Tilden for President. A fine choice—a man who had opposed the

372

Tweed Ring. Just recently the papers reported that the Government had finally located the fugitive. To think that Boss Tweed, who had once held all of New York in the palm of his hand, was now a convicted criminal, dodging pursuit in out-of-the-way corners of the world. If the news was correct, they had caught up with him finally in Greece, or Turkey, somewhere. He had been dealt with strongly and the country would profit thereby.

By God, they ought to do the same thing with other groups and individuals at home who were causing so much trouble. Those labor champions—the hotheads who talked about strikes and organizing. They needed to be well chastised, that's what. The country was in a bad enough way without those people causing more dissension. The voters at the polls should turn out the crooks in office, and put in honest men. It was as simple as that. Then the economic wrongs that were behind the labor unrest would be righted. The scandals like the newly uncovered Whisky Ring would be ended. Whipping posts, that's what was needed; then business and labor, officials and politicians, would settle down like good children and behave themselves.

In his heart, Mr. Rogers knew this would not happen, and that if it did, the results would not be as he expected, but as these views would not have comported with his present line of reasoning, he ignored them.

He returned to the Bald Eagle Hotel, and left instructions that if anyone came to see him, he was to be called immediately. He retired for his morning nap, but found sleep impossible. What was going on at home? What had Gussie done? Was she worried as to his whereabouts? Had Zena reached New York safely? There was a risk in women's traveling alone so far.

Gradually his brain tired and he dozed off, although he would have denied that he actually fell asleep in the state

373

he was in. At the same time, it took three knocks on the door before he answered, and then he jumped from bed with the agility of a startled bear. "Duffy at last," he thought, but there was only a note from the priest: "No sign of Mrs. R. If she does not come by four o'clock, I shall stop in and see her on my parish rounds."

He was desolated! After a quarter-century of marriage, Gussie had not cared enough to try to find out what had happened to him. Then he thought: "Perhaps she has appealed to the police—after all, you don't run to your priest to find a missing husband." He and Duffy had been wrong. She wouldn't go to the priest at all. Pride would prevent, and besides, Gussie was one to do things for herself. She wasn't one to run sniveling to someone else in case of trouble.

Meanwhile, he would have to do something to pass the time. A man would go crazy just waiting for something to happen. He couldn't make up his mind whether to take in an afternoon performance of the minstrels or go to the cyclorama. The theater might make him forget, but on the other hand, he was so preoccupied with his trouble that he might miss the point of the jokes. The cyclorama won. In the first place, it was educational, and then, if later Gussie wormed out of him how he spent his time during their separation, she might feel hurt if he took the matter no more seriously than to go to the theater.

The cyclorama was different. One couldn't object to so refined a way of spending the time—and it was marvelously interesting. It was almost like being at the place itself, the illusion was so perfect. The thought also struck him that he could say later, at a proper moment, that he had chosen it because they had last gone together to a similar entertainment, "The Siege of Paris," out at the Centennial.

This was about Paris, also, by the way. "Paris by Gaslight"—a laudable and interesting subject, surely, and proper entertainment for a husband as unhappy as he was at the moment.

He just did not feel like walking, nor did he want Mr. Quinby to have to stand in the heat, so he left him in the stable below the hotel and took a hansom up to the Coliseum Building at Broad and Locust streets, which housed the beautiful and gigantic work of art. It was a full hour before the tour of Paris after dark was completed, and he spent a good part of the time standing on the platform wishing that Gussie were along, to enjoy the sights with him as the guide pointed them out on the huge oil painting.

He returned to his hotel not a whit improved in mind by his experience. In fact, he worried all the way back for fear Duffy was waiting for him, and his heart was still heavier when there was no message from him at the office. And then he opened the door to his room, unaware that it was already unlocked, to hear the pleasantest music he could imagine.

"Jesse Rogers—don't you think it is about time you stopped this foolishness, and came home?"

He was so overjoyed he forgot entirely the state of the relations between himself and his wife, and caught her in a hug that lifted her completely from the floor and disarranged her bonnet. Finally, after coughing a few times to clear his throat, he managed to ask:

"Did you see Duffy, finally? How did you learn I was here?"

"Father Duffy? Of course I didn't see him. I'll take care of my family myself, without calling in the Church to do it for me. Your name was in the paper this morning, large as life, as one of the newly arrived guests here. I waited to see if you would have the common sense to come home, and when you didn't, I came in to fetch you."

375

"But Zena?"

"Good riddance, I'd say. You needn't worry about her. If I was wrong this time, she knows in her heart I would have been right in the long run."

Mr. Rogers beamed. "Gussie—you admit you were wrong this time?"

She gave an impatient shrug. "I got from Mary what she heard, and put two and two together. You'd hurt Zena's feelings about those two poor dogs. . . . Honest, Jesse, the way you carry on about the dear little animals aggravates me beyond words—no wonder she was distressed, and all this trouble we've had just because you insist upon an unreasonable attitude toward them. I hope this is a lesson to you."

"Good old Gussie, trust her for a way of wriggling out of things!" thought Mr. Rogers. He was delighted, but then looked worried again. "All right, my dear, it was all my fault, but what about your sister? You should really apologize. Blame me, of course, but admit that you misjudged her."

"I'll do nothing of the kind. I didn't misjudge her at all, as she very well knows. She was out for you, Jesse. It was merely your ill-considered outburst that brought the thing to a head at the moment. However, I will write her presently as if nothing ever happened, and she'll be sorry enough for the trouble she caused, and the whole episode will be forgotten, I assure you."

Knowing something of the prior relations of the sisters, Mr. Rogers accepted this assurance, although he determined to write to Zena himself at the first opportunity. One thing was still unexplained, however. "Tell me, my dear, how did you get in the room? I left it locked."

"I merely told the clerk I had arrived a day sooner than

376

expected. You don't think he would disbelieve me, do you?"

"My dear, who could ever say you nay? Now I'm anxious to get home, and I'm sure Mr. Quinby misses his nice stall. Let's go!"

2

Mary let them in, a wide grin on her face. She twisted her mouth in the most impossible grimaces to whisper, "Father Duffy is in the parlor, ma'am, and he's awful upset about somethin'."

Mrs. Rogers looked her most determined. "I'll settle him, right now, poking his nose in my affairs. Mary, let me by."

Mr. Rogers tried to restrain her, but when his wife was determined enough, no force could hold her. The effect created was that of an avenging female dragging in a sorry culprit of a husband, and it was a few minutes before the priest realized that all was again well with his charges.

"You and that husband of mine are a fine pair, I must say. Well, your little plans miscarried because I still can read the newspapers. I suppose you conspirators forgot they print a daily list of arrivals at the hotels, because of the Centennial?"

Father Duffy's face was a study in conflicting emotions. He had difficulty in repressing a smile when Mr. Rogers appeared to be towed along by his determined though diminutive spouse, and again at the reason for the failure of their stratagem. He was trying to decide how to handle the matter of the quarrel, and this turned his features to a more serious cast, the while he sought to understand the state of affairs at the moment. Of this he was soon apprised.

"Jesse saw fit to drag you into this little misunderstanding—for the life of me, I can't see why, busy as you are, Father, with all your parish duties—and I apologize for him."

As Mr. Rogers stood to the rear of his wife, the priest could see him grin, grimace, and indulge in a series of winks designed to show that everything had been satisfactorily arranged, but in spite of these, his face grew grim and implacable. Mrs. Rogers rattled on with her account against a growing feeling that she had incurred the good Father's displeasure.

"Imagine all that fuss over a couple of dogs—you've seen them, Father? Aren't they little dears?"

"I have, and excepting, as I have remarked recently, that they have a little more of the old Adam about them than would seem natural, I have nothing against them whatever."

"What in the world is he talking about?" Mrs. Rogers wondered. But she hurried on, "I've forgiven Jesse, and we've forgotten the whole episode, which was made too much of anyhow."

When Father Duffy wanted to look stern, he appeared hard indeed. He began to talk in a low, biting voice, in which every syllable was given an equal value of scorn.

"Augustina Rogers, you may twist things around, distort facts, bamboozle your husband, and blame helpless beasts for your own sins—but you shan't bamboozle me, and I'm doing some straight talking to you. You call me Father, and as such I have a duty toward you which I wouldn't escape if I could. You have sinned, and I intend to admonish you."

At this moment, as if by prearranged signal, Moody and Sankey scampered into the room and made a circle of it. Everyone was forced to look at them, and even Mr. Rogers couldn't help smiling. By the Lord Harry, he'd swear if their hind legs were a half-inch shorter they'd plow up

378

the Wilton! After a pause, Father Duffy continued as if there had been no interruption.

"In a moment of levity, I said those beasts were possessed of the old Adam. I say to you, there is too much of Mother Eve in you. You've been guilty of jealousy, Augustina Rogers, and I expect an honest confession of it, right here and now!"

As he finished his demand, the priest's voice was as loud as ever his own had been, Mr. Rogers thought. Railroading developed the lungs, and maybe preaching helped as well! He watched his wife covertly—she'd frazzle Duffy! But no, she lowered her head, and stood for a moment like a guilty schoolgirl. When she spoke finally, her voice was low and childlike.

"Yes, Father, I've been jealous." Gradually, she seemed to become her mature self again as she went on, "But so would you, if you were a woman and had a husband as handsome as my Jesse, and as gullible."

Father Duffy relaxed and put a hand on each of their shoulders. "It's an awful thing, jealousy. I intend to preach upon it shortly—I don't suppose you'd come to hear me, Rogers?"

The irrepressible master of the Rogers household threw back his head and roared:

"Why should I, Duffy? I know all about it after almost losing my home from its effects. But when you do preach on it, follow the old Methodist rule for sermonizing:

"Begin low and go on slow,
　　Rise higher and take fire.
When you want to impress,
　　Be self-possessed.
At the end wax warm,
　　And sit down in a storm."

379

Chapter 6

THERE were many things to disturb Philippe's peace of mind, and all of them were feminine. First, the beautiful Algerian, busily engaged in rearranging her wares at the booth opposite. He never saw the girl without feeling self-conscious, and remembering the scene his fiancée had precipitated over her. The exotic creature had been the cause of many domestic rifts since that time, although he was never amused when some male was angrily dragged away from the presence of the charming Oriental by an irate feminine companion. In a city filled with beautiful girls, why did this one create such a sensation? She was pretty. Yes, in her way, but even so, she would never have caused such a furore in a more cosmopolitan city. In Paris, for instance. Here in this provincial atmosphere she had the charm of the strange and the unknown. If the girl collected clippings, she must have a scrapbook filled by now with all the newspaper and magazine accounts. And in the main, American editors had been boorish and unchivalrous, in their desire to please their womenfolk. However, the amount of business she had done probably compensated the Algerian for the tone of the articles about her.

The narrow, uninteresting lives Americans led were responsible for the interest shown, he was sure of that. They had the shallowest kind of interest in art, music, and literature. Even in their food they seemed to demand only quantity and speed of service. Their whole energies were given to the making of money. If they couldn't make it by honest trading, they made it by swindling and bribery. The whole population boasted about the smart trickeries of men like Fisk and Gould.

Their manufacturers produced the cheapest possible materials. There was no pride in quality, in craftsmanship.

All one had to do to prove this was to visit this great, boastful display. The best showing was in the machinery and printing-press sections. Most of the American art was atrocious. Its ironwork was meretricious, its china poor. There was a little good silverwork, but in the main it was cheap and ostentatious. The good displays in these fields came almost entirely from foreign sources, and then were incomplete, because few manufacturers wished to show their goods where a high tariff discouraged their sale.

This strangely beautiful girl had succeeded, quite unaware of her own powers, he was sure, in opening to American men (at least) a vista that stretched beyond the uttermost dollar sign. A vista of exotic countries, other fascinations, unholy beauties. . . .

Philippe realized, guiltily, that he must have been staring at the girl while he was thinking about her, and he walked around to the other side of the display before continuing his unhappy reflections.

Disturbance number two was Zena. Why had his favorite aunt fled so suddenly from Philadelphia? She was mercurial enough, he knew from past experience, but it was unlike her to have left without a spoken word of good-by to him, particularly as she had been so enthusiastic about the details of his approaching wedding. Of course, if there had been a man in the offing—no, that was impossible. Zena had confided in him before about her love affairs; she would surely have let fall some hint now.

It was most mysterious. She had sent him that note, but it had explained nothing satisfactorily. The heat was too much for her! Zena, who had spent a whole summer in Martinique! She hadn't complained about the heat at all, anyway. No, that wouldn't do. Besides, the heat wave had broken two days later, and this early September weather

381

was delightful. If she had gone on to New York for that reason she could easily have returned afterward.

There was a deeper reason, and it lay within the Rogers family. He noticed a peculiar restraint whenever he was with them—or did he? There was no indication on the surface. Teresina, who had been a little nervous and difficult during the earlier days of their engagement, had been pleasant and serene for weeks. If she appeared a little cold, it was purely as a defense against his own ardor, and he admitted to himself complacently that he must be difficult to resist at times. If there was some kind of restraint in the house he couldn't put his finger on it. Mr. Rogers was perfect; he was hearty, frank, and quite his usual self—a man after his own heart, as he repeated to himself every so often. Mrs. Rogers also seemed friendly and cordial. She and Aunt Zena were so much alike it was amusing at times, with their sudden enthusiasms, their warmhearted impulsiveness, and also, it must be added, their unpredictable tempers and quick excitements.

Was not the feeling within himself, and caused by that blonde minx of a Georgina? He had never believed a word she said to him, and couldn't forget one of them. It was purely accidental that he hadn't seen Julia for some time, and that Teresina herself, or Mary, let him in when he called. He was so sure it was merely a coincidence that each time he pulled the doorbell he looked forward with the keenest anticipation to seeing Julia's slow, pleasant smile. He was disappointed, increasingly disappointed, when it was someone else. "Julia did promise, though, she would never, never see you again." That child's words kept coming back to him, and he imagined her pointing a finger at him, with that expression of naïveté mixed with roguery, and repeating "I told you so."

"Julia did promise, though, she would never, never see

you again." He banged his fist on the top of a case. By Jove, he wanted to see her again. She was a nice girl. She was good fun, too. A lot better fun than Teresina, and easier to talk to, as well. He had enjoyed the conversations he had with her almost every evening, and he missed them now that they were apparently over. There, the truth was out that he had repressed so long! He did miss seeing Julia, and if she evaded him again tonight, that would be proof that at least a part of Georgina's seemingly preposterous tale had been true. It required considerable restraint to keep him from leaving the Exposition grounds then and there, and putting his new resolutions to the test. If he didn't see Julia tonight, he would find out why!

There was nothing like walking for a state like his, Philippe decided. The exercise would be good for him. He left the main exhibition building and set off at a good pace for the little French Building, which was also under his charge. The cool weather had finally brought the crowds. The wide expanses of the park, deserted under the summer heat, were now alive with people intent upon getting their fifty cents' worth. It took Americans to do things on a big scale, he decided. The scene was more impressive than he had ever seen it before. On the opening day it had been too unfinished. He could think of only one criticism now —all the banners and decorative buntings had faded during the summer and lost their original bright, gay look.

From the French Building it was but a few minutes' scramble down a steep bank that followed the Schuylkill (impossible name, he thought, though no one tried to pronounce it in the Dutch manner) and he was on Lansdowne Drive, the fashionable roadway that began at Girard Avenue. At the moment, early in the afternoon, it was empty of the carriages that usually filled it. He appreciated the solitude, which came as a relief after the Centennial crowds.

383

The river at this point was wide, and with the high, picturesque bluff on the opposite side of the valley, presented a noble view. Here and there a coal barge, heavily laden, nosed along the bank, towed by mules. Although the current undoubtedly set in their favor, it seemed to help them very little. One could plainly see the taut muscles strain and the animals' bellies push groundward with the effort.

This was the great coal river of America, he thought. What a tremendous tonnage of that fuel it had borne seaward! He wished he might have the time to visit the mines and mining country at the head of the stream, and he meant some day to make an excursion down-river to a point where the coal barges assembled to begin their sea voyage under steam tow to Boston, Baltimore, and other American coastal cities.

The country's rivers were its blood streams, he observed to himself, and decided it was no original thought and not altogether true. Easy money and free land had caused the building of more railroads than the population warranted. The various lines were already underselling each other, and in the process of open competition, the rivers, and their supporting canals, were fast losing out. There seemed to be a waste of natural resources in this national passion for change. The French had a healthier regard for their heritage. He couldn't imagine their scrapping one form of transportation at the expense of another. Somehow the two would be worked into an economical and efficient relation.

Toward the other bank, several empty barges moved up-river, and in midstream a little passenger steamer lifted a white plume of smoke. While the setting was different, the scene reminded him of the Seine, probably because of these steamers, which were similar to those that ran from

Paris to St. Cloud. He determined upon a ride in one of the little vessels, and strode along the drive until he came to the nearest landing, the one used by Centennial visitors. It was crowded at the moment with members of some religious sect, apparently, from the strange black garments they affected. The men wore long beards, and their hair, tied up under their hats, also seemed of unusual length.

Philippe understood enough German to know they were conversing in that language, and he determined to question Mr. Rogers, when he saw him, as to their probable identity. Now these folk had robbed him of the peace of solitude, and he regretted his decision to take the steamer ride. It was too late, though, to change his mind. More people were arriving all the time, and these pushed him forward inexorably as one of the steamers churned to the landing and took them on.

2

The room which had once so appealed to Julia no longer gave her a sense of refuge from the world. She loathed the narrow chamber, with its plain walls and iron cot. Instead of being a willing recluse up here on the fourth floor away from the rest of the family, she felt like a prisoner. Once she had looked out over the rooftops and dreamed of Paris. Now she merely saw the flat, homely roofs of Kensington houses, with lines of green foliage marking the streets. In this part of the city, the gridiron arrangement of streets which William Penn had planned with so much pride had succumbed to geographical necessity, and the pattern of the streets formed city blocks of many shapes other than rectangular.

Where once she had loved her room, and spent much of her time in it, embroidering or doing lacework or dreaming, she stayed there now merely to escape contact with her sister, and in the evenings, or Sundays, to avoid Philippe. Since the day of that scene with Teresina when her sister had actually tried to stab her with the hatpin, she had not seen him. She had made the promise to end a distressing occasion, and she had lived up to it to the letter, though she bitterly regretted having given it. The unhappy evenings spent there when she knew Philippe was downstairs contributed to her dislike of the place.

She never gave up hope that something would happen which would bring them together, and a visit from Georgina encouraged her. She distrusted the motives of her younger sister. Gene had some reasons of her own, that was certain; but while she reproved her for what she had said, at the same time she couldn't help feeling it might lead to something. She had seen Gene get her own way before. And yet, in thinking it over, just what had Gene said? Merely that she was on her side. It was silly to take anything so seriously. She had talked of putting a flea in Philippe's ear, but her attempts to find out just what Gene had told him proved in vain. She had just shaken her head, and looked mysterious. There was one thing to which she had been adamant, Georgina's urging that she meet Philippe outside in some way that she would arrange. It was silly, she knew, to be so affected by the goings-on of a mere child, especially when she had insisted so strenuously that Georgina should cease her connivings.

To escape her room, Julia had got into the habit of going for walks much more frequently than she had ever done before. It was extremely bad form to be seen unaccompanied on the streets, except perhaps when one was shopping. In the evenings, of course, no self-respecting lady would think of going out alone. Not that Julia would have dared this latter course, even when the presence of Philippe downstairs made her room seem a prison indeed;

but in the afternoons she did brave public opinion and the city's dangers when the weather was pleasant for walking. Among her new clothes was a becoming and practical walking dress of purple silk and gray cashmere, cut in the new princess style and form-fitting to the knee. She changed into this, trusted her mother wouldn't encounter her, or if she did would not ask for explanations, and started, casually enough, on her great adventure.

Once out of the house, Julia considered what to do. It was a beautiful afternoon, and the Centennial drew her like a lodestone, but, no—that would be wrong. Once in the grounds, she couldn't avoid searching out Philippe. Fate, she told herself, would eventually draw them together, and an arrangement of fate dishonestly come by would always be on her conscience. On the other hand, she didn't dare take the horsecar into the city, much as she wanted to be away from Kensington for a while. After all, she was alone, and how could she tell who might accost her in a public conveyance? The steam trains were safer.

Suppose she took the train at Richmond, went to the Centennial station, but avoided the Exposition grounds entirely. She could enjoy nature alone, walking down some of the pathways that ran along the Schuylkill. Her dress was admirably suited for walking. Its hem little more than touched the ground, and her shoes had good high tops that came well up to the calf and provided adequate support for her ankles. Yes, she was well equipped for a stroll in the park. She was also glad that she had brought along her parasol. While the sun did not seem hot, still, one couldn't risk tanning, and beside, the parasol made an excellent defensive weapon in case one was attacked by a wild beast. Julia had no idea what creatures might be encountered on a trip such as she contemplated. It was a daring thing to attempt, this she realized, and it was well to be completely prepared. She enjoyed a feeling of self-reliance as she set out.

It was indeed an adventure to make so extended a journey alone, and she enjoyed every minute of it, except for momentary distress when a strange man gazed too often in her direction. This incident occurred in the train that shuttled back and forth between Richmond and the Centennial grounds. A tall, dark man with sideburns and drooping mustache was seated on the other side of the coach, and he stared at her so continuously that she was sure he must belong to one of the vice rings about which her mother often spoke, that lured young girls to their doom. While she trembled from sudden fear, she looked straight ahead, giving the man no least cause to believe that she would listen to any proposals he might suggest. Recognizing her sterling character, the man's attention turned elsewhere, and in the excitement of her little trip, she forgot him entirely by the time the train reached its destination.

The adventure affected her like a tonic; her cheeks glowed with color, and she palpitated with the joy of living. Shantytown, where she and Philippe had so enjoyed themselves, beckoned to her with bright buntings and all the lure of its sinful life, but she knew if she went there alone she would be undone indeed.

She tried to imagine what might happen. Suppose she should be led into one of those traps for the unwary girl. She could never afterward go home. Her parents would be distressed, of course. They would search everywhere, but would they ever think of looking in the dens of Shantytown? The answer was obvious, of course. There she would remain, to become a dancer, or something even worse, luring men on to sin while her own heart was broken, and then, some day, Philippe and Zena would come in—

388

happily married now—and they would see her leading a life of shame.

There had been a play, the saddest thing imaginable, with much the same plot, and Julia could never forget the poignant distress of the heroine. In this case, Zenie would turn away in disgust. Zenie wouldn't care what happened to *her*, Julia, just so *she* got Philippe; but his eyes would follow her sadly, and he would wipe away a furtive tear. He would never be able to lose a sense of sorrow at seeing her gone beyond reclaim, and it would give him a melancholy disposition for the rest of his life. Even as they left the dive, he would look back reproachfully as Zenie pulled him along.

While Julia's imagination took no account of time, or realized that the Exposition had only a couple more months to run, it was sufficiently harrowing to turn her footsteps in an opposite direction. In a mood in which exhilaration and apprehension succeeded each other, she walked down Elm Avenue, filled with beggars and sidewalk merchants and fakers.

A path curved away from the busy street, but she decided it was too lonely. Who might be in ambush, waiting for unsuspecting females behind that nearest clump of bushes? There was greater safety on the avenue. She walked a little farther, and found a path that seemed more to her liking. A number of persons were walking along it, and if she had been more observant, she would have realized they were going toward some definite objective. The path wound down to the river, and at last she realized that it led to a pier of the Schuylkill steamboat line. One of the little vessels was alongside, and apparently about to cast off. On an impulse she made no attempt to understand, she dashed for the narrow plank that formed the gangway just as the bell clanged a signal. This was the very last thing she had expected to do, go for a boat ride!

There were a number of Pennsylvania German Mennonites on board, and she felt at home, and safe, with these good people. They were like Mr. and Mrs. Schaffhauser, the Mennonite farmers in the market from whom her mother bought scrapple and cottage cheese, and other farm produce. She walked over to the rail, and watched the tree-covered banks as they fled by. It was as if she stood in a new kind of cyclorama. The boat was the platform, but instead of turning around to behold the picture, the painting itself moved by her at dizzy speed. The breeze caught at her skirt, and except that the silk was well stitched to its buckram foundation and to the inner lining, might have caused a shameful display. Even so, Julia felt no sense of security concerning it. At any moment, a zephyr stronger than the others might do unthinkable damage. She decided to leave the rail. . . . But then she would lose the feeling of being alone, on some distant tributary. She tried to picture the Rhine, and built imaginary castles on the Schuylkill's pleasant reaches. The Thames—how did it look? She dared not think of the Seine. When she had been in Paris she had not been much impressed by the river, but now it had a tremendous glamour. The passing barges also reminded her of the busy traffic on that other, distant stream.

The parasol was unmanageable in the breeze, and she had lowered it as soon as the boat started. Now she could feel the warmth of the sun on her face. It would be disgraceful if she became tanned by this outing! She moved across the deck to another empty space at the rail, on the shady side of the vessel, and she felt less like a lonely female, for here were clustered the two or three other women passengers who were not Mennonites. There was a man next her at the rail who was as tall as her father, and almost as broad. She imagined to herself that it was Philippe, and that they were traveling together, on their wedding journey, perhaps. It was an immodest thought, and she blushed, and was glad the man could not know her imaginings. Nevertheless they persisted, and she entered into long mental conversations with the stranger.

"Look, Philippe, that barge is so prettily painted, red roof, green walls, and yellow shutters—the house on it, I mean. Do you suppose the family lives on it all the year round? I see two children. No, there is a third, handling that pole, near the center. He must be the oldest. Do you think the bargeman and his wife love each other as we do?"

There were so many things to point out with the phrase "Look, Philippe" that the time came when she forgot entirely that hers were imaginary conversations, and she spoke aloud. The stranger at her side seemed to be startled. He turned around suddenly, and Julia began to blush. What in the world had she done? Her imagination had led her into the most frightful indiscretion. The stranger was looking at her curiously, and he had assumed the very appearance of Philippe. She was demented—it couldn't be possible. She closed her eyes and opened them. She was still seeing Philippe! He was holding her two hands, a flesh-and-blood grip that threatened to crush them. It was Philippe! And she had been standing next him all that time. It was he, it was, it was! She was so overjoyed it was difficult to restrain herself from hugging him. Then he spoke:

"Julia, Julia—it's so good to see you. . . . But how did you get here? How long were you standing there before you spoke to me? You're not *alone*, are you? Why didn't you let me know sooner that you were there?"

It was impossible to answer so many questions in order,

and to one at least she didn't dare a reply. How could she explain that she had been romanticizing, that he had heard the end of a fancied dialogue between them?

They stayed on the steamer clear to its destination at the Falls of Schuylkill. Now her eager interest found a real and living foil.

"Look, Philippe, that canalboat. The one with the white mules. Isn't it pretty? Imagine living in a little cottage on a floating island. See, they have a garden, and a white picket fence. I wonder, Philippe . . ." No, there were still things that had to be left unsaid. They watched the passengers embark or disembark at the various landings, and Julia explained about the Mennonites. "Their beliefs are somewhat like the Quakers, Papa says. A great many of them wear a habit—it is gray, with a little white linen showing, much more attractive than the Quakers wear."

"I suppose if your father hadn't married Aunt Zena's sister you would now be a little Quaker mouse in gray," Philippe teased.

"Perhaps I would. Grandfather Rogers wore plain clothes, I remember. He died when I was small. And he used plain speech—thee and thou, you know. He was very much upset when Mama wouldn't allow us to do the same. I don't think he liked Mama, and she didn't like him, for that matter."

"I think it's nice that things happen the way they do. The union of a fiery Italian temperament with a sensible Quaker heritage intrigues me, although both you and Teresina look more Italian than Quaker, I should say."

"And Gene is all Quaker. . . . You see, we didn't mix properly. Perhaps it is like oil and water. . . . Papa and Mama are *too* different."

The mention of Georgina reminded Philippe of a great many things which had disturbed him. "Tell me, Julia, why have you been evading me for so long? I've missed seeing you. . . . What was the reason?"

Julia turned her head away and pretended a great interest in the landscape, but Philippe was not to be denied an answer, and she replied, finally, "After all, Philippe, you are engaged to Zenie, you know, and not to me."

Philippe had taken Mr. Rogers' favorite expletive for his own, and he used it now. "By the Lord Harry, Julia, it's you I really love. . . . I didn't realize it until now—seeing you again." There, it was out! An entirely different kind of declaration from his romantic proposal to Teresina; but this was really from the heart.

He knew it had an effect upon Julia. She disengaged her hand from his. Until then she had been hardly conscious that he held it. Her face took on a deep, worried look—a saintly quality, he thought.

"You can't—really you can't say such things, Philippe. You've given your word . . . and I have, as well. I promised I wouldn't see you again. I've been faithless."

"So you did promise . . ." Philippe interrupted quickly. "I knew there was something. . . . Tell me, Julia, *did* Teresina attack you—with a—with a hatpin? It sounded preposterous, but that younger sister of yours told me."

"Gene is a meddlesome child who shouldn't say such things."

"Thinking back on it, I'm certain she hadn't meant to. . . . It just popped out in talking to me," Philippe defended.

Julia thought differently. So that was the flea Gene had been talking about! "I'm sure she made a little spat seem too important. Zenie has an Italian temperament, you know, and when she's angry enough might do something she would regret afterward. If *I* was engaged to you, Phi-

393

lippe, and someone else tried to take you away, I'd scratch their eyes out—I would, indeed."

They had completely forgotten their surroundings until a touch on their elbows startled them. "End of the line. . . . Return fares, if you're goin' back." The steamer was tied to a pier, and all the other passengers were gone! Philippe seized Julia's arm and they hurried ashore in embarrassed confusion. Just ahead of them was the stable of a public house, and in front of it their fellow passengers of a few minutes before, the Mennonites, were already engaged in hitching horses to farm wagons and ramshackle carriages and buggies.

"They evidently leave their teams here, to avoid the heavy traffic into the city," Philippe remarked, and then, noticing another sign, suggested: "There seems to be a steamer that goes still farther upstream. 'To the Wissahickon,' the sign says. Let's keep on voyaging as far as we can go."

The scenery, which had been beautiful, took on a rugged grandeur almost comparable with that of the Alps, lacking the snow-topped mountains, Philippe thought. This was untouched wilderness, the haunt of the savage Indian. The name of the stream ahead was that of a famous chieftain. They were practically alone on the vessel, and made rapid strides in their new understanding and intimacy. When they disembarked a second time, Philippe had another suggestion.

"Voyaging makes me hungry. Suppose we try that tavern and take potluck on whatever food they have."

There were tables and chairs on a wide porch fronting the inn, and the sound of their footsteps, or the scraping of chairs as they took seats, brought the innkeeper.

"Do you have any food for a pair of hungry wayfarers?" Philippe asked.

394

The man peered at them suspiciously. What kind of English was this? They must be some of the foreigners that came over for the Centennial. He held for America for Americans, and answered surlily:

"There's catfish—and I guess I could kill a chicken, if you wanted it."

Philippe looked questioningly, and Julia clasped her hands together. "Let's have catfish, Philippe. Haven't you eaten them yet? They are a Philadelphia delicacy. A good catfish supper is a real treat, I assure you."

Catfish—the name didn't sound very inspired, nor did their host appear able to furnish a meal of very high quality. However, if Julia liked them . . .

"Catfish it shall be, and some good ale, or stout, to wash it down—eh, Julia?"

The long wait made the meal seem even more delicious when it finally arrived. There were at least a dozen whole fish, fried to a delicate brown and banked on each side with potatoes. They both protested inability to eat more than one or two of the fish, but the rich white meat, the absence of all bones except the spine, the utter deliciousness of the flavor, and the heady quality of the stout, which proved to be more like a porter, kept them eating until nothing remained on the platter but a sorry heap of bones.

Discreet inquiries by Philippe gradually won over the innkeeper, and before they left he was answering questions cheerfully enough.

"A path? Of course there's a path, there's a dozen of 'em, more or less. But if I was goin' walkin' with a young lady, I'd go up to the Devil's Pool. It's a ways, but when you get there it's worth it."

"The Devil's Pool? What happened there? Did the Devil jump in and drown?"

The innkeeper laughed. "He ain't drowned yet, I don't

395

believe. Leastways, you wouldn't think so, seein' what I see in my business." After giving his establishment somewhat the air of a den of iniquity by this remark, he went on to explain. "It's bottomless, that's why they named it like that. They've sent down plumb lines hundreds of feet —and no nearer the bottom than they ever was. It's a real nice walk up there, too. No brambles for a dress to get caught in, and easy on the shoes, and real scenery when you get there."

"Capital! It's easy to see you have good taste in walks, and experience as well—besides having an excellent cook. How much do I owe you?"

"The cook is my wife. . . . I proposed up to Devil's Pool, by the way, and it got me a good cook, if I do say so myself—and the bill is a greenback. That was a full serving of catfish, plus the stout. You could have divided a serving for less, but I see you didn't leave none."

"A cheap price for such a delicious repast, I assure you— and I think we'll take your advice. Do you feel up to the Devil's Pool, Julia?"

When they were beyond earshot, Julia said: "Philippe, you remind me so of Papa. He has the greatest knack of making friends with people, the way you do. You don't laugh as loud, of course."

"I've never had to shout over the noise of locomotives, Julia; that develops the lungs. . . . As for making friends, I like people, and I want them to like me—and as for catfish, I never tasted anything more delicious—and as for company, it's divine."

"Don't be silly. And this must be the place we turn off—a bridle path to the left, didn't he say?" Julia was glad she had worn a proper walking suit, though even so the skirt caught at every little root and rock, and the wide ribbon at the knees became increasingly dusty. The path climbed gradually, but she grew tired from her new corset, which threw her torso forward in the fashionable Grecian bend. As the innkeeper had told them, they couldn't miss the pool if they followed the stream, and eventually they came to it. A large flat rock made a point, or cape, and Julia instinctively threw herself down on it to rest.

The Devil's Pool lived up to all expectations. Another little stream fed into the Wissahickon, tumbling over tortured rocks for a final plunge into the forbidding pool. It wasn't more than twenty feet across, and the water was black. Rocky ledges overhung its margin and cast evil, purplish shadows. One rocky stratum slanted off into the pool itself, and suddenly they both noticed that it was occupied by what appeared to be a large water snake. Finally the reptile turned and slithered back into the depths, and Philippe announced, "It's an eel—and a monster. I've seen them in Belgium."

They sat quietly for a long time, content with each other's nearness, and gazed into the almost circular depths as if it were a fortuneteller's crystal globe in which they were trying to see their future. The rock on which they sat had been warmed by the sun all afternoon. It was not uncomfortable, for generations of lovers had worn the granite to velvet smoothness. Everything combined to create in them a state of sweet languor, so that when eventually they found themselves in each other's arms, there was no urgency, no demand, no surrender. It was merely right that they were there. By the time Julia was conscious of Philippe's lips pressing against her own, and the crisp vitality of his beard, in which she seemed to drown, she was beyond caring about anything but his nearness. There were no defenses, no fears for the morrow, no torturings of conscience. This was right. They were the only two people in a world of oak, chestnut, and beech trees. In a world of bluejays and squirrels, who looked down upon them and chattered approval.

No matter what happened later, this moment was perfect, a consummation of all of life. External things seemed not to exist—they were not even aware of clothes hampering them. Later, much later, Julia wondered if other human eyes might have seen them. The sense of seclusion within the dense walls of forest might have played them false.

They remade their toilets carefully. Philippe recombed his hair and brushed his beard with a pocket set he carried for the purpose. Julia's dress had survived surprisingly well, but she borrowed Philippe's comb to undo the ravagement of her hair. The walk down the Wissahickon Valley seemed short, compared with the ascent. Julia felt tireless when at last they reached the little steamboat landing and found a vessel waiting, but she dropped readily enough upon one of the benches fixed to the wheelhouse.

"Oh, Philippe, it has been a perfect day, and I shall never forget it. There is one thing I must know. What shall I tell Teresina about today? We can't go on behind her back."

Philippe was serious. "I made a mistake, Julia, and no words will rectify it. I am certain now that you are the only girl I shall ever love, and I realize you love me in a way that Teresina is incapable of ever knowing. I shan't let you out of my sight until we are married—that will be the easier and kinder way."

"Do you still want to marry me, after today, Philippe? I thought it was the end—a kind of glorious finale. I've been completely unwise, and I don't care, but you mustn't be as well."

"My dear, you are a little goose, a little American goose. We'll be married tonight, if possible. One can have civil ceremonies, I know, as in France."

398

"You really mean it, Philippe? You know, Papa's people, the Quakers, just accept each other as man and wife in the presence of their Meeting. The birds and the squirrels saw us, and that is enough for me. I would, though, like just a little religion, I guess. We couldn't get a priest to marry us so quickly."

Philippe put his hand gently over Julia's lips. "Please don't say another word—I want to remember what you said about the birds and the squirrels. We shall find the right thing to do, never fear. You can send a note to your mother by messenger, so she won't be too worried about you. We'll go to the hotel now, and I'll make inquiries. Now look, there is the canalboat we passed going upstream, do you remember? With the white mules and the picket fence?"

Now Julia could complete the question she had not then dared to ask. "Philippe, do you think the couple on there—it looks so clean and neat and homelike—do you think they can love each other the way we do?"

Chapter 7

THE EVENING paper carried first reports of the fire under the heading CONFLAGRATION AT THE CENTENNIAL. Rumors spread quickly that the whole exhibition was one great blaze, although the paper expressed the opinion that it was confined to Shantytown, where it had started. The water supply was very low after the long season of drouth, and there was little the firemen could do but watch the blaze and prevent it from spreading. Saloons, variety shows, restaurants and shooting galleries, games of chance and freak exhibits, all were being consumed. There was an editorial question-

ing the good judgment of the city fathers in allowing rows
of wooden shacks to become a fire menace to the valuable
exhibits in the Centennial buildings proper. Stress was
laid on the fact that the great Exposition was educational
and cultural, and people did not attend it to be amused
and entertained by variety shows and lewd displays.

While Mr. Rogers read the accounts with gusto, his wife
paid little attention to his recital until Julia's extreme tardiness began to cause her worry. The supper hour came and
passed without sign of her. Mr. Rogers made ready to
leave for work, bemoaning, as he regularly did, the necessity which had forced him to turn into a night prowler,
as he called himself.

"Jesse, I declare I don't know what has become of
Julia. She sneaked away this afternoon without an aye,
yes, or no to anyone, and I've seen neither hair nor hide
of her since."

Mr. Rogers snorted. "Gussie, if you would stick to
plain language, instead of embellishing your statements
with meaningless if alliterative phrases, it would be easier
to understand what you are saying."

"Oh, bother—I'm worried. The girl knows suppertime
perfectly well, and she went out alone. Something must
have happened to her."

Mr. Rogers was inclined to take a more optimistic view
of the situation. "She's probably down at Lucius' place,
playing with those pickaninnies of his."

The explanation did not satisfy his wife, nor did it
actually sound logical to him. "Jesse, do you think she
could have gone to the Centennial? Perhaps she was
trapped in that awful fire!"

"Alone? Without a man to watch out for her? Don't
be absurd, Gussie. Our girls may be foolish at times, but
they are not foolhardy."

"You know Philippe is out there, and she is head over heels in love with him. I wouldn't put it past that girl to be sneaking over there to see him. She's been out a great deal lately by herself, and comes in with long tales of the walks she has taken."

Mr. Rogers expressed the most extreme surprise. "Julia in love with Philippe? I never heard of such a thing. He's engaged to Zenie. Madam, are you sure your imagination isn't playing you false again?"

"Jesse Rogers, you are blind as a bat. Julia is in love with Philippe. Everybody knows it but you. Teresina and she have had the most terrible quarrels about it, and you go on, unconscious of everything."

"Am I the head of this family, or merely its breadwinner? Why don't someone tell me these things? It is a situation I would have put an end to quickly, I assure you. While I am struggling to gain us a livelihood, and a few of the comforts of life, my family is indulging in shameless intrigue."

"And just how would you put an end to it? Philippe is the most eligible bachelor the two girls are ever likely to see. He picked out Zenie, so of course Julia is sure her heart is breaking. You would command her to stop, I suppose?" This in tones of withering sarcasm, which were immediately succeeded by fretful ones. "The more I think of it, the more I'm sure that is what has happened. That little minx of ours has been carrying on with Philippe behind our backs. They've had a rendezvous over in that awful Shantytown section, and now, like as not, they are both burned to a crisp. God in his wrath has been hard on them."

For the second time Mr. Rogers snorted. "If God were in the habit of sending fires from heaven to burn up evil-doers, there wouldn't be a Republican left in the country."

401

Mrs. Rogers dropped into a chair and held her head in her hands, in an attitude of complete despair. "Good heavens, Father, with your daughter probably lying in the morgue at this minute, you switch the talk around to politics! You'd try the patience of a saint."

With the promise that he would make inquiries on his way to the freight yard, Mr. Rogers escaped the house, certain that his wife was borrowing trouble. Her own uneasiness increased when seven o'clock came, and half-past. Philippe always called before that hour, and Teresina now joined with her mother in pacing to the front door for a sign of the truants. There was no longer any question in either of their minds but that they were together.

"If she has been meeting him out at the Exposition, I hope they did get caught in the fire," Teresina declared, vindictively. "I hope she isn't killed, though. I should just like to see her disfigured—horribly."

The twins were dispatched to the end of the street, to bring the news if Philippe's rig came in sight, and Georgina took the opportunity to voice her own thoughts.

"I told you I would fix things, and what do you bet I have? I wouldn't be surprised if they have run away, and will lead a life of sin. Wouldn't that be perfect—showing up Zenie, who's so stuck on herself, and Mother could see at the same time that Julia isn't the plaster saint she's always made her out to be."

It was after eight when a messenger boy arrived with an envelope for a truly frantic household. As he held it toward them both Teresina and her mother clutched it with gestures so sudden and so violent that the poor youth retreated in fright.

"Zenie, if you will take your hand off that envelope I'd be obliged. Things have reached a pretty pass if I can't open my own letters."

402

"It's from Philippe—I know it is, and I have a right to know what it says." Teresina turned sullen at the look in her mother's eyes, and released her grip. "I suppose you don't care that my feelings are being played with."

By this time, her mother was reading the letter rapidly, drawing in her lips in a familiar expression of disapproval, and Teresina's voice faded away while she waited to know the worst.

"Well, they weren't in the fire, anyway—they never mention it, in fact. This will be a blow for you, Zenie, although, as I've always said, there's more than one pebble on the beach. Besides, as I warned you plenty of times, you weren't handling . . ."

"Mother, stop, please!" Teresina interrupted in a choked voice. "It's Julia, of course. The little sneak. I long since found there is only one way to get the interest of a man like Philippe, with his French morals. If Julia cared to stoop to anything like that, she can have him." Her mother passed over the note, and she read it, hastily.

Dearest Mama: I am running away with Philippe, for we love each other, and life without him would be intolerable. My heart grieves to cause you worry, but this is the only way. Explanations would have been impossible to anyone of Zenie's jealous nature. I know you will understand that. Please don't worry too much.

Yr affte daughter
Julia

Now that the irrevocable had occurred, Teresina assumed the cool, detached pose that could set her apart from the rest of the family so completely. She returned the letter with a bored, almost disinterested air.

"My goodness, Julia takes herself seriously. What ex-

403

planations are necessary in a situation of this kind? The whole thing is too transparent."

"If you think any daughter of mine has been up to anything improper, you can disabuse your mind," Mrs. Rogers snapped. "I've raised you all to be good Christians, and I have perfect confidence in all of you.". . . "Excepting Georgina," she added in her own mind.

Teresina walked toward the stairway with her most languid, regal stride. "Indeed I hope you are right, Mother, but you notice there is nothing at all said in the note about marriage—or did *that* escape your attention?"

"Teresina Rogers, will you get out of here! With your high and mighty airs you make me sick, and you might as well know it. I can read, can't I? I suppose I should know what the letter said and what it didn't say, but if Julia ran away with Philippe without marrying him, she's a worse fool than I think she is. Now hush up, for here come the twins, and the less they know of this shameful proceeding, the better."

2

As Teresina climbed upstairs, her mind labored over the greatest profusion of ideas, attitudes, plans, and projects, most of which she discarded as quickly as they occurred to her. Never, never would she believe a man again. She convinced herself, in quick succession, first, that she had loved Philippe dearly, then that she never loved him; and by the time she reached her room, she came to the final conclusion that she had loved him at first, had learned his true nature, and was just waiting the proper moment to tell him off when her sister saved her the trouble.

It was not enough to decide the course of events to her

own satisfaction. She had to do something, make some gesture to show her rightness. The best move would be an immediate engagement to someone else. She nodded her head in great determination. That would put the shoe on the other foot, she assured herself. She turned in her thoughts toward Gus Palmer for refuge, and not toward Harry Naylor. Except for his potential future, the politician always repelled her. No, Gus would understand. He would sympathize. He would believe completely in her version of the affair. He was utterly devoted, utterly dependable.

He was around the house all the time, calling on Julia. The horrid thought occurred to her—supposing Gus also had fallen in love with Julia. It seemed incredible, but no more so than what had already happened. There could be no mistake about it, Julia had been seeing Gus every day. She had been trying to wean him away from her. Perhaps she had succeeded. This line of reasoning made Gus suddenly most desirable. She hurriedly changed into her most becoming dress and hastened downstairs. She determined to be present if Gus came around, so she could be the first to tell him what had happened. By this time she was beginning to believe that she had actually sent Philippe packing, and he had turned to Julia in revenge, but even her consummate egotism could not quite accept so obvious a distortion of the facts.

It was almost nine o'clock, and a late hour to expect Gus. She felt almost angry with him because he was not within call the moment she needed him. Her mother came into the parlor and sat down opposite her.

"Well, if Mother expects any hysterics from me, she will be sadly disappointed," she thought with satisfaction. The important thing was to let no one, not even her mother, think that she felt anything but relief.

405

"I declare, it's been a wearing day," Mrs. Rogers cut across her daughter's thoughts. "I must say, Zenie, on the whole you've taken things more sensibly than I thought you would."

In that moment, Teresina forgot all her elaborate plans. She was a hurt girl, desperately hurt. In a dramatic gesture that was most unusual for her, she jumped up, darted over to her mother, and knelt at her feet. Her head found a resting place on Mrs. Rogers' ample bosom, and she began to cry, deep sobs that shook her convulsively. It was a long time before she quieted; then, gradually, her mother's soothing pats began to have an effect, and she was like a sleepy, fretful child again, crying for a lost toy.

"He was so good-looking, Mother. He was most good-looking, and so rich, besides, and now Julia has him."

Mrs. Rogers understood perfectly. She would have felt just the same way herself, she thought, but in a gentle voice she began to give her daughter some advice.

"We all have things happen to us, and we have to be brave, and not do anything foolish. A girl with your looks won't ever be wanting for a man, but right now you want to beware of doing anything unconsidered that you'll be sorry for later. See Gus, if you want, he's good company, but don't be too hasty. Now run to bed, like a good child, and you will feel better in the morning."

For the first time in her life, Teresina really appreciated her mother. She was so—so understanding, and at the same time so practical. Perhaps it was a good thing Gus had not come along. She might have thrown herself at him without further consideration, just to avenge herself for one mistake. Tomorrow she would try to see him. There was no one who could make her forget as he could, but she wouldn't lose her head again, never fear.

She spent a long time in undressing and preparing for bed, until at last her mother called back to her:

"Zenie, you better put that gas out and get a good night's sleep. You'll feel better for it in the morning."

Chapter 8 · WITHIN a few days, Teresina was able to look back upon her loss as an experience that was over. A necessary but perhaps useful lesson. She had seen Gus several times, and he was as devoted as ever. Imagine questioning his love, even for a minute! Poor Gus, perhaps he deserved a better reward than she was prepared to give, yet he had seemed completely happy just to see her again on the old basis.

She studied her mirrored reflection as if it were a work of art, which it actually was if the perfectness of nature can be so styled. She imagined all kinds of terrible ravages to her features from the emotional stress she had been through, but she could discern no change. Lines? None. No tenseness of the muscles around the mouth, no looseness in the skin under her eyes. Her hair might have turned gray overnight. She had heard of such things happening, but it seemed black as ever, with no hint of silver; its depths still held their vibrant purple shadows. It was a beautiful face! She was beautiful, surpassingly beautiful. Julia had not bested her through superior looks; her mirror assured her of that. She had played other cards, that was all. Julia, the member of the family who had always pretended to be so good, had run away with a man!

Teresina was quite ready to believe the worst. "He'll never marry her," she thought vindictively for the tenth time. "In a few weeks he will cast her aside, like a crumpled rose"—this latter thought was the effect of Gus's ballads—and what must have transpired before they fled no decent girl like herself dare even think about.

Nevertheless, Teresina's mind skirted very close to every possible likelihood. Hadn't she herself been forced continually to avoid or resist Philippe's importunities? Suppose she had succumbed to his advances? Right now she would be in the disgraceful position of her sister. It was almost a week since they had run away, and not a word from them. Well, she hoped that when Julia came crawling back to the house, she would be refused admittance!

Teresina felt no anger at all; the days of suffering were over. She took the loss philosophically, once she was convinced that she had not been vanquished in a contest of good looks. That would have been a loss indeed, for it would have robbed her of her pride and her belief in herself. In the quiet of her room, in the company of her reflection, she was able to assess things calmly. Philippe was rich, so she had been assured, but how rich? What were the standards by which his wealth was judged? And his investments were probably in French and English industries. Who knew what might happen to them? They were not good safe American securities. Besides, Aunt Zena herself had warned her how difficult Frenchmen were to manage. They insisted on running things. As for herself, she wanted a husband she could manage, and none other.

To that extent, Julia had done her a real favor. "I never had so much fun in all the time I knew Philippe as I had last night with Gus," she told herself.

Gus loved her, she knew that, and yet he wasn't trying to paw her all the time. He was respectful, and perhaps he was right about his future. Maybe he would be a great success. She might be the wife of a famous doctor. His arguments sounded logical. Most doctors treated everything;

therefore a man who became known as a specialist in one field might be able, as Gus argued, to command higher fees for his services. Even an ordinary doctor didn't live too badly. With her to keep pushing him along, Gus might go far.

Then there was Harry. She hadn't yet decided how to let him know that she had decided marriage with a Frenchman was impossible. Should she wait until the session of the legislature was over, or should she send him a note to Harrisburg? Still deep in her thoughts, she descended to the dining room, to find her father and Georgina already at their places. With Henry working, and Julia (good riddance to her) gone, the table seemed empty, somehow, although as much food as ever appeared to grace it.

Her mother came in from the kitchen and took a seat opposite. For the first time that day Zenie felt a strong sense of irritation and annoyance, although she gave no indication of it.

"If Mother would only stop looking at me that way, as if I was going into a decline at any moment!" she thought. "Can't she understand the whole thing is over and done with, and that I'm glad of it?" It was fortunate, really, that things had come to a head when they did. Another two weeks and the invitations would have been out. Then it would have been difficult to face the world with an announcement that would immediately be interpreted to mean she had been jilted.

"Zenie, do eat your dinner," her mother interrupted her thoughts sharply. "You must keep up your strength, child, or you will lose weight. That's a nice loin of pork I bought specially."

"I'm perfectly all right, Mother. I was thinking about something entirely different. Gus was singing a new song

409

to me last evening, and I was trying to remember how the words went."

Georgina looked up, with her too innocent, vague stare. "Oh, was it 'Waiting at the Church,' Zenie? It's so sad!"

Teresina determined that some day she would murder her young sister—in a subtle fashion, so that the crime could never be attributed to herself—but she evinced no sign that she had understood the sly dig. To prove once and for all that she was not languishing for a faithless lover she ate two good thick chops from the pork loin, and a half-dozen of the potatoes that had been roasted with it. The garden greens were just about over, but there was new sauerkraut, and she had a heaping mound of this delicacy to top off with. In her determination to prove that her appetite had been unaffected by her experience, she ate too much, and when Mary hobbled around with the first pumpkin pie of the year she almost decided not to accept any of it. But that would have been a confession, to Mary as well as to her mother. The old woman was worse than her parent; she kept gazing at her with an infuriatingly sympathetic leer.

Mr. Rogers, meanwhile, was too busy reading the paper to notice anything. It was filled with details of the storm. Trees had been uprooted, roofs torn off dwellings. Many of the buildings at the Exposition were ruined. The water had leaked through the Main Building, damaging thousands of dollars' worth of merchandise. "Strange, how the weather has been a constant stumbling block to the Centennial," he philosophized. There was an amusing story in the paper, which he read at length. A tree had fallen across Spruce Street, close to an intersection of the horse railways. The driver of an eastbound car, seeing his way blocked, unhitched his horses, fastened them to the branches of the tree, and pulled it out of the way, little caring that in so doing he tied up the track of the rival northbound line. Rehitching his horses, he sped merrily on his way, to the amusement of his passengers, who visualized the difficulty which would face the first driver on the intersecting line. Mr. Rogers roared: "Imagine us doing tricks like that. My dear, you see the difference between amateur and professional railroadmen." The paper continued with the tale; when the northbound vehicle finally appeared, its driver unhitched his horses and reversed the process. All day long the game of moving the tree from one track to another continued, until finally the poor maple or cottonwood wore out and fell to pieces.

2

Teresina left the table before the end of the story, a tiny segment of the pie still remaining on her plate. She was no sooner out of hearing than Mrs. Rogers began:

"I declare, Jesse, the way Zenie is taking this worries me. An appetite like a bird's. She never leaves Martha's pie on her plate—and pumpkin at that! . . . Fortunately, she has Gus Palmer, and he may bring her out of it. Sometimes I think he mightn't be a bad match for Zenie, if Harry Naylor is occupied elsewhere by this time. He really loves her, and that is something—and his prospects may be better than one would think."

Mr. Rogers threw out his chest until the tent-sized napkin that covered his beard and coat billowed up like a sail.

"Heavens, Gussie, we married for love, and it hasn't turned out too badly. I wouldn't be so afraid to trust our children to the tender passion."

Georgina tried to make herself as inconspicuous as possible, to enjoy a conversation over a matter in which she felt an almost motherly concern. Hadn't she assisted materially in causing the whole situation they were discussing? She was almost smirking with satisfaction over the outcome of her efforts when her mother sharply interrupted her thoughts.

"Gene, what in the world are you dawdling for? You can get along with yourself right away—your father and I have something to talk over." She waited impatiently while Georgina pushed back her chair and left the room, taking as long as she could to do so. When Mrs. Rogers finally decided she was beyond earshot, she took up the conversation at the exact place where it had stopped. "Love is all very well in its place, Jesse, but there are practical considerations as well."

"Bosh, pure bosh. By the Lord Harry, I don't agree!"

"All right—look at what has happened to Julia. That is what comes of your love. Nothing practical there, was there? Without so much as a by-your-leave she's decamped. What do you suppose anyone will think of her—or of my training?" Mrs. Rogers' features gathered in a little knot that gave her a peculiarly childlike expression. The appearance of a little girl that had been robbed of a favorite doll, and was undecided whether or no she should give way to tears over the loss. "Yet, in spite of everything, I would forgive her—the ruin of all my plans for the wedding, poor Zenie brokenhearted—if I only, only knew he did right by her. The day I know for certain they're married will be a happy one, but I'm afraid my sister's influence, when she lived with her in Paris, corrupted the child."

Mr. Rogers answered in full voice. "Bosh again! What you need, Gussie, is more faith in people. Faith in your daughter and faith in a fine gentleman like Philippe is— in spite of the French blood in his veins. I tell you right now, I'm not worried about either of them, and as for Zenie's being brokenhearted, she was never in love with

412

him in the first place. I know you, and that was some of your doings—what you call making a good match."

It was seldom that her husband interfered in her plans for her daughters, or was so outspoken regarding them, and Mrs. Rogers appeared more than ever ready to burst into tears. She twisted her hands together in a gesture that was unusual for her.

"It has been so long, almost a week. If they had married, what could be the reason for waiting so long to let us know? They could have sent us word by the telegraph as easy as not. Pet, I tell you, I shall never be able to hold up my head again if a daughter of mine has actually run away with a man without getting him to marry her."

"We Quakers hold less store by the sacrament over which you evince such concern," Mr. Rogers began in oracular tones, but his wife headed him off.

"Julia is no Quaker, thank goodness—two of them in the family is enough. I hate to think of the trouble Henry will cause us some day. He's been thrown out of school already, and I expect to see him come home sacked almost any time."

"To the point—to the point." Mr. Rogers grew exasperated at criticism of Henry. "By Christopher, Gussie, I never saw anyone could derail a man's ideas by throwing a red herring across the track the way you can."

"For the last time in my life, Jesse Rogers, I am not a railroadman, even if I was unfortunate enough to marry one. Whatever you mean about fish on the track . . ."

"An unfortunate mixture of metaphors, which I regretted as the words escaped my lips." Whatever else Mr. Rogers intended to add was never spoken. Georgina could be heard shouting from the front door, and then she came running into the dining room with flushed, excited face.

"They're back—they're back! . . . They're just driving

413

up outside, and they're married! I can tell by the look on their faces."

In spite of her excitement at the news, Mrs. Rogers paused long enough to tuck a thought away in her mind. "That child knows entirely too much for a girl of her years —and I bet she was listening, as well. I'll settle her hash later." She reached out and caught her husband's coat as he started for the door.

"Into the parlor, Jesse," she commanded. "We'll let them come in and make their explanations for their behavior. After all, they have both acted outrageously, and I don't think they should be forgiven too quickly."

Against his wishes, Mr. Rogers followed her instructions. "A moment ago, all you wanted was to see them back. Now they are here, you want to go into the parlor and sulk because young people are young people. I declare, Gussie, women are beyond my ken," he grumbled.

"Just so you realize it, you'll be all right. Now don't sit there looking pleased as Punch. You can look angry enough at times, and this is once you can act it, if you don't feel that way. As for me, I intend to give those two a piece of my mind."

Mr. Rogers sank down uncomfortably into the divan. Now that Zena was gone he began to regret the comfort of the old furniture. It was designed for sitting, not lolling. A man just couldn't sit properly on this heathenish contraption; you wallowed in a mire of upholstery and pillows. Mrs. Rogers, meanwhile, had taken the Turkish rocker, and was working it so furiously that its combination of springs, levers, and cradles began to squeak loudly in protest. There was a peal at the doorbell, and Mr. Rogers jumped to his feet, to subside again after a sharp caution:

"Jesse, Mary will answer the door." She listened for a moment, and with a second peal, shouted angrily, so she

414

could be clearly heard in the kitchen. "Mary, will you answer that doorbell? It's rung twice." In what seemed like an age of time to Mr. Rogers, the old woman could be heard as she slowly hobbled down the hall, all the while keeping up a running, whispered conversation with herself. Poor old Mary—she had failed greatly since the summer.

"I swear, Mary is going dafter than a loon," Mrs. Rogers observed angrily, forgetting for a moment her determination never to allow the old servant to upset her again. A moment later, her welcome of the returned elopers still more incensed Mrs. Rogers, and largely undid the effect she had planned. With one of her high, keening cries, Mary leaped upon Julia and smothered her in hugs.

"Well, my own little girl—it seems only a couple of years since I was puttin' diapers on her, and here she is, coming home married." A suspicion entered Mary's head, and she looked up slyly. "It's married you are, ain't it?"

"Of course we are married, Mary." Excitement at her return, mortification at the old woman's remarks, and a kind of sentimental response to the toothless kisses all combined in Julia's expression. "Where are Mama and Papa? Were they very much worried?"

Mary confided in a loud, wet whisper: "I think *she* is waitin' in the parlor to haul you over the coals, but don't either of you pay a mite of attention. She's been eatin' her heart out since you left so sudden-like."

The parents, who could hear the conversation perfectly, reacted differently. Mr. Rogers was annoyed to hear himself described as Papa, but forgot about it upon viewing his wife's expression of helpless consternation. She jumped from the rocker with an "I never heard anything so outrageous. I'm going to send that old harpy packing this minute," but her anger lasted no farther than the doorway. She saw her daughter, sweetly pleading for forgiveness, and forgot everything but the fact that she was back. Her performance actually was very similar to Mary's. She gave a high shriek and caught Julia to her, kissing her frantically on both cheeks.

Mr. Rogers seized both of Philippe's hands and boomed: "Well, my boy, Gussie had prepared a difficult scene for you, but it looks as though it fell through. Personally, I should have had a hard time playing the angry father, and I'm glad all was forgiven without that."

Georgina, meanwhile, had been circling around, awaiting her opportunity to greet the returned pair, when she had another idea, which took precedence. She bounded for the stairway and mounted it two steps at a time. Zenie was in her room, all right. The door was open on a crack. She pushed at it, and shouted:

"Zenie, Philippe and Julia are downstairs! Aren't you coming down to welcome them home?" She waited with avid gaze to enjoy the pleasure of Teresina's anger, but her sister looked up, apparently unmoved.

"I'll see them later. There's no hurry, I suppose, and I can't right now. I'm busy writing a letter." She turned to her desk, and continued with the difficult epistle to Harry Naylor while Georgina, disappointed, thought: "I believe she's even glad she got thrown over. And all the trouble I went to, too."

She walked downstairs at a slower pace, but in good time to add her own welcome; then her mother bustled her away.

"You two better take the back room Zena had. I'll give you a few minutes to wash up, and then I want to hear the whole story. And, Gene, you can run out and play a while. You're getting too many ideas already."

The evening was a typical Rogers occasion. The master of the house arranged with the railroad to come in late because of his daughter's marriage. Martha stayed and made ice cream, the twins behaved like children again, putting aside the grown-up manners they were now accustomed to use for most occasions. A celebration was in order and they intended to celebrate—an impossible undertaking if you were grown-up. Early in the evening they became possessed of a great idea, and several times withdrew to the shed to engage in excited discussion regarding it.

Mr. Rogers was in fine fettle. Philippe had none of the bashfulness and embarrassed modesty which ordinarily characterizes the young bridegroom, and Julia was vivacious, and immensely proud of her husband. Teresina, once more adamant against emotion in her shining armor of beauty, wished bridegroom and bride well in a manner that deceived the former completely.

"I'm glad things worked out as they did," she drawled. "Long ago I realized we were completely unsuited to each other, but I had hesitated to speak, to spare your feelings."

Mary limped about like one possessed of more youthful energy, and when there was nothing to be done, she made herself noticeable by adjusting pictures, dusting the whatnot or a table, or with a tsk-tsk of regret at the lapse in household symmetry, pushed a vase on the mantelpiece a fraction of an inch one way or the other.

When the ice cream was served, Mr. Rogers knocked on the wall for the Peales, and when they came over, the happy couple had to tell all over again of their elopement. With appropriate deletions, Julia described their chance meeting on the Schuylkill steamboat, and the mutual realization that absence had indeed made the heart grow fonder.

She made the trip to the Wissahickon seem like a real adventure, and the Devil's Pool a spot of eerie fascination. She told of their decision to marry, and then, because she was such a shameless person, she had given assent to an elopement. Philippe hastened to assume the blame for their impetuous behavior, and carried on the tale.

"I learned of a minister who marries eloping couples, and we drove down to his place by carriage, and routed him out of bed."

Julia interrupted. "It must have been after nine o'clock —the poor man looked so amusing. Still yawning, and stuffing his nightshirt into his trousers."

"Married by a Methodist, imagine!" her mother interjected, so there were, for part of the time, three voices going at once. She shook her head as if to imply that the very worst had happened. "Married by a Methodist—it will have to be done all over again, that's all I have to say. It's good the man wasn't a Baptist. They probably would have had to stand up to their necks in water while they said 'I do.'"

Mrs. Peale took umbrage, her large bosom shaking with indignation. "Indeed, Mrs. Rogers, Sol and I were married by a Methodist, and it took as well as any priest could do, even that Father Duffy you are so fond of. As for Baptists, they are far inferior to Methodists, of course, but you have got them all wrong, indeed you have. They wed on dry land just like anyone else does. It's only at christening they try to drown a body."

The ensuing pause was used by Mr. Rogers to shout: "Who'll have another helping of ice cream? There's another freezerful in the kitchen."

The room seemed unusually quiet, and Mrs. Rogers asked, suspiciously, "Has anyone seen the twins?" No one had, but as she was as anxious as anybody else to hear the rest of the story again, she allowed herself to be lulled by the thought that they had probably gone to the Naylors'. An interim dictated by modesty occurred at this point in Julia's account, which skipped to the next morning, and the trip to Cape May.

"As romance budded on one vessel, what better plan than to have it blossom on another." While Mr. Rogers blotted out the narration with this sentimental observation, Julia talked on underneath the overwhelming sound.

"Philippe had the brilliant idea of taking his rig along—they have regular stables on the boat, and we had such wonderful rides later. It was a beautiful trip, and I shall never forget the good old steamship *Richard Stockton*. We left Philadelphia at nine o'clock, and it took most of the day down the bay to the Cape."

Mrs. Rogers could not resist interpolating: "You might at least have written and let me know where you were, or telegraphed."

Julia was instantly contrite. "I'm so sorry I worried you so, and you, Papa."

It was an opportunity for which Mr. Rogers had been waiting. He had been out of the focus of interest for too long. He shouted, "I will *not* be called by that odious name—don't *Papa* me, I won't stand for it."

For the first time in her life, Julia was not the least bit afraid of her angry parent. She ran her fingers through his beard the way she had been doing to Philippe's for the past week. "My dear Papa," she teased, "what will you do to me if I don't obey you? Remember, I have somebody to protect me now, and he is quite as big as you are."

Teresina looked more bored than ever during this pretty speech, but actually her mind was deep in her own plans. Mr. Rogers, surprised by the change in his daughter's behavior, laughed at the joke on himself.

"Philippe, marriage has been good for her. I wager she's gained twenty pounds during the last week."

The bridegroom laughed complacently. "She is getting to be quite an armful, I assure you." Julia colored, and her father let loose a roar that rocked every vase, knick-knack, and piece of statuary in the house.

With Father getting in one of his more boisterous moods, Mrs. Rogers steered the conversation so as to avoid further embarrassment for Julia. "And just think of all that happened while you were gone. You missed the fire at the Centennial. It happened the day you two ran away, and I feared you were caught in it."

"And the storm—did the wind do any damage at Cape May?" Mr. Rogers asked, and then, not waiting for an answer, went on: "Pretty nearly wrecked the whole Exposition, I tell you. Blew out the whole side of that French restaurant . . ." He stopped in the middle of his description as a new idea struck him, and his face turned serious. "You know, it's too bad your Aunt Zena isn't here today —she would have enjoyed this, even though things worked out differently from what she planned."

At this, Mrs. Rogers jumped up as if she'd had a cake in the oven and could smell it scorching. "Good grief!" she remarked, and the heavy silk in her dress crackled as she dashed for the stairway and raced up it. Everyone looked at everyone else in surprise, the unexpressed thought of all of them being that she had left the tap running in the bathroom and had just now remembered it. There occurred one of those moments of complete quiet that occasionally afflict a roomful of people. Not a spoon rattled against a dish. Not a chair scraped. No one spoke, nor did the Turkish rocker squeak. It was a quiet before the storm. Suddenly, from the upper regions of the house bedlam broke loose. There was a cry of terror, the sound

420

as of a whole kitchen full of pots and pans clanging and banging. An army seemed to be running through the hallway. There were shouts and cries of vexation, and then—complete quiet once more.

Before anyone could be aroused to action, Mrs. Rogers descended into view, leading the protesting twins. She did not slow her advance until she stood immediately before her husband. By this time, everyone noticed that she was covered with a kind of pearly-white grain. It was rice, of course, and it lay in her hair and on her bosom, and in the folds, pleats, tucks, gores, and bows of her dress. As she talked, a shower of the cereal fell on the parlor Wilton.

"Jesse, I want you to take these two hyenas and thrash them within an inch of their lives, and when you are finished, I'm going to start."

His wife's agitation and the appearance of the twins struck him as amusing, but he made a determined effort to be serious. "Will you please tell me the meaning of all this?" he boomed.

Henry tried to speak, but his mother forestalled him. "It means that these devils filled a bucket with rice, and fixed it over the door in some fashion so that when I went in, down it came."

Georgina broke in, eager to set the record straight. "We didn't mean for Mother to get it, honest we didn't. We fixed it up for the bride and groom."

Henry wanted credit for the ingenuity they had shown, even if it meant a licking afterward. "We filled the bucket with rice, and put it on the top of the four-poster bed by the door. Then we put a string across the doorway, down near the floor, so when someone stepped against it, they would get a rice shower."

"Mother had to spoil it all, running into their room the way she did—then taking it out on us," Georgina wailed.

The cleverness of the trick completely won over their father, and he held his sides. "I declare, I'll burst a boiler laughing. . . . And Gussie trips over the string and gets the rice intended for the bride—ho—ho—*hah*."

"Yes, and the bucket too, if you must know," Mrs. Rogers began, to be interrupted again by Henry.

"We didn't think about the bucket coming down. It wouldn't have, either, only she was going so fast she pulled the string harder than we figured on."

Mr. Rogers collapsed on the divan, speechless; tears coursed down his cheeks. His amusement did not cause any abatement in his wife's anger.

"If you think it's a laughing matter to have a bucketful of rice come crashing down on you when you least expect it, I don't. I was never so overcome in my life."

Between gusts of laughter, in which by this time their company had also joined, Mr. Rogers remembered that there was one detail in the explanation still lacking. "A bucketful of rice! But, Gussie, we never use rice. It's a wicked waste to buy things in such a fashion that you'd have so much of the stuff around the house. I hate it, and so do the children."

Mrs. Rogers' head lowered between her shoulders while her eyes darted lightnings and her voice was sharp, cool steel.

"Jesse Rogers, do you really want me to tell you where that rice came from?"

A light burst with startling clarity. No further explanation was necessary; he recalled all too well. Instead of answering, he responded with another question. "What in the world sent you up to the back room in such a hurry?"

Mrs. Rogers made a gesture of extreme annoyance. "There, I don't have it again. A letter from Zena came yesterday, from Paris. Mary brought it up when something or other happened, and I laid it on the bureau. I clean forgot it until you mentioned her."

"A letter? From Zena? On the bureau?" Mr. Rogers turned to Henry. "Streak up and get it this minute, but don't open it—you hear!"

As Henry dashed off, hoping the rice episode would now be forgotten, Mr. Rogers beamed around the room. "Evidently Gussie's sister got back to Paris all right."

He interrupted himself to hold out a demanding hand as Henry reappeared, triumphantly waving a square blue envelope. It was from Zena, all right, and her writing was as difficult as ever. So many words were underlined, some of them two or three times, and the letter was written over so many sheets of paper that seemed not to follow each other consecutively, that he was quite a time assuring himself that he had interpreted it correctly. There was no doubt! Zena was in love again! The Rogers timbers shivered once more.

"Whoops, Gussie, your sister is in love, with a Quaker!"

Mrs. Rogers, still overcome by the prank of the twins, made a hurried recovery. She jumped up, put her hand to her breast, and exclaimed, "What will Zena come to?"

Her husband strode into the center of the room and cleared his throat importantly. He was completely the center of interest as he held up the letter and prepared to read from it. The occasion called for all the graces of delivery of which he believed himself a master, so he proceeded slowly, with a heavy emphasis on the underlined words, until Mrs. Rogers declared, impatiently:

"Do hurry, Jesse, and give us the gist of it. You can be the most tantalizing man."

Scorning the interruption, and sparing the company none of his artistic efforts, Mr. Rogers read on: " '. . . the vessel

423

was most *steady* and as the wind was *favorable*, the sails were set to aid the engines, when this *gentleman* spoke to me. He was most *interesting* and explained the whole management of the ship. By a *coincidence*, it turns out he is a sea captain, retired, the same as an old *friend* of mine, who died in the East.

" 'This made a *bond* between us, which was firmly *cemented* during the rest of the voyage. Two days out from Le Havre a storm arose, which I am *convinced* would have wrecked the vessel, except that Captain Porter, my *friend*, offered his assistance and advice to the Captain, who was thankful for the help of a more *experienced* navigator, and that *saved the day*. Captain Porter is extremely modest, and I had to *worm* the facts out of him, afterwards.

" 'He knows all about you, and Jesse, and I told him what a . . .' " At this point Mr. Rogers became almost hopelessly lost in the puzzle of paging, so that he had to read over most of the letter again to himself until he found the proper spot, while Mrs. Rogers began a tirade over her sister's gullibility.

"Can't you see Zena, taking up with the first man who paid her any attention? Sea captain indeed!"

The Peales were bored by this time, but tried to be polite, and the twins had begun one of their endless conversations. Mr. Rogers coughed, stuck out his beard, and went on:

" '. . . what a fine and *highly principled* man he was, and a *Quaker*. Coincidence number two, Gussie, can you believe it, Tom is *also* of that faith, although he hasn't actually *trembled* for years.' "

"Trembled? Good grief, Jesse, does she think Quakers have the ague? Of all the old fools, taking up with a Quaker, no less!"

Mr. Rogers took on an air of extreme aggravation. "Indeed, Gussie, how am I to do justice to this epistle with these constant interruptions? I am at the very marrow of it now. Will I be permitted to finish, or must I leave your sister on the high seas for the rest of eternity?"

"La, get on with it, by all means." Mrs. Rogers shrugged, but by this time the impatience of his hearers had become so noticeable that Mr. Rogers chose to feel that his wife had deliberately spoiled his performance. All right. She had asked for the gist of it and that's what he would give her!

"She says if it hadn't been for you, she would never have met him, and she is sending you—she is sending you . . ." He frowned, and his mouth fell open while Mrs. Rogers wondered, "Good grief, what has Zena written to put Jesse in such a state?"

Julia used the pause to take Philippe by the arm, and say quite shamelessly, "Come, dear, I think it is time we retired."

As the Peales also arose, Mr. Rogers thrust the letter into his pocket, its reading unfinished, but his clouded brow carried storm warnings which his wife did not miss.

Teresina had already vanished to her room, and no sooner had the twins clumped noisily toward the third story than he retrieved the offending letter and began to indulge in noises appropriate to an expression of his feelings. Mrs. Rogers forestalled him by asking, with one of her inquiring, sparrowlike glances:

"Pet, what do you think of this conquest of Zena's?"

"What do I think? I hope he marries her. A Quaker with salt in his marrow! She needs someone to look out for her. Do you know what that sister of yours has done?"

Pursing her lips and shaking her head, Mrs. Rogers put him off by ignoring his question and continuing with her own thoughts. "I hope for the best, of course, but there are too many coincidences in that man's story to sound natural. I suspect he is nothing but an adventurer, after Zena's money."

"She needs someone to take care of her money," Mr. Rogers went on, "and a good, hard-fisted Quaker would be the man . . ."

"Why, Pet," Mrs. Rogers protested. Whatever Zena had done, the longer Jesse was put off telling about it, the less violent the explosion. She feigned extreme concern as she continued: "If Zena marries, our other poor girls won't have her wealth to fall back on. I'm not so worried about Teresina, in spite of what's happened. It's a good match for Georgina disturbs me."

Mr. Rogers' impatience could no longer be restrained. "And I'm not worried about either of our girls!" he roared. " 'Love will find a way,' I say. There's something else does worry me. Because of your ceaseless interruptions I've had no opportunity to tell you, Mrs. Rogers, that your sister is starting in again. First the dash-hounds, and now this."

He caught up Zena's letter and held it in agitated fingers. "She has sent you, as a token of reconciliation"—he squinted, and read with overemphasized inflection—" 'a most *handsome* life-sized *oil* painting entitled *The Retreat from Moscow.*' " He shook his head, his arms fell to his sides in a well-studied gesture of despair, and he lowered his voice to the tones of one reasoning with a difficult child. "Gussie, where in this house is there room for even a shattered remnant of Napoleon's Army, let alone the immensity of the wide Russian steppes?"